D0040689

HADRIAN'S WALLS

HADRIAN'S WALLS

ROBERT DRAPER

ALFRED A. KNOPF   NEW YORK   1999

THIS IS A BORZOI BOOK
PUBLISHED BY ALFRED A. KNOPF, INC.

Copyright © 1999 by Robert Draper

www.randomhouse.com

Knopf, Borzoi Books, and the colophon
are registered trademarks of
Random House, Inc.

Library of Congress Cataloging-in-Publication Data
Draper, Robert.
Hadrian's walls / by Robert Draper.—1st ed.
p.   cm.
ISBN 0-375-40369-8
I. Title
PS3554.R2398H34   1999
813'.54—dc21   98-43203
CIP

Manufactured in the United States of America

First Edition

For Meg

My deepest thanks to Sloan Harris, Sonny Mehta, Sarah McGrath, Judy Frels, Rebecca Orr, Joe Malof, Loma Hobson, Art Cooper, Marty Beiser, Greg Curtis, Paul Burka, and my friends in Huntsville, Texas, and Venice, Italy. Each has, in one way or another, helped make this book possible.

HADRIAN'S WALLS

1

There's more than one way to get to Shepherdsville, but the route I took isn't found on any map, being as how the old mulecart roads of East Texas are unnumbered and, when it comes down to it, ungoverned by the state. You damn sure wouldn't want to get lost on them, even if you're partial to the woods. I'm less partial than I used to be as a kid, for reasons I hope to make clear soon enough. Still, deep East Texas is where I'm from. I have never blamed the bad in me on anyone or anything; but credit for the good in me—and it's there, despite what I once believed—must surely go to these thickets, these river bottoms, these pigtrails and sloughs and battered clay roads, and to the people here who have drawn from their environs a rough, elemental goodness, and did what they could to pass it on to me.

That these most obscure of roads outlined the very path I'd taken in an earlier year, though in the opposite direction—belly-down, recoiling from the moonlight—naturally suggested something. But I wasn't about to consider it. After all, a man who not only distrusts his instincts but actively fears them . . . well, he's got to find a way to live with himself somehow or other, and so he leaves it to others (and to that evil little meter humming somewhere in the oblivion of his guts) to register this latest demonstration of ill judgment and most likely conclude that his lust for badness is proof of badness incarnate. No, better for me to keep it simple. I had to get to Shepherdsville, and it's the prettiest way to go, and to me the most gratifying—not to mention the slowest, and I was in no hurry to get to Shepherdsville.

In my shabby off-yellow Impala I passed through the surly lushness
of the lowlands, a panorama blemished here and there by caved-in produce stands, cemeteries choked with kudzu, and squatty missionary
Baptist and Pentecostal churches that secreted a dark sorcery of their
own. The debris of a tribe that never stood a chance. But no: I knew for
a fact that people lived out here, on by-roads that made this one look
like a tollway. "Get on, you old mule," I said as I gave the gas to my car,
which I'd picked up somewhere in the Missouri boot-heel a year ago,
from some Amway drifter who took my two hundred and grinned like
a jackass eating bees. His miscalculation. I'd put four thousand miles
on the Impala since then, not counting this journey I'd begun the
afternoon before.

Then again, I'd generally spared it roads as unruly as these. Red
clay swirled through the open windows, and I squinted and spat as it
coated me. "Dust to dust!" I hollered out—a meager battle cry, the
best that I could manage on this day I hadn't seen coming, this August
day that deserved to be the greatest day of my life. Today it was official:
I was free. Not rodent-under-the-floorboards free as I'd been the last
eight years. No, this was the real thing, the wide-open invitation to
take the outlaw roads in broad daylight, rebaptize myself in native soil,
and make a mess of myself all over again. And maybe the joy would hit
me after the dust did. In Shepherdsville, they made bricks out of this
clay, and walls with the bricks; and without those walls and men to stick
behind them, there might as well not be a Shepherdsville. But look
around, I told myself. No numbers here for roads or for men. No
keeping track. I kept the windows down, taking the dust with the
free air.

Fatigue and the heat pressed against my neck. I'd been too jumpy to
sleep for the past seven hundred miles, ever since I flew out of the
Western Union office in Cape Girardeau like a bazooka shell with five
Ben Franklins throbbing in my shirt pocket along with the telegram
that hollered out: ALL FORGIVEN HAH HAH STOP. PAPER NEEDS YR
SIGN STOP. GET ON HOME STOP. LOVE GUESS WHO STOP. How familiar the voice, and the marvel of how readily the years withered against
it had preoccupied me for much of the way. Now I could barely grip
the wheel. I flicked the FM dial over to the Shepherdsville station. The
voice belonged to an East Texas boy, fellow by the name of George
Jones. "Now we liiiive . . . in a two-story house . . . It's splendiiid . . .

But there's no love about . . ." I joined in: "How sad it is, we now live in a, two-story house . . ."

Then old George's voice was lost in a blizzard of static. It was still a good fifty miles to town. Presently the road cut past a meadow where a half-dozen Branguses stood up to their haunches in a stock tank, motionless and blissfully dim in the coppery pool. "Now that's how you spend a summer day, God love 'em," I said, and with that came, at last, a smile.

An entrance gate appeared on the left. My stomach flinched with the memory, but then I took a second look. The sign above the gate bore an unfamiliar name. Somebody Farley was the new owner of the ranch. The rush of air whistled out of me. I hadn't thought about Del Sparks when I set out on this road. Likely Del would've thought about me, and then gotten up to fetch his deer rifle. I couldn't hold this against Del, who had been a pallbearer at my father's funeral. Hopefully the new sign didn't signify that he'd come to a bad end, and hopefully he'd gotten back the horse I had stolen from him. It wasn't his best horse, not even his second or third best. Beyond that, there was nothing more to say. I'd done what I had to do that early morning eight years ago. And no doubt if Del Sparks laid eyes on me again, he'd do what he had to do.

That misdeed, if not the others, had been a fluke of geography. Just east of the old Sparks ranch, the meadow gives out to the Minerva River, which is too far from the road to be seen, though it runs fast enough that you can hear it when the air is still. It's a high, rattling whisper of a sound, like cottonwood leaves shuddering in a summer afternoon breeze. From this distance, and if you weren't from around here and you'd chucked your map and bellowed Gimme some country Lord and made for the mulecart roads—from this distance, you would imagine the Minerva to be one of those shady little streams where you took your girl for a picnic on the first warm day of spring, and you bit your lip a little as she sat on a flinty overhang and hootched her lemon dress up to just above her knees and danced her candy toes against the surface of the water, and looked up in time to catch your stare, and blew you the lightest kiss. Well, God help your girlfriend's toes. I've seen catfish pulled out of the Minerva that, once gutted, belched out the slimy remains of squirrels, raccoons and small dogs. For that matter, many's the night I saw my dad—who was Shepherd County's veterinarian for all of his adult life—depart the dinner table to go milk the leg of some fool who had invaded the sanctuary of a Minerva cottonmouth. The river exists in no postcard. Even on the calmest of evenings, it froths and flails like the devil's own handmaiden. Come late autumn she is swollen like a tick; come the winter rains, and by early spring she explodes across the river valleys, gathering up pigs and cattle and crippled shut-ins and infants, and it's a month of Thanksgivings for the catfish. Well into spring, uprooted trees lay mangled along the banks or straggle out in the rushing water. As to whether this suggests that the river's evil—and possibly everyone else's—has its seasons, I wouldn't know, except to say that it was a low-water August eight years ago when the Minerva nearly killed me, and on this August day I intended to stay clear.

In a mile, the clear-cut meadow surrendered to the thicket. The air abruptly became soupy, the road a ragged carpet of pine needles. The odor stung like buckshot. To live out here, you had better love the smell of pine, and I most certainly did. This ignorant affection did not please my grandfather, who would pshaw me when he'd see me lifting my nostrils high as we roamed the bottomlands together with our deer rifles. He'd say, "Now, y'see these white oaks? Or those sweetgum up yonder? Those tupelos we passed back at Shapleigh's Baygall? You pay them a good look. Shee. Used to be thousands upon thousands of 'em here before the timber barons come down from up east. Brought their steam skidders into the woods. Dragged off every hardwood they could get. Barged 'em down the Minerva. I was your age then. Watched it all myself. Watched 'em pull up a whole dang forest like it was a bunch of carrots."

His eyes keen through the dirty spectacles. "Now, Hadrian, you ain't gonna live here forever."

"I am so!"

"Shhh. Mind the deer." But then, with a hand on my shoulder: "You'll go on. Ain't no judging it. People just go on. But don't take a whiff of those scrawny ol' sumbucks with you. Hell! Mama went into town the other day, said at the supermarket they put it in spray cans now! Make your toilet room smell like you done crapped under a pine tree!"

And after we both finished laughing, grandfather and grandson only too happy to scare off the deer, he sighed a little and cleared his throat, and I knew the next words would be solemn. "Now you listen," he said. "You need to remember these hardwoods. 'Cause there ain't any more like 'em in East Texas. And when you come back to visit, I lay you what. These'll be gone too. Big ol' giants, cut down dead and dragged off. Don't you forget 'em, y' hear me?"

Pawpaw might as well have been talking about himself. I took my foot off the gas pedal and stared up at the rows and rows. I'd sooner forget my own name than forget him. But he was long, long gone, and so was that floppy-haired little brat beside him, and so were the hardwoods. Just me and the pines were left.

"Still," I said out loud as I picked up the speed again, "I do love the smell of these pines."

Five miles down the road, a one-lane wooden bridge took me over Bernadette Creek. The icehouse was still there. Over the peeling white paint someone had begun to apply a shade of blue usually seen on the bottom of swimming pools. The sides of the icehouse remained unpainted; empty buckets lay rusting in the grass.

An old mutt huddled under the wooden porch steps. It growled a little as I climbed above him, and fleas danced about my legs. Fastened to the screen door by a leather shoestring was a wooden sign that announced Live Minnows. It was darker inside than out in the woods. I could smell plastic worms and beef jerky, but above all, a human staleness.

An old fellow with a spotted face and a lumber company cap sat on a stool, reading the want ads in the back of *The Shepherdsville Light*. "Some sumbitch here trying to sell his '89 Homeyer outboard for one hundred fifty-five dollars," he rasped, not looking up. "Dumbass! An '89 Homeyer? That couldn't push a goddamn tadpole!"

Shaking his head, dragging his finger to the next ad, he rumbled, "We're out of minners."

"Where's your bathroom?" I asked.

"Toilet's busted."

"I just need to change clothes," I said.

The man looked up for the first time, brows mangled as he glared at the bag draped over my shoulder. I'd bought the outfit yesterday from a discount store in Little Rock.

"Just go outside," he said, returning to the newspaper. "Ain't no law gonna bust you for being nekkid."

A few minutes later, I returned through the screen door. Leaning over the glass display case filled with plastic worms, I adjusted my tie. I could feel the old man's smirk.

"Does Dutch Wilson still own this place?" I asked.

He folded up the paper and trained his heavy-lidded eyes on me. "You from the Liquor Board?" he demanded.

"I borrowed something from Dutch, and I need to make good on it," I said.

"Borrowed something. Didn't know he had so much as a piss-bucket to borrow from." The man looked me up and down. "Well, I'm his cousin. You can give it to me."

"It's money," I said.

He shrugged agreeably. "Like I said. You can give it to me. I'll see that Dutch gets it."

I looked at my watch. Ten minutes before five. "All right," I said. "You have anything to write with?"

He offered me a pencil, then fished around behind the counter before slapping down a scrap of paper. Something was printed on the other side. When I flipped it over, the face of a huge-headed man with a sharply sloping nose and eyebrows like caterpillars grimaced back at me. RE-ELECT SHERIFF BO WORLEY, it said.

I found myself smiling. "Old Bo Worley," I said as I turned the paper back over. "You voting for him?"

Dutch's cousin spat loudly on the floor. "I'd sooner vote for that dog laying outside there," he said. Then he let loose a long and tangled but heartfelt string of curses inspired by the Shepherd County sheriff, and it had to be fully a minute before he came up for air and said to me, "But my vote don't count none anyways. Them big boys in Shepherdsville, they ain't gonna let a shiteater like Worley lose."

Warily, he added, "I hope Worley ain't your buddy."

"He's not my buddy," I said, and began my note to Dutch Wilson. After signing it, I pulled out my wallet and removed fifty dollars. Then I glanced at the window on the far wall. A piece of plywood was nailed up over it. Nothing ever got fixed in old wrecks like this, but that didn't remove my burden. I took out another fifty and folded up the bills inside the note.

The old man was pretending he hadn't been watching. "Where you heading off to?" he asked.

"Shepherdsville," I said.

"Figgered," he grunted. "You got prison business?"

"I didn't know they had any other kind of business in Shepherdsville," I said.

The old man snickered. "You got that right," he said as he settled back onto his stool. "Crime sho nuf pays in that town, don't it! Yeah buddy. They got it all figgered out in Shepherdsville. That old prison boss, Sonny Hope. He sits up there like the king of God. Ever politician and businessman in Texas lives to kiss his ass. Now," and Dutch's cousin reached back to the cigarette shelf and opened up a carton of Camels, "ol' Thunderball taught his boy that. Purvis Hope, Sonny's daddy? See, he was prison boss also."

"I know who Thunderball Hope is," I said.

"Well, then you know how he was. He was plain folks, Thunderball was. But he could dance them politicians, too. He was sho nuf stout. But," he added, chuckling low as he lit up his Camel, "not like his ol' Sonny. Shee-it. Sonny Hope, he's got stroke his daddy never thought of having."

He looked up to see if I was appreciating all of this. "Hell, you're probably going to see him, too," he grinned.

I offered back a smile. "I probably am."

"Well, if you're going to see him and you're coming back thisaway, I'd sure as hell like to know something," the fellow said, his eyes narrowing viper-like.

He pulled on his cigarette for awhile, making sure he had my attention before saying, "I hear it was ol' Sonny Hope that talked the governor into pardoning that sumbitch who killed Judge Castlebury umpteen years ago and then killed some other damn convict and ran out of the prison farm a week before they was fixing to parole him. You remember all that? Goddamn my sorry ass, what was his name? Doc Coleman's boy. Though he sure as shit wasn't like ol' Doc. Goddamn animal. Remember how he strangled that blind judge and cut his fuckin' eyes out? Anyways. Then, when he's down on the farm, he kills that convict. Only now they say he didn't—some other con did. But I guess Doc Coleman's boy—hell, what was his name?—I guess he figgered no one's gonna believe a killer like him, so he done run off. And so seven years after all that, ol' Sonny Hope he calls all the newspapers. Says the true killer of that con done confessed. And so Doc Coleman's boy, he's been cleared of that killing and then they went and pardoned him for escaping. But he done escaped too good for them to find him! Nine months they got those pardon papers sitting! And Doc Coleman's boy, I betcha he's somewheres in China by now eatin' rice and fish heads and killin' babies for the Communists!"

Through his wheezing and his cigarette smoke, he surely couldn't see me.

"Well," I finally said, and edged towards the screen door.

"But what I want to know is," he continued, in a suddenly composed voice, "why in the hell is some big ol' prison boss like Sonny Hope going to all that trouble for some sumbitchin' convict? Why should he give a good rat's ass which damn con killed which?"

I leaned against the screen door, steadying myself.

"Fact is, he done escaped, and I'd want his ass punished for that. I'd drag his ass back and do somethin' u-nique to him right there in front of all those other convicts. Send a goddamn message, that's what I'd do. But Sonny Hope—he's gettin' that sumbitch pardoned! And I'd sure as hell like to know why."

He squinted at me. "How well you know Sonny Hope?" he asked. "Y'all friends?"

Those were two very different questions.

"We're best friends," I said.

"Well hell! He might tell you after all! He just might! Though I tell you what."

His voice fell to a near-whisper. "Ol' Sonny, he didn't get that con pardoned on account of the Bible told him to. Nah. Not ol' Sonny Hope. He don't do squat for free. So if you're comin' back thisaway—"

"I'm not," I said, having heard enough.

"Wh—" he began, crestfallen.

"But I appreciate you giving that over to Dutch when you see him." I threw a wave as I walked out.

I was well out the door when I heard Dutch's cousin holler, "What was your name again?" But as I drove off, he came back into view: standing with the screen door open, the note to Dutch held out in front of his face, and him not so much reading it for what it said, but instead reading it, long-jawed and marble-eyed, as nothing more and

nothing less than a judgment on the puny sum total of his own sorry-
ass life—a life which, if I were all he thought I was, I would not leave
up to the dirt kicking up from my Impala to erase, to bury as he'd have
me buried, in the red clay dust to dust . . .

As I drove into Shepherdsville, I did all I could to retrieve the memory
that is surely stowed away somewhere—that of the country boy I was
who, on his first-ever Saturday ride into town, saw for the very first
time the legions and legions of men in white, stooped along highways
and in cotton fields and in the courthouse garden. That moment, when
I first laid eyes on justice's whipping boys, should have formed a powerful impression. Today, I could tell you everything about the first and
last deer I ever shot, at the age of five. I could tell you about Mawmaw's
fatal heart attack during a supper prayer, and how I ran away from
home when my sister Mimi was born, and about the catfish that jerked
the cane pole out of my hand and dragged it down the Minerva, and
about driving in Pawpaw's pickup to the big city of Houston to see the
Colt . 45's play Sandy Koufax and the Dodgers. And of course I could
read you chapter and verse about my first kiss, with Flo Wattleston the
prison chaplain's daughter, at the age of thirteen, and the taste of her
mouth and the sweat of her palms against my back and the sweet desperation clawing inside of me.

But then I thought of Pawpaw's big hardwood trees. If they could
be dragged to the ground, what made a memory of mine so almighty
that it couldn't buckle to its intended destroyer? Prison was that
destroyer. It not only took from me what might have been; it took
from me what actually *had* been. And so as I drove, I could only imagine the virgin shock that comes with observing the hoe squads and the
cotton-pickers and the rosebush-trimmers and all the other forlorn,
sullen losers in their ghost outfits, spread across the Shepherdsville
terrain like dirty white fertilizer. I was long accustomed to the spectacle. To my eyes, the cons were nothing more than semi-animated
infrastructure, kindred to the town's fire hydrants and dumpsters.

Their awful homes came into view, one after the next: the Purvis J.
Hope Prison Farm, six miles from town; the Carter Unit, for incorrigi-
bles and death row cases, three miles further in; the Farenthold
Women's Unit, just off the interstate at the city limits; the Diagnostic

Unit, wedged between First Presbyterian, First City and the Wal-Mart; and the historic Shepherdsville Unit, also known as Big Red, which sat two blocks east of the courthouse in the heart of downtown. Even spread apart from each other as they were, you would be inclined to see the prisons in tandem, like bones strung along a pagan tribal necklace, or as some cancerous continuum blighting the town. What you would really be looking at was Shepherdsville's artery. Prisons fed money to the core, money to the outskirts, money everywhere. They were the common bond. They employed people, paid people, gave people something to talk about—gave them a whole new language, so that perfectly ordinary grey-haired matrons could be heard clucking at the D.A.R. luncheon, "They tell me the Winston boy's been in ad-seg ever since the lockdown," or, "Buddy says he wishes he could put an end to that turf battle over at the Carter Unit between the Aryan Brotherhood and the Mandingo Warriors, but after the last excessive-use-of-force citation he says he'd better leave it up to the CO-1s."

Unlike the typical small town, there's always something to see in Shepherdsville by looking up—namely, the prison lights, the picket towers, the curls of razor wire, and if you're lucky, the sight of a helicopter tracking some poor bastard who'd scampered off of trusty duty. It had never occurred to me that this dismal skyline might change. But it had. To my surprise, I found myself driving past several gaudy new buildings, tall and prominent as they poked out of Shepherdsville like great gleaming spires awaiting a congregation of giants. They were state offices for prison bureaucrats, properly bland, but their presence was so alarming that I couldn't for the life of me remember what had been there beforehand. Texas Department of Criminal Retribution—Prison Industry Division. Texas Department of Criminal Retribution—Managed Health Care Division. Texas Department of Criminal Retribution—Legal Affairs Division. Texas Department of Criminal Retribution—Victim Support Division. Texas Department of Criminal Retribution—Inmate Education Division. And no doubt there would be more.

A final building presented itself from the far east side of town: less boxy, composed of craggy limestone likely quarried from the hill country of central Texas and plunked down at the western edge of the Pine Curtain. I knew that had to be the Administrative Division. Sonny never was much for wandering in the forest. But up there, behind his one-way glass, he could be one with nature. Fond amusement welled up in me—replaced, then, by something else, and I shivered.

At the light I turned left onto Walls Boulevard. A few blocks up ahead, the clock crowning the olive Italianate courthouse gonged six times. A sensation overtook me—one, I thought at first, of confinement. But this was different. It was the feeling of being trapped. I thought about the liver-spotted old cracker back at the icehouse by Bernadette Creek. What were the words of wisdom he'd stumbled upon: *Not old Sonny Hope. He don't do squat for free.*

A honk of a horn slapped me awake. Here I was, in the belly of Shepherdsville. The familiarity of my surroundings brought a surge of joy, followed by a cascade of aching. The day-shift guards and deputies filing into the courthouse square café. The college students huddled in broad-shouldered, fancy-haired packs outside the Grizzly Bar & Grille. The fuzzy-eared coots feeling their way with their canes down those familiar well-ordered walkways bordered by shocks of azaleas and petunias . . . And extending out of the right hip of the square stretched the avenues, with their once-impressive procession of antebellum estates now hideously tricked up by the wives of Sonny's entrenched lieutenants. Except for one. I knew, without daring to look, that the old Estelle mansion remained fixed to the spirit of noble dilapidation upheld by its owner, a man who for some time now had been accorded the chortling deference of a crackpot king long dethroned and consigned to his piles of obsolete currency. The Estelles meant nothing to the town they had founded—meant less than its minions in white, which was reason enough to draw me to the family. But by no means was it the only reason. I might have chanced a look down the avenue if it were.

Instead, I stared at my hands clenched around the steering wheel. "Look at you, you skanky old con," I muttered, and pulled into a convenience store, where I bought some fingernail clippers.

The prison director's mansion sits directly across the street from where I lived for five years, the Shepherdsville Unit. Both are composed of the same red brick, poured and pressed a century and a half ago by inmates, who also constructed every inch of both buildings. I had forgotten how handsomely the bricks sparkled. Or perhaps I'd never noticed it before. Big Red was a terrible place. And until today, I had always regarded the specter of the mansion as one designed purely to spite the tenants across the street. A con would see it that way, naturally. He wouldn't consider it the other way around.

Several parking spaces remained unclaimed in the director's lot. But I couldn't see my crusty Impala among those polished state-issued sedans, and as I realized this and idled further down the block, a stage-whisper issued from within, imploring: *Keep driving. It ain't just the Impala that doesn't belong. Leave this town.*

I pulled over to the curb and fumbled with the ignition. What the hell. I'd bought the suit already. I'd driven eight hundred miles. My papers were waiting. I owed it to myself. Or to Sonny. Or . . . Well, I was here now. I stepped out onto the street.

A magnolia petal dropped from the trees and fell to the sidewalk in front of me. I picked it up, smelled it, and my youth here returned to me that instant. I walked to the corner. There rose the red tide, the Shepherdsville Unit wall. Thirty feet higher still, the guard manning Picket 1 leaned over the tower rail and appraised me with slightly bared teeth. I grinned and waved. He continued to stare. From somewhere behind him and the wall, a procession of half-buried words burbled out of the main loudspeaker. *Clear the mess hall and walk that line back to your shitters you sweet little bitches . . .* The picket guard kept his eyes on me. I straightened my tie, told myself not to look up again, and stepped onto the walkway of the mansion.

A silver Range Rover with state-issued plates glimmered in the driveway. From thirty paces I could make out my scarecrow reflection in it. The other space in the driveway was empty. I continued up the walkway. The soil beds alongside me were almost frantic with color. The flowers weren't native, as far as I could tell. Sonny wouldn't have been the one to depart from the usual indigenous varieties. So, I thought: they're still together, Sonny and Jill.

I walked between the fat white pillars, and at the front steps I took a deep breath. The baroque clang of the doorbell bounded off the mansion walls. From the other side of the door, I could hear rubber heels against marble. The door opened halfway, and a hulking black man with ash-colored hair and standard-issue prison whites peered out at me. He was holding a butcher knife, and from the tip of it, a shred of what looked to be chicken skin dangled.

"It won't be a fair fight, Vermiel," I said. "At least give me a spatula to defend myself with."

Watching his scowl melt was a marvelous thing. "Jesus . . . Coleman! Lord have mercy, it's you, you little shitass! My!"

He threw his arms, sticky with chicken blood, around me. Vermiel Crenshaw had to be seventy by now. It had been nearly a half-century since he'd slashed his stepfather's throat, and no one was really sure why the parole board had overlooked him year after year. The best theory had it that a director might be indisposed to free a con who'd trained under Luis Wyatt-Chenault at Delacorte's in New Orleans. Any number of inmate writ writers had offered to file suit on his behalf. Vermiel told them to go on. He wasn't one of those pathetically housebroken cons who dreaded the free world. It was just that he couldn't abide disappointment. No rash promises. No temptation. To be hopeful was to court hopelessness. To take solace in the everyday was the only way to keep the days coming. He'd passed these admonitions on to me, and they'd served me in good stead when I followed them. For the life now ahead of me, Vermiel had less expertise to lend than I did. But God, it was good to see him.

"Look at that monkey up there in that tree," he chuckled into my ear, and easing away from his hug I saw that the picket guard was on his feet now, staring at us and fumbling at his control panel. "Hey Jackson! 's all right, man! He's here to see the director!"

Leveling his gaze, he shook his head and said, "The damn COs, they've gotten even dumber, if you can imagine that. It's the truth! They're building too many prisons too damn fast, and staffin' 'em with fools like Jackson up there. Now look at you!" he exclaimed, stepping back. "You ain't but a twig, Coleman! How long since you had an honest bite?"

I smiled and shrugged. "Too busy running to sit at a table," I said.

"Hah! But you ain't running no more!" he said, and laughing he slapped my shoulder hard enough to rearrange the bones. "I want to hear *all* about that. Mister Sonny says you're staying for dinner. Coq au vin in your honor. That gonna suit you? Hah!"

Straw-legged, I proceeded behind Vermiel through the sweeping foyer, past the ornately framed rogues' gallery of prison directors past staring down at me—some outraged, some knowingly amused, but most of them looking as vapid as turtles; down hallways buffered with

regally hued Persian rugs that had to be Jill's acquisitions; past the
darkened bedrooms traditionally occupied by visiting wardens, prison
board members or redneck celebrities who had an abiding fetish for all
this jailbird stuff; and finally into Vermiel's haunt, the mother of all
kitchens, where two young men, one white and the other Hispanic,
looked me up and down in the trademark peripheral way of cons as one
chopped the onions and garlic while the other uncorked the bottles of
red wine.

Vermiel leaned against one of the refrigerators. On the cutting
board beside him sat a magazine of crossword puzzles. Seeing that I
noticed, he giggled a little as he gestured with his kitchen knife: "That
oven's new. New dishwasher over there. New paint job. Otherwise . . ."

"Yes," I murmured. Sidelong, I could see the two houseboys looking sidelong at me.

The kitchen door leading to the back yard was open; a round of
guffaws rippled through it. I recognized more than one from among
that testosterone-freighted chorus. "Hey Vermiel!" bellowed the most
familiar voice of all. "Vermiel! Sheriff needs another Jim Beam on the
rocks! And Mister Aspromonte says that cabernet's breathed all it
needs to. Get it on out here."

"I'll do that, sir!" Vermiel hollered back.

After the Hispanic houseboy had finished assembling the tray, the
director's chef said, "Get on back to breakin' up the chicken, Benavides. We're gonna let Mr. Coleman take the drinks out."

Vermiel winked at me. "You gotta let me have my fun, Coleman.
Ain't much of it to go around."

I took the tray from Benavides. "Anything to brighten your day,
Vermiel," I said, hoisting the platter in a manner that came, after all
these years, awfully damned easily.

The houseboy must have caught on. He gestured to Sheriff Bo
Worley's whiskey glass and leered, revealing a gold front tooth. "You
don't need to spit in it," he said. "I already did."

"Well! Get out your autograph pads, fellas. It's the man who walks
through walls."

His voice was jovial, but only that. All very proper, I told myself; I
understood what we had to do here. Sonny lifted himself up from

behind the wrought iron patio table. He'd added to his paunch, of course, and his cheeks still begged for pinching. But the deep puncture of a chin cleft along with the crescent-like dimples gave his face the sculpted valor of a swordsman, while that immortal flourish of golden hair remained in place above his mint-green eyes. As Sonny reached out his hand, so did a second man—taller, coarse by comparison but equally sure of himself: state representative Randall "Foots" Taylor, whom I'd known since toddlerhood. His lips peeled back to reveal that familiar asymmetrical country grin.

"Welcome back, you ol' dog," said Foots, and indeed he grabbed the nape of my neck as if to drag me back to the litter. "You've been missed."

A third fellow rose: barnacle-faced, with a ghastly inkblot of a toupee and a powder blue double-knit suit. It took a minute for me to place him. Once I did, I nearly burst out laughing. His name was Kirby Morris. He'd been the assistant warden at the Creel Unit down in Sugarland, where I spent my first year in prison. Kirby was a frightful bumbler, and it was widely assumed that he'd pulled some politician's pecker out of a mousetrap, else how could a zero like him be drawing a state salary? But there was something deceptively resilient about the man—owing not so much to slyness as to that drowsy staying power common to beasts of burden. Plus, he was at least nominally skilled in the art of ass-kissing. A stranger to the Texas Department of Criminal Retribution would look at a Kirby Morris and figure him to be chewed up and spat out within a calendar year. But I was no stranger to the TDCR, and when I saw old Kirby on the mansion's patio, I knew I was looking at Sonny's deputy director.

I took their hands: "Hello, Mister Director. Good to see you, Representative Taylor. It's been awhile, Warden Morris."

Sonny brushed his free hand against my shoulder and then quickly returned to his chair. But I saw his eyes go momentarily glassy.

"I'd like that whiskey of mine sometime before the ice melts," came a voice off to Sonny's side. It was Bo Worley, muttering through his toothpick.

"Don't get up, Sheriff," I said as I lifted the drink over to him.

"Don't worry," the sheriff said. He pulled the gristled remains of the toothpick from his mouth and examined it before tossing it onto the lawn. "You do that waitressing pretty good, Coleman. I think you got a real future in the free world."

Sonny nudged Worley's boot with his spit-shined loafer. "Now, Bo, we can't all be Renaissance men like you. And I'll tell you and Kirby what a Renaissance man is in just a sec, but I've gotta make this introduction."

Sonny handed one of the two wine glasses over to a man I hadn't seen before. He was slightly built, though with a honker as big as Worley's, and that was all they had in common. He wore a striped red shirt, a violet tie, and burgundy patent leather shoes. Unless Shepherdsville had changed more drastically than it appeared, I felt safe deducing that the fellow wasn't from around these parts.

"Now Wick," said Sonny as the other hopped to his feet, "you *were* the most famous man on this patio 'til just now. I want you to meet the only man who has ever successfully escaped from the Hope Prison Farm. Wick Aspromonte, this is—"

"Hadrian Coleman, sweet Jesus, what a pleasure!" exclaimed the man. He actually made a show of clutching his heart. "Well heck, my lucky timing and whatnot, I was just in town for a little business, Sonny was gracious enough to let me stay for this historic—well, I've read all about you, you became quite a *cause célèbre* there, not to mention you've helped revolutionize, what with all the taut-wire high-intrusion fence innovations that came right after you, you . . . well, heck! Son of a gun! It's my lucky day!"

I thought he would wiggle out of his clothes. Responding to a grunting noise that came from the sheriff's direction, Wick Aspromonte stammered, "Well, Jesus, Bo, I mean the man's paid his debt and then some, now doesn't there come a—"

"Why don't you hire him, then?" said Worley, and put one of his dusty booted feet on the table as he threw back his whiskey.

"Well, who knows? Who knows?" He grinned feebly at me. "Though, heh heh, you might've had your fill of my line of work. My shop's called Global Corrections, Inc. We build prisons."

"Wick just made the front page of the *Wall Street Journal*," said Sonny as he slurped at his wine glass. "Australia decided to privatize its entire federal prison system, and GCI got the contract for the whole shooting match. Little old Shepherdsville, we're just a pimple on Wick's butt now."

"Aw, get outta town for Chrissake Mister Director, heck, Texas is GCI's home away from home. Beautiful bouquet to this cab,

Sonny. Just exquisite. You land the Wickster a case of this reserve and I swear we'll renegotiate the PIPD. Sorry," he said with a flash of a glance my way, "that's per-inmate-per-day. My wife hates when I talk prison-ese. I hate when she talks period, heh heh. No, we're delighted with the Australia contract, but heck do I want that on my epitaph? I mean, who gives a shit about the fucking Australians, right boys? GCI wants to make its mark right here. Especially here in Texas."

"Well hell, Wick, you done made your mark here," came Kirby Morris's thick-tongued drawl. He blushed and fingered his toupee upon noticing that he had the floor. "I mean, you already got two maxes and two minis here, plus them contracts we drew up last week for the juvie and the sub-abuse. I'd've figgered you'd be done with us by now and gone off to Oklahoma or some such place."

Both Wick and Foots Taylor leaned forward to reply, but Sonny's insistent tenor carried. "Now Kirby, I know you haven't used your comp time since Noah put out to sea, but Jesus boy, at least read a newspaper once in awhile," he said, grinning all around. "If Oklahoma had twenty times its population, a federal court order to end over-crowding, fifty thousand paper-ready cons backlogged in county jails and no beds to send 'em to, and a pissed-off public that wants anyone who stole a popsicle stick to go down for five minimum, then yes, Wick would be sitting with a bunch of Okies today instead of us genteel folk. God dawg, where're my manners. Vermiel! Get Mister Coleman—what'll you have?"

"I'd take a beer if you had one," I said.

"I need a refill, too," said Foots Taylor.

"Vermiel! Two Dos Equis!"

"Yessir," came the hollered reply from the kitchen.

"And bring out that cheese and bread! I'm goin' faint!"

"Alright, sir."

Within a minute's time, Vermiel hustled out with the snacks and the Mexican beers. I smiled at him, but his eyes were averted, and he retreated as quickly as he'd arrived.

"Damn, I'm about to boil," muttered Sonny. He snatched up a fist-ful of cheese cubes and tossed them like peanuts down his gullet. With a wink in my direction, he said through his mouthful, "You missed Fitch. He ducked out a half-hour ago. Sent his best."

Cal Fitch had been Thunderball Hope's deputy for nearly two decades. He had covered the director's ass better than anyone could have. But when the walls started to crumble and the feds started swarming, Fitch took care of Fitch.

An unseen phone bleated. "That's mine," said the director as he fished the receiver out of his navy blazer pocket. "Sonny here. Yeah, Bobby. You got that inmate Parker moved into ad-seg yet? . . . Then double up, I want him in there and away from the general population. His cousin's the reason we got the low utility rates in that unit . . ."

Foots Taylor leaned over to me. "I was sorry about your mom," he said. "I made it to the funeral. Saw your sister there, by the way. You talk to her yet?"

I nodded. "That newspaper article mentioned where she worked," I said. "I only had a few quarters, so we didn't talk long. How did she seem?"

"Well, she sure looked hotter than a two-dollar pistol. There was some fella with her. She introduced him to me as her husband. What's that, Mimi's third? Fourth?"

"Somewhere in that range." Mimi hadn't mentioned her recent marital status to me, and I had been afraid to ask.

To Wick Aspromonte, who had been straining to eavesdrop on Sonny's phone conversation, Foots said, "Hadrian and his sister had just about the finest man for a father this part of the world's ever seen. Doc Coleman. My family would've been out of the quarter-horsing business thirty years ago if it weren't for Doc. He gave this county a lot."

"He gave us a goddamned killer." So spoke the sheriff, who had been staring at me throughout. My fingers tightened around the arms of my chair. Foots looked away. Kirby Morris listlessly picked at his fingernails.

"Well heck," said Wick Aspromonte, giggling nervously, "my pop was a Lutheran minister, and I'm not sure I turned out just quite the way he—"

"But did you go around killing blind men?" demanded Bo Worley.

"Well. Maybe not that, but—"

"Did you go around strangling public officials? And then gouging their eyes out with a broken whiskey bottle?"

My chair trembled against the red brick patio. I could feel myself rising, and I saw that Worley was standing to meet me.

Then came Sonny's voice. "Bo, will you quit living in the past, for Pete's sake? Now, Coleman's slate is clean, and as long as we're on that subject . . ." From underneath his chair, the director retrieved a large manila envelope.

His mouth gaping with delight, Sonny waggled the envelope in front of me like it was a chicken drumstick. "From the governor with love," he cooed.

From across the street, I could hear the slamming of the sallyport gates to Big Red. "The governor's gonna regret he ever let you talk him into doing that," said the sheriff to Sonny.

"Well, you just be sure and tell him that the next time you've got the governor's ear," snickered Sonny. The others laughed. I didn't. "But I'd take care of my own neighborhood if I was you, Bo," the director continued—his voice as genial as before, but somehow the patio darkened. "I know for a fact you've got better things to do than chew on Coleman's ass. You still haven't talked to that fucking Coushatta tribe, and we're getting on deadline to expand the Carter Unit."

The sheriff's face soured. "They're not breaking any laws," he said.

"Only every five minutes! Jesus H. Christ, Sheriff, they're growing pot on their reservation—"

"That's in Polk County. That's not my jurisdiction."

"I'll tell you what's in your jurisdiction. The damn Carter Unit's in your jurisdiction. And if we don't build that expansion on account of some pile of Indian bones, some goddamn sacred burial mound no one gave a rat's ass about 'til we started digging—if you don't get those Coushattas out of my face, then upwards of a hundred fifty jobs in *your* jurisdiction are gonna go the way of the buffalo, Kemo Sabe. And I will let the right people know, some time before election day, who let it all happen on account of he was too busy harassing an ex-con. And then: when the governor asks me why we can't get those beds ready for those gang members he told the voters he'd get tough on? I'll sure tell him, Bo. *Then* you'll have his ear!"

Worley's face soared crimson. Sonny eyed him dead-on. Then he looked away, and as he pulled two stiff sheets of paper out of the envelope, his grin was one I hadn't seen before. "Just don't test me, okay,

Bo?" he said as he perused the document in his hand. "You go pop those Coushattas on something. Run their damn licenses. They've got it coming. I offered to dig up their ancestors' bones on our nickel and hand 'em over, and they give me this 'sacred land' crap."

He snorted. "Ain't nothing sacred in the state of Texas but jobs and safe streets, right Foots? Ain't we doing the Lord's work, all of us here? They want some sacred land—Bo, you go stick 'em in your most sacred county cell block. But before you do, I need you to put your X-mark on the witness line here after Coleman signs his."

Sonny thrust the documents, along with a gold pen, in front of my face. "Two copies," he said. "One for you, one for the governor's office. Sign both where your name's typed."

As I read over the leaden, severe prose of the document that would sanction my freedom, I tried to ignore the conversation, in which Bo Worley swore that he would under no circumstances participate in this savaging of justice, followed by a few dire threats on Sonny's part and then Foots Taylor's interjection that he would be happy to sign on as the state or local elected official who witnessed this conferral of liberty. A minute later, the signed documents were back in the envelope and we had returned to our drinks—all but the sheriff, who stood over me and fingered the brim of his Resistol.

"You better not be thinking of moving back to Shepherd County," he said.

I could think of no reply.

"'Cause I don't want you anywhere near my jurisdiction. You got that? You so much as jaywalk here and I will stick you in a hole where you will be buttfucked by sweaty niggers all day long."

"Hey. Bo. Were you just listening to wh—"

"Don't you tell me what to do, Mister Director!" Now the sheriff was yelling. "Once he's in your system, as I guarantee you he will be, then you can mollycoddle him all you want, like your daddy did! But not in my jurisdiction you can't!"

Worley wheeled on Wick Aspromonte, who shrank back in alarm. "See, I *know* this son of a bitch!" he hollered at the prison entrepreneur. "I don't care what that piece of asswipe says with the governor's signature on it! The governor don't know this scum of the earth like I do!"

Then he pivoted deftly on the heel of his boot. His face near mine, the sheriff dropped his voice to a nearly feminine whisper:

"And *you* know you're the scum of the earth too, don't you? Don't you?"

The others may have seen him go. I don't know what I saw.

"Cocoa what?" the deputy director was asking.

"Coq au vin, Kirby, but I don't think it's best suited for your discerning palate, now you get on home to Jeanie's pot roast," Sonny said, and stood so that his subordinate would do the same.

Kirby Morris rose. "We got that eight a.m. at East Texas State to go over the new inmate curriculum," he said, gravely adding, "Don't forget."

"I wish I could forget. Give the little ones my best."

When Kirby was gone, Foots crossed his legs, took a swig of his beer and observed, "That is without a doubt the most nonfunctional second-in-command I have ever seen."

"Ah hah! And that, in and of itself, is a function." Sonny's eyes were alight. "You think I want someone else around to talk prisons with the governor? It's bad enough that you're around—and speaking of which, Mister Representative, I've seen *your* chief of staff on the House Corrections Committee. He doesn't look like he could clean out an ashtray without setting his hair on fire. And Wick's vice-president, he—you all right over there, Wick?"

"Jeez." The prison businessman loosened his purple silk tie. His pinched face was pale and knotted. "Sorry, guys. I'm just—I mean, Jeez. What a hostile man."

When Wick turned a baleful expression my way, Sonny exclaimed, "Ohhh. You mean Bo's hard-on for Hadrian. Well, shit. That goes way back."

The director turned to me. I waved him off, looked down at the cracks between the red bricks on the patio. "Go ahead," I said. "I don't care."

"Well," said Sonny, "the man Hadrian was sent to the pen for killing, Judge Castlebury? He was a dear friend of Bo's daddy. And the silent partner of the bar Bo's daddy ran. When Bo first announced for sheriff, Castlebury just pretty much made that deal happen. Just pretty much put his arm around the incumbent and told him it was time he got himself a bass boat and a rocking chair. He was a stout man in these parts, Judge Castlebury was. Though . . ."

I believe Sonny took great care not to look at me, for fear that his voice might quaver that much more. "Though he was . . . one of the most . . . *obscene* . . . creatures. Just rancid with evil. And it would take being the kind of man Bo Worley is, and the kind of favors done to him by Judge Horace Castlebury, to make a man sentimental—"

"But Sonny, it goes back way further than Judge Castlebury," interrupted Foots. The local legislator picked at his beer label. "See, the Worleys, they were Ku Klux Klan when Bo was growing up. And Hadrian's daddy, Doc Coleman, was the local chapter's sworn enemy. All that stuff with Castlebury was just icing on the cake."

"Isn't that something. Jeez Louise." Wick Aspromonte fluttered his eyelashes, shook his head. "Not that we didn't have our own neighborhood melodramas in Newark, but . . ."

"Aw, don't make us out to be Sodom and Gomorrah. Shepherdsville's just Mayberry R.F.D. under lock and key." Sonny followed this with a bored yawn that might have fooled Aspromonte. But I knew why he'd had enough of that subject.

"Gentlemen," he then announced, "I've done all the pardoning I can do on an empty stomach. Vermiel!"

Breaking free of myself, I contemplated my dubious presence at the great oak table with those captains of an ancient industry, while the three uniformed figures shuffled from setting to setting as I once did, serving Sonny his extra helping of meat as I once did. Sonny glanced across the table once, his expression neither careworn nor placid but somewhere in between; and then it gave way to a smile befogged with . . . with, good God, was that nostalgia? Only that? No, something else just now. But then the director took a whiff of his entree, and he fell joyously into his food.

We were not far into our meal—which was the best I'd had in years; Vermiel was still the master—when Sonny blurted out, "Okay. Let's hear the debriefing."

He shifted just to the right so as to face me. The light in his pale green eyes crackled like fuses set to fire. "Debriefing," I said vacantly.

"Yup. I'm braced for the humiliation now. Come on, bubba! The debriefing! The terrible tale of how you brought shame to the proud reputation of the Purvis J. Hope Prison Farm. Git to it. Sing for your supper."

"I don't remember much about it," I said.

"The hell you don't." He slurped at the chicken breast he held with both hands. "So. Once you got over the fence, you waded through the slough until you took that pigtrail and crossed Highway 392."

I had to close my eyes for a moment. "I think that's right," I said.

"And then you—"

"Let the record reflect," cut in Wick Aspromonte, "that GCI's taut-wire variety would never, ever have been so flimsy as to, not meaning any offense to your heroics of course Hadrian but our tech—"

"Wick, it was a different world then, no one's disputing that, eight years ago you were still in Newark selling hospital supplies," Sonny commented wearily. With his palm extended Wick's way to ward off further digression, he continued, "And then from the highway, you hoofed it to the railroad tracks."

"Pretty much," I said. "I rested in that cabin for an hour or so."

"Which is where the Chadwick Unit dogs picked up your scent," said Sonny.

"From the back of the Hope Farm to 392," mused Foots. "Hell, that's twelve miles right there. And ugly miles at that. How long did that take you?"

"What? Oh . . ." I'd been thrown by Sonny's words. *The Chadwick Unit dogs* . . . Wiping my napkin against my mouth, I chanced a look at Sonny. Our eyes met, and lest anyone see him, his gaze was low-lidded, neutral. But I saw the encompassing glow, like twin ferris wheels . . . Now I had to swallow. I had to look down. It was Sonny's doing. It had to be. As deputy director, he'd given the order, that morning eight years ago, to send the Chadwick Unit dogs after me and leave the Hope Farm dogs in their kennels—the kennels where I'd worked my last nine years in the system, raising from pups and naming and feeding and laying tracks for the very dogs who knew my scent better than they knew their own, and who could have tracked me to the bottom of the Gulf Coast or to the outer mists of heaven . . . And when, in the years and years of evenings spent in the devastating solitude of lumberyards or dispossessed tin shacks, I'd conjure up something, anything, to make the next breath one worth taking—well, I believed I could hear Sonny's reasoned voice singing it out to his gravely nodding inquirers:

"Please do not misunderstand me, there is no dog sergeant more disciplined or relentless than C. C. Holliday. But to put him in a position where he would have to hunt down a young man who'd been like his only son was something I would sooner avoid. Nor, gentlemen, did it seem altogether damned prudent to send out a pack of dogs that Coleman had, with very little supervision, trained all by himself. Trained to do what, you'd have to wonder. For all we knew, he'd been planning this escape for years and had some trick up his sleeve that only he and those Hope Farm canines knew about. Would you take that chance?—Especially when you had the best set of dogs in the system only forty miles away, at Chadwick?"

Vintage Sonny Hope. All of it true and in the end, total bullshit. Though it might have killed him to do it, Sarge Holliday would have shown me no mercy. And yes, I'd trained those dogs: I'd trained them to track my scent, chase me down, pin me to the dirt and gnash away at my padded armor. And at night I'd hear them moaning in their kennels, plagued with fever dreams in which their jaws at last clamped down on my jugular. They, not the Chadwick Unit dogs, were uniquely trained to track my ass through the river bottoms and make goulash out of me. But only someone inside the system would understand this. And inside the system, in Shepherdsville, things got around, but nothing got out . . .

Except me. I got out. And I knew Sonny had been there for me. I just knew it.

He was talking. "—have a watch on him, Foots. But he left Sarge Holliday's office just before six a.m. And then the Chadwick Unit dogs got the scent at the barn around noon, which was maybe an hour after he'd left. So you figure in the nap he took, and I'd say he legged out those twelve miles in a little over three hours."

"Christ Jesus," said Wick Aspromonte. "Though I'd venture to say you know those woods pretty well."

"Damn skippy he knows those woods," said Sonny as he gnashed at his chickenbone. He looked my way, winked. I felt a great settling take place inside of me, and I drew a long, long breath.

"But then you got to the railroad tracks," Sonny continued. "Now Wick, what you're about to hear is vintage East Texas Houdini."

He took a sip of his wine and cleared his throat. "This sumbitch ran three solid miles on the tracks. You know why he did that?"

Foots cut in. "All those incident reports came to my committee," he said. "Apparently those railroad ties and that gravel on the tracks ripped up those dogs' paws pretty good. Now Hadrian, how'd you know to do that?"

Sonny wouldn't let me reply. "Oh, that's not the best part," he said, and held the chickenbone out like a conductor's wand. "This isn't in the reports, 'cause it was months before Holliday and I figured it out. Those dogs followed him along those tracks. Limping and stumbling, but for three miles they followed him. And then . . . no scent. I mean, *none.* Last they picked up on was a telephone pole where they figured he'd leaned on to catch his breath. And they done lost his happy ass after that. I mean, Hadrian Coleman done vanished like Halloween."

The legislator and the prison-builder turned their eyes on me. But Sonny's eyes—God, look at them, I thought, he's begging, he's still that spoiled little shit.

"You tell them," I said to Sonny.

"He climbed that fucking telephone pole," Sonny proclaimed. "And then for almost two miles, he scaled the telephone wires. *Man!*"

As Foots and Aspromonte gasped and Sonny hooted, I couldn't suppress a smile, though for a different reason. Sonny didn't any more figure it out than do the escaping himself. He'd gotten it all from C. C. Holliday. The dog sergeant had heard the telephone-wire trick from the same place I had: Kittycat Nelson, a black kennelman who'd been in and out of the system maybe fifteen times in his sixty years, a friendly old mess who couldn't spell his own name or brush his teeth, much less walk a straight line . . . but he sure could tell Sarge Holliday and me about witchcraft and juke joints and the mind of the catfish, and how to turn a dog's nose inside out.

"And then," shrugged the director, "he dropped down into a slough. And as far as we could figure, he took it all the way to where it fed into the Minerva. And that's where we lost him."

Sonny then leaned back and gestured for me to tell the rest. I nodded, but the words were slow to come. To them it was a puzzle. I understood that. To me, though, it was a nightmare in fragments, like a mirror dropped to the floor, with some pieces flipped over and others catching more than their share of the light, and all in all a frightful composite. A nightmare. Because I hadn't been some frolicsome wizard who knew without a sliver of doubt that he would sit at the big table someday and chortle with his pursuers about how he had outfoxed them. I was a hunted creature, crashing through burrs and

branches like a poor dumb rooter hog. That I knew those woods intimately meant that I knew they could defend me against only so much
and for only so long before turning fatally against me. For two days, I
was utterly consumed by the notion of death and its near presence. In
that frenzied timespan, the only other noises I remember hearing,
besides my own panting, were the distant chorus of the tracking dogs
and the whirring of police helicopters; and I could not possibly convey
to these three men, even if I wanted to, the overwhelming reek of fear
I wore for days thereafter. It was nothing to revisit—except, of course,
in my dreams, when I had no choice.

But did I have a choice now? I owed this to Sonny. So I went along.

"Where did you look?" I asked him.

Laughing in exaggerated astonishment, he said, "Where didn't we
look? We combed the riverbanks some fifty miles south, way past
Shepherdsville, all the way to Liberty. Though most of all we kept an
eye on your mom's place. That's where I figured you'd turn up. See,"
and he turned to the other two, "I never for a second thought he killed
Wexler premeditated. A week before his parole? Not a chance. No,
considering Wexler's disciplinary jacket, it looked like the typical case
of a lifer jacking with a guy who's on his way out. So it had to be self-
defense. Meaning spontaneous. Meaning we have a guy without a
plan."

Shrugging, he said to me, "I was positive that you'd come home to
your mama's place to regroup. But we waited there a day, a week, a
month. We eyeballed that house twenty-four/seven for six months,
you bastard! And you never showed up! Now where the hell were
you?"

"You say you went fifty miles south of the slough," I said.

"At least! Found one of your damn inmate shoes hung on a tupelo
stump about twelve miles downstream. Hell, the Texas Rangers
wanted your ass so bad they even dredged the Minerva! Or tried to.
Dumb sons of bitches. It was like dragging a net through a briar
patch."

"All that was south of the slough," I said.

"Well, and hell, we ran the dogs up both shores upstream a mile or
two. Maybe it was five miles. Why?"

"I swam upriver," I said.

"You . . . For how long?"

"I don't know exactly. All night and all the next day and through the night again until before midnight."

Their shared stupefaction was not unlike that of the cattle I'd seen earlier today, paralyzed in the middle of the stock tank beside the mulecart road.

Finally, Foots spoke. "Where did you get out of the water, Hadrian?"

"At Bernadette Creek."

"No!" Foots Taylor dropped his fork against his plate. "You got that wrong, Hadrian. Couldn't be. Do you have any idea—"

"Yes. But that's what I did. And then I waded the creek 'til I got to the first bridge."

They were still gaping at me, so I went on: "I got to Dutch Wilson's icehouse, and I broke into it and got some new clothes and some food, plus the twenty dollars that was in the cash register. And then . . ." I put my head back against the chair and stared at the shattered light of the chandelier. "Then I ran a few more miles in the woods. Somehow. I could barely stand. But I remember it looked like only two or three more hours 'til daylight, and I needed to get someplace safe before the sun came up. So I made it on foot as far as Del Sparks's ranch. I took one of his horses and rode it, I don't know, five or ten miles, into the pine uplands, and I let it go. And there was a little home out by the Neches River, and the folks there took me in."

"Who?" Sonny asked.

"I don't even know if they told me their names. They were cooking speed out there. You wouldn't invite them home for Christmas dinner. But they damn sure saved my ass."

"And then?" asked Wick.

"Nothing worth telling," I said. "I got the hell out of Texas. And then I got the hell out of every other place I was at."

"But that, that couple you saved! That, those honeymooners from Houston who were driving to Chicago and got hijacked—I mean, c'mon Hadrian, I read all about it in the Houston paper, don't hold out on us, give us the dirt!"

He blanched when he saw how I looked at him. "Sorry, I just meant—"

"Mister Aspromonte," I said.

"Please. Wick."

"Wick. This was not a movie. I was not playing a role. I was an escaped convict. I was wanted for murder. And any time I went out in public, whether to have a cup of coffee or to drive those two kids to the hospital . . ."

I closed my eyes. It did not feel over. It did not feel far away at all. "Any time I stepped outside," I said, "I could hear those dogs. And I could see those sirens. And that made me feel just about as good as dead."

That last word lingered. When the kitchen door swung open and Vermiel burst into the dining room, I found myself smiling. He'd been eavesdropping. Somewhere on that side of the kitchen door, there was an imprint of my ear as well.

Vermiel reached for the dishes. "But," Sonny then declared, "the good guys won."

To my surprise, he hoisted his wine glass. "That couple told the story back home to the one and only Sissy Shipman. She wrote it up in the *Houston Chronicle*. The Missouri papers picked it up off the wires. And you found out you'd been free as a sneeze for the last six months. So why don't we leave the rest to history and drink to the good guys winning for once, just once, in this sorry-dog lifetime."

So now I was among the good guys. With an unsteady smile, I joined the others in the toast. Still, the simple motion of lifting my glass seemed to squeeze the last drop of energy out of me. *Among the good guys*, I thought blearily. As recently as this morning, I'd been somewhere else. No telling where.

Not long after the dishes were cleared, Foots Taylor and Wick Aspromonte thanked their host and headed for the door. I trailed along behind them, but Sonny pulled me back and we retreated to the den on the south side of the mansion. There, in the mahogany-paneled room where I'd served God knows how many thousands of Tanqueray-and-tonics to Sonny's father and fed the fireplace whole forests of cedar and oak, we sat under the dimness of a single endtable lamp, trading clumsy words—waiting, I guess, for the old language to resurface, or to see if it had died somewhere in the infinity of space between us. Reclined in plush leather, the spot where for decades a stiff-backed cypress chair creaked in protest of old Thunderball's huge posterior, the present director swished his single-malt beneath his nose and cracked open a Nicaraguan cigar. (I had declined both and stuck with my Mexican beer, which was plenty good.) Shmoozer though he was, Sonny seemed at ease with the stillness, and especially with his new props. His grey slacks had hootched up, exposing calves as pale and flabby as fish bellies. He'd always loved calling himself "the consummate indoorsman"—though with the new job title came golf with lobbyists and deer and quail hunts with politicians. Thunderball, a fanatical hunter, hated the game of golf with equal fanaticism. He liked to brag that he'd never stepped on anything greener than a snake. That wouldn't be a proper epitaph for Sonny's dad: it wasn't lack of experience with a putter that did him in. Instead, you could say this about old Purvis "Thunderball" Hope: he would not change when the unwritten rules of the game did, as if sticking to the rules he'd mastered amounted to the noblest stance of all, when no matter what rules you were talking about, the game itself was corrupt beyond measure. And it was on account of that basic hypocrisy that, at least in my eyes—though I'd loved Thunderball like the father he truly was to me—the old prison boss came to appear deranged and pathetic, and thus unfit.

If he could see his son, his betrayer, now. Through the glaze of his bitterness and enfeeblement, might he discern anything in the boy—his only child—to stir up any remnants of fondness? I, for one, always got a hoot out of watching Sonny. The way his plump hands made everything he clasped tightly in them seem so worthy of possession. The way, with a hitch of his neck, he tossed back the corn silk filaments of yellow hair from his forehead, and the way, then, that those eyes, silver-green like mountain springwater, shone from his full moon of a face. The way he walked with a jubilant bounce, with the hair on the back of his scalp springing even lighter . . . And of course there was his grin, dazzling and idiotic and cruel in a way that did not offend. He'd put on his usual show this evening: we'd all been thrown in orbit around him, even Bo Worley, whom he'd brought low, which alone was worth the price of gas getting back to Shepherdsville. Still, moments like this one were when I think I was always most drawn to him. The moments of repose, when Sonny kicked back—toys in hand but all other devices stowed out of sight—and luxuriated in the world that was triumphantly his.

Vermiel appeared from the shadows of the doorway. "Kitchen's all clean, sir," he said as he wiped his hand against his grimy white pants. "What can I bring y'all?"

"We're squared away, Vermiel," said Sonny. "Get on home."

"Alright, sir. You take care now, Coleman," he added, and turned and departed out the front door, headed for the sallyport across the street.

Sonny said nothing. I smelled the smoke from his puffing.

"I'll never know how to thank you," I began.

More puffing as my next words faltered.

"Well," Sonny said after a time. "Sissy Shipman, bless her frosty little heart, set the table with that first story of hers. I guess you didn't see that one. The one where Digby confessed he was the one who killed Wexler."

He put up a hand to ward off my protests. "I know, I know," he laughed. "But Digby *did* see the whole thing. He said you were making your bed when Wexler came at you with his shank. Hell, there wasn't any physical evidence to hang it on you anyway! Only that you ran off. Digby was the one who dragged Wexler back to his cell. Digby was the one who mopped up the blood."

"But Digby didn't kill him, Sonny."

"Hadrian. Would you listen to me real carefully? Digby confessed to it. He confessed it to me, confessed it to the D.A., confessed it to Sheriff Worley, confessed it to the Rangers, and confessed it to Sissy Shipman. Right there on his deathbed. Told the world he wanted to go to the other side with a clear conscience."

His lips smacked loudly against his cigar.

"Told me a little more than he told everyone else, obviously. On account of he knew you and I went way back."

Before I could interject, he laughed and said, "Relax, babycakes! Digby's dead, Wexler's dead, and you are fully and unconditionally absolved of the legal consequences of the crimes of which you stood accused, with all civil rights restored that would otherwise blah blah blah get the picture bubba?"

I watched his face glow with pleasure beneath the haze of his smoke. "Anyway," he continued. "Give yourself a little credit. You were a hell of a lot easier to go to bat for when you played Good Samaritan up there in Missouri. You hadn't done that, they wouldn't have come to

Sissy with their heroic tale, and Sissy wouldn't have interviewed Mimi and written that come-out-come-out-wherever-you-are story. You'd still be on the run. By the way. Sissy made me promise to set her up an exclusive with you. I don't see any way out of it, but bubba, need I remind you: Sissy Shipman may have been on the side of the angels this one time, but she ain't your friend, and she damn sure ain't mine."

His eyes bulged with dire thoughts. "No one ever needed to tell me to quit talking so much," I reminded him.

"No, Mister Loquacious would not be you," he said, and knocked back the dregs of his Scotch. With a groan, he got to his feet. "I'm bringing back the damn bottle. Whatcha need?"

"I'm fine," I said.

"No you're not. The taxpayers owe you one."

From the kitchen he called out, "Jill's gonna be sorry she missed you. She's at some inane D.A.R. banquet at the country club. Against my advice, she recruited the TDCR general counsel to be the guest speaker. In case you hadn't heard, that's Aynsley. So she ought to be home some time before Christmas."

I listened to the obscure sounds of Sonny rooting through the cabinets. "Are you and her doing okay?" I asked.

"Me and Jill? Yeah, we're fine. Her daddy still hates me and my mama still hates her, but other than that . . ."

He padded back in, cigar between his teeth, and put my beer on the coffee table in front of me. "What about kids?" I asked.

"Arrgh. It's come up. Always goes away, though."

He smiled weakly at his drink. It was time to change the subject. "It was good to see Foots," I said.

"Hasn't changed a hair, has he? He nearly didn't make it when I told him Aspromonte was coming over. I said Foots, I don't wanna hear it. Hell, Sonny has to deal with clowns like Wick all damn day long. I'm sitting on top of a three-billion-dollar budget, and there ain't a minute goes by that some yahoo isn't in my office trying to sell me his new state-of-the-art institutional crapper or Velcro standard-issues or high-grade cell padding or a ton of synthetic beef with a shelf life of twelve million years. Shee. At least Aspromonte knows how to entertain when I'm up east. My God, you should see his wife. A hundred twenty pounds of blonde and collagen and a dumper that'll put wood in your drawers . . . Damn."

He returned to his puffing. "Don't be worried about Worley, by the way," he said. "He's gotta talk that talk, just so he can convince himself that badge really means something."

"It sure meant something the last time he arrested me," I said.

"Yeah. Well." The low, dark voice seemed to be coming from somebody else. "I wasn't prison director then. Bo Worley knows I could have him thrown in his own jail in one fucking heartbeat. He couldn't cross the street without my go-ahead. He's nothing."

With a vague gesture he concluded, "So don't worry about Bo."

But the tone of his voice said that something else was bothering him. He flicked his ashes and missed the ashtray, muttered "Goddammit" and tended to the mess with exaggerated care, his pale eyebrows crossed. He muttered again, something I couldn't catch. Then he fell back into his leather chair, puffing slow and deep. Whatever he was gazing at was not in this room. A current of air from the ceiling vent caused a few strands of his hair to flutter back from his forehead, just barely, and so too did the smoke warp and drift all around him—distorting him, but still I could see him clearly. He was forty. A very young forty, but an old forty as well. And now it hit me, the folly of imagining him as the emotionally unburdened throwback to days that had to be as gone for him as they were for me.

"It's Tempesta," he said. His voice was now as clear as ice. "Tempesta's the one to worry about."

He put down his cigar. Then he put his thumb to his mouth and began to chew on his nail.

The name took a moment to register. "You don't mean Ricky Tempesta," I said. "Is he still bribing your people down at the Hope Farm?"

"The—what the hell are you . . . Oh. I keep forgetting how long you've been gone."

He took a swig straight out of the bottle, wincing down the swallow. "Tempesta's been out seven years. His capital murder conviction got reversed by the Court of Criminal Appeals."

"You're shitting me."

"And he's set up shop here," said Sonny. His tone of voice was flat, expunged. "Three years in the Hope Farm, and he figured he liked Shepherdsville so much he'd just send for his things once the court sprung him."

At least that part didn't surprise me. Ricky Tempesta had bought off so many guards, had so many local hookers ferried in, had so much blow and good whiskey available in his outsized cell, had so many diamonds on his fingers, had so many lawyers and accountants and rare book dealers and stereo repairmen filing in to see him at the Hope Farm—Tempesta had so much of Shepherdsville as a con that he used to love to brag, "I don't need a fucking key to my cell. Why bother? I've got a key to the whole fucking city!"

That he'd decided to keep a good thing going was no shock. That he'd been let out was what I could not fathom. Even the cons who had committed far more brutal offenses saw Ricky Tempesta as a superior breed of predator. You could look all the way down into him and discover only the mind, manner and morals of a hammerhead shark. Tempesta bought and sold "property"—meaning land and buildings, but also drugs, guns, bodies . . . anything of value. I'd heard all the stories firsthand. Maybe only half of them were true. Tempesta was a braggart, a shit-starter, the kind of con you were best off avoiding and not for a second trusting. Still, you had better consider his words, on the off-chance that he was shooting straight. That, and you had better not underestimate him.

"So what's he doing in Shepherdsville?" I asked.

The noise that came from Sonny sounded at first like an expulsion of mirth, until it curdled in his throat.

"Well," he began, and he almost seemed to smile as he poured the Scotch into his tumbler. "It seems Ricky Tempesta has decided he's going to bleed Shepherdsville dry. He's incorporated a new town the next county over and he's building a half-dozen prisons in it. And he's gotten the legislature to call for a public referendum to decide whether to contract out every inmate in the state to the care of private business. Like Wick Aspromonte did in Australia. Meantime, he's paying off half the people in the system to feed him dirt about TDCR so he can slam us in television ads. He's declared war on us. On Shepherdsville. Oh, and I forgot to tell you the name of his new town. Trust. Trust, Texas. Now, how's that for shit in your sandbox."

I couldn't help it—I erupted in laughter. "That's beautiful," I managed. "That's just beautiful. What a country."

But Sonny wasn't laughing along. He shook his head, over and over, his mouth twisted against his face. "Come on," I protested. "Who cares what the Court of Criminal Appeals says? Tempesta's a sleazebag. No one's going to let him get within ten feet of a prison, unless he's wearing white."

"Wrong, bubba. He's been in the prison business since six months after he got out."

I was too stunned to respond.

"That idiot Aspromonte. He's the one that got Tempesta started. He was new in town and fell for Tempesta's big talk about old-time Texas connections. Used him as a developer—the guy who'd go to some down-in-the-mouth town, taking the mayor and the local dumbo from the chamber of commerce out for a steak, telling them how to reap the goddamn harvest like Shepherdsville did. Instant economic salvation. That's what the privates like GCI sell. And Aspromonte used Tempesta to do the selling."

"But not anymore?"

"Shit, no. Tempesta swindled him. Kickbacks on every level. And Wick couldn't squawk for fear the state would shut his prisons down. He just stopped using him. But by then, Tempesta already had references and lobbyists on his payroll."

I had to laugh again. "Sounds like business as usual to me."

"Well, it's not, believe me." His tone was offended, his sharp glare reproachful. "It's as crooked as a snake. By all rights he should've gotten the needle. And now he's trying to preside over the Texas criminal justice system? Jesus." He drew back into his chair, taut and nervous, blowing out hot smoke from between his teeth.

It still seemed farcical to me. "If you've got the goods on him, Sonny, then blow the damn whistle," I said. "It's not like he's got more stroke than you do."

"Shit. Money buys stroke, Hadrian. He's got more of both than I'll ever have. Besides."

He turned to the endtable, fidgeting about for his drink. His hand was shaking. The ice rattled; his lips trembled at the lip of the glass. I had seen Sonny this upset only once before. At the time, he was eighteen and I was fifteen, and we were both huddled over the corpse of the man I had just killed.

"Besides," he said again, but he was interrupted by the sound of the front door opening, followed by a soft ruffling and a jangling of keys. The door closed. Two soprano heels came clicking our way.

"For God's sake, Sonny, are you conducting some kind of seance or did the state forget to pay the electricity bill? This place is dismal enough without . . . Oh my . . ."

"Hey, honey," said Sonny, cheery and cock-eyed again. "Look who the cat drug in."

She wore a sleeveless silk dress that clung to the hips and waist. I remembered that now. She always wore white in the summer.

I stood. "Hi, Jill," I said.

"Well . . . hello." She seemed not to be seeing me—but instead considering, for the first time in ages, the idea of me.

As if drawn out of a trance by a finger-snap, she was instantly recomposed. "Well, the cat deserves a bonus, for once. Hadrian! Where have you been all of our lives?"

I stepped over to her and we hugged. The discreet scent of her cologne—when had I last smelled something such as this . . .

Her hand was examining mine. "And you've taken good care of your nails," she sang. "Hadrian, would you please loan your nail clippers to Sonny? He seems to have misplaced his somewhere in his mouth."

"Enter nagging," mumbled Sonny. "That's my girl."

"That's very good, dear. But in fact, I'm quite patient. Otherwise Aynsley Reeves would be tied to the Shepherdsville Country Club flagpole, his entrails gathered at his feet."

"Did I tell you?" exclaimed Sonny, now standing. "I told you he was the black hole, Jill—but you insisted, on account of he's cozy as lice with your daddy. Honey, you knew! How many times has he pinned us to the wall at cocktail parties, going on and on about the history of Shepherd County's land deeds?"

"But I thought he'd be better in a set format," she pouted, "with all those pugnacious-looking matrons bearing down on him from behind their platters of angel food cake! I had no idea he'd filibuster so! I mean, it was one thing to talk about inmate mail restrictions, and the bit about the court-ordered showerhead spacing requirements was edifying so far as it went. But then to go on, like one of those car alarms that wails all night for no reason whatsoever, about the Open Records Act! As if Harriet Bridges might one day put down her sewing needle, turn off her soap opera, shutter all the windows, and draft an Open Records request demanding to know the annotated dental history of Inmate Bugsy Knucklesworth!"

Jill let out an exaggerated sigh. "I'm sorry, I'm sure I was interrupting something more urgent," she said. "Were you two talking about golf?"

"Join us for a drink," grinned Sonny. "And there's leftover coq au vin if you're not all stove up with angel food cake."

"I'm stove up with Aynsley, but thanks." She turned to me. "Your sister called me and told me you were on your way back."

At last came the frown that was sweet enough to be a smile. "It's so wonderful you're here in Shepherdsville again," she said. "I won't ask you what lunatic notion compelled you to come back. You've been terribly missed."

It must have been my expression that made her suddenly glance her husband's way. "Anyhow," she said, "Sonny's been in serious need of a true friend. Even a true enemy would be refreshing. No one who hates him wants to take the first swing."

Sonny rolled his eyes. "She's a nag *and* she's paranoid."

"Exhausted is what I am." She turned again to me. "Plan on Sunday brunch with us, won't you? We'll go somewhere where Aynsley Reeves won't find us. And don't forget to loan Sonny your nail clippers."

And then, in a brisk flapping of white, like a magician's handkerchief, she was somewhere else.

As I was leaving, but before the front door was opened to expose us to the picket guard, Sonny held out his arms. He hugged me hard, and for a long time.

"Jill was right, you know," he murmured. "I have needed you back in the worst way, bubba."

I didn't know what to say. That I needed to be back? Maybe I did. Maybe I did.

And then he asked: "Are we even now?"

But even as he uttered the question, his body seemed to sag, and he let go of me.

"No."

It was him talking, not me. "No. We won't ever be even. That's a fact."

Still, I stepped out into a night that was warm and forgiving, and I passed under the picket guard and got in my car and drove off. And I had Sonny to thank for that.

2

Mimi had left me the key in a flower pot beside the front porch. I entered my parents' house in darkness. It had been over twenty years, but I was ill-equipped at this late hour of this interminable day to reckon with the ghosts. I kept the lights out and made for my old bedroom, shucking my clothes in the hallway.

The bed was where it had always been. For a moment I wobbled over it. Fifteen years on a slab in a cage. Eight years under bridges, or beneath heaps of garbage, or on the floors of condemned shacks, or in the back of my car. What I was standing over was the last real bed I had ever slept in. I crumpled against the kid-sized mattress that, the moment I fell with a moan against it, whispered back the breath of the little boy I'd once been. A fluttering of wonderment, then of regret, and sleep was soon to follow.

It was not the roar of morning light through the bedroom window that awakened me, but instead, a knocking. On my way towards the front door, I fetched up yesterday's dress shirt off of the sofa. I pulled back a flap of the living room curtains. "Holy shit," I muttered. It was Aynsley Reeves, general counsel of the Texas Department of Criminal Retribution, knocking on the glass of the front door window with the knuckle that glinted with his Harvard ring.

"Cockle-doodle-doo, sunbeam," he sang as soon as I opened the door. Peering up and down from beneath his horn-rimmed glasses, he added, "My my. Did you dress up on our account? The following bulletin may be a little hard to take before your morning coffee, but there's been an ever so slight shift in fashion sensibilities since you last showed your backside to Shepherdsville. People wear pants now. May we come in? Official business."

With his left hand, the one that hadn't been tapping at the window, Aynsley held up his briefcase, along with a white plastic bag the likes of which I'd seen a million times before—though what the general counsel was doing with an Inmate Processing property bag was beyond me. Scratching the back of my hair, I stepped from behind the doorway. "I heard you got work, Aynsley," I said. "Congratulations. Good to see you."

"Likewise," he replied, bowing curtly. "Though perhaps not so much all at once. Not meaning any offense to your family jewels. They appear, at the briefest possible glance, to be surprisingly untrammeled, and not everyone who's been chased by the hounds of hell can say that. This will take only a minute, and then you'll be back in the horizontal in no—What are you laughing at?"

"You," I said as he followed me inside. " 'This'll only take a minute.' You wouldn't tie your shoe in a minute."

He frowned at the floor. "Well. Not without informing it of its rights and forfeitures, of course not."

In the kitchen I put water on to boil, while Aynsley stood beside the drainboard where the plastic bag now sat. He held the ancient brown leather briefcase by its handle with both fists. I couldn't help but recognize it, since the last time I had seen it was when it was the property of Colbert Reeves, Aynsley's dad, who happened to be my attorney back then. I took the transfer of the briefcase to mean that Colbert had at last put himself out to pasture on account of his shot nerves. Like Sonny, Aynsley had gotten heftier around the waist. Like me, though to a lesser extent, his hair had greyed. Otherwise, he hadn't changed, not one syllable.

"I heard you gave a real barn-burner at the D.A.R. dinner last night," I said as I measured out the coffee.

"Yes, barns were burned," he said with a modest nod. "That the purple-haired empresses require their evening's constitution before bedtime necessitated a woefully truncated elaboration of the Open Records Act, but *che sarà sarà*." Tugging at his whiskers, he managed a crippled kind of smile. "Presumably your information came from our esteemed director's betrothed, who did not exactly conceal the fact that she was staring at her watch throughout the entirety of the speech."

When I didn't say anything, Aynsley smirked and went on, "Maybe she was trying to figure out what time it was in Paris. Or maybe she was regretting that the topic of the speech wasn't something she knew more about. Something like, 'The Tradition of Pissing on the Family Tree, from Cain to Pattys Hearst and Reagan.'"

So Aynsley still had it in for Jill. "How is old Tobias doing, anyway?"

"Professor Estelle is fine, the soggy condition of said tree notwithstanding," the general counsel said. "We breakfasted together this morning, in fact, while others were, ahem, still drooling on their bedsheets. Are we alone, by the way? Or did you choose to spend your first night in Shepherdsville pinning and mounting one of the local butterflies?"

"Just me and the moths, Aynsley. I hate to disappoint you."

"On the contrary, my fine seminaked friend. The last thing we need in Shepherdsville is another perfectly ordinary male behaving like a correctional officer."

In his unsinkable Ivy League lilt buttered here and there with local off-colorisms, Aynsley went on for a fair amount longer while I slurped at my coffee and marveled at how such a priss could also be so lewd. But there was only so much who-did-whom I could take before I finally asked him, "Are we getting to the official business any time soon? Because I'm getting a little hungry and there's nothing around here to eat."

"Yes, rude former felon, we were coming around to that," came the huffy reply. "And we'll begin with the message—which we deliver to you free of charge though tips are always appreciated—that our Mister Fitch wishes to buy you lunch. Now then. Hand us yonder bag."

I brought the white plastic bag over to the coffee table. Aynsley's face was almost completely inside his open briefcase. "Come out come out wherever you are, Inmate Property Requisition Form And Attached Form 3812 Notification Waiver Of Property Rights . . . Here, my little red-taped Fido . . ." His fingers rustled through files and scraps of legal paper. "Hmmm . . . Well, there's the writ of mandamus filed by Inmate Willoughby we were looking for yesterday."

He looked up from his briefcase, dryly snickering. "Our man Willoughby, it seems, is not only an accomplished kiddy-diddler and self-appointed legal giant, but also a devout Igbo chieftain, and he simply cannot go about his business of communing with the spirits in his ad-seg cell without a fresh quart of goat's blood every morning. Destined to become a landmark freedom of religious expression case," he intoned before diving headfirst back into his briefcase.

I was about to get up and pour more coffee when Aynsley cried, "Ah hah!" and withdrew a manila folder. "Now then. We have here the usual property requisition form, which would ordinarily require your signature. But instead, notice the alarming red-inked notation at the bottom."

"'Inapplicable—See Form 3812,'" I read aloud, though I had no idea what I was reading.

"And so, *voilà*, said Form," continued Aynsley as he slid the other sheet of paper in front of me. "It is, of course, a masterwork of bureaucratic doublespeak, and a highly recommended bedtime read. But what it basically says is that your spontaneous outburst from the Hope Farm, while forgiven as a criminal deed by the governor and the Board of Pardons and Paroles, nonetheless is *not* forgiven by the Texas Department of Criminal Retribution insofar as your right to your inmate property is concerned."

I rubbed my eyes. "Would you please just tell me what the hell you're talking about?" I asked.

"By choosing to vacate your inmate habitat and in the process abandoning control of said habitat's personal contents, you have *ipso facto* waived your requisition rights to said property, as well as to your properties warehoused fifteen years earlier by TDCR, the rights to the latter properties having been relinquished under the stipulations of the penal code, chapter twenty-three, section fourteen, point thirty-one, more colloquially known as the You-Boogie-We-Burn Clause. And so, without further ado . . ."

He plopped the white plastic bag in front of me. "What's this?" I asked.

"Besides being a white plastic bag, you mean? It's the container for the worldly possessions you brought into the brave new world with you—what, twenty-three years ago? Twenty-four? Anyway, it says on the form."

"I thought you just said I couldn't have my property."

"We said no such thing. What we said was that we aren't *responsible* for your property. So don't come after us if a lucky rabbit's foot or a snapshot of Miss Clodhopper '73 is missing from your stash."

I upended the bag and let its contents drop to the carpeted floor. A musty odor wafted, along with some other smell, familiar but elusive. "I'll be goddamned," I murmured. There, heaped before me, were the brown suit and brown penny loafers my mother had brought me to wear to my sentencing.

"You could try on the slacks, but they may be somewhat binding in the Horn of Plenty region," Aynsley allowed. But he shut up after that. I held the jacket in my hands, rubbing its cheap polyester material with my thumbs. A memory bubbled to the surface, and I lifted the right sleeve. The stitching was torn out of the cuff. That had happened when Mimi grabbed me as they were leading me off. She was only nine then, and screamed like a cat in a storm when the bailiff pried us apart. The kids at school had told my sister I'd be sent back home in little pieces . . . I let the jacket fall away from my fingers and picked up a shoe. It seemed like a toy in my hand. I had been a tall kid—but, I now thought, not really so big after all.

The pale beige shirt I didn't recognize. In fact, as I lifted it, I nearly blurted out, "This isn't mine." Just as quickly it came to me: it hadn't been mine, it was someone else's. It was Sonny's. The morning of my sentencing, one of the drunks in the county jail took a swing at me, and I beat him to the floor but he bled on my dress shirt. Colbert Reeves took one look at me and said, "Good God, son, you look like a cannibal. You can't go before the judge looking like that. Does your mother have any more shirts for you?" And I said, "Get one from Sonny Hope." And then, in a whisper: "Tell Sonny he owes me a shirt. At least a shirt." But Sonny didn't need convincing. He handed one over. And though he wasn't there for the sentencing, I think he would have agreed that the shirt didn't look half bad on his pal Hadrian, if a little short in the sleeves.

I wadded up the shirt and threw it against the heap. My mood had changed for the worse. "So where's the property I had in my cell?" I asked.

"Ah yes. Well. You'll have to sue us for that." Aynsley smiled agreeably. "Of course, more than one vengeful writ writer has been impaled on the tusks of the You-Boogie-We-Burn Clause, but who knows? You could be the primate who types Shakespeare."

"I didn't say I wanted it. I asked who had it. Do you?"

He appeared puzzled. "No."

"Does Sonny?"

"Unlikely, but you'll have to ask him. If this is a pivotal issue, then perhaps—"

"It doesn't matter," I snapped. "I'm sure they went through everything when I ran off. Anybody who wanted a look probably saw it then."

"Was there—"

"Just forget it," I said, thinking: it was only one picture. Not even a photograph. A drawing, and not by me. And if he saw it, he saw it, and what would it change . . . Still, I wished to hell I'd taken it with me. I'd kicked myself plenty over that.

It was momentarily quiet. I looked up to tell Aynsley that he'd finished his business and could go now. But he beat me to the silence. "The place hasn't changed much, has it?" he observed, looking around. "Still Rockwell Under The Pines. Mimi threw the usual post-mortuarial winging here, but we couldn't make it to send your mother off to her reward. Dear old Warden Musk was in federal court in Tyler on drug smuggling charges. Alas, a prison lawyer's job is never done."

Rocking back and forth on his heels, hands in pockets, head craning this way and that, he continued his appraisal for a moment. "So," he said with a grin. "Planning to redecorate? Maybe counterpoint the middle-class nirvana with some of the old Hope Farm sensibility? Wallpaper by *Hustler*, perhaps?"

"Fuck off, Aynsley," I said, but without much gusto.

"Apologies," he replied. My old schoolmate sighed, and then his voice lost its sarcasm and became almost tender. "It's really got your old man all over it, doesn't it? Funny how widows don't change things. She lived here alone for what, twenty some-odd years? And yet, taking nothing away from your mother, she's not who you feel in here. Is she?"

I looked up at him, astounded, but he was already wandering around the living room, brushing ashtrays and chair arms with his hands. "Doc Coleman used to sit in that rocking chair," he observed, pointing. "He sat there and read books. Yes. A rarity in Shepherdsville. A man who read actual books, containing more words than pictures. He sat there with those silver wire-rimmed spectacles, sucking on his pipe. That silver pin flashlight of his always clipped to his shirt pocket—except when you took it to school that one day, and Sonny kept shining it on my face in the lunch room and Miss Finkel sent me to the nurse because she thought my facial glow to be a tad unnatural."

He stepped towards where his briefcase lay. "Well, back to the warehouse," he sang. "At eleven tonight we make a pin cushion out of Inmate Glover, if the court allows, and it may not. Sheila sends her best, by the way. And congratulations on the pardon. Of course, owing to that little waltz with Judge Castlebury, you're forbidden to become a dental hygienist, an auctioneer, a labor organizer or an embalmer, among other lofty trades. Still, being a pardonee puts you in far more illustrious company. Remember the two Kiowa chiefs, Satanta and Big Tree? Class of 1873, courtesy of Governor Davis. Have you plans, by the way?"

"None," I confessed.

Aynsley folded his arms against the old seersucker jacket I knew to be his father's. "Um. How, may we ask, will you eat?"

"My mother left me some money in her life insurance policy," I said. "I'm okay for a few months."

"Um. Well. Sheila's turkey pot pie, as you may know, is somewhat mythic, and she tends to make them by the gross. So . . ."

"I appreciate that, Aynsley."

The smirk returned. "Then there's Trust, of course."

"What . . . Oh, you mean Ricky Tempesta's town?"

"Indeed. A fellow could make a fresh start in Trust. Or so goes the slogan. In any event, he pays well."

"Do you speak from experience?" I asked.

Aynsley's smile was meditative. "It was only an offer," he said after a moment, and then shook his head. "Not for us. After all, we know Mister Tempesta."

"So do I," I said.

"Then you'll remember," he said as we shook hands.

It should have seemed quiet then. But Aynsley was right. You could still hear the voice all over the house. His was never the loudest, but always the one that got heard. I turned towards the rocking chair, then drew back, half-expecting him to see me here, naked from the waist down, unshaven, my hair already as grey as his. Trashed out before my time. He wouldn't have said anything. He would've just peered out from behind those mangled glasses that had been knocked to the floor a million times by squirming dogs and shying colts—peered out at his only son and the mess I'd made of myself, pulled his pipe out from between his lips, flexed the little fist of a muscle between his eyebrows, stared for a brief eternity, and then he'd look back down at his veterinary trade journal. Nothing spoken, and that, too, would be heard.

My father was not what you would call an idle man. Even sitting, his hands and mouth worked the pipe, his eyes fixed themselves on books of learning, and all the while he rocked soundlessly in that chair with its tacky upholstery of dogs and mallards stitched onto it several birthdays ago by my mother, who idolized her husband as much as I did—but in a way that made her happy, as worshipping on Sunday made her sing all afternoon in the kitchen . . . while after church I myself made for the woods, feeling more restless and less fulfilled than ever. That energy came from my father. As to where the lack of fulfillment came from, I couldn't say. But my father knew I had it in me, and I know this because I could see the worry in his eyes when he looked my way . . . and what my own self-doubt had begun, his quiet fretting pretty much finished off. Or so theorized Doctor Green over at the Creel Unit, where I spent the first year of my sentence. Doctor Green said it was all about "transference." He was maybe half-right: it was about plenty of other things, too. But I didn't expect him to know that, since I'd kept my mouth shut about the rest.

Today, my father's dog-and-mallard rocking chair looked forlorn and more than a little idiotic—the first relic in the house to be discarded, assuming I'd have the nerve to do so. Amazing, I thought, that a man of my dad's masculine elegance would not be diminished by such a clownish throne. He was a striking presence, crystal-eyed with deep lines stamped into his forehead from decades of consideration, his peppery hair left just long enough to graze those wrinkles, but never so long as to pose a moment's distraction. He stood just over six feet, as I now did, and though I got my slight case of birdleggedness from him, from the waist up my dad was a powerful man, with shoulders that never gave in to a distressed mule and hands that never lost a grip. Men called him "one hell of a good-lookin' fella" without blushing. Women called him "sure enough handsome." Whatever vanity inhabited him, he hid well beneath his flannel or denim shirts and his simple work boots. Of course, I knew he was vain, because I was his son. I was a threat to his pride every time I stepped out into Shepherdsville.

He'd built this house himself, with the help of his dad, my Pawpaw, in the spring of 1959, putting the last layer of white paint on the wood siding six months before I was born. Set back off of Highway 12, the house represented a typically sensible compromise for my father, who didn't want to live in town but knew that's where his business increasingly was, and who knew also that the feds and the lumber companies were in a horserace to buy up all of the bottomlands where he and Mama had lived since birth. The two acres my father acquired were quiet and wood-shaded, situated just two miles from school, so that in dry weather I could hoof it with Mimi in tow while Mama helped out with the usual flurry of early morning business at the veterinary clinic, which sat between the house and the highway, with a wide semicircular driveway so that the trailers could pull in and out without tearing up the lawn. In other words, my dad was thinking of everyone when and where and how he built the house; and yet both the effort and the finished product bore no gaudy reflection of his calculations. He was just naturally right about things. There wasn't a man in the county who could touch my father in a popularity contest—nor a man or woman who would vote my dad into some kind of elected position, so badly did they need him to remain just where he was.

The previous veterinarian, Doc Pollard, was a funny fat man who, I'm told, could do a fine impersonation of every character in *Gone With the Wind*—particularly, of course, the mammy. But he was a bad drunk, and being as how Shepherd County was still very much a rural community, his jokes wore thinner as the body count at his clinic rose higher and higher. My dad was the silver bullet with Doc Pollard's name on it. He was twenty-four, fresh out of Texas A&M's vet sciences school, but by no means a kid. By no means. Confrontation wasn't his style. He just hung up his sign and did his work and allowed the word to spread. Within two years, Doc Pollard had closed up shop. They say Doc Coleman's emergence provided his predecessor with a way out of a grueling vocation to which his lifestyle was not suited. They say he was relieved. But many years later, while sitting in my cell or while driving at night from one fugitive haven to the next, I'd think about poor old far-from-perfect Doc Pollard, and I'd wonder just how much of a favor it was to him that the white knight came galloping in and threw so fierce a light on the old vet's warts.

It was my father who discovered the early symptoms of brucellosis in one of Teddy Milton's dairy cattle. And though the resulting quarantine was unpleasant business, the disasters that the cattlemen way out west suffered from the epidemic later that year convinced the folks in deep East Texas that they had a hero in their midst. And it was my father who ferreted out a crippling bone disease from the ranks of the Taylor quarter horses. Those were monumental deeds, but a vet is appreciated most of all for his reliability, his surehandedness and his caring, which meant at times his charity. I had only seen my father turn down a customer once. A retired lawyer who'd started up an exotic animal ranch near Jasper brought in a chimpanzee and wanted it castrated to "settle it down some," in the owner's words. Dad wouldn't do it. That night at the dinner table, he cursed the man. "The goddamned barbarian," he said, conversing with himself. "He'd have us all castrated. Goddamn his kind." And then he stormed out, later to return and sit in an apologetic stew.

Only on two other occasions did I hear Earl Coleman curse. The more celebrated of the two came on a summer night, when a knock at the door interrupted our dinner. "It must be Jensen's squirrel hound," my father said as he scooted out of his chair. "He said its hind leg was swelling up again. Excuse me, Wanda." My mother nodded and carried his plate over to the oven to keep it warm, as she had done dozens of times before.

Presently we could hear him at the doorway. But he was talking to a man whose voice was not Mister Jensen's, and replying in a way that he would never talk back to a friend. "I'm sure you do, and I really don't care," we heard him say in a clipped voice. My mother looked up towards the doorway, the whites of her eyes bulbous. But she didn't get up. Beside me, my three-year-old sister dug a hole in her biscuit with her index finger.

Then I heard my name. "Hadrian. Would you come here, please?"

"Earl, no," said Mama, her voice quavering.

"It'll be alright, Wanda. Hadrian?"

I put down my napkin, slipped out of my chair and walked around the corner towards the doorway. There, on the front porch, stood three men in white hoods. At first I nearly laughed out loud, because Halloween was a month off, and besides, since when did adults go trick-or-treating? But my father wasn't smiling. His right hand trembled against the knob of the door he held open.

One man stood in front of the other two. He wore a khaki shirt and jeans underneath his hood. His gut was comically swollen. I'd seen it somewhere before. "Send your boy away, Doc," said the man. The words were muffled, but I knew I'd heard the voice in another place. "This ain't kid stuff we're talking about."

My father ignored them. He put his left hand on my shoulder. "Hadrian," he asked me, though his eyes remained on the others, "how old are you?"

"Nine," I said.

"And how old is your sister?"

"Um. Three."

"Do you remember last week, Hadrian, when your mama told me that you had locked your three-year-old sister in a closet 'til she cried?"

Instantly humiliated, I mumbled, "Yes sir."

"Do you remember what I said to you after your mama told me what you'd done?"

I looked up at the hooded men. They were shifting their feet, and their red eyes peered out at me.

"They were three little words, Hadrian. I want you to tell our visitors here what those words are."

My face went hot. "Shame on you," I said.

"Look up at them, son. Say it to their faces. Or what you see of their faces."

First I looked at his right hand. It was trembling so hard that I thought it would rattle the doorknob to the floor. Suddenly I heard myself holler, "Shame on you!" into their hooded faces, and they all jumped. My dad squeezed my shoulder—whether out of embarrassment or out of pride, I would never know.

"And shame on your daddy," barked the man in front, "for getting in the way of our business! For being a niggerlover! Did you know your daddy was a niggerlover, boy?"

Now I was shaking. My father's hand on my shoulder tightened again. "Let me tell you what they're talking about, Hadrian," he said, and his voice became even and reassuring. "You remember yesterday I told you about that black man, Mister Rivers, and the mule he brought in?"

"The mule that got shot?" I asked.

"That's the one. Well," and with a casual gesture, as if pointing at roadside wildflowers rather than three simmering menaces on our doorstep, he continued, "these men are with the Ku Klux Klan. Have they taught you about the Ku Klux Klan at school? Maybe in history class?"

A shudder went up my back. "Yes sir."

"And, well, son, the Klan *is* history, for the most part. But in East Texas, I'm afraid, there are still some people living in the past. Like these three fellows here with the sheets over their heads. And from the way it was explained to me, Mister Rivers has a cousin who's moved here recently from up north to attend East Texas State. And that cousin went to a bar the other day, and the bartender told him black folks weren't allowed. And Mister Rivers's cousin told him it was 1968 and he was offended, and that he'd talk to Mister Rivers about getting a lawyer somewhere to sue the bar. And so yesterday morning, someone went into Mister Rivers's pasture and shot his mule in the stomach. And like I told you yesterday, I pulled out the slug and patched up that mule. And now these men are telling me I shouldn't have done that. Do you understand?"

I nodded, though in fact I'd become confused, as something else was taking shape in my mind. Then it came to me, and I blurted out, "I know which bar you're talking about! It's his bar!"

Pointing to the man in front, I said, "It's Mister Worley's bar!"

I felt a harder squeeze on my shoulder. I dropped my hand.

The man's eyes narrowed. "You need to teach that boy of yours not to talk so damn much, Doc," he said.

I could feel the explosion, from the tremors in the floor and against my shoulder, a half-second before it occurred. "Don't you *dare* tell me how to raise my son! And don't you *dare* tell me how to do my job! And don't you *dare* tell me to give you back that bullet slug, because it's mine and it will stay mine until the D.A. asks for it! Now get off my property! Go back to your caves and die there, you primitive sons of bitches!"

He took a step back, jerking me back with him, and made to swing the door closed. But before he did, he yelled, loud enough to throw his voice out: "*And shame on you!*"

That night, my father stepped into my bedroom, but not to tell me goodnight.

"I shouldn't have put you through all that," he said through barely moving lips. "At the time, I thought it was something you needed to see. A history lesson, I suppose. Anyway, I wasn't thinking. I'm sorry."

I was astonished. But in the darkness, he couldn't see my hurt expression, or I his.

"It wasn't good parenting," he then mumbled. Looking away, he patted me on the leg and said, "Sleep well," in a tone indicating that he would not.

There had been only one other time he'd cursed that I knew of. It happened not at the house, but at the funeral home, on the night Pawpaw lay in state before his burial the next morning. The viewing had ended, and everyone filed out, sniffling, with their arms around each other. But I snuck back in. And for a long, long time, I knelt there with my arms around that hump-backed old fable-spinner, and with what was left of him to keep me company, I cried my eyes out.

At some point I looked up from Pawpaw's casket and saw the leaning of a familiar shadow. I said nothing, did nothing, did not even turn my head. I only waited for him to say whatever he had come to say. And then I heard the words, whispered in the manner of a prayer:

"Goddamn . . . goddamn . . ."

And just as quietly he left the room and walked on home with Mama and Mimi, and I caught up later.

Westward into town I drove half-blind from the August sunlight splintering off of the distant towers, the brilliant new prison-palaces of my birthplace. They lunged out of the dark forest like God's own pale fists. I'd never imagined that one could see Shepherdsville from this far off—or that one should; or, in either case, that this is how the town would present itself from afar: as a city, a civilized city, blasted out of the murk, making the forest look puny and colorless. That was my youth, the blackened forest. All of that up ahead, the now-unfamiliar city, was where I'd become a man. No wonder I feared it so.

I first passed the spangled limestone building that bore the engraved notation, Texas Department of Criminal Retribution—Administrative Headquarters. Though I didn't look up, I wondered if Sonny was looking down. The parking lot was crowded with both civilian and state-issued automobiles, and with well-dressed men and women milling about. I kept my eyes to the road, which at this mid-morning hour was fairly calm, aside from the occasional testosterone burst of an East Texas State boy's sports car. From close in, Shep-herdsville looked small again. On the county courthouse steps, a dark-suited clump of attorneys wheezed out laughter and cigar smoke. Just below their feet, at the bottom of the steps, two inmates scraped gum off of the cement—both of them expressionless but, I imagined, furi-ously attuned to every word of the courthouse gossip, since you never knew what you might pick up that could be bartered off to make your life easier in the joint. Off to my right, a third inmate tidied the shop-side walkways with a push broom, while three others squatted in the flower gardens, appearing almost dainty as they pruned and plucked and watered and patted.

A flatbed Ford rattled past, and at the sight of the driver—a beet-cheeked hoss with a camouflage cap pulled tightly over his skull—I stuck my hand out the Impala window, all set to greet Clifford Horner, a pal from childhood and kin to half the folks in the river bottoms. But just as he craned his massive neck in my direction, my guts spun with panic, and I jerked my hand back inside, turned back to my windshield and punched the accelerator. My tires skidded, and through my rearview I could see the attorneys and the inmates look up.

"Jesus!" I shouted, and smacked the steering wheel with my fist. "Jesus! What the hell am I doing here?"

Three blocks south of the courthouse, I pulled into a metered space and sat there for a spell. Behind me sprawled the director's man-sion, as well as Big Red. Eyes closed, I measured my breaths, tried not to think about what was there to see or who might be seeing. The town seemed deathly still. Then, from somewhere behind me, I heard laughter.

When I stepped out of my car, I beheld a sight I'd all but forgotten about. A procession of males, maybe forty in all, sauntered down the sidewalk parallel to Walls Boulevard, whooping it up and pushing each other, whistling at female passersby. They wore blue short-sleeved shirts, like those of auto mechanics, along with ill-fitting plaid or khaki pants and black rubber-soled shoes; but you could not have convinced these boys that they weren't the suavest damned rat pack Shepherdsville had ever seen. They were ex-cons, freshly processed out, and this was their march to freedom.

Specifically, they were marching from Inmate Processing to the bus depot, and to the secondhand clothing store next door, where they would buy what they thought were hip sunglasses and pay what they thought was a fair price for cigarettes. They'd snatch up some loser's former straw hat off the rack, stand before the cracked mirror and pronounce themselves altogether transformed. And they'd buy some baggy-ass jeans and a tight polyester shirt and roll up the sleeves to show off those tough-stud tattoos they'd acquired down on the farm. And then they'd make for the pay phone to call their poor dumb faithful honeys, tell them to put on their reddest nail polish and their trashiest underwear and fluff that hairdo like a big ol' storm cloud, 'cause Big Daddy just checked out of Big Red bigtime, and come two o'clock the bus would be rolling up, free at last and look out for the big swinging johnson, look out world!

They swung their white plastic bags as they walked. Some carried manila folders in their other arm: the precious legal material, cases still pending for these self-styled writ writers because now, *now*, they were free to scour the law books all day and all night, twenty-four/seven, and without fear of reprisal sue the TDCR into oblivion, that's what they'd do now that they were out on the streets, be avengers, make a little law, make history . . . but first get on back home, tip a few at the old bar, check in with the homeboys, maybe do a little weed, a little blow, figure out how to get some more, how to get some money to get some more, knock off a gas station, *oops* . . .

Poor stupid bastards, I thought as I watched them saunter. As Thunderball Hope's houseboy, I used to sit on the balcony of the mansion after cleaning up the kitchen, and watch this swaggering scene repeat itself every morning around eleven. Some of them I'd seen before; most of the rest I'd see again. And the ones who'd walked this walk some years back would grin along with the rest, only not so boldly, and they looked at nothing but where they were walking, barely trusting their feet to keep them upright. They scared me, because they knew this little trip came with no guarantees; and from where I sat, privileged among cons but still nothing but a con, I wanted to take that trip in the worst way. But Lord I wanted a guarantee . . .

"Hey man! You got a light?"

He was twenty-one if that, a black kid, with clunky black plastic standard-issue eyeglass frames. The hem of his blue-and-white checkered pants rose above his ankles.

A fugitive always carries matches—for warmth, for illumination or just for company. "Hang on," I said, digging around in my pocket as he strolled on over my way. "You heading home today?"

"Shit, I heard that," he muttered as he dropped his property bag to the concrete and stood there fidgeting with his unlit Marlboro. "This is one sorry-ass town, y'know what I'm saying? I'm going back to Dallas. And I'm planning to stay straight—but if I don't? If I fuck up? They ain't taking me back to Shepherdsville, y'know what I'm saying? Shit no. They have to kill my ass first."

I produced a pack of matches and handed them over to him. "Where've you been?" I asked. "Big Red?"

"Shee. They put niggers like me on the farm, pilgrim."

"Hoe squad?"

"Then chow hall. Then laundry. Every sorry-ass nigger job they got." He looked up while igniting his cigarette. "You a CO or something?"

"No. I did five years at Big Red, eight at the Hope Farm."

"And you ain't gone yet?" He regarded me with amazement and disgust. "Shit, then you ain't got the sense God gave a monkey, 'cause let me tell you what. The way Shepherdsville makes its scratch is by putting your ass in the joint. You ain't no good to 'em out here! They ain't got no job for you, homes! But they put you in the joint, and then the state of Texas pays some peckerwood to wear grey and guard your ass! You listening to me? The state pays Shepherdsville to keep your ass in the pen. Shit, that motherfucking fair-haired punk they got sitting up there? Sonny Hope? He's got one hundred forty thousand inmates. You know what his salary is? I ain't talking about the money people stick in his pockets. I'm talking about his official state salary. You know what it is?"

"No," I said.

"Check this out. *One hundred forty thousand dollars.* One inmate for Shepherdsville, one dollar for Sonny Hope. Now you tell me, homes. Would Sonny Hope rather see your ugly white ass out on the street fucking up his view, or would he rather have that dollar in his pocket? That's what I'm talking about."

I smiled. "Thanks for the advice," I said.

"Yeah whatever. Thanks for the light."

He turned, then stopped. "How long you been out?"

"Eight years," I said.

His brows furrowed underneath the mask of black plastic. "And they still ain't snatched you back up?" He shook his head. "Shee. Don't you test your luck no more, pilgrim. You hear me? Be cool."

I waved at the back of him. Then, as I stepped towards the street, a passing sedan screeched to a halt in front of me. A bald, pudgy man in a red cardigan fussed his way out of the driver's seat, slammed the car door and stalked over my way, his hands balled into little fists.

He stood right up against me, looked up at my chin and declared, in a midget-like voice, "You're a no-good crook, you know that? You're a killer and a liar and a no-good crook! And no piece of paper is ever going to change that! You hear me? I hope you rot in hell!"

His face went purple even as I felt the blood vacate mine. "Who the hell are you?" I managed.

"You know who I am, you piece of dung!" he screamed, and then he scrambled back into his car and drove off.

I stood there for awhile before it at last came to me. Damn, I thought. Dillard Bunch. He'd been Judge Horace Castlebury's clerk for some twenty years, until I displaced him by killing his boss.

I put my hands in my back pockets and kept walking. Looking back towards the depot, I could see my ex-con friend through the window of the thrift shop. He had his hands on an Oakland Raiders cap, and he was sure smiling.

Cal Fitch was waiting for me in the parking lot of the Inmate Processing office. He folded up the day's edition of *The Shepherdsville Light* and held out his hand. "I didn't make the news, and neither did you," he said. "That's cause for celebration, youngun."

"It's great to see you, Cal," I said, and it was true.

The former deputy director nodded to indicate our surroundings. "Thought I'd meet you halfway, save you a few stares," he said. "You'll get a lifetime's worth this afternoon. Sissy Shipman phoned this morning. She heard you and I were getting together. Told me to tell you to meet her at The Guilty Dog at six."

"What the hell is The Guilty Dog?" I asked.

Fitch's smile spread all the way around his face. "It's what you've been missing out on all these years," he said. "Get there before Sissy does. Five-forty at the latest. You listening to your Uncle Cal?"

"Sure," I said. "And where are we going?"

"Someplace quiet," he promised.

Fitch drove us west of town, away from all the prisons, and into cotton country, where as recently as the era presided over by Thunderball Hope the plantation owners leased inmates from TDCR to pick their summer crop. Today the fields were untended. Fitch asked me questions and I answered them, nothing too probing just yet, simply passing the half-hour before we made it to the town of Barrister, and to a little diner where farmers mumbled to each other over their platters, and where the waitresses all seemed to know Cal Fitch.

Fitch was black, but he had a way of entering places like this one that put everyone's mind at ease. He smiled and waved and held his head high, just short of cocky, in a manner to suggest that there was nothing he would change about himself. That air of self-satisfaction invited a second look at him, since on the first take all you might likely see was a somewhat squatty, dark-skinned fellow with a mat of tight goofy curls roosting atop his cube-like head. But upon closer inspection you would observe that he was keen-eyed and tended to work his long, thin lips against each other, the better to keep most of his words to himself. Fitch barely had a neck to speak of, so that when we sat in our booth, his head seemed to disappear halfway inside the collar of his blue button-down shirt. It might take awhile before you recognized that this was not a posture of cowering—rather, that the short, stocky object sitting before you was in fact all coiled up like a copperhead. Some thought of Fitch as dangerous. After all, truth was his venom. Fitch could stick you with reality, and God help you if you weren't prepared for it.

"So why Inmate Processing?" I asked once the waitress had taken our orders.

Fitch chuckled privately. "You mean," he said, "why that instead of something else. Like chief of Treatment Programs, which was last year's model. Or chief of Educational Services, which got all the blue ribbons the year before treatment did. Or chief of Victims' Assistance, which is what's getting ink now, along with Managed Health Care. Or chief of Construction, where all the action is. Or," he said, just barely smiling, "director."

"They offered it to you," I pointed out.

He shook his head. "I knew what they were offering," he said. "After they chased out Thunderball, the new director was going to be a eunuch. But here's what I'm getting at. There's always something to be said for the flavor of the month. And if you want to be that flavor, well, make the most of it. But youngun," and he crinkled his ginger-colored eyes, "I've been around a long time. I've seen the taxpayers say, 'Let's rehabilitate those poor misfortunates.' And then I've seen 'em turn around and say, 'Make those evil bastards bust rocks.' The pendulum swings. But no matter what, one thing remains constant. Inmates coming in, inmates going out. Processing."

"Job security," I said.

"You know it, youngun. Besides," he added, and it seemed as if Fitch didn't want to grin but just couldn't stop himself, "you see who's coming and who's going, and why. You've got access to every report from every warden in every unit across the state. Access to every inmate grievance, every disciplinary report. If Inmate Smith's folder says he had trouble out at Sheffield, I can call up Aynsley Reeves and get every classified document at that prison unit, no questions asked."

He examined his thumbnails. "You know more about what's going on than Sonny does," I said.

"Well now. Don't go underestimating Sonny. He knows a few things." Fitch tore off a corner of a Sweet-N-Low packet and poured the contents into his tea. "Like how to go up to Austin, where they can't find money in the state budget to pay for schools or services for the elderly, and come back with forty million to fund the construction of six TDCR office buildings in Shepherdsville. That didn't happen by accident."

"Just how did it happen?" I asked.

Leaning forward, Fitch declared with relish, "The silkiest pitch you ever heard. I was there. He addressed the legislature five years ago. You had to listen hard to hear what Sonny was really selling. He was selling Shepherdsville. Proposing that they make it the center of the universe. Make all the roads run through it. Basically, he told them, 'Want to satisfy the courts and save the multi-million-dollar legal fees fighting the overcrowding lawsuits? Build more prisons. Want to get tough on crime? Build more prisons. Want to create jobs? Build more prisons. Want to stimulate private enterprise? Build more prisons. *Want to get re-elected?* Build more prisons. Or your political opponents will hang every paroled murderer in the state of Texas around your neck 'til the damn thing snaps.'"

"But those aren't new prisons they built in Shepherdsville," I protested.

"Aw, quit getting nitpicky," Fitch said, and burst out laughing, his belly jiggling and his teeth agape and finally, mirthful tears collecting around his eyes.

Gradually Fitch composed himself. He took a few gulps from his tea glass. "No," he said, "there's plenty of new prisons. You just haven't seen 'em yet. Some are out in the Panhandle, some are in the Rio Grande Valley, a couple are around the Trans-Pecos, and a couple others are south of town yonder way. In five years, we've tripled the number of prison beds."

He corrected himself. "Not 'we.' It was Sonny. No one else could've done it. It took a man who was part cheerleader, part tyrant. Sonny saw to it that, over a five-year period, we built more prisons in Texas than at any other time in the recorded history of the free world. You think of that, youngun. One hundred thousand new beds. One hundred fifty thousand we've got now! I asked my secretary to look this up: seven of the fifty states in the U.S. don't even have a *city* with one hundred fifty thousand residents. And now Texas has beds for one hundred fifty thousand criminals. And they're filling fast, and Sonny will build more. Some kid throws a rock at a schoolbus. You want to send him to jail? Sonny Hope will build him a bed. You want to keep that kid there for five years, rather than, say, six months? Sonny Hope will build *ten* beds. Lengthen everyone's sentence. Give everyone a bed for life. Sonny's proved it can be done. And what amazes me is that there are still some people around here who underestimate Sonny Hope."

Fitch's gentle eyes were trained on me. "Don't you underestimate him, now," he said. "Hell, you grew up with him. Has he ever been anything other than who he is? Has he ever done anything that's surprised you? Anything? Because if he has, youngun, that's *your* fault."

Those last words were like a suckerpunch that makes your bones rattle and sends a buzzing to your ears. I sat there, eyes more or less fixed to the formica tabletop while sweat seeped out of my fingers. Now I knew why Cal Fitch had asked me out to lunch. He wanted to see if I knew what the hell I'd gotten myself into.

"Then I have a question for you," I said, but just then the food came, and Fitch chatted up the waitress while I brooded. When she slid the plate under my face, I took one look at the clutter of yellow, brown and grey matter that constituted standard East Texas fare, and I nearly got sick.

"You're not gonna find a better chicken-fried in the county," Fitch exhorted me as he picked up his dining implements. "Corn bread's fresh out of the oven."

I heard him chomping away, and so I picked up my silverware, tried a bite of the steak and was immediately glad to have done so. Fitch ate away, patient as always, his expression dreamily neutral.

Halfway into my meal, I wiped my mouth and said, "I'd like to know why you think Sonny pushed to have me pardoned."

Fitch arched an eyebrow but otherwise remained attentive to his food. "Did you ask him that question?" he asked.

"Not directly, no."

"You should've," he said. "Because let me tell you something. Contrary to what most people think, Sonny Hope is not a fundamentally dishonest man."

I laughed. "But not fundamentally honest, either," I said.

"But not fundamentally honest, no."

"Or trustworthy."

"Well, now, that depends on what you mean," Fitch said as he dunked an oversized piece of steak into his mouth. "Is he an out and out liar? I wouldn't say so. No more than the rest of us. Now, can you trust him to do the right thing? I wouldn't. But: can you trust him to be Sonny through and through? Absolutely."

I put down my fork and scratched at the back of my head. "Damn, what were his words," I said. "Something like . . . I remember now. He said, 'I have needed you back in the worst way.'"

As he chewed, Fitch's eyes gleamed.

"What the hell does that mean," I murmured. "'. . . needed you back in the worst way.'"

Fitch shrugged, chuckled into his napkin, his eyes still burning.

"Ricky Tempesta," I then said.

Something flickered in his eyes—twin candlelights dancing; then out again.

"What about him?" he said.

"Sonny's worried about him. All this stuff about Tempesta building a new prison town run by private business. I guess Sonny sees it as a threat to his job."

"Hmmph. Among other things."

I looked up. "What do you mean?" I asked.

"Oh . . ." Then he burst out laughing, another full-fledged belly-bouncer, and he reclined against the corner of the booth for awhile. His laughter subsided into a wide smile, which itself became, gradually, a wince.

Shaking his head, he murmured: "Stupid, stupid, stupid."

Leaning forward, his voice breathy, Cal Fitch said, "You were there at the Hope Farm when Tempesta was. All those conjugal visits he got in the library with his wife and his girlfriends. All that fancy furniture and stereo equipment. The booze and the drugs. Now, didn't all that strike you as being out of the ordinary?"

"Sure," I said. "But I'd heard that kind of stuff happened all the time."

"Did happen. *Did.* Twenty years ago when Thunderball was boss, sure. Youngun, where are your eyes? You were in the system for fifteen years. Other than Ricky Tempesta, did you ever see or hear about any inmate having orgies in a prison library?"

"I guess not. But what's your point? Everyone knows Warden Grissom was getting cash money from Tempesta. He got fired over it. I read about it while I was on the run."

"Mitch Grissom didn't get fired," said Fitch. "He got demoted and transferred. Then three years later Sonny gets kicked upstairs to director. Would you like me to tell you who he made his chief of Treatment Programs? At a salary roughly twice what a unit warden makes?"

Flustered, I said, "Maybe Sonny thought Grissom was right for the job."

"He owed Grissom, Hadrian. Sonny was in on the conjugal-visits deal. From the git."

"And getting money from Tempesta in return? Come on, Cal. Sonny's not that stupid."

"Not that kind of stupid, you mean," he said. "Sonny's not dumb like Mitch Grissom was dumb. He wouldn't walk into a cell block and lift up an inmate's pillow and grab the wad of bills and stuff it down his boot in full view of the closed-circuit cameras."

"What do you mean? They didn't have closed-circuit cameras in the Hope Farm cell blocks. Not when I was there, at least."

Fitch grinned. "And thanks to you, they got installed four days after you broke out," he said. "And when those cameras caught Grissom in the act, he knew he'd screwed up in a way Sonny hadn't. He knew he'd have to take the fall. But he also knew Sonny would be in a position to help him later, if he just played dead for awhile."

I nodded.

"But you'll be seeing a lot of Sonny," he said, his voice low and close. "And eventually, he's going to tell you about this little place he's got. East of town, on the banks of the Minerva. Beautiful riverhouse. You'll see it. He loves to entertain there."

He scanned our environs before going on, "Well, it's in his wife's name. Jill's lawyers did all the paperwork when they got the deed. But she told me she didn't buy the house. She said Sonny got it for her as a gift, and for tax purposes they put it in her name."

Again Fitch looked over my shoulder. His voice descended into a near-whisper.

"The deed records show a promissory note in the amount of one dollar," he said. "Nothing to finance. It was all cash up front."

He shrugged. "Like I said. You'll see what kind of place it is. And either Sonny paid up front, in cash, on his state salary, what it was worth. Or he paid . . . somewhat less."

"Tell me who sold it to him," I sighed.

"Fellow by the name of Lester Broom. He's an investor based out of Houston. Anyway, his name's on the deed. But he only had the property for a year. You look back in the records, and the year before Sonny got it from Broom, Broom bought it from a lawyer named A. P. Whitfield. He has offices in downtown Houston. A friend of mine works in the same building, on the same floor. He sees Ricky Tempesta going in and out of that office almost every day. Are you ready for the good part?"

"Probably not," I said.

"This new town Tempesta's incorporated over in Minerva County? Well, that used to be Estelle land. The professor gave it to Jill some years ago, as a college graduation gift. When they did the pre-nups for Sonny and Jill, the lawyers made such a fuss over the family bank accounts and the stockholdings that they felt obliged to toss Sonny a bone. He and Jill got joint ownership of the land. The same year they bought the riverhouse, they sold the acreage. You want to guess who bought it?"

"Oh, Jesus. A. P. Whitfield?"

"And then who bought it from Whitfield two years ago?"

"Lester Broom. Son of a bitch! So Sonny basically swapped property deeds with Tempesta?"

"So it would appear. As a cover, I guess. If people come around wanting to know how Sonny could afford to buy his wife a riverhouse on his prison salary, he can prove he liquidated some assets."

"But he couldn't have known what Tempesta was intending to do with the land."

"Oh, I seriously doubt it," said Fitch. "But you can see how it's just one big fork in Sonny's eye. Tempesta got the luxury treatment at the Hope Farm as part of the deal he made with Sonny. Today Tempesta's story is that he deliberately bribed and extorted his way through prison so he could demonstrate how hopelessly corrupt the system is—and how we need a whole new system, built on land he got in that same crooked deal!"

Shaking his head, the chief of inmate processing said sadly, "It'd be almost poetic if it weren't so cruel. He's got Sonny screwed coming and going. And the only thing that would make it worse would be if Sonny opened his mouth about it."

I held my head with both hands. "My God," I gasped. "There's no way out for Sonny, is there?"

At about the time I realized Fitch had not answered me, a sickness filled my insides. When I looked up, Cal Fitch's face was not three inches from mine. The amusement had faded from his eyes.

"If Sonny told you he's needed you in the worst way," he said simply, "then you had better believe him."

I passed on dessert.

"Now, when I had him, he was the purtiest little punk you ever saw. And housebroke! Wasn't 'til he gone over to the Hope Farm that he got all wild. But bless his heart, he's come home to his master, haven't you, Coleman?"

The proprietor of The Guilty Dog, former Shepherdsville Unit warden Scotty Folger, pounded my back as he tittered. From the shadows of the bar came a caustic voice: "Yeah, we all know how you mastered thatun, Scotty. You like to broke his elbow makin' him drink all that whiskey with you."

Amid snickers, Folger proclaimed, "And I'm agonna make him drink some more, unless there's something in that pardon of his't says his old boss can't serve him up a tequila!"

"Just a beer is fine, Warden," I said as Folger eased past me on his bad right leg and took his position behind the bar. As Cal Fitch told me on the drive back to town, Folger's departure from Big Red was compelled by a sexual harassment lawsuit brought against the warden by three of his female subordinates. The lawsuit had been thrown out when it surfaced that two of the three plaintiffs had enjoyed relations with an inmate, while the third had been arranging for extended inmate visits to family members at the rate of fifty dollars per additional hour. But the facts of the case were sufficiently damning that Sonny thought it best to transfer the warden to the basement of the TDCR Public Affairs office, where Folger would wind down his career censoring the inmate newspaper before his thirty-year state retirement pension kicked in.

I couldn't decide which of these details surprised me least. Folger was fifty-five going on fifteen, numerously divorced and DWI'd, with his bad leg a consequence of having fallen drunk out of a deer blind. Nonetheless, he'd lasted thirty years in the prison system for the same reason he was now running a successful bar—namely, he was impossible to dislike, unless it happened to be your skirt his hand was up. My stay at Big Red had been turbulent, but hardly because of Scotty Folger. What sanity I'd retained I owed to the warden's salty, aimless banter.

The Guilty Dog sported the lewd ornamentation of a frat dorm, with NRA bumper stickers and beer posters of half-naked women plastered across the grimy concrete walls, accompanied by the throbbing odor of yesteryear's Lone Star. As I situated myself upon a barstool, I saw a hand go up from one of the far booths. It was Wick Aspromonte, the prison hustler. His teeth glinted like quartz as he called out my name. Three men in short-sleeved dress shirts sat around Aspromonte. They wore the dreary expressions of TDCR middle managers—site selection or construction management, I figured. Influential in their own middling way, and only too happy to be bought. A couple of booths down, I spied Sonny's deputy, Kirby Morris, sitting with two men who by their cheap neckties and spit-polished cowboy boots advertised themselves to the world as wardens. Morris returned my stare with a furtive wink. I got the message. To show me any greater warmth would be to invite disrespect from the bosses around him. They hated me, I knew, for the grief I'd brought the system by escaping, and for now having to watch Scotty Folger buy me a round. Maybe Kirby Morris didn't hold it against me; maybe he couldn't, given that I was his boss's childhood buddy. I suspected, though, that Kirby Morris hated Sonny with a quiet passion.

Playing shuffle and pool were a few first-shift correctional officers who still wore their grey. They cued up, snuck a peek over at the booths to see if rank was watching, knocked back their shots and stuffed the jiggers in their shirt pockets. Before long, I figured, one of them would get into a fight in the presence of their superiors, and get tossed by Scotty Folger, and by tomorrow he'd be turning in his grey and looking for work in the lumberyards. The few women in attendance gaggled at the far end of the bar, where they drank Miller Lites and munched on little goldfish crackers and bemoaned an impending audit of the purchasing department. Now and then they gave me the eye, nervously. How, after all, was I to be regarded? As a minor celebrity? As a convicted murderer? As someone to forgive, or at least forget?

When the door opened slowly, all conversations faltered. "Why, it's Miss Sissy," cooed the ex-warden. "You here to make me famous?"

"Just keep your hands on the bar where I can see them, okay, Folger?" she replied through her barely smiling teeth. Without looking my way, Sissy Shipman strolled past, dispersing her terse greetings: "Hello, Wick. Kirby. Warden Twombly, Warden Miles. Hello, Wheatley. Johnson, I thought you had a little class. It'll break your wife's heart when I tell her where I saw you . . ."

Nodding with each acknowledgment, both hands clutching the strap of her purse, she sauntered through the gauntlet of scowling prison officials who grunted their hellos and sullenly checked out the wiggle in her beige linen pants. Sissy claimed the booth in the corner. Squinting, she scanned her environs. Upon picking me out, she raised her head upward in a partial nod of greeting, which was as close as Sissy Shipman would ever get to a bear hug.

"Hello there, Coleman," Sissy said as I brought my beer over to the booth. She blinked almost coquettishly as she shook my hand. "It's been awhile. How do you like The Guilty Dog? I figured it was your kind of place."

I laughed with her. "You've always looked out for my best interests, Sissy," I said.

"Mm-hmm." She was looking over my shoulder. "Son of a bitch. I thought we'd run into Aynsley Reeves here. Well, he can't hide from me forever. He's dicked me over for the last time on open records requests. No more Miss Sweetness and Light."

From her purse, Sissy pulled out a microcassette recorder and a slender notepad already half-filled with her shorthand scrawl. She fiddled with the recorder. "Fucking batteries," she muttered, and tossed the device back into her purse. Then she pushed her wavy rust-colored hair behind her ear and regarded me with grey-eyed amusement. It was fair to say that Sissy Shipman stood out from amongst the rogues of Shepherdsville, and in her early forties she was a damn sight better preserved than I was at thirty-eight. A little chunkier than she used to be, and with permanent frown lines bordering her eyes and mouth, but still a creamy-skinned, torch-haired duchess. And as warm and fuzzy as a lizard.

"I was surprised to hear you're still in town," I said.

For a fraction of a second, her eyes went into a rueful drift. But then she laughed sharply and said, "Hell, they pay me to be here. What's your excuse, Coleman?"

"Free rent," I shrugged.

"You always managed to get free rent in Shepherdsville, didn't you," she observed. "So you're staying at your parents' old place. What are you going to do with yourself now that you've been corrected and pardoned?"

She flipped her notepad to a blank page and did not look down as she wrote, the pages turning every minute with a bare fluttering of a finger, a purely nontransferable skill like so many I'd learned behind bars—how to dry off after a shower with a hand towel, how to time my strides so that I didn't have to slow down for the opening of the picket gate, how to squirm inside a padded suit so as to avoid the clutches of the tracking dogs' teeth, how to sleep while surrounded by screaming lunatics . . . Her questions floated like whiffleballs, and she lobbed them with a bored expression and a flat, barely audible voice, just to let me know that her stupidass editors had put her up to this blowjob of a story, that it was my lucky day if not hers. Only it was an act. I'd heard about it from Thunderball, Fitch and Sonny. They'd talked about this game of possum Sissy played, and sure enough, when I dropped my eyelids a little and made as if I wasn't paying attention, I could see her little grey eyes dart around to the others watching us—and, it occurred to me, her tape recorder inside her purse was probably on, catching what her pen couldn't.

Then it came, the high heat. "Did Digby's confession surprise you?" she asked.

"I guess," I said.

She waited to see if that was all I had to say. Then: "Did he get his AIDS from you? The rumor was that you two were lovers."

"Jesus," I laughed. "No and no."

"So you didn't kill Wexler. Digby did. Is that your story?"

I knew I had to stare her right in the face when I said it. "That's right," I said.

"Then why did you have to escape?"

"Because," I said, feeling suddenly very tired, "I already had a murder on my record. I didn't think anyone would believe . . ."

"You ran because you feared you'd get tagged with it."

"That's right."

"How about that." Her eyes were having a good laugh. "When I interviewed Digby before he croaked, he told me he'd always assumed you'd run off to divert the investigation away from him. He went to his grave thinking you were doing him a good turn."

I knew better, of course. "Is that a question?" I asked.

She stared at me, tapping the butt of her pen against her notepad. Finally, weary of the stalemate, she said, "And what do you have to say about the allegation that you've gotten special treatment? That you got a pardon others wouldn't have gotten, just because you and the prison director hung out in the same sandbox?"

The question had no answer—no good answer, anyway. "What does Sonny say?" I asked.

Her annoyance brought a smile to my face. She turned to a page near the front of the notepad. "He says, 'Sure, we played together as kids. Shepherdsville's a small town. But the point is that he had done his time for murdering Judge Castlebury. That's undisputed. He forfeited his teenage and young adult years. John Wesley Hardin killed over twenty men and served sixteen years in the Texas prison system. Hadrian Coleman, as a teenaged boy, killed one man and served fifteen years. The parole board decided that was enough. Then a jealous hard con went after him during his last week. Wexler tried to kill Coleman, and Coleman's cellmate got in between them and turned Wexler's shank against him. We can all sit here and second-guess Coleman for running. But it never made sense to me that a thirty-year-old man who'd served half his life behind bars would go looking for trouble during the last week of his sentence. Trouble found him. That's how I saw it, and that's how the parole board and the governor saw it.'"

Sissy looked up. I shrugged. "I don't have anything to add to that," I said.

"You're a regular quote machine. So what do you have to do for Sonny in return?"

Betraying myself, I looked down at the table. "The pardon is unconditional," I said.

"So it says. Have you thought about why you killed Castlebury and gouged his eyes out?"

I looked back up. It was a challenging smile she wore. "There's no more thinking to be done on that subject," I said. "What do you want me to say, Sissy? I wish it hadn't happened."

"That's very moving, Coleman." She scrutinized my face. "Give me one reason why I shouldn't write that you're the same killer today you were then."

Now I understood why she'd brought me to The Guilty Dog. A portrait of remorselessness, that's what the *Houston Chronicle* reporter had in mind. She wanted to see me making merry with the old bosses, tossing back a few, drinking to the governor's health, then pissing on Judge Castlebury's grave. My heart pounded with the realization of what Sissy would have written had she gotten here earlier, when Scotty Folger was loving on me. Cal Fitch had said it: "Get there before Sissy does." He'd saved my ass. And no sooner was I counting the ways in which I despised Sissy Shipman than I recalled Sonny's observation last night—that I wouldn't be a free man today were it not for her deathbed interview with Digby, and later, her faithful recording of what the star-crossed honeymooners from Houston recollected, which was that a Texas drifter named Hadrian had saved their lives in the backwoods of southeastern Missouri. In print, she'd as much as called me innocent—and later, a hero. Now she wanted to call me remorseless. What the hell did she believe, if anything? I knew what I believed. I believed I wasn't any of the above.

"Fine, Sissy. You write whatever you want," I said, but I noticed Sissy wasn't paying attention. There was a general clamor at the doorway, and before I could turn to look back, I heard the name hollered out from a dozen mouths: "Foots!" The local state rep had arrived, sleeves rolled up, blazer slung over his shoulder and held there by the crook of his index finger as he negotiated his way bowlegged towards the bar, clapping backs and trading genial bullshit as he proceeded. I turned back to Sissy to see her studying her notepad, but an obvious change had come over her face. I'd forgotten. She and he had been high school sweethearts, just at the time when Shepherdsville High's star quarterback had earned his nickname on the gridiron for quick-kicking into a swirling thunderstorm, a trick play that literally backfired when the ball got sucked into a fierce wind current, carried back over his head thirty yards and landed with a plop in the end zone, where it was recovered by the other team for the winning touchdown.

Randall Taylor wore his new moniker like an old hat—comfortable with the knowledge that the ball would bounce back his way in the end. And indeed, seven years later, as a twenty-four-year-old candidate for the state legislature, he recounted the tale of the botched quick-kick with drawling relish, and to such great effect, that the incumbent, a tired old fatass named Arnold Bluffer, charged rather pitiably that young Randall had deliberately punted away the ballgame so as to curry sympathy from his future constituents. It was a laughable notion, but by then Cecilia Shipman was only there to write it down, not to bask onstage with the victorious Foots. She'd been dumped some years back in favor of Susie Clemens, a San Antonio girl he'd met at Texas A&M, and who was as vivacious and affectionate as Sissy was edgy and scornful. He'd broken Sissy's heart; it was all but public record. And not long after that, she insured her disinheritance by bolting from the family paper, *The Shepherdsville Light*, and hiring on as the prison beat reporter for the Houston daily, from which perch she bashed Representative Taylor with one exposé after the next, each of which he took with a mournful shrug, saying only, "That's Sissy." And eventually she stopped, and wrote a few that were in his favor, and a few that weren't, and that was Sissy too.

She tore out a page from her notepad and handed it to me. My sister's telephone number was written on it. "If you feel like doing a good deed," Sissy said as she snapped her purse shut, "you might want to move her back home with you. She's hanging with rough company in Houston."

I folded up the paper and stuck it in my front pocket. "I've never been in a position to tell Mimi how to run her life," I said.

"You're her big brother," she shot back, with more emotion than either of us seemed prepared for. Then, more distantly: "If you can sleep knowing your sister's getting smacked around by a lowlife pot dealer, that's your business."

She reopened her purse, rustled through it and pulled out a ten-dollar bill. "Give that to Folger for the drinks," she said. "The Astros are on cable in ten minutes. I need a little diversion before I go over to the Carter Unit at the witching hour and watch them give Glover the secret sauce."

Sissy slid her purse back into her lap. But then she smiled a guarded halfway smile and said, "You know what I remember most about you when you were a kid?"

"I'm sure I don't want to know," I said.

She said, "I remember having to cover Little League baseball for my dad's paper the summer before I went off to UT. And I guess because you were so tall for your age, they let you play with the fifteen-year-olds. Though you would've been, what? Thirteen?"

"Twelve." I knew where she was heading.

"But you were still kind of scrawny," she recalled, "so you were really more a batboy than anything else. Anyway. This game I remember, your team was up against a team that had imported some big old farmboys from Madisonville. In fact, now that I think of it, Bo Worley was their manager. God, he couldn't have been more than thirty. And of course, your team's manager was—"

"My dad," I said softly.

"Doc Coleman. Exactly. And so they just blew right through your entire pitching staff, and somehow your team kept scoring right back. And it got to be the last inning, with your team up at the plate, down something like sixteen to thirteen. And with two outs, Aynsley fooled everyone and bunted his way to first. And then they walked the next two guys. And there weren't any pinch-hitters left but you."

Laughing, she continued, "And so you went up there and you just knocked the fool out of the first pitch! Sent it all the way to the wall. Everyone came home, you wheeled around third, slid into home, beat the tag. Your team wins, seventeen to sixteen. And everyone pours out onto the field, and the team's got you on their shoulders. And then suddenly Bo Worley's grabbing his catcher and pushing him towards where your team is celebrating, and the catcher comes up and tags you. And Bo Worley starts hollering to the umpire that you didn't touch second, and that only two of the baserunners had scored by that time. And I remember your granddad came hobbling down from the stands and started clobbering Bo Worley with his cane, calling him a lying sack of shit, and there's all this confusion and you're off their shoulders and milling around with a lost look on your face. And that's when Doc Coleman walked up to the umpire and said he saw it, too, that you'd missed the bag. And so Bo Worley's team won, sixteen to fifteen."

I tried to study the table. My throat felt swollen.

"And that was the old ballgame," she said. "I drove over to the paper and wrote up the story. An hour later, I drove back to the ballpark, and there was one car still there. It was your dad's car, and he was sitting in it. He was waiting for you. And you were sitting out there on the field, right where the second base bag would've been, and crying your little eyes out."

I barely heard her say the next words: "And I just wanted to go out there, and give you the biggest hug . . ."

I stared at my hands. Ravaged old things. The fingers bent and crinkled. Then I felt her cold little hand brush up against my face and give my pinch a cheek. Her smirky litany of goodbyes faded out the door.

"You missed the punch line," I muttered. And she had. There had, in fact, been two pinch-hitters available for that final at-bat. And in fact, with the bases loaded, my dad had looked down the bench and said, so that everyone could hear it: "Get on up there, Sonny."

Only Sonny wouldn't get up. Wide-eyed, grinning frantically, he just sat there. "Let Hadrian," he insisted. "Give Hadrian the bat! He'll clear the bases!"

And he nudged me and said, "Come on, slugger! Hit a damn tater!"

My dad pulled back his baseball cap and scratched his scalp in momentary thought. Finally, he said, "That's awful gracious of you, Sonny. Your at-bat, Hadrian."

And I was only twelve then, an innocent bumpkin. Still, I remembered distinctly the thought I had as I advanced to the plate: *Gracious my ass. Sonny just doesn't want to catch hell from everyone for striking out and losing the game.*

I'd saved him the trouble. That was the story. That was the history. "Goddamn it," I suddenly said, and I set my beer mug on top of Sissy's ten-dollar bill on my way out the door.

There was still plenty of light by the time I pulled off of the clay road and hiked down to the shores of the Minerva River. The spot I picked was a familiar one, on a dusty slate ledge situated beneath the bulky reaches of two cottonwood trees. There I sat for awhile, sipping on a tall can of beer while the dirty old river and everything it conveyed hurried past me. It wasn't as ugly as I'd remembered it, especially in this dissipating late summer light. Somewhere off to the east, in the preserve of the thicket, I heard gunfire, and I wondered what the poachers had made off with. I thought again of Pawpaw, whose basic respect for the law did not extend to hunting regulations. The land was everyone's—that's how he'd been raised, and when the ethic didn't take with his own son, he waited 'til I came around, and by the time I was old enough to walk he'd awaken me before first light and lead me into the bottomlands, where we took great care to respect nature, but less care to respect man's barbed wire fences.

I'd made my way to the river today along a legal footpath. It wasn't the way Pawpaw liked to go. He had what he called his own footpath, a zigzag through lumber company property, and as we crunched through the leaves and the pine needles I would hear him murmur his laments the moment we came upon a freshly cut stump of a vast hardwood squatting morosely before us. Pawpaw had himself worked in a planing mill, his single greatest source of shame and the reason for his humped back. In a prior, happier life, he'd been a trapper, a guide and even a taxidermist. But come the Depression he had run out of bullets and customers, with a pregnant wife to feed, and so in turn he swallowed his pride. But his was an unforgiving heart, and I believe he died from being broken so completely in two: half of him a lover, the other half a hater. There was absolutely no question how he felt about his bottomlands and about his grandson. And because he loved us the way he did, it drained the sweetness right out of me every time I saw Pawpaw on one of his binges, his back to me and to the woods, flailing at the walls of his cabin with his feeble old fists.

Pawpaw's regard for his own son was a strange thing to behold. "Your daddy was up all night reading those fool veterinary journals again," he'd say to me, and then with a crinkle of his nose, add, "Can y'imagine?" Or, "Earl Junior just spent all morning delivering two colts for that colored fella, and all he took for payment was five prune pies. Five prune pies! Can y'imagine?" At times his awe was plain, and Pawpaw was careful never in my presence to term my father anything harsher than "strange." But even as a kid, I could see that the father envied the son for his sure place in the world—and probably resented him for finding that place entirely on his own, for becoming a man before Pawpaw ever got the chance to shape him. I could see how Earl Coleman, Sr., quavered in the shadow of Doc Coleman.

I, of course, quavered alongside him. Once we sat together at this very spot, Pawpaw and I. It was a late summer day like this one, and we'd begun it with me shinnying up a cottonwood and cutting a couple of tall limbs with Pawpaw's ancient buck knife. Out of those limbs we fashioned cane poles, and whiled away the day casting out our minnows while a family of raccoons peered out from the plumegrass and scarfed up whatever spent bait we threw their way. We'd used up a hundred summer days like this. But what was notable about this one was that at a certain point I looked over and noticed he was staring at me, his white mustache drooping into the glummest of frowns, and he reached over and brushed my hair with a hand that smelled like minnows.

"He should've called you Earl the Third," he said.

Looking back towards the lake, he shook his head, sighed and said, "Your mama was for it. I only had your daddy to convince. I said, 'It's a family tradition, God dawg it! Now, you name the next youngun whatever you damn well please, but my daddy named me his firstborn son Earl after his daddy's best friend who got killed in the War Between the States, and I named my firstborn Earl, and I don't see how it's gonna put you out so damn much to name *your* firstborn Earl!'

"But your daddy, 'course you know, if pure stubbornness is strength why then he's stronger'n Nellie's breath. He says, 'Pop, I don't want my son to feel beholden to family tradition. I want him to set his own goals. Be his own man.' And so when I asked him just what name he's got in mind that could be so hellfire special, he said, 'I'm naming him Hadrian, after the great Roman emperor. He loved hunting, poetry, philosophy, athletics, justice—he was a man without boundaries.'"

He blinked hard, scowled, and then he said the words: "Can y'imagine? Can y'imagine?"

And then looking away and nearly whispering, but I could still hear: "Naming a boy after some fella who could do slap anything. Tellin' a boy it ain't enough just to be a good ol' Earl . . . Tellin' him to go forth and be a king . . . Can y'imagine . . ."

But that, I knew, was a wounded father talking. Dispensing with the recollection, I stretched back into the silver plumegrass, poured the rest of the beer directly down my throat, and then just lay there for awhile, expended but at peace, watching the light dim through the branches. Beneath the ledge, the Minerva rumbled on and on. It drained the worries from me. Limply I smiled at the graceful collapse of the day.

I must have fallen asleep, because the next thing I knew the night had drawn itself all around me. I got up, brushed myself off, stomped the beer can into a snug little aluminum disc and stuck it in my back pocket. I clawed my way up the riverbank to the footpath and walked the half-mile towards my car. A few strides into it, I stopped and took a deep breath. It was a glorious evening. There'd been no evenings like this in my life for a long, long time. Here is home, I thought: the skies clear and pine-scented, the belches of bullfrogs clamoring with the puny screeches of cicadas and obscure rustlings of spooked beasts, the chanting of the Minerva in my ears . . . I should never have strayed. Somehow, I thought—no longer walking, my back now against a tree and my face upturned to the rash of stars—somehow I should have left Pawpaw's funeral and made my way towards the woods, and just stuck it out in the place that I loved; just lived and starved like a lover, and if I died, if I died, what great loss was that up against all the losses I inflicted, and what great pain would it have caused me up against the torture of the last twenty-three years . . . I slid down the tree, sat in the plumegrass. My fists pulled at my hair and I stared down into the well of my lap and cursed myself, not even with real words—just hard, spitting sounds and tried to crush my eyes with my eyelids, shutting them so hard my face might explode.

My head flew up from my lap. "Goddamn it!" I screamed. "Why are you keeping me alive, goddamn you!"

The only reply was the heedless chorus of the creatures in the woods. They hadn't missed a beat.

After awhile, I got to my feet. Wiping my eyes, I mustered a sorry laugh. "You worthless piece of shit," I said. "You're as lost here as you were when you were running."

Then I said to myself, "Well. Let's get on, killer." And I made pretty good time after that.

Even in the darkness, I could see that the Impala was not sitting right. Someone had let the air out of both of its left tires. I cut the engine, turned off the lights and slammed the door shut with my foot. Fucking East Texas, I thought. There's people out here who would set the woods on fire just to have something to light their cigarettes against all night.

It was a three-mile walk before I reached the highway. My watch at that point read ten minutes after ten. I hadn't eaten dinner, and at this rate I'd be lucky to make it home for breakfast. I walked backwards for a bit, and before long some headlights appeared off in the distance.

The car had a familiar shape to it. I stood and waited. It was a cop car. Slowing to a crawl, the vehicle edged up beside me. Its door emblem read, Shepherd County Sheriff.

Bo Worley lowered the passenger window. "What are you doing out here, Coleman?" he wanted to know.

"I'm walking home," I said. "My car broke down."

"Are you looking for a ride?" he asked.

"I'm all right," I said.

"Good," he said. "Because hitchhiking is a crime in this state." And with that, he sped off.

A few other cars whizzed by after that, but I didn't even bother to look at them. The night had lost its charm, and I was just trying to make it before the hateful appearance of the sun.

Some twenty minutes after Worley had kicked up his dust in my face, another car slowed as it passed me. A hundred yards ahead, it pulled over to the shoulder.

The vehicle glowed and sputtered. Soon a voice came out: "Is that you, Hadrian Coleman?" It was a female.

I walked over to the cheap economy car. "That's me," I said.

"It's me!" she said, and jumped out of her car. She wore a grey correctional officer's uniform, was tall and stout-hipped, with a ponytail draped over her right shoulder, her dark bangs obscuring her eyelids. "It's me, Bonnie Bierbauer! Remember me? I was Mimi's best friend growing up!"

"Damn. Bonnie . . ." Then her grey-sleeved arms were around my neck.

"I've been reading all about you!" she exclaimed. Her eyes bulged and glistened. "You're the most famous man in East Texas! Now what the hell are you doing wandering around here at night? Are you having trouble getting civilized?"

I laughed. "Little Bonnie Bierbauer," I said as I hugged her back. "What the hell are you doing in grey?"

"Fixing to take your ass to the slammer," she giggled, and gave me a soft push in the chest. "I'm a CO-II over at the Hicks Unit. I just got off second shift and I am redd-dee to par-ty!"

I couldn't believe what was happening. "Take me anywhere," I said, "unless you're going to The Guilty Dog."

She hooked an index finger through my belt loop and pulled me towards her. "Honey," she said in a husky whisper, "they don't have a dance floor at The Guilty Dog."

As we sped off, she slapped a cassette into the deck, rolled back the sun roof and pulled out a bottle of Cuervo Gold tequila from underneath her seat. The music was so loud I couldn't tell who or what it was, and the wind through the sun roof was blowing so hard it undid her ponytail and her face was lost to me. She put the bottle to her lips and turned it up, then thrust it into my chest, and as soon as I took it she put her hand on my leg. "Yeeeee!" she suddenly shrieked out the window, and turned off the highway onto a farm-to-market road, barely making the turn. "Yeeeeee!" she shrieked again, and laughed, and then I laughed too and handed her the bottle, regretting the sudden absence of her hand, my heartbeat returning only when her hand did. We blazed onward, and a family of deer stood statuesque as we passed—looking at us, then at each other, and then resuming their own obscure rituals. Bonnie slowed only just a little as she leaned over to kiss me. It was as if I'd stuck my mouth into a bowl of warm honey.

The song, whatever it had been, ended, and she said, "Oh Hadrian," conferring spirituality to my name, and turned back to the windshield and sped furiously for another minute until she pulled into a long private drive. It led to a dark high-arching gate, behind which a single light winked some fifty yards away. She put it in park, and we began to wrestle, a clumsy tangle of fingers and tongues, and throughout it all not a single coherent thought entered my skull—only a long, blissful pant.

But before any article of clothing was removed, Bonnie's lips said to mine, "We've got all night. I want to dance first. You finished with that bottle?"

It was lying somewhere underneath me. "It's empty," I said as I produced it.

"Give it to me," she said. When I did, she flung it over the gate, and again hollered, "Yeeeee!" We were off again, the music was on again, and my breath was somewhere else.

Between songs, I asked her, "Where were we just then?"

Bonnie looked at me. "You don't know?" she sang. "My God. You *have* been gone a long time. It's that awful bitch's house."

"Who?"

"That rich bitch," she said. "Sonny's wife. It's where she goes to fuck niggers while her husband's catting around."

Sometime in the middle of the night, the phone rang. She heard it before I did.

"Aren't you going to get that?"

"Wh—? Oh." I stumbled naked out of my bed, my head singing like a beehive. Picking my way through the house, I made it to the kitchen, where the ring was so shrill I fairly lunged for the receiver.

"Hello?"

After a pause, a quiet, familiar voice: "Hey boy."

"Sonny?"

"It's late, I know. Least you ain't working tomorrow."

A sigh. Then: "You got company over there, hot stuff?"

"Yeah," I managed.

"Who? Between us girls."

"Bonnie Bierbauer."

"Oooh. You done good, bubba. She's a morsel, ain't she?"

Something about the way he said it . . .

Then came his next words: "Look, I need to see you."

I sat down on a stool. "I know you do," I said.

"I don't mean Sunday brunch. Jill still wants to do that. But this has gotta be between you and me and the fencepost."

I listened to his breath, quiet but not so steady; and I imagined I could see him now, deep in his leather chair, his belly nudging over his pajama bottoms, his Nicaraguan stogie smoldering in the ashtray beside him and his wispy eyebrows pinched together in the slightest pout.

He said, "Hadrian. Bubba, I need you."

I shut my eyes. "You can't do this to me," I hissed. "And besides, I don't—"

"Not over the phone. Bubba, you need to hear what I've got to tell you. But not over the phone. Come by the office at about seven tomorrow. We'll go where we can chat. Okay, Hadrian? You there?"

"I'm here," I mumbled.

"This isn't just about me," he said. "You got a big, big stake in it."

I closed my eyes. "See you tomorrow," I said, and hung up.

It took awhile before I felt able to go back to the bedroom. But when I did, she didn't even ask who it was on the phone or why I'd been gone so long. She just said, "C'mere." And I had never in my thirty-eight years felt a body so warm. It remained warm throughout the night, and I believe that's why I was able to sleep at all. But not even so tender a presence as hers could prevent me from seeing, with the dreamer's wide-open eye, the boy in the brown suit and the brown shoes and the shirt that almost fit just right.

3

"And thus while the murder victim may not have, in the strictest legal sense, *deserved* his grisly fate, this court—moved, as always, not merely by the usual juridical imperatives but also by the ecumenical sweep of the matter—held that the son of a bitch had it coming."

Horace Castlebury, judge of the 78th district of the state of Texas, did not wait for his guests' reaction. He threw back his massive bearded head and shook with glee, his cheeks burning purple and soon glistening with tears that leaked out in crooked streams from the ducts of his blind eyes. He shook from head to toe, wheezing out of his gin-blossomed nose as he did, and though the carriage rattled and the seat cushion underneath him gasped, the two mules did not so much as stamp a hoof or shiver off a horsefly, so accustomed were they to their master's outbursts. A gulp's worth of bourbon plopped out of his cocktail glass and stained the left leg of his khakis, which were grimy already from other such explosions. If the judge noticed, it only made him laugh harder, and soon his mouth was wide open and he was bawling like a lost calf, his red hand slapping the hand of Sonny, who was laughing right along with him.

"He didn't deserve it, boys, but he goddamned well had it coming," Judge Castlebury managed as more tears oozed out from behind his wraparound sunglasses. And, "Didn't deserve it but damn sure had it coming!" was Sonny's howling echo as the two of them tittered on and on about the town's hapless Casanova, a pulping laborer named Riddle, whose weekday afternoon jaunts with the wife of local insurance giant

Harvey Cubb earned Riddle a fatal hole in the cranium courtesy of Harvey's twelve-gauge, after which the judge assessed the guilty party a nominal fine for the crime of voluntary manslaughter and solemnly accepted one hundred thousand dollars in cash from the grateful insurance mogul some time later. The judge didn't mention that last part, but the whole town knew it, and he knew that they knew it, and that was Shepherdsville, and that was Judge Horace Castlebury.

And now here was Sonny, eighteen years of age and just three weeks shy of his first classes at East Texas State University. He wasn't a man yet, not even close. But on this day, August 5, 1974, he seemed in the prime of—what was it? Post-adolescent splendor? Pre-adult bravado? Or just sheer goldenness? It didn't matter that he had virtually flunked out of high school, and that no major university would have a thing to do with him, and that East Texas State would not have accepted the local boy were it not for his father's influence over how much state prison money would be diverted to the ETSU Department of Criminology. And somehow on this day it could be overlooked, if not ignored, that he was transparently ingratiating himself with Judge Castlebury so as to shortcut his way to some goal he hadn't even contrived yet. Because Sonny Hope was, at that suspended moment, in full possession of all the bliss that can be wrenched from life—an absolutely brilliant spectacle you couldn't resist any more than you could understand it. And so you stayed close, bedazzled and strangely protective, ever slack-jawed. That was me, at least, because already enough had occurred in my life to convince me that this condition of Sonny's, whether permanent or fleeting, was not infectious—that if I didn't see it in him, I'd never know it at all. And even then I'd have only the barest understanding, since how could someone so in the sway of joy be expected to describe it?

So instead I listened to his bell-like laughter, his shameless brown-nosing of the most crooked elected official in Shepherd County . . . and felt, underneath my sweat from the August heat and underneath an altogether different burning from a year's worth of devastation, a pale but penetrating warmth. That, and a large deer rifle at my feet.

"Ah me," sighed the judge. Then, boozy but authoritative: "Publius Aelius Hadrianus! Why the silence, boy?"

"I'm just watching the blueberries, sir." And that was more or less true, for spread out before us were fifty acres of mangy dark green bushes, some extending as high as fifteen feet, rashed with fat purple berries.

"And my felons?" he demanded.

"They're still picking away," I said, and as I made the remark, a trusty barked, "Move on there, niggers!"—he himself being black, and a few of the twenty-one not being, but the trusty stood in the shade, enjoying a Marlboro, while the others clanked through the fields with chains on their legs and four-quart pails sagging about their waists. They worked in three groups of seven, each group manacled together and positioned beside the giant bushes, atop wooden platforms they'd spent the morning hammering together—standing there with their hands cupped under the berry clusters, so that their dreary work looked barely like work at all, but instead a form of prayer. Their white uniforms were smudged with purple, and they wore bandanas or old T-shirts over their heads to ward off the sun.

"Git on now! You niggers be working from Can 'til Can't, y'hear me?" came another voice, that of a second trusty, who wore mirror shades and moved between the rows on horseback, now and then swatting an inmate with a three-foot-long thick leather strap attached to a wooden handle. The noise, upon contact, sounded like the instant sizzle of a chicken breast against a hot grill. The inmate would gasp or grunt or yelp, and the trusty would growl, "You daisy-ass, you better squeeze those bushes or you gonna feel the bat all day long, y'hear me?" And then, "Yes boss," and onward with the picking, and every few minutes or so the trusty on horseback would holler, "'mon up," and the inmates as one disorganized, cursing unit would clank their way up to the next step on the platform and reach for the higher berries. After a row was picked, the three groups hoisted the platforms and shuffled off to the next row. When one stumbled, so did the others nearest him, and they would fall upon him and smack him around and spit in his face until the trusty on horseback would right things with the bat. In the five days I'd observed the harvesting of Judge Castlebury's blueberry farm, the other trusty had not once strayed from the shade, leaving the rest of us to wonder how he had gotten his job.

It had all been an eye-opener to me that first day, when the judge, as a favor to my recently widowed mother, hired me on to drive the flatbed truck into the town market every evening at seven and unload the heavy field boxes from the pallets. My mother liked nothing about me driving underage, or being surrounded by inmates, or toting a rifle, or being in the presence of a man like Judge Castlebury, about whose private habits there had always been queasy rumors. But she knew she had to do something: it was still summer, and the juvenile authorities were bearing down on her, saying they understood the situation, hoped themselves that this was just a passing phase, but Hadrian needs direction, a firm grip on the boy is essential, we can't have him out on the streets every evening, find him something . . . And though things were roiling around inside of me, there was something that first day about watching those surly misfits on their chains that spellbound me; and at six-thirty, while I observed them loading the last pails into the field boxes, and the field boxes onto the pallets, I sat with the judge on his mule wagon and ate fresh blueberry ice cream that the judge's in-house chef, a prison inmate, made from scratch that very afternoon.

But by the third day I was already tired of the inmates, tired of the bat, tired of the heat and sick to death of blueberry ice cream. Above all, I'd had my fill of Judge Castlebury and his Lincolnesque beard stained with blueberry ice cream and his pants stained with whiskey, braying on about this pathetic nigger he'd sent to the chair or that rich murderer he'd liberated because the victim may not have deserved it but damn sure had it coming. Laughter did not come easily that year, five months after burying my father, ten after burying Pawpaw. And by the fourth day I realized that the judge, through his own hilarity, was in fact listening, and hearing nothing out there from me by way of awe or gratitude, and that was not what he'd had in mind. And so, "Tomorrow, bring the Hope boy with you," and at the time I felt great relief . . . not knowing that this was how it would begin, how the first domino would fall—with me, a boy insufficient with life, failing to laugh, when laughter is all it might have taken to have saved everyone from the whole sorry mess.

"Dad says these are all mainly new boots," Sonny said as he stretched his legs out to the front edge of the mulecart and put his hands behind his head as if he were watching the whole spectacle on television. "A few discipline jackets, but mainly new ones. Fresh from the county jails. See that scrawny little redhead, Hadrian? The one on the right end of the chain gang closest to us? He'll be somebody's punk by chow time if not before. By tomorrow he'll be washing the old boots' socks and underwear. Come the end of the week he'll be calling himself Felicia and giving the COs blowjobs to smuggle him in some lipstick and panties."

The redhead, pale and nervous, already with a welt below his left eye, heard every word. The bushes trembled around his hands, and the inmate next to him said something, which made the others laugh and the redhead's bushes tremble even more, in turn causing the trusty on horseback to holler, "Shaddup, girls!" While Sonny cackled, the judge licked his lips and seemed to survey the sky through his impregnable sunglasses. "Justice," he said, "is not a poem sung aloud. Alas, it's a single sentence chiseled rather crudely, and often repeatedly, using whatever tools may be at hand. Do you boys know why?"

Without waiting for an answer, he ran his fingertips through his unkempt white-and-blue beard and said, "Because men don't understand poems sung aloud. Particularly vermin like these," and he waved a hairy backhand at the chain gang. "And without an understanding of the calibrations and causalities of justice—that Y, a universally recognized sufferance, has been meted out as a consequence of committing X—there would be no justice. None! Justice isn't poetry, boys," he concluded, and took a noisy sip of his bourbon. The whiskey jostled something in him. In a much louder voice, he proclaimed, "Justice is not poetry at all. If it were, my bench would be occupied by Dante Alighieri. And the director of the Texas prison system would be named Pavarotti, not Thunderball."

Judge Castlebury fell into wheezing then, accompanied by Sonny, who also pounded the judge's back. I watched the mules stand there, heads just cocked, their eyes welling with some obscure yearning. "Snap out of it, bubba," Sonny then said, and nudged me with an elbow. His tongue was purple from berries; against it, his teeth shone like porcelain. "Think fast," he said, and the last syllable was barely out before he flicked a berry with the middle finger of his left hand from the palm of his right, and the berry bounced off my nose. I held up a fist, and Sonny cringed and squeaked, "Your Honor, make Hadrian sing me a poem!" The judge threw his arm around Sonny, bellowed, "Sing out, oh justice!" and Sonny sneered at me and yelled, "Sing for your berries!" and I said, "Like hell I will" and turned back to the mules while Sonny cut loose in a reckless warble: *"I am a lineman for the coun-teeee . . . And I drive the main rooooad . . ."*

The judge was enjoying this. "Sing along, Publius Aelius Hadrianus!" he roared, and I muttered, "No thanks," and Sonny stopped long enough to say, "The poor bastard can't carry a tune like we can, your Honor," before resuming his awful noise. Eventually, the judge commanded the trusty underneath the tree to find a felon who would sing in exchange for a rest period. After some discussion, a yellow-eyed black man with burn scars all along his neck clanked forward. His body seemed misshapen and twisted, with one leg shorter than the other and arms crookedly adangle. Peering up at the judge, the inmate said, in a voice that sounded like he'd just swallowed a plateful of ground glass, "Just any ol' song?"

"Something that's got a good beat, that you can da—Ow!" hollered Sonny as I frogged him on his thigh.

"Settle down, boys," commanded the judge.

To the inmate he said, "Whatever moves the spirit—if," he added doubtfully, "you *are* capable of singing."

"I 'spect I am, last I checked," he rasped, chortling a little.

Then he put his hands behind his back, took one deep breath. *"Oh Shenandoah . . . I long to see you . . . Aaaaaway . . . You rolling river . . ."*

"God," I whispered.

It was the deepest, most beautiful voice I had ever heard. It carried over the blueberry fields, and the world fell silent for him. Looking up at the mangled figure in purple-stained white, his arms now raised in the hybrid manner of scarecrow and diva, I imagined all of Shepherdsville entranced, wardens frozen at their desks, the pencils of students slipping out of their limp hands and onto the floors, inmates rising from their stooped postures, farmers squinting up at the sky—and from the lawn chair behind the big mansion on the grand avenue, the girl's eyes opening, seeing something for the first time, whispering, "Could it be . . ."

". . . 'cross the wiiiiiide Mii-sooo-riiiiii."

And then, heartbreaking silence. The inmate hung his head, shrugged and snickered modestly.

Quiet prevailed for a time. Then the judge asked, "What are you in for, mister?"

"Aggravated assault with a deadly weapon, suh," the inmate replied.

The judge nodded. "And how many priors?" he asked.

Shifting from one foot to the other, the inmate squinched up his face. "Oh, now let's see . . . Well. I been on probation two times, been to the pen three times. And I reckon I got a mess of DWI's . . ." He shrugged, snickered again.

Said Judge Castlebury, "You are a hideous waste."

To the trusty he declared, "Get this blight upon humanity back to work. Get them all back to work. I want all those bushes picked by five o'clock."

By five-fifteen, the last field box was loaded and the chain gangs clambered up into a converted school bus, which the trusty who'd stood in the shade drove back to the prison farm while the trusty on horseback galloped off behind it. I watched the white figure disappear into the swirl of red dust. It triggered something in me—I saw other ghostly figures, frail and blurry, moving as if through snow rather than air. I'd seen these people before. They were all at my father's funeral, a great lurching tide of them. Somewhere in there I also shuffled, just beside my mother, who held Mimi's hand. But I couldn't feel anything inside—only the bulk of mourners all around me, whose grief clanged in my ears like a can kicked down an alleyway. All those people whose lives he had touched . . . But I, feeling strangely untouched, just wanted to sit by the river and hear Pawpaw one more time tell about the trapping of the last grizzly in deep East Texas, about the naked Dutchman who raised panthers out by the old Hooks baygall, about the Confederate deserters and the moonshiners, about Caddo graves. And instead there was only his grave, and six months later, his son's— and I wanted nothing to do with either.

I wanted nothing to do with anything or anyone, except for Sonny and the girl I'd seen by the university. Only a girl (though older than me), but surrounded by young men the way I'd been surrounded at the funeral of Doc Coleman; and her look not so different from mine. Untouched, unfeeling, but maybe, maybe not unreachable. When I ran to fetch Sonny at the director's mansion, the houseboys said he'd gone to the picture show. I snuck my way in through the back door, and among a scattering of matinee viewers, there was Sonny, splayed out in his chair, magnificent in his laziness, a big tub of buttered popcorn resting on his stomach. "That's Faye Dunaway up there, you asshole," he protested, but he abandoned the movie and followed me out the door anyway, taking his popcorn with him. He ran as I did, laughing as the popcorn flew everywhere, and finally he dumped the remainder on top of my head and I snatched the cardboard container away from him and whacked him upside with it, all the while still running.

We were both out of breath by the time we reached University Park. She was still there, half-reclined on a lone lawn chair among those twenty acres of grass. The same blonde ponytail, the same skin-tight white shorts, the same impossible legs, the same uncompromisingly bored expression, and for all I knew, the same cigarette held to her cherry-red lips, unlit, while perhaps even more young men than before jostled and groped with their lighters extended. A hundred little torches for the princess of the park.

"That's Professor Estelle's daughter," whispered Sonny from our vantage point behind a chestnut oak. "She went to Hockaday in Dallas."

"Went?" I asked.

"She just graduated," he said. "She's going off to college up east this fall. Yale or Princeton, I think." Then: "God fucking Friday. She makes Faye Dunaway look like a big steaming turd."

"What's her name?" I asked.

"I don't know," he said. "I've just heard the jocks at school talk about how there was a piece of ass living in the Estelle haunted house. This is the first time I've ever laid eyes on her."

"Oh, shit," I said as she suddenly looked up and through her sunglasses gazed out at our direction. Before I knew it, I was running. That night I went to the Quik-Stop and shoplifted a cigarette lighter. The next morning at the juvenile office, Mister Scott wanted to know how long I'd been smoking. He asked other questions, too, but I found it hard to concentrate, because inside I was saying over and over: *He didn't run, and you did. Now here you are, and where is he and where is she—that's the difference, you ran and he didn't, that's the difference . . .*

"I brought the rabbiteye to Texas thirty years ago," Judge Castlebury was telling us as we walked on either side of him through the rows of shorn bushes. He had a hairy hand around each of us, but walked surefootedly, almost daintily, in his scarred calfskin boots. "It's native to the southeast, and you'll find it as far west as Louisiana. No other grower in the state thought it would work here. They didn't do the research. It fell to a blind man to do the reading."

He wheezed a little. "Where's that bottle?" he coughed, and I handed it to him. As he chugged from it, a golden rivulet of whiskey ran down the side of his face. The judge let forth a satisfied growl and thrust the bottle back into my chest, then replaced his hand around my shoulder. "The rabbiteye species, I learned, has a hexaploid ancestor from these very woods," he continued as we strolled. "And if *Vaccinium amoenum* could thrive here, why couldn't *Vaccinium ashei*? Here," he said, flourishing his hand to indicate his hundred-acre spread of pastureland four miles south of town, "here we have the same dry upland climate. The same soil pH range. The same low propensity for late spring freezes and the same winter rest period. And, of course, since *V. ashei* is indigenous to stream banks . . ."

With a sharp index finger, he pointed just off to the east, where the field tumbled down into Vero Creek, the fast-running slough feeding out of the Minerva that ran a jagged route through the judge's property until petering out somewhere near the county line. "Well, your Honor, it's like my dad always said," remarked Sonny, his hands jingling coins in the front pockets of his Bermuda shorts as he strolled. "Some folks couldn't walk a straight line if you put 'em on a conveyor belt."

The judge wheezed his approval, mussed Sonny's yellow thicket of hair with his hand. "What the hell does walking a straight line have to do with growing blueberries?" I demanded.

"You ignoramus, I'm saying there's some people who can't figure out how to do what's easiest," retorted Sonny. "Do you want me to draw you a picture?"

I spat on the ground. "You don't even know what the hell you're talking about," I said.

"Lick mine," he sneered. "Don't pay attention to Hadrian, your Honor. He's just crabby because no one's giving him a blowjob on his birthday."

Blushing, I mumbled, "I could give a rat's ass."

"Birthday," said Judge Castlebury, his bearded chin slack with wonder. "You didn't tell me. How old are you, son?"

I shot Sonny a dirty look, and he returned it with a mocking, weaselly grin. "Fifteen," I said.

"Fifteen," the judge marveled. "When I was fifteen, Woodrow Wilson was just beginning his first term as president. Even as a blind boy, I was determined to be president myself someday. Boys don't dream much anymore, do they? Tell us what you'd like to do with your life, young Hadrianus."

I shrugged. "He'd like to be a bouncer at one of those titty bars out by the airport," cracked Sonny. "You're probably wondering, your Honor, why I'm associating with such a worthless little punk. And well, it's a weakness, I know, but I'm just a big-hearted slob."

"Shit," I muttered, and batted my hand against the naked bushes as we walked past them.

"Our youthful emperor here needs a mature influence," the judge said, his fingers fumbling around my chest for the bottle until I handed it to him. Half of what he put to his lips dribbled down his face. Bronze beads of whiskey hung from his blueberry-smudged beard. Instantly his voice was louder, bolder, and obviously impaired. "He stands on a most precarious fulcrum. So says his worried mother. The onslaught of adolescence, a lingering tendency towards the life-style of the dreaded American Loner . . . And then, of course, the sudden removal of his male role models, just when a boy needs them most."

He shook his furry head. "Quite a man, Doc Coleman. A saint among mortals." His voice had turned strange. I looked up. The smile he wore was more like a baring of teeth. "Never one to play favorites," he continued. "Never one to stoop to the indignities of politics. Not Doc Coleman. He preferred the refuge of his manger, and the beasts of the holy barn. Yes, yes. My mules shall mourn him forever."

Could he tell that I was eyeing him? The judge cleared his throat and said, "And so in the face of such a loss, one can only expect our young Hadrianus to falter. I've offered up my assistance to his mother. A little summer labor for the idle hands. But as you can see, the harvest is over. So you would do him a further service, Purvis Junior, by diverting him from some of the community's less desirable elements."

"Lord knows I try," Sonny said, sighing so hard I thought he'd expire on the spot. "But the kid's like a monkey in a jungle. I can't keep up with him."

"Not on that conveyor belt of yours you can't," I said.

"Lick mine twice. But if I say so myself, your Honor, I've done as well as anyone could have. I've kept him out of the bars, the bowling alley, the convenience stores, pretty much all the typical—"

"I am referring mainly to the Estelle girl," said the judge.

I stopped on the spot, as did Sonny. In turn, the judge pitched forward ahead and then turned around to face us, a sliver of a smile on his liver-spotted face. "I have my eyes, of course," he said, and descended again into wheezing laughter.

Sonny and I looked at each other. His eyes rolled heavenward with both recognition and dismay just as mine did. We said the name together: "Dillard Bunch."

"Dillard drives home late after our dinners here," said the judge of his clerk. His malignant grin was the same as the one he'd worn when speaking of my father. "And on his drives back, he has seen our wayward emperor in the shadows of the Estelle mansion—"

"That's bullshit," I said. "And if I'm walking down a street, that's my own damn business."

"—Standing in the front yard," the judge continued merrily, drunkenly, while Sonny cackled in the background, "behind that ancient magnolia, and gazing up at the southmost window on the second story, which seems always lit—"

"Bullshit! Bullshit!"

"—Always lit, and his gaze upon that window is not that of a petty thief, nor of an assailant . . . but that of the smitten."

"Oh, screw your little faggot clerk," I yelled. I could see Sonny's eyes bulge in horror, and him mouthing something to me, but I was too far gone. "What the hell does he know about me?"

My throat felt suddenly clogged. I didn't want to cry in front of Sonny, but the first tears came too quickly. "He's just a nosy little faggot who'd be chased out of town if it wasn't for you! He can go to hell! And so can you!"

When I managed to control myself, and could see, I noticed that the judge had not moved at all. But he had changed. It was his face—so much of it hidden beneath a mask of liver spots and hemorrhaged blood vessels, beneath that filthy beard and the greenish black lenses braced tightly against his wasted eyes; so much of it hidden, but now I could see it. The face knew that I was afraid. With that knowledge, its flesh tensed and twitched, barely able to contain its hunger. It was the look of a man who lived off of fear. His life was devoted to it—first instilling it, then exploiting it. Darkness had served him better than light served others. He had occupied the bench of the 78th state district court for over thirty years, unopposed in every election, though that never stopped him from amassing campaign donations, or from throwing lavish fundraisers wherein lawyers, politicians and businessmen would be obliged to make their support public as they kissed his ass and stuffed his pockets. Day after day, Judge Horace Castlebury held dominion from his highback red velvet perch, slurping Rebel Yell whiskey out of a hollowed-out lemon which his faithful clerk Dillard dutifully refilled while surveying the courtroom so as to keep his master apprised of the visual goings-on. Outside of Shepherd County, no one knew much about Horace Castlebury, or had any reason to know or care. But inside the county, buildings bore his name, protégés like Dillard Bunch and newly elected Sheriff Bo Worley carried out his will, his learnedness and wisdom were mythologized in a million fondly told tales, and the 78th was his for life. So potent was their fear of him that the residents of Shepherd County could only embrace the senile and alcoholic blind man who lived with kingly arrogance on his lush blueberry farm—supported by a state salary of thirty-eight thousand dollars, free prison labor, and an incalculable host of bribes. They could only muster love for one so hateful, lest they face their own cowardice.

I faced mine now. Watching him, I knew that in his darkness, he watched me as well. And what I learned then was something that no one else knew about Horace Castlebury, except perhaps his devious little manservant. At that very moment, a different wave of fear overcame me: sheer terror at first, thoroughly paralyzing, until I felt my legs tremble inside my jeans; but then it subsided into something else, and I knew then and there that I had his number. The judge seemed to sense that a battle had been joined. His head tilted a fraction upward, a half-nod of half-approval. Sonny stood a few feet from both of us, another dimension away. It was just me and the judge. For the moment, at least, we had an understanding.

"The Estelle girl," he continued, now stone-cold sober, "is the end product of a disastrous bloodline. I know her father, knew her father's father, and the father before that. Oafs one and all, and harmless enough now that their pitiful vision of a feudalistic Shepherdsville is a century dead and buried. If that idiot professor wishes to pretend otherwise, I say let him. Delusionary behavior is not itself a crime.

"But the girl." His face was as hard as his voice. "She is the tawdry Omega. The decadent culmination. I don't doubt for a moment that all of the rumors about her are true. But her affection for pornography and the county's Negro population barely tell the half of it. She is an empty vessel, I tell you. She has no center. No purpose. The wealth, the physical beauty—of what use can they be to such a creature, except to gull the unsuspecting, so that they might share in her doom?"

Sonny let out a jittery chuckle. "And so, Purvis Junior, it would be a service to our young emperor if you were to discourage his nightly sojourns to the Estelle mansion." The judge bared his grey teeth again. "Though this might prove too tall an order for one similarly inclined."

Instantly Sonny's face went crimson. "Well, now, hang on," he protested. Facing me, he said, "I've only seen her twice. That day out at the park after you left, and then once when I was taking Sparky for a walk. Jesus, Hadrian, I ran into her on the street! Was I supposed to ignore her?"

"And," prodded the judge gleefully, "at this cinema this past Wednesday . . ."

I watched Sonny's mouth flap open and shut. "You told me you went by yourself," I said.

"I did, damn it! I didn't even know she was there 'til we ran into each other on the way out! Your Honor, meaning no offense, but this Dillard Bunch—man alive, he's putting two and two together and coming up with twenty-two!"

"Well," chuckled the judge. He drank the dregs of the whiskey bottle. Sighing with pleasure, he flung the bottle far over his shoulder and into the bushes. "Well," he said again, his smile now little more than a flesh wound on his rancid face. "Just so we all stay out of harm's way."

He reached out for me. Petting my shoulder, he declared, "So we have a birthday to celebrate! Who's for a dip in Vero Creek? Young emperor, be so kind as to take the mules back to the house and bring us back some towels from the hall closet. And the blueberry ice cream, of course. And another bottle if you would be so kind. And whatever interests you from the icebox."

"An ice-cold beer!" Sonny hollered as I made my way back toward the mulecart. When I turned around and shot him the finger, his eyes welled. "What?" he demanded. "You don't believe—"

"Big-hearted slob," I muttered, and turned away.

The living room wall gleamed darkly with the judge's multitude of honorary plaques. It was an unsettling place—tidy and filled with handsome wooden furniture, but absent any lighting fixtures. An odor of stale human breath rankled the air. I didn't want to be here; I didn't want to go swimming. But I didn't know where else to go. I'd been seen, and now Sonny knew—and yes, he'd made his own play for her, but I had expected that, and it was all silliness anyway, so impossibly distant was she from either his reach or mine. Yet I'd kept on dreaming . . . I still had Sonny. I had my friend, until the fall, when he would begin college and I would enter high school, assuming the juvenile authorities would permit it.

Somewhere in the house, the clock struck six times. My mother would be home washing the dinner vegetables and battering the steaks. I had asked her not to bake me a cake, but I'd already seen the little bag of candles sticking out of her purse when I headed off this morning in the flatbed Ford to pick up Sonny on the way to the blueberry farm. It was more for Mimi, I thought. She was nine, and for her sake, we had to prop ourselves up. I opened the judge's icebox, pulled out two Budweisers. An aluminum bowl covered with foil sat prominently in the freezer. I lifted the foil and stuck my finger into the ice cream. Today it tasted sweeter than before.

Using the towels as a tray, I carried the whiskey, the beers and the ice cream back out to the mulecart. The two beasts were not anxious to return to the heat. "Get on, you dumb bastards," I yelled, and lashed them hard. When they both jumped, shame overtook me. "Sorry," I said to the mules, and eventually they resumed their usual sluggish gait.

At the edge of the pasture, the land tumbled into pine bottomlands. I could hear the splashing, and Sonny's loud crooning: *"We all live in a yellow submarine . . . yellow submarine . . . yellow submarine . . . "* I hopped down from the cart. Their clothes were heaped in the grass. I pulled out one of the Budweisers from underneath the towels in the carts. Only twice before had I drunk beer, both occasions being with Sonny at the prison director's mansion late at night. Getting past the sour taste to the drowsy euphoria was a chore. But on this late afternoon, the cold liquid rolled down my throat with ease. I belched, tossed the bottle into the grass and considered drinking Sonny's. But then I hard his voice from the creek: "Get those suds down here, bubba! I've got a man's thirst!"

I left a towel on top of the big aluminum bowl to shade it from the heat. The other towels I took with me, along with the whiskey and the remaining beer. I stood beside the two heaps of clothes for a moment, contemplating the judge's soiled khakis wadded up next to Sonny's Bermudas and loafers. Sweat glued my T-shirt to my chest. Peeling it off, I shivered for a moment and hugged my bare torso. The blueberry fields looked naked themselves. By winter they'd be a wretched sight; but come springtime, the judge had told me, the bushes would burst open with long, tubular pink petals, and two months later the berries would emerge once more. At that moment, I felt an overwhelming desire to see the blueberry flowers—to endure the coming months, this early winter of mine, and sustain myself with dreams of the early bloom . . . My clothes were now a third heap. The sun felt wonderful against me. I bared myself to it, stretching out my arms. My entire naked body, with its new dark hairs and its modest suggestions of muscle, surged with life. I closed my eyes, happily alone, privileged: it was my birthday.

The slope was snarled with burrs and vine branches, carpeted with pine needles. My feet had lost their tough padding over the last year, and once again I thought of Pawpaw as I made my way through the brush. But the memories were scattered by the intrusion of Sonny's voice: "*We all live in a yellow submarine . . . yellow sub*—Hey, Ringo! Get your butt down here! The judge has got the best damn swimming hole in Shepherd County!"

It was definitely a sight. There, where a serpentine twist of the fast-moving Vero thrashed its way past a series of boulders and opened out into a thirty-foot-wide bowl of clay-colored water, Judge Castlebury stood, submerged up to mid-chest, wearing only his sunglasses, his splotched and wrinkled body now just that of any old fart as he gaped with timid pleasure; while above him, dangling from a rope tied to a large cypress branch, swung Sonny, naked as Jesus, his blonde hair plastered wet against his round, hilarious face. "You're probably wondering why I've called this meeting," he greeted me. "Come on in, dear, the water's fine. What'd you do with your nads, by the way?"

"Did you bring the elixir, boy?" called out the judge.

"Yes sir," I said, and began to wade in. The water was not too cold. It rose up to the base of my neck by the time I reached the judge, whose outstretched hands collapsed lovingly around the bottle. He unscrewed the top, which promptly slid out of his fingers and drifted downstream, but the judge had the bottle to his lips and was in a world of his own.

Dangling from the rope, Sonny nodded to the beer in my other hand and said, "Throw that buddy up where I can swing out and catch it." In a throaty voice, he droned, "Drew Pearson heads out into the flat . . . runs a textbook perfect route . . . Staubach sees him . . . He heaves it . . ." I cocked my arm and threw, and Sonny lunged from the rope in midair and of course fumbled the bottle and landed with a crash of water that drenched the judge's face in mid-swig, causing him to gag for a moment. "You couldn't catch a cold, you dumb fuck," I said, and paddled after the bottle, only to be pulled back by Sonny, who had ahold of my ankle. "My baby, officer, he snatched my baby!" he gurgled in the water, and down we both went, scrambling and kicking at each other and yanking each other's hair. I got to the bottle first. Just as my fingers wrapped around it, Sonny's hand lunged forward and gave my testicles a savage jerk. I curled up, losing my grip. By the time I'd come up for air and finished coughing, Sonny had already twisted off the cap and now offered me the very archetype of a shiteating grin—while a few yards away, the judge was proffering his whiskey bottle to the cloudless sky, singing: *Oh Shenandoah, I long to see you . . . Aaawaaay . . .*"

A half-hour later, we crawled out of the swimming hole and wrapped ourselves in the towels. The judge surrendered his bottle long enough to be lent a hand as Sonny and I led him up the banks. Back at the pasture, we spead out the towels upon the first sunny patch we could find and dropped to the ground. The judge's breath was somewhat labored, though contented. I could feel myself smiling. It had not occurred to me before that what I might need more than anything else was simply to feel as young as I was—to splash around in a dirty creek, to hold myself up to the light with nothing on my back, unburdened . . . Stretching out under the sun, I didn't think about what might come next for me. I almost forgot where I was, until I felt Sonny give my ribs a soft slug.

He murmured, "Happy birthday, bubba."

I smiled at the thought. Then I got up and walked over to the mules, who had maintained their bleary standstill where I'd left them. I petted them both for a moment before fetching up the aluminum bowl. Most of the ice cream had melted. We took turns holding the bowl up to our faces and slurping the contents. The judge had reached an agreeable plateau in his inebriation. He and Sonny lay on their backs, groaning blissfully. Bloated with ice cream, I fell back and submitted to the sun.

"We'd better get those blueberries into market," the judge said.

"Shit," said Sonny. "I'd forgotten all about it. Can't we just let the buzzards have them?"

"Well, here's an idea," said the judge, and using Sonny's thigh as a grip he sat himself up. His mottled flesh hung in lifeless clumps. "I'll phone up Dillard and tell him to bring us whatever we want for dinner. Why don't you both stay over? Hadrianus, you could come back here in the truck after you've unloaded. By then, we'll have food on the table. And of course," he added with a feeble smile as he turned to Sonny and rumpled his hair, "we have no shortage of Budweiser."

"You just dialed my number, your Honor," Sonny said as he clapped his hands. "Bubba, get those buddies off to market and haul ass back here."

My heart sank as I remembered. "I can't," I said. "My mom's cooking me dinner for my birthday."

"Aw, tell her your birthday's tomorrow," said Sonny. "C'mon! We'll tip a few and swim under the moonlight."

"If Mrs. Coleman is expecting her boy home for dinner," the judge interjected, "then I want him home for dinner. But do this. Take the berries off to market. Go home and eat your mother's cooking. Then call over here when you're finished." He shrugged amiably. "If the festivities are still in progress over here, then you should feel free to drive back over and join us."

I put on my clothes, said goodbye and started the truck, peering through the rearview at the sight of the two figures in repose, the sun paling above them. Then I took off, and everything behind me disappeared in a dusty red puff. I followed the tire tracks of the prison bus a half-mile to the entrance gate, which the trusty on horseback had left open. I climbed out and locked the gate behind me. On my way back to the driver's seat, I reached into one of the field boxes and popped a couple of blueberries into my mouth.

It was almost seven-thirty, but I took the drive slowly—for the blueberries' sake, and for mine. Already the afternoon was well behind me. The old gloom, familiar as night, began seeping through. But there was a difference now: I fought back, my teeth gritted as I began the drive along the farm-to-market road, telling myself *Snap out of it bubba please snap out of it* . . . I thought of Sonny, who didn't have any more ambition than I did but still somehow knew exactly what he wanted—who saw the very same girl I had, from just as unfathomable a distance, but did not for a second consider the distance itself. All he'd seen was the prized possession. And I'd withdrawn from it, from her, saying *Oh no* even as Sonny was saying *Oh yes oh yes.* Inside me a voice screamed: *God show me!* My knuckles were white against the steering wheel. I let out a hoarse growl, wrestling to the death with the brutish despair that had all but smothered me in convincing me that I was born wrong, had lived wrong and would always live wrong, would be underneath or upside down and always, always distant from the sweet, pink blossoms of the spring . . .

Except for Sonny.

The engine burbled as I sat there, my forehead resting against my hands on the steering wheel. I knew I had to get home. I owed it to my mother to be her birthday boy—to be, if not the man of the house, then at least the son, and not the cold-eyed monster Sheriff Worley was already telling the juvenile authorities I had become. "You've got a chance here," I said out loud, quoting Mister Scott or one of the others. The words, whenever they were first said, entered me like a long, cold dagger, because having a chance only meant racking up another failure. But now, saying the words myself on this day, the completion of my fifteenth year, I surprised myself by thinking: Maybe. Maybe it was not too late to break out of this awfulness, to suffer the winter like a man and find the boy in spring—or at least, at the very least, to walk the straight line. "Conveyor belt my ass," I mumbled, with a dark snicker that was still a kind of laugh as I thought of Sonny, and just then wondered how he was going to get home if I didn't come back and get him.

I lifted my head from the steering wheel. Off to my left, the sun teetered on the horizon. Dillard Bunch would give Sonny a lift the next morning, I figured. But the realization—a physical reaction, beginning with my hands which suddenly melted in sweat—came over me that the clerk had always arrived punctually at seven. And then I remembered the judge's words to me: "Call over here when you're finished." Judge Castlebury's number at the farm was unlisted. He'd never given it to me. The only person entrusted with it was Dillard Bunch, and he wasn't here—he wasn't coming. And now, with a wild sickness rising up in me, it reappeared, the face of the old man with the dark glasses forbidding anyone to see what I had in fact beheld with my own misery-blinded eyes.

I jumped a split-second before the distant sound of the rifle shot. "You idiot, you knew!" I yelled as I wheeled the truck around with such force that one of the field boxes rocked and tumbled out of the flatbed, the blueberries swirling with the red clay dust and then bouncing every which way. The engine groaned as I floored it. The truck shook wildly; blueberries flew in wild arcs, oozing against the windows while my mind screamed out *You saw the way he was with Sonny you saw the way his face went and you saw the goddamn rifle you stupid idiot you knew you knew!* I veered off the road, grinding through rocks. Another field box tumbled out. I steered back on course, trying to slow down just enough to be able to regain control, but my breath was coming out in yelps and the whole world went red and purple. At the sight of the gate, I slammed the gear in neutral and jumped out. My fingers trembled against the padlock. "Oh God oh God," I wailed, but when I finally squeezed it tight in my fist and stared at the little digits on the lock, my mind went not so much blank as awash in numbers, millions of them, and the combination was lost to me forever.

I climbed over the gate and began to run. Within the first few strides I knew I'd finally done something right, and I could feel my breath return to my control even as I picked up speed. But my heart pounded so crazily that I believed I could feel tissues give, sinews snap; I feared it would batter its way right through my chest. I ran anyway, telling myself *Think think think goddammit.* I was on foot—maybe too late, and vulnerable myself. But, but: I had the element of surprise, he would've heard the truck, and if he didn't hear it, he wouldn't expect me. If I was quiet, if I was careful . . .

I saw the farmhouse from the distance, darker than ever. But the shot had come from the deer rifle, which I had left in the mulecart somewhere between the blueberry fields and Vero Creek. So I cut away from the clay road, towards the back of the residence, and when I reached it after a final sprint, I fell against the back wall and sank to my knees, gasping and shivering. *Get up you stupid bastard there's no time . . .* I slid back up the wall and looked around the corner. The land looked just as I'd left it, though now the sky shimmered a furious orange over the dark bushes off in the distance.

Tiptoeing, I moved to the front of the house. I crouched against a pillar, and for fully a minute I did nothing but stare at the unobscured meadow that separated me from the bushes. In that span of time, a sober calm embraced me. They were both out there. Staying where I was would do no good. To save Sonny, if he could be saved, I would have to head for the fields, out in the open. Out where the rifle had been fired. There it was. I took a deep breath. At last, a reason.

And so I walked in the direction of my destiny, quietly but steadily following the mulecart path towards the bushes a quarter of a mile away. In thirty minutes or so, it would be pitch dark. As the fields began to take shape, I slowed my approach and searched for any twirl of a leaf, any turn of a shadow, anything. But there was nothing. Not a movement, not a sound. Perhaps a hundred yards from the fields, I stopped and got down on one knee. From that vantage point, I squinted hard at the uniform rows of shorn bushes. My eyes fell on the northmost edge of the field. Flush against the furthest row of bushes sat the wooden platform the inmates had built. If I could make it there, I thought, I could stand on top of the platform, obscured by the bushes, and see out towards the woods.

I got on my stomach and began to crawl, propelling myself by my elbows over the rocks and burrs. The darkness was coming on fast. I could feel the skin on my forearms peel away, and I realized also that my throat was aching from thirst. Soon the bushes loomed before me. I crawled sideways towards the platform at the edge of the field. As I did, I craned my neck upwards, staring ahead with such concentration that I felt certain I could see every speck in the air, every bug on the ground. But it took some time for the still grey mass, directly underneath the platform five yards in front of me, to materialize, and announce itself to my eyes as the face of Sonny.

On my belly, eye level with him, I could see only one side of his face. But the glassy eye and the gaping lips told me that he had not been shot, and that he was scared out of his mind. And then his mouth moved, and what he said was well beneath a whisper. I didn't hear it. But I saw it from the movement of his lips and the fear in his eyes—and I'd already guessed it anyway:

"He can see."

I made a motion with my hand for him to stay where he was, and I rose slowly to my feet. Maneuvering sideways, I eased over to the first step of the platform. I eased up, then listened. I took the second step. Again I listened. There was one more step. I took it, rose slowly to my full height, my face up against the bushes, which I then parted, leaf by leaf, so that I could peer out beyond the field towards the creek, where I knew the judge would be.

Before me stretched a sullen grey field. Minutes passed. The last bronze wisp of daylight fell into the jaws of the evening sky. Just then, the mulecart appeared from over the slopes of the riverbank, with Judge Horace Castlebury holding the reins, clicking his beasts forward. He was fully clothed again, and still wearing his dark glasses. But I could see him lift his head, turn it from one side to the next. I could also see a long object laid across his lap. He was steering the mules towards the blueberry fields.

I ducked, then crawled down the platform steps on all fours. "Sonny," I whispered.

The voice that came back was quiet but hysterical: "He's going to kill us."

"No he's not." I said it before I'd even considered it. "No he's not," I repeated, and leaning under the platform, I saw Sonny, huddled like a possum, still naked, his eyes mad with fear. "If he starts talking to you, I want you to talk back."

His eyes widened further, but he said nothing.

"I want you to talk back," I said again. "I want him to come into the bushes."

He let out a gasp of protest, but the mules were drawing nearer. I scrambled on my belly past the platform and wedged myself between the bushes two rows away.

The jangling and the creaking of the mulecart now resounded in the stillness. When it ceased, I stared ahead with my cheek to the ground, but I couldn't see their hooves. He was maybe twenty yards away.

"Purvis Junior?"

The voice, calm and even genial at first, quickly hardened.

"I want you to come out from the bushes."

Say something, damn it, I pleaded silently.

I could hear him shift his weight on the mulecart pillows. "I'm sorry I shot at you, Purvis Junior," he said. "I was not aiming for you. Though," and then came a laugh not like the laughter of his I'd heard before, "my aim is not very good anyway. My eyesight is still very poor . . . whether you believe that or not . . ."

His voice trailed off.

"But you ran from me," he then said, with a note of wrath in his voice. "You ran from me, and that was rude of you, and a very bad mistake. Because then I had to chase you. And to chase you, I had to give up my secret to you. So now you must give up your secret to me. You must show me where you are."

Total silence followed. The game had changed now. For the moment, vision was a useless commodity. Now all of us, perhaps even the mules, were only listening.

"Purvis Junior!"

It was a terrifying bellow. My teeth began to chatter.

But then, to my amazement, Sonny spoke. The voice quavered, but was otherwise plainly his.

"You'll kill me if I come out," he said.

The seat cushions squeaked. He had deduced that Sonny was in the bushes furthest from where he sat. But the voice wasn't muffled—which, I realized, meant that Sonny had leaned his face out from underneath the platform. He was thinking. He would play his part.

"I won't," said the judge, a little too anxiously, and he knew it, for his next words were soothing. "I won't, Sonny," he said, using the nickname for the first time. "It wouldn't make sense. There's nothing to be gained by it. I want us to be friends, Sonny. You know, of course, how fond I am of you. I should think I've made that quite apparent. Sonny? I can help you."

The last words came out in an awkward rush.

"Help me?" echoed Sonny.

"Yes. I can help you. Help you with your life, your career. I—I didn't mean to scare you when I pulled you towards me, Sonny. It's just that I'm used to getting what I want, you see. But I return favors. You may ask anybody."

And after a moment of silence, the judge spoke again, gently but warily: "I'm going to come down from the mulecart, Sonny. I'm going to walk over to where you are. Here—I have your clothes with me."

"Where's the rifle?"

"I'm leaving it in the mulecart."

"Prove it."

The judge uttered something I couldn't catch. He was taken aback, perhaps angry as well. But quickly he restrained himself. "Well, I'll do what I can," he said.

The seat cushion groaned, as did the wheels of the cart. His boots thudded to the ground.

"I'm putting the rifle in the cart now, Sonny." An emphatic collision of metal against wood followed.

"And now, Sonny, I'm walking towards you. And I want you to show yourself to me." But as he spoke, I heard, and knew that Sonny heard, the soft sliding noise of the judge lifting the rifle away from the floorboards—the slightest noise, ordinarily beyond our range of hearing, but the situation wasn't ordinary, and that was the miscalculation of a man whose own senses the world had long misgauged: for some time now, in our blindness, Sonny and I had been able to hear as never before.

But now he was taking his first steps our way, with a loaded rifle, and Sonny had certainly been right: the judge had no intention of letting him live. I began to panic. The bushes provided scarce cover. All he needed to do was walk to the edge of my row, and I would be seen. And I could hear him headed my way.

Then Sonny said, "Stop."

The judge did so. From his voice, I could tell that he was maybe ten yards from the edge of the fields.

"Yes?"

"Prove to me you've got my clothes. Shake them in the air so I can hear them."

When the judge complied, holding up the T-shirt and the Bermudas and flapping them noisily in the air, it dawned on me what Sonny was up to. Knowing that I was our unexpected weapon, he had spoken again to lure the judge further from my direction. But the genius—vintage Sonny Hope, but the other wouldn't have known this—resided in the particular request. For it seemed only the imploring of a boy, trapped and frightened, seeking to allay the primal core of his fear, brought on by his nakedness; a child's naive query, put to an old man for whom childhood was a memory long erased, who now knew only how to coax trust from the weak. But that wasn't it. Not at all. Knowing, as he and I did, that the judge had his rifle in one hand, Sonny had asked the judge to announce, in effect, whether his other hand was free. In that single, deceptively brilliant reading of the available angles, my friend had literally disarmed Judge Castlebury.

"Can you hear them? I've got them right here. Now. Will you come out, please?"

But I knew that Sonny wouldn't speak again. Likely the judge knew this, too. He didn't wait for a reply. I could see his boots now, walking directly towards what he believed to be the location of Sonny's voice— one footstep and then the next, cautious but undeviating, his movements set on a path slightly diagonal from the western edge of the fields . . . Before long, I could see his full outline. Tall in his boots, no longer the wizened and pink-eyed figure splashing about timidly in the swimming hole. His right hand, pressed against his flank, held something that glinted in the new moonlight. The rifle. His head turned towards one row and then the next.

At the edge of the row where I crouched, the judge suddenly stopped. He leaned into the bushes, scanning them. Thirty feet, if that, separated us. Then he stepped forward. Another step. I shut my eyes. The leaves shifted against my back. The footsteps stopped. The judge, I was certain, had fixed his eyes on me. Slight movements of fabric, followed by a vague thud. He had lifted his rifle. I opened one eye, expecting any moment for it to be shattered by a flying bullet.

But the judge stood there, twenty feet away, the firearm lifted yet not aimed. His jaw was slack; his shoulders were hunched towards his head. He was uncertain. He sensed something, but he couldn't see it. Though I could now see him, every inch of him, he couldn't see me. *My eyesight is still very poor* . . . He had given himself away twice now. And though the gun, the property, and the power were all his, I could see the doubt cloud his face. He turned his head sideways, trying to listen.

And Sonny obliged him. From two rows away, a single bush rattled. The judge braced himself, and a second later he looked upwards and must have seen the lone bush swaying at its tip, for he dashed right past me, two feet from where I crouched, and I watched the legs stride alongside me but my fingers went suddenly numb and too late I realized I'd blown my single opportunity, that all of Sonny's maneuvers had predicated themselves on that one moment—and I had failed him, failed utterly. Swiveling, rising up from my crouch, stupefied and nauseous, I watched the back of Judge Castlebury as he strode purposefully, confidently to the northern edge of the fields, mounting the platform step by step, and set the rifle to his shoulder and gaze into the sights . . .

. . . And he gazed, and gazed. Swinging the barrel slowly to the left, then to the right. Aiming, but, but . . . Couldn't he see? All that flatness before him, and he couldn't see his prey fleeing? No! It came to me then—Sonny didn't run, he hadn't gone anywhere, he'd only reached out with an arm to shake the nearest bush. And just then I saw the judge turn away from the pasture, back towards me but looking down rather than up, cursing his own foolishness as he suddenly realized, but not before the platform flew out from under him and the judge gasped and landed on his back with an anguished holler, against the wooden edge of the platform.

Sonny got to his feet first. Naked and dirty, he took off, churning his chubby legs eastwards towards the farmhouse, screaming, "Help! Help!" With a groan, the judge pushed himself up. Then he reached for his rifle on the ground, scooped it up with one hand while lifting up his sunglasses with the other, and took three long strides, where he set himself, raised his weapon and aimed for the kill.

He must have seen me and heard me a full second before I reached him. But perhaps he didn't comprehend me—an altogether new presence, a creature stirred by the prospect of violence. I comprehended fully. This was me, never so sure of myself as I was now, lunging straight for his neck, grabbing it with both hands and with such force that the rifle flew out of his hands in midair. We hit the ground before it did. I felt his arms go up, his fingers claw at the back of my head as we crashed into a bush that buckled against us as we rolled over it, and against and over another bush, strange noises now in my ears, noises from us both, and then a wild roar that could not have come from a normal boy but had not come from the judge—and then, just then, a noise so definitive, so singular and final, that the skies themselves seemed to dissolve into a purple light . . .

And from another galaxy came Sonny's voice—closer and closer, but still far away: "You got him, goddammit! You got him! You got him, Hadrian! You snapped his fucking neck like a chicken's! I could hear it all the way from—man, you got him! He's fucking dead as a fucking hammer! You got him, bubba! Hahahaha! The son of a bitch, he's fucking graveyard dead! Oh man! You fucking got him! Hahahaha!

He didn't deserve it but the son of a bitch had it coming! He had it coming, the son of a bitch! I knew you could do it! I knew it!"

He knew I could do it? . . . He did?

"Hadrian . . ."

My hand found it. It was put there for me.

"Hadrian . . . What . . ."

Sitting on top of him, on top of the shivering corpse of State District Judge Horace Castlebury, I pulled the sunglasses from his dead face. And rising up, crouched over him, breathing fumes, breathing death, I took what was there for me, what was in my hand, the empty whiskey bottle he'd flung, and with all the resolve in me tilting at last in one deadly certain direction, I brought down the bottle against his open right eye. A shattering, a gushing. Then down against his left. And looking down at my fist, blinking past the shards and the blood, I saw only a jagged fragment, which I drove deep into the twin lidless caverns of that mess of a face, deeper with every scream of Sonny's, driven by the certainty of the scream, and by the certainty that I'd found myself.

Then I felt him brush past me, my only friend, whose life I'd saved; saw the hand reach for the clothes, the soft hand almost feminine as it retrieved the shirt, the shorts, the underwear, the loafers; saw him run from the fields, still naked, the clothes bundled against the crook of his right arm; saw the golden hair bouncing, waving goodbye, as he disappeared into the darkness, bound for Vero Creek.

And who knows how many minutes or hours passed before I myself ran, shedding the blood of the judge; who knows how I even made it as far as I did, past the farmhouse and over the gate and back into the flatbed truck with the engine still running and the blueberries scattered like a coarse black rug all along the clay road which I took almost to its conclusion before the truck quietly swerved off the path and into a meadow, where it drank the last drop of gas and then expired.

The metal door swung open. "I'm Colbert Reeves, your attorney," said the man, a gaunt and oily-haired figure wearing crooked horn-rimmed frames and an unpressed seersucker jacket. "I believe you know my son Aynsley."

"Sure. Yeah, I know Aynsley." I sat up from my cot. He held out his right hand, while his left held a battered leather briefcase with gold monogrammed initials: CCR. I shook the free hand. It was clammy, trembling. A strange medicinal odor emanated from his pores.

He looked me up and down, taking note of the paper clothing. "They've got you in suicide sweats," he said. "You haven't tried to hurt yourself, have you?"

I shook my head. "Did Aynsley go off to Harvard?" I asked.

"He did, and I'm sure he'll antagonize every professor there, but right now let's talk about the trouble you're in, shall we. May I sit?"

I moved over. The odor of him tingled in my nostrils. He unclasped his briefcase and pulled out two pieces of paper. "Let's talk about your statement, first of all," he said. "Is this your handwriting?"

I looked at it. "Yes."

"And you gave this statement willingly?"

"Yes."

"Hmmm." He fidgeted with his glasses as he read. "And so you admitted to killing Judge Castlebury," he remarked.

"Yes."

"You said it was self-defense."

"He was going to shoot me."

"Because . . ."

"Because he . . . he wanted . . ."

"He wanted to have sex with you."

I nodded.

"And," he said, frowning as he read, "you're saying the judge could see."

"He could see."

"And how did you find this out?"

"Because he told me. And because he chased me, and pointed a fucking gun right at me and shot at me."

"Calm down, Hadrian. I'm just ascertaining what you believe happened."

He chuckled a little. "You know," he said, "I always suspected it. Others did, too. I used to pull stunts in the courtroom. Make a sudden movement, make a face, that kind of thing. But he was good. He never flinched. And with those heavy shades, and Dillard whispering in his ear—"

"Dillard!" I exclaimed. "He has to know! He knows the judge could see!"

"You're probably right," said Colbert Reeves, and smirked as he pulled out a yellow legal pad and jotted down a note. "Of course, he'll never admit it. But maybe we can court-order a polygraph."

He laid his notepad on the concrete floor and turned to face me. His eyes were sad and bloodshot. "Our problem, not only with the issue of the eyesight, but with the whole incident, has to do with—well, with the disfigurement," he said. "Breaking a man's neck in self-defense, a jury could buy that. But the other . . ."

My eyes filled with tears. "I know," I managed. "I know. I just . . ."

His hand was on my shoulder. And then my face was pressed against that grubby seersucker, and I sobbed against it for awhile. When I was finished, he handed me a handkerchief—also dirty, also smelling of medicine. But I took it and wiped my eyes with it and thanked him.

"Hadrian," he then asked, "would your parents have had any reason to lie about when you were born?"

I looked up, puzzled. But he was serious. "I doubt it," I said.

From his briefcase he pulled out a dark photocopy. "This says you were born on August fifth, nineteen-fifty-nine," he read as he adjusted his glasses, "at five-thirty-five p.m. at Shepherd County Memorial Hospital. Does that sound right?"

I shrugged. "Sure."

"Not August sixth. Not the seventh."

"No," I said. "The fifth is my birthday." And remembering my birthday, my eyes filled with tears again.

Colbert Reeves stood and began to walk in a tiny circle on the floor of the tiny room, his fists thrust deep into his front pockets, his lips working themselves against his teeth as he studied his scarred Hush Puppies. "Has anyone mentioned the term 'certification' to you yet?" he asked.

"No," I said. "I don't think so."

He nodded. Then he stopped pacing and leaned against the metal door. His fists came out of his pockets, and he folded his arms around his small chest as he stared towards the ceiling. "You are, of course, a juvenile," he said. "You're not an adult. You can't vote, can't drink, can't be drafted, can't do any number of things. And thus, when you've been in trouble in the past—and I've seen your folder . . ."

I looked down, nodded.

"Each of those times, you were taken to the building where we are now. The county juvenile probation center. Though," he added, "your records don't reflect that you've been in the detention wing before."

"No sir."

"Well. So you know, then, that juvenile crimes are handled by the juvenile authorities." He took in air, whistled it out. "But in certain extraordinary cases, a juvenile offender may be certified. Meaning, certified to stand trial as an adult, in an adult court, before a jury—and, if found guilty, to be sent to an adult prison."

I stared at him.

"To be eligible for certification," he said, with a sad smile, "the juvenile must be fifteen years of age."

I closed my eyes.

"Now, this is very important, Hadrian. So you must listen. Eight years ago, the U.S. Supreme Court prescribed a series of guidelines for the courts to follow when they consider whether to certify a juvenile. First, the juvenile must be subjected to a complete diagnostic study. You will be evaluated by psychologists and social workers who will ask you lots of questions. They will ask you about your juvenile history, and naturally they will ask you everything about this, this incident. They'll also ask about your background. About your family."

"My family?" I said. "Why do they want to know about my family?"

"To evaluate you, Hadrian. To *understand* you."

"What's my family got to do with understanding . . ."

"Listen to me, Hadrian. I want you to think about this. You *need* to think about this. You had never been in trouble with anyone until your grandfather died and your father died. You weren't the world's greatest student or the most popular kid, but you weren't a troublemaker, either. Look at me, Hadrian. Your life is at stake here. You are a child. What happened out there was not the kind of thing a child does. But you need to make people *see the child*. You need their sympathy. You need to make them understand why you would do what you confessed, in that statement, to doing."

"He made me!" I yelled.

"In point of fact," said Colbert Reeves, his head cocked, "Judge Castlebury did not make you stick a broken whiskey bottle into his eyes *after*, by your own admission, he was dead. That will be a very hard story to sell in a courtroom. Are you with me?"

I nodded glumly.

"After the diagnostic evaluations, what's called a transfer hearing will take place. It'll take place in juvenile court, before Judge Winkler, whom you've already met. It'll be very much like a regular trial, except that it won't be public, and what takes place in there will remain sealed. On your side, I will try to convince the judge—hopefully with the diagnostic evaluations to our advantage—that you should be adjudicated as a juvenile. If we prevail, then the worst that can happen is that you'll get sent off to a state reform school until your eighteenth birthday. On the other side, the district attorney will try to convince the judge to transfer you, as a certified adult, to state district court.

"Judge Winkler," he continued, holding out his fingers, "will be obliged to certify you if he determines four things, in keeping with the Supreme Court guidelines. First, that the alleged offense was a felony—and, unless he buys our plea of self-defense, the felonious nature of the offense is indisputable. Second, that you were fifteen or older when it occurred—and unfortunately, you were. Third, that no other juvenile hearing with regard to this offense has taken place—and none has. And finally, that after full investigation and hearing, it's shown that because of the seriousness of the offense, *or* the background of the offender, the welfare of the community requires criminal proceedings. That's the X-factor, Hadrian. We want to convince Judge Winkler that yes, Judge Castlebury was killed in self-defense . . . but also that what you did to him is not proof that the community should fear you. Do you understand?"

I sat there in my paper clothes, looking down at my hands—for the millionth time in the past day, but always as if for the first time.

"Hadrian?"

"If he certifies me, then what?"

"Well. Let's hope for a little wisdom from Judge Winkler. But if he sides against us, there'll be a public trial. Not here, of course. First thing I'll do is get a change of venue. Only a lunatic would assert that you could get a fair trial in the 78th District."

"What if they find me guilty?"

He nodded, took off his glasses, wiped them against his smelly white shirt. His eyes looked like those of a cave dweller. "They can't give you the death penalty," he said quietly. "The Texas penal code won't allow it. But they can give you . . ." He cleared his throat, shrugged. "They can give you a lot of years. An awful lot. And in a Texas penitentiary, a lot of years is . . . well . . ."

He put his glasses back on. "I'm a very good attorney," he said shakily. "Your mother couldn't possibly afford my services. But that's not why I'm waiving the fee."

Stepping towards his briefcase, stuffing the papers and the notepad into it with shaking hands and reeking skin, he muttered, "It could just as easily have been my son. Except that Aynsley wouldn't have fought back. He wouldn't have been able."

And then: "He was a terrible man."

He left, and when I no longer could hear the stamping of his shoes, I let out a yell and tore off my paper outfit, and fell naked onto my naked bed.

And before long I was wearing a blue T-shirt and sweatpants. After that, an orange jumpsuit with black stenciled letters across the back that read, Property of Shepherd County Sheriff's Department. And then the brown polyester suit, the nicest outfit I'd ever worn, with Sonny's shirt—his only contribution, the only one I'd asked for; he gave the shirt to Colbert Reeves and otherwise was left out of it. And after that, after they led me down the corridor, past mobs of strange faces and strange lights, with only Sissy Shipman among them recognizable to me, but she like the rest blurting out strange questions in the strangest, most insistent tones, I wore a different orange jumpsuit all the way to Sugarland, in a white bus with iron grates over the windows, chained to my seat alongside adults I did not dare look at, though they all looked at me. And there, in Sugarland, at the Albert Creel Unit, they fitted me in white, and showed me the fields, where for a year I worked from Can 'til Can't, through Thanksgiving and Christmas and the new year, through the frost of winter and the bloomless spring, through the dead of summer and through my sixteenth birthday, and no one sang "Shenandoah."

4

Mimi leaned over the balcony, the slight pudge of her belly pressed against the cypress balustrade and her shoeless feet dangling just above the floorboards. "How killer," she murmured for the seventh or eighth time as she surveyed the vista of the surging Minerva and the pine timberland further afield—taking it in as if she'd never before laid eyes on her native land. "How very, very killer." Spoken with her usual endearing disregard, intending no harm, just as she meant no offense as she hoisted her butt—which appeared to have been poured like flour into her Levis—directly into the field of vision of her appreciative male host. If she should have known what she was doing to Sonny, that was probably more my fault than hers.

She looked back our way, eyes dazed with wonderment and envy. Alas, nothing about Mimi had changed. She still had our mother's soft apple face, our father's dark curls, and a waywardness all her own. Today's emblem of the latter was the purple crescent under her right eye, a souvenir from her latest ex-husband-to-be. Mimi had a knack for such encounters. Rare was the time that she wouldn't show up during inmate visitation hours sporting some new war wound veiled by an extra coat of make-up and her dizzy amiability. She'd think she was doing me a favor, being so brave. But today the sight of her brought back those moments when I blinked through the plexiglass at my pert punching bag of a little sister, a prisoner to the recitation of her inno-cent misadventures, while the CO took no pains to conceal his stare as her breasts jiggled in cadence with her monologue. She'd become something else besides my own flesh and blood. She'd become a part of my punishment—the part that constituted a life sentence.

This morning, she materialized on our parents' doorstep—bruised, sniffling, with a bad case of the hiccups—and, with a squeal and a hug and a hiccup, said all that she had to say about all that had been. "Somebody smells like Bonnie Bierbauer," Mimi sang as she stepped inside and tossed her fake Gucci suitcase on the kitchen table. Her fourth marriage was down the toilet and her three daughters were presently in the care of two topless dancer friends in south Houston. But all Mimi could talk about was my grey hair, the scent of her friend Bonnie (who'd departed two hours earlier, wiggling up against me in her grey CO uniform before speeding off for the morning shift), the cute AAA guy who'd fixed her flat tire an hour ago on the interstate just outside of Conroe—and now, the view from Sonny and Jill's riverside house, where we'd just finished our Sunday brunch.

"Hell," she said, again awarding us a view of her backside as she appraised the panorama, "if I had this kind of spread, you couldn't budge my happy ass with a cattle prod. I wouldn't need nothing else!"

Then, considering, and inquiring over her shoulder: "Is there a hot tub here?"

"Does the pope shit in the woods?" shot back Sonny with a giggle.

"Yessss!" hollered Mimi, pumping a fist. "Maybe after we digest our food . . ."

"I wouldn't." Jill's voice was grave by comparison. She smiled carefully at my sister. "The hot tub is in no condition for civilized company. Sonny was entertaining some wardens on Friday."

"Oh," Mimi snickered as she swiveled against the balustrade to face us, "I'm sure I've been in a hot tub with worse," and "Oh, well," was Jill's reply as she stood to clear the table, but when she reached towards Sonny's plate her husband hunkered protectively over the remnants of his omelet and he said, "Don't listen to Jill, kid. She's got a hard-on for all wardens on account of the one night I let Rennie Gribbs from the Dunston Unit stay over at the mansion." He flipped back his hair and then with the same hand stuffed the last two slices of bacon into his mouth. "Warden Gribbs had an inmate over there who brewed a pretty raw hootch out of his cell toilet. Kept the warden pretty fragrant, 'til after that night at the mansion. We shipped that inmate out to Luling where the whole town smells like shit anyway. But regardless, I wouldn't let Rennie Gribbs clean my hot tub much less swim in it. No, we had some first class gentlemen over here on Friday, by Shepherdsville standards anyway."

And Jill by the kitchen doorway murmured, "Yes," but Sonny paid her no mind as he recited the role call of his recent guests: Warden Powell with the FBI background, Warden Luckett the lay preacher, a visiting criminologist from Georgetown, Lichtenstein's director of prisons, a Hollywood screenwriter researching prison gangs, and several others whose names I ignored. It was all a lie. None of them had been to Sonny and Jill's retreat on Friday. It was just Sonny and me, sitting on the balcony where my sister now luxuriated. I found myself thinking about how much Mimi would have loved the view that was wasted on me and Sonny that evening. We had sat there for hours, Sonny and his cigar and his single-malt, me and my beer, and under a magisterial pageant of stars we talked not about God or love or even life and hot tubs . . . but instead, murder.

And murder was all I'd thought about since. "God, you were growling like that girl in *The Exorcist*," Bonnie said with a nervous laugh before telling me goodbye this morning. And then, kissing me lightly on the lips: "You're a free man, Charlie Brown. Start sleeping like it."

But Sonny wouldn't let that happen. Since Friday night, he had phoned me four times, always employing some transparent excuse. "Jill wants to know if you'll eat oysters." "Jill says you don't have to be here before eleven if you were planning on going to church." "Just calling to make sure you remember the passcode to get through the gate." "Hey bubba, couldn't remember what you told me about the oysters." Nor could I.

The food, as it turned out, was delicious: chive biscuits, the oyster omelets and the bacon, pan-seared salmon, mimosas and chicory coffee from New Orleans. I hadn't figured Jill for a cook, and in fact she looked vaguely comical in the kitchen as she frowned at her recipe book and handled each egg like it might detonate in her hands. But after shooing us off, she emerged an hour later with plates so fabulously assembled that Sonny could only gasp, "Why, Betty Crocker . . ." to which Mimi—already zany from the mimosas—replied, "Betty Crocker my ass, this here's Martha Stewart and girl I am *moving in*!"

"We've got a spare bedroom," Sonny replied with a look of such phony earnestness that I could not bear to look at Jill. Instead, I started on my food and considered what Sonny had said about Bonnie the other night, and what she had said about Jill, and what Shepherdsville had always said about my friend and his wife. And while eating and half-listening to Mimi and Sonny banter and horse-laugh throughout the Sunday brunch, it dawned on me that he would probably be screwing my sister any day now.

Meanwhile, Jill said almost nothing. Her movements were elegant but economical, her countenance modulating ever so slightly between dreamy and morose. There wasn't a line on her face, not a single hair gone white; at age forty, she'd aged even less than Mimi, eight years younger. Only the veins, an opaque blue web of them beneath her pale forehead, hinted at the strain she endured. Now and then she politely asked Mimi about her daughters or her employment outlook, or reproached Sonny with a barbed aside while moving the food platters around the table. Otherwise, she kept to her own untouchable world.

At one point, her voice shifted discreetly my way, like a note slid under the table: "How is your omelet, Hadrian?"

"It's terrific, Jill," I said, and she received my words with that quiet, pained smile of hers, just as Mimi echoed, "Killer!" I fell into a deeper malaise and said nothing more for a while. Instead, I worked away at my food, determined to make a show of my appreciation, though my appetite was shot from the moment I began tormenting myself with the image of my sister and my best friend entangled loudly in the hot tub.

I came to at the sound of my own name. The others were talking about the story Sissy Shipman had published yesterday in the *Houston Chronicle*. "Boy, and you could see ol' Sis gnashing like a rottweiler to find something crooked with that pardon, the poor thing," Sonny chuckled as he dragged a biscuit against his plate to sponge up the juices. "See, now that's the press for you. It ain't even that the glass is half-empty. It's that it's half-full of rat poison."

"Or bile," murmured Jill.

"I loved the story!" said Mimi, her dark eyes pinwheeling with light and her baby cheeks flush with sudden vigor. "I read it all the way through—three times! I wanted to go out on the street and tell everyone, 'See? See what I told you? My brother ain't no crook! He's a hero!'"

She leaned over, smudged my cheek with her lipstick, and it was all I could do not to get sick. For it was a crook she had kissed. *Killer.* Yes. I had killed not one, but two—the first to save my best friend's life, the second to save my own; but I had killed. And only two nights ago, I had heard myself say it: that for Sonny's sake, and possibly mine, I would kill a third. I would kill Ricky Tempesta. My best friend had asked this of me. He had done so not simply because he trusted me, but because he clearly believed that I was a crook. And for all of the days and nights I had struggled with the question no human being should have to ask one's self—namely, not "Who am I?" but "What am I?"—the answer was now unavoidable. This time around, I would kill with deliberation, unprovoked. I would end someone's life for the convenience of my own. Only a crook could, or would, think in such terms.

And Sonny, who had been around crooks all his life, knew this best of all.

He had asked me to visit his office on Friday evening at seven, when the building would be vacant. My shoes clapped against the marble floors. On a wall just in front of the elevators, an inscription announced: THROUGH THESE HALLS PASS THE FINEST MINDS IN AMERICAN CRIMINAL JUSTICE. The laughter that burst out of me drowned in its own echoes, which themselves trembled into nothingness while the inscription's boast gleamed stoically as before. In the mirror-walled elevator, I punched Sonny's passcode and the button 10 for the top floor. The reflection on all sides of me was familiar enough. A rumpled grey stick figure stuck in a cage.

Everyone on the top floor was out to play. No receptionist, no ringing phones, no tapping against computer keys, no muted life within the cubicles. Only Sonny's genial tenor somewhere down the hall. I followed the voice. There he sat, behind a large and paper-cluttered desk, on top of which his shoeless feet rested as he puffed on a Nicaraguan cigar and chattered into a sleek black cordless phone. Behind him, a wall of tinted glass separated him from the abyss of the bottomland pines. I stared in pure amazement for a moment. It had to be the most splendid view in all of East Texas. I had no doubt that Sonny's back was to it all day long. But that in itself was something, the way the explosion of wilderness offset itself against him, highlighting him, so that the fresh-faced bureaucrat appeared theatrically pale, authoritative, a king of the jungle and all that it might contain. A track of lights trained soft beams on his beaming facade. He seemed borderless, and perhaps a little ghostly—but indisputably larger than life.

Another track of lights, just off to Sonny's right, danced at angles against a far wall where his plaques and photographs hung. Honorary professor of this, distinguished speaker at that. Pictured here with the president, there with the governor, and there with a hundred grinning cub scouts, with him right at home among the preadolescents. As Thunderball Hope's houseboy, it used to take me all morning to dust the old director's commemoratives, which he kept in the study of the mansion, where all the deals were brokered. Yet Thunderball's collection was barely half that of Sonny's, and had reflected the provincial scale of that era: crude gifts from wardens and inmates, Kiwanis Club trophies, a tangle of deer antlers, a pair of medieval leg irons, his East Texas State diploma, a framed *Time* magazine story from 1962 billing the Texas Department of Criminal Retribution as "The Most Miserable Place On Earth." Seeing the grandeur of the son's office triggered in me the first and only tender feeling I would have on that barren day.

"Pssst." Sonny had flipped the mouthpiece away from his lips as he snapped his fingers and pointed to a spartan white wooden chair situated a few feet from his desk. "Sit down there for a second."

Among the furniture in his office, the chair seemed the least comfortable. "Hold on a second, Frank," Sonny said into the receiver. Then his face split open into a grin. "C'mon, bubba," he urged me. "Just for a second. Sit down there."

I did. Sonny began to giggle. "What the hell is this all about?" I demanded.

"Look at that little lightbeam on the chair just above your left shoulder," he said.

I turned. A small green light winked. "What does it mean?" I asked.

"It means you ain't got a shank concealed up your bunghole," Sonny said. "That's an all-new Body Orifice Security Scanner. The latest in contraband detection. Works with pussies, too."

"Jesus." I stood and turned my back to Sonny's guffaws. As he resumed his conversation, I scanned his office ornaments. Near the door hung a series of framed photographs. One row was devoted to Sonny's professional evolution, from a clueless-looking CO to a stern, determined warden to a preppy but keen-eyed prison sociologist to an almost alarmingly sober deputy director to the present incarnation, the director with a somehow different smile—a little cockier, a little more sculpted, unquestionably meaner . . . Below that row hung three other pictures. The first was of young correctional officer Hope and his father the director, the former appearing somewhat effeminate and tongue-tied as he shook the enormous mitt of Thunderball, who seemed to be regarding his son with threadbare patience. In vivid contrast, the next picture showed Sonny and his mother—he as a college boy, yet babied by Mama Jean across whose lap he sprawled, laughing while she pretended to whack him on the butt with a prison bat. I wondered who would've taken the picture. Not Thunderball, I thought. He wouldn't have had any part of this.

I knew what the third picture would be. I managed a sidelong look at them, the bride and the groom. Then I turned away. Now there was a completeness to my mood. I was facing a long burgundy leather couch situated against the far wall. I knew what it was there for. The Bonnies, the Mimis. I closed my eyes and shook my head hard.

"You all right?" Sonny's hand was cupped over the phone receiver. "Give me a couple minutes more. Here," and he opened a drawer that was actually a small refrigerator door, and from behind his desk he flipped me an ice-cold beer. Winking, he returned to his conversation, which I now followed for the sake of self-distraction:

"Well anyway, that's how rumors get started, bubba. Never say never, but here and now Sonny ain't running for governor or anything else . . . Aw, hell, Frank. Polls might as well be polygraphs for all the stock I put in 'em. Crime rate's down, they're thanking Sonny. Swing that pendulum and it'll be me they blame. Shit, I'm just a corrections lifer, Frank. I ain't no governor. Besides. You ever tasted the food over at *his* mansion? My houseboys eat better than he does."

He winked at me. "Oh, Shepherdsville's not so bad," he continued as he fished around in his refrigerator for a beer of his own. "You lobbyists are all alike. Y'all think God created Austin on the seventh day . . . Well, then He would've been better off taking the day off, but that's a country boy talking. Look, Frank, I've gotta make it git in a minute here, but here's where I am on your client's bid for the maximum security gig in Lufkin. This is between us girls, okay? . . . Now, Frank, I'm serious as a train wreck. If this gets out, then I don't see much work for your client in the state of Texas in the near future. Really and truly. So let's not fuck up. Bastille Systems is good people, and I think we both agree Wick Aspromonte's got too big a slice of the pie. I was just telling Foots Taylor how I think the prison system might could stand a little more competition. Better for private enterprise, better for the state of Texas. But I need to see lower bids, Frank . . . How low? Say around $28.30 per inmate per day . . . Hold your tongue and hear me out.

"Now here's where it gets sweet, and you keep a lock on this. In case you've been dead and ain't heard it yet, this is an election year. You remember the governor had us build all those boot camps up northeast so he could get some photo-op mileage out of him standing there like fucking Mussolini while all those cons did push-ups on the pavement? Well, after November we're gonna need those beds for harder cases. And I'd just as soon farm out that conversion job to the privates. Like Bastille Systems, Frank. And the kicker is that I could get emergency approval on those, and then due to proximity, tie that project with the max at Lufkin—That's right, Frank, emergency means waiving the competitive bidding. All those beds would be Bastille's. Silver goddamn platter."

Sonny listened for awhile while slurping his beer. Presently his eyes and smile narrowed. "Well, Frank, it's just my way of demonstrating how I've always been in the forefront of prison privatization. Hell, Sonny brought the privates to Texas! Y'all do more business here than anywhere else in the world! And Sonny did that! And as long as Sonny's here, y'all are gonna be in the chips—*within reason*."

He sat up in his desk chair. "And the Tempesta Plan is way beyond the bounds of reason," he said. "See, Frank, there's always got to be a dance between government and business. Like my mama always said, 'A place for everything, and everything in its place.' Truth be told, I don't know why any businessman would *want* my job. But regardless, *it is not a job for business*. These are wards of the *state*. These—I mean, Jesus Christ, Frank, under the Tempesta Plan, we'd have a private Death Row! People making money killing cons! Don't you know the goddamn writ writers will have a field day—court challenges up the wazoo—and killers'll end up getting sprung and there'll be blood in the goddamn streets, mark my words, Frank! You think Sonny's gonna stand by and let the Texas penal system become the laughingstock of the nation the way it once was? You think I'm gonna let everything I built get perverted beyond recognition and moved lock, stock, and barrel to some fucking joke of a Gomorrah-town that a career criminal has the fucking hair to call *Trust*? You think Sonny's gonna go quietly? *Do you?!!*"

I marveled at the burnished purple in his neck and cheeks. Sonny held a pen tight in his right fist as he listened. "Well, I'm glad you agree," he then said in an even but austere voice as he lifted his feet back onto his desktop. "But see, Sonny says these things publicly and the reaction is, 'Sour grapes.' I need help getting the message out, Frank. I need your clients to come forward and say, 'We know where we belong, and where we don't belong. This Trust, Texas, pipe dream is greedy and it's dangerous and we want no part of it.' You get Bastille Systems to produce a damning critique of the Tempesta Plan, and submit it to the legislature, and these beds are yours. We'll supply all the research if you want. I've got a whole cadre of support staff to furnish the particulars. Hell, just retype it word for word on Bastille's letterhead, I ain't proud . . ."

The reply compelled Sonny to reach for his cigar. He puffed for a moment. "That's right, Frank," he then said. "It is asking for a lot. But nothing's free, bubba. Y'all are looking for a way in? Well, here's the way in. But consider this. If it's bad PR you're worried about, imagine how history's going to treat the people who didn't stand up to this craven weasel Tempesta. Imagine what's going to happen when the Tempesta Plan explodes in our face—as it will. I'll tell you one thing that's gonna happen. Sonny's gonna be the private prison industry's worst nightmare. I'll turn on every last one of you like a fucking howitzer. You'll be out of Texas before you can say Jack Robinson . . . Look, Frank, I understand. You're worried about going toe to toe with Ricky Tempesta. I'm just trying to draw the lines for you here. *You don't have a choice.* If you're for him, you're against me. Ain't no middle ground. But think about this. Either of us could be your enemy. But will Tempesta ever be your friend? 'Cause Sonny sure will be. Sonny can make a big difference in your life. One way or the other."

A plume of smoke swayed over him. "You do that, podner," he said. "And give Mindy a hug for me. 'Bye now."

Sonny turned off the phone and put it on the desk. With a roll of his neck he threw his hair back from his forehead. Then he set the cigar back into his mouth and worked it for awhile, his eyes slitlike beneath the smoke. I wondered if he had forgotten his guest.

Then he looked down at the ashtray and muttered, "Some of 'em you've got to draw the footprints on the sidewalk so they'll know where to walk."

When I didn't say anything, he looked up at me. The stony-eyed man I beheld was one I knew faintly, if at all.

"Is that what you're about to do for me?" I asked.

He winced, stabbed the butt into his ashtray. "Hadrian, please. That was just some greedy shitass who wants something for nothing. He ain't my friend, for God's sake."

"I just sat here and heard you tell him different."

Sonny's eyes executed a dramatic roll. "Will you quit pretending to be so naive? *He* knew what I was saying."

He stood, brushed off the ashes and touched a button on his desk. All the lights were extinguished. "Let's jailbreak, bubba," said Sonny as he made for the doorway. "It's Friday."

The riverhouse was all Jill, from the mottled terra cotta walls to the painted tiles in the kitchen and the rustic wood furnishings scattered throughout. "She copycatted some villa in the Yucatán she went to," said Sonny as he kicked off his shoes and stepped over them where they lay on the hardwood floor.

He waited there while I took in the brightly painted furniture, the imposing rail chandeliers, the smoked glass and the fanciful Latino pottery, the rugs tossed across the aged terra cotta and cypress hardwoods, the walls stained in rich mineral hues lit here and there by copper sconces, the countless books and plants and paintings . . . And not a photograph in sight. A place of invisible ownership, I thought, as it had been when it was Tempesta's.

Sonny held out a palm and, by way of explanation, said, "It's her never-neverland."

"It's really beautiful," I said.

"Yep. Yep, it sure is. I don't come by here much."

His expression fogged, but I could see the genuine remorse and aloneness. I could see Sonny again—Sonny the boy, lost in the life of Sonny the man.

"Where's the grub?" I asked.

I knew the subject of food would brighten him. "Oh, babycakes, have I got a feast in store for us," he exclaimed as he pounded me on the back and led me to the refrigerator, where he pulled out trays of beautiful steaks, ribs, sausages and shish-kebabed vegetables. "I've been waiting for this," he continued breathlessly as I followed him out to the balcony, where a large grill stood beside wooden chairs and a long table. "Jill won't eat red meat anymore, and it just fucking kills me. Here I am, sitting on this embarrassment of riches, and I hardly get to take advantage of it."

The sly grin reappeared. Flipping his hair back, he said in a voice trembling with delight, "This is Hope Prison Farm bovine, bubba. We've been selling the choice cuts to the East Texas school districts and feeding the—well," he blushed, "you remember. The other stuff to the inmates. Anyway. Last months we had an unanticipated surplus of our swine stock. So I sold seventy-five percent of the surplus to a farm in Idaho and made a goddamned *killing*. Took the other twenty-five percent and sold it to the schools in place of the equivalent weight of beef cuts at fifty cents on the dollar. And lo and behold! We got a balanced ag budget and a dozen extra bovines sitting in the slaughterhouse."

I choked out a surprised laugh. "Is—is that legal?"

He puckered his mouth gleefully, lowered his voice. "It may not be legal," he said. "But it sure is tasty."

After he'd wound down his laughter, Sonny said, "Besides. We're donating half of the beef to homeless shelters in Dallas and Houston. So my conscience is clear."

He turned towards the grill and proceeded to assemble the charcoal. Thinking better of it, but then finally unable to resist it, I asked, "That half you donated to the homeless shelters—did it include the choice cuts?"

Sonny peered back over his shoulder. "Did anyone tell you that you are one cynical sumbitch?"

"So," I went on, "who got the choice cuts, besides you?"

"Foots, the head of the Legislative Budget Board, and the lieutenant governor." And then his head tilted skyward with laughter.

He fell against the balustrade, shoulders trembling as he savored the joke he'd played on the state. "Oh me," he finally sighed, and leaned back towards the grill. "What can I tell you?" He pulled out a pack of matches and fumbled with it over the coals. "Sonny does all he can to spread the damn wealth. I'm just a big-hearted slob, is all."

The coals burst into flames. While I nudged at my plate of choice cuts—abundant, befitting a sentenced man's last meal—Sonny lustily chomped and babbled.

"Never was any mystery to it," he explained to the charred heap upon his paper plate. "Just redefine the terms. Prisons don't cost. They provide. Shit, look what they've done for Shepherdsville. Hell of a lot more than any Estelle did. So I'd buttonhole those gutless twits down at the capitol and I'd tell 'em, 'You want to do good? *And* do well? Tell you what to do. Snatch those funds out of state welfare and elderly infirm care—bless their hearts, they ain't voting anyway. Just be a man and do it! And you give that money to the Texas Department of Criminal Retribution, to ol' Sonny, and I'll stuff it in Wick Aspromonte's pocket and tell him to build a 500-bed max in the dark part of town and hire all your illiterates and pave all your roads and triple your tax base and create an economic ripple effect that'll light up the community like Caesar's Palace. And not only will they sing your praises at the local Kiwanis Club, but when you're fixing to run for higher office, you can righteously thump your chest and say: "You wanna know who's responsible for the 39 percent decline in violent crime statewide over the past five years? Little ol' me, your next U.S. Congressman, that's who!"'

"You get everyone involved," he went on. "Developers. Academicians. County judges. Even the goddamn press. Big fucking tent. Cut 'em all in. Together we make money. Together we make—history! But you *never*," he added gravely, "demystify it. Hey. When it comes to the logistics, leave it to the experts. The best and the brightest and the Texas Department of Criminal Retribution. You've been there, bubba. Corrections ain't for the faint of heart. It ain't for the random gun-toting bloodsucker. Or some goddamn hobbyist, for crying out loud. Man, it takes a *lifer*. Sonny was raised on this shit. My daily bread! Hell, I knew crash gate specs and lockdown procedures before I knew the multiplication tables. I *knew* . . ."

At last he ran out of words. By and by the sun commenced a brilliant finale of copper and crimson. Sonny leaned back in his chair—a lion sated, with a mound of barren bones criss-crossing his paper plate. Darkness was all but complete when I emerged from my stew.

"Tell me about Tempesta," I said.

At first he didn't seem to hear. Gradually the eyes narrowed, though not with hostility or discontent. He appeared to be lost in a fond memory, or maybe struggling to remember, or to impose fondness upon what had come to mind.

"Old Thunderball," he began in a faraway voice. "He always said there wasn't a damn thing wrong with doing inmates favors. Hell. He said it was wrong if you didn't. 'It ain't doing no con any good to teach him that life's a Got damn level playing field,' he'd say. 'Teach him that, he goes out into the free world and slides off the edge, just like before. Now. You got an inmate who shows a little initiative—well hell, you reward that con. If he makes you a nice pair of boots in the leather shop, you give him hall privileges. If he whispers in your ear that there's fixing to be a riot in the B wing, you clean up his disciplinary jacket for him. You're his boss. An underling makes his boss's life better, he gets something back. That's what you call Real Life.'"

Sonny chuckled darkly, as did I—it was a passable imitation of the gruff old prison boss. But Thunderball's son was laughing about something different. "Biggest fucking rationalization you ever heard," he spat. "As if he gave a rat's ass about what a con did once he left Shepherdsville. Naw, old Thunderball, he got and gave. Gave and got. Like a damn banker. Fitch said that, I think. Called Thunderball a banker right to his face. And of course, Daddy fires back, 'You're damn right! Deposits and withdrawals! That's life, Calvin—only you best make damn sure the books look like virgin snow. I do the banking, you do the accounting, and we'll close up shop early and break out the hootch.'"

He laughed, more fondly now, and I joined in. For that was Thunderball, bless him: banker, boozer, scoundrel. So wise, and so fatally ignorant.

"As long as there's control." I looked up to see that Sonny's face was now obscured by his hands.

"Control," he sighed as his hands fell away. "And I believed I had control over Tempesta. Lots of slack in the rope, I know. But I believed I could give it a yank at any time, and he'd be mine. By the throat."

He took out a cigar from the pocket of the suit jacket he'd let slide from his chair to the balcony floor. He studied the cigar, scowled at it; lit it, and pulled hard, that the smoke might take him away.

"That's how it would've been," he said. "If the court hadn't sprung him, I mean. I know: he'd turned his cell into a Hugh Hefner playpen, and everyone was going in and out . . . He had it pretty sweet, no denying that. But I still had him. He was my con. He was mine."

His fist was clenched at the level of his chin. It looked, to my surprise, like a fist that could do real damage.

"Thunderball didn't have to worry about the goddamn courts," he muttered.

The words surprised me. Sonny knew better. "You mean, until the *Herrera* lawsuit," I ventured carefully.

"Well, obviously *Herrera*," he snapped, blushing a little. "I'm talking about before. For twenty years, Thunderball had it his way. He was your goddamn master. You so much as blink too loud and you got a hot poker up your hiney. You so much as *think* of snitching on the boss and you got a world of hurt, bubba, you got lye down your throat and your shit on some trusty's dick and those Dr. Pepper bottles you gotta stand on for twenty-four solid or that bat's gonna rearrange your brains and do a—"

"Sonny," I interrupted, almost yelling. "I was there, goddamn it."

"—hell of a dancing beat on your ear, and then you get slid into the Oven, man oh man, the freaks I've seen after one week rolled up like a human meatball inside that goddamn Oven . . ." He shook his head, pale and suddenly sweating from his forehead, his eyes big and his mouth open wide like that of a catfish gasping on the shore. A memory fought its way to the surface, and for the first time in years I saw the single grimy *Houston Chronicle* passed around from cell to cell, all day long, until it was nearly illegible from greasy thumbprints: the edition discussing Sonny's shocking breakthrough testimony in the *Herrera* lawsuit, testimony in which—"speaking in an emotional but resolute voice," as the story's author, young Cecilia Shipman, put it—he brought low the whole big system, and in so doing, buried his daddy alive. For weeks, it was all the cons would talk about. Instead of celebrating a federal judgment that promised to improve their lot a thousandfold, they seemed, to a man, spellbound by this peculiar act of heroism and treason. "Why'd the kid do it?" The question went round and round, but always made its way to me, because every con knew I was thick with both Hopes. I had no answer to give them. Not for the first time, and not for the last, the whole *Herrera* saga had left me in a staredown with my own near-total ignorance of my best friend.

Now he sat before me, consumed by awful memories. Any fool could tell that Sonny was genuinely disturbed. But disturbed about what? That humans had been treated like animals? That he had to publicly step on his old man's back to make his own way to the top? Or was it just that he was a big baby who didn't like to think about bruises and blood?

"I know you were there," he said quietly. Frowning, he added, "But you weren't . . . I don't know. Somewhere different. In between. You know what I mean?"

"Somewhere," I nodded.

"I mean, you saw both sides. But you didn't see everything of either side. That was where Thunderball had you."

I was about to interject something. But then he blurted out, "And that's where I had Tempesta, you know? That's where I had him. In the middle. He was another one. A special case. Not like you, obviously. He was . . . a different special case."

His cigar rose towards his lips. But the hand holding it came back down again, and he said, "Tempesta had money. And goddammit, what do you do? Jesus Christ, let's be adults! Let's face it! The fucker had millions! He could buy everyone in sight! And faced with the prospect that he could spread his money around to every CO, every gang, turn everyone against each other, turn the whole thing upside down just as Sonny's getting it rightside up . . . What do you *do*?"

He stared out beyond the balcony, his grimace dark as the purpling Minerva. "Everything he taught me," Sonny said, and I knew he was speaking of his father, "ain't worth shit. It went the way of the Oven and the bat and the twenty-five-cent matinee movie. And when they replaced Thunderball with that doofus Etzler from Minnesota, and kicked me upstairs to deputy, it takes me about five seconds to see that Jamie Etzler couldn't wipe his butt if the paper came with instructions. And I ain't got no help. Goddamn Fitch bails on me, scrambles over to Finance. Every warden hates me, even though they hated Thunderball—'cause it's change they hate the most. Here I am, suddenly running the whole fucking circus. And first thing I see is we've got some capital murderer over at the Hope Farm who happens to be richer than Solomon."

I smiled faintly, remembering. "You did what Thunderball would've done," I said.

"Did what he would've done," he nodded. "Brought him to the office, sat him down. Put on my game face and said, 'Mister Tempesta, I have a big problem that's fixing to be someone else's bigger problem.'

And of course, he was grinning like a jackass eating bees. He knew I couldn't turn right around and do to him what I'd just testified about in federal court. And I just up and admitted it. But then I used that old Fitch line. 'You know, I can hurt you a lot more with this pen than with this fist. The Texas Department of Criminal Retribution is still a bad place to spend the rest of your days—and I can see to it, Mister Tempesta, you little piece of shit, that you get written up for every blink of an eye, until your disciplinary history reads like a Sears catalog of impropriety. And that leads to very dismal work for very long hours, and a very small cell with a very undesirable cellmate, on a cell block full of queers and lunatics, where you will fuck or fight and thereby end up with either an asshole that looks like a cauliflower or a disciplinary jacket too heavy for the parole board to *lift*, much less read . . . Unless you tow the line, boy.'

"And unbeknownst to me, while I was giving my little speech, his blue-suits were chewing their way through the appellate process. But Tempesta wasn't leaving anything to chance. So he just asked it: 'How much do you want?'

"And I swear, Hadrian. I told him, 'I don't want your money. That's my point, Mister Tempesta. I don't want your money *anywhere*.'

"Well. He just looked at me. You remember how his lips smother against his teeth when he smiles like a couple of worms? He gave that grin, and he said, 'Mister Hope, you don't really want to spend every minute of your day watching where my money goes, do you? Don't you have other responsibilities? Don't you need to spend time with that beautiful wife of yours? Don't you need at least an hour of sleep each night? 'Cause Mister Hope, you'd have to be on me every minute of every day to keep my money out—and that just sounds like an awful waste of your time.'"

Sonny heaved a sigh. He lowered his gaze to the balcony hardwoods. "So he told me about this riverhouse. How it was in his lawyer's name, and since it looked like he wasn't going to be seeing it anytime soon, I might want to take a look at it and see if it was the kind of thing I'd be interested in buying."

He chanced a look at me. That I wasn't gaping in shock gave him some relief. "He told me not to worry. Said it wasn't traceable to him, that his lawyer had property all over East Texas. That I could buy it from the lawyer straight up. And I said, 'Like hell. Drug lords may buy houses on the water, but prison bosses don't.' But then I remembered that land in Minerva County. Just a bunch of shitty old pines."

Then he mumbled something and reached for his single-malt. "I didn't know about the hookers," he said. "He just told me he wanted conjugal visits with his wife. When I heard he was bringing three or four of them at a time in the prison library, I thought about calling him in again. But," and he let out a hard, throaty laugh, "he had me! One hundred per cent! I bring him into my office, it only calls attention to it! And *now*," he moaned loudly, "Tempesta has the gall to say he was setting us up all along! That the only reason he'd been bribing Mitch Grissom and all the COs was to make a goddamn point about how corrupt the prison system is! And I can't say *jack*!"

He threw his cigar to the floor, where it rolled a few feet, throwing off sparks. Sonny covered his face in his hands, and there he gurgled like a child.

"Why didn't you give him the house back?" I asked.

Through his hands came the muffled words: "Too late. Too late."

Waving his hands suddenly in the air, so that I was distracted for a moment from the reddened misery smearing his face, he said, "Take a look around you, Hadrian! Look what—look what she's done to this place! It was just space with a view and, Christ, she flew to Milan, flew to Oaxaca, brought in consultants from Dallas and Houston, I mean *look at it*!"

His eyes went glassy again. His voice pleaded: "Hadrian. You should've seen the look on her face when I surprised her with it. You should've seen . . . oh God, the way she—she hugged me, she ran from room to room, crying and laughing, I don't know how long it's been . . ."

A fat tear rolled down his cheek. Then another. "'scuse me," he stammered, and pushed himself out of the chair. I watched him lumber off, sag-shouldered, his cowlick bouncing somberly. Then I turned to the river, thinking: *He still loves her. Even if his magic's worn off. He'd still kill to bring her joy.*

A moment later, Sonny padded back outside. He wore a drowsy, almost beaten expression. With a grunt he bent down and retrieved his cigar from the floor. He relit it, and then plopped back down into his chair.

"If I took it away from her," he said simply, "she'd leave me. And if I told her why I wanted to get rid of it, she'd leave me for that, too."

He laughed wistfully, shook his head. "I'm fucked, bubba," he said. "I been fucked the moment I tried to do the right thing about Ricky Tempesta."

The sky was indigo now, and moths appeared and flopped against the porchlights. I felt a cramping in my stomach. He was almost there. We both were.

"He called me the day the court reversed his case," Sonny said quietly. He smacked loudly against his cigar a few last times before stubbing it out. "Called me from Inmate Processing on his attorney's car phone. Bastard didn't waste a second. He said in that piss-ant smug voice of his, 'Mister Deputy Director, it's no secret you're about to get the top job. And soon it won't be any secret that I'm fixing to get into the private prison business. So we're gonna be crossing paths a lot, you and me. Let's not cause each other any hardship. Let's be friends.'

"I told him, 'I don't make friends with reptiles.'

"And he says to me, 'Do you make enemies with them?'"

Sonny descended into gloom. "But it looks like you've got it taken care of," I protested. "I heard you talking to that lobbyist on the phone. Let his clients shoot Tempesta's plan down, you're home free."

"Shit," Sonny mumbled.

"Well, then, just let it happen," I said. "Let Tempesta build his own little prison town. Maybe it'll be a disaster, but it won't be your disaster."

"No," Sonny said emphatically.

"Why not?"

He shook his head. When no words followed, I exploded. "Look," I said, "I know you're just piss-proud of this empire you've built, and you don't want to be upstaged, and your ego's on the line, and—"

"No!" he hollered, crimson-faced. "That's not it at all!"

"Well, that's sure as shit what I heard you telling that guy on the phone, that you don't want your legacy to—"

"Will you fucking forget about what I said over the fucking phone? He's a fucking *lobbyist*! You're not supposed to talk to them like they're regular human beings!"

He sprang from his chair and began to pace. "And yes, okay," he admitted testily, "I'm not going to pretend like my ego's not in this. I'm goddamned proud of what I've done. You ask anyone. Ask Cal Fitch. Sonny's turned the whole prison system around. Hell, you remember what it was like! And now," he declared, stopping suddenly and poising himself erect, punching the air, "it's second to none. Second to none! Do you have any idea what it took to take these pestholes and make them constitutional? And then to fucking *triple* the number of beds in five years?—build more prison space, in sixty months, than has ever been built anywhere? At any time? Do you have any idea what those sixty months were like for me? How many miles I logged from one construction site to the next? How many times the phone rang in the middle of the night? Do you know what," and now the tears flowed steadily, "what it cost me in my personal life? What it did to Jill and me?"

"Okay, Sonny. Jesus. Calm down."

"They forget about Sonny," he said, pacing again, his voice choking against the tears. "They think it all happened by divine fucking intervention. They forget about Sonny."

He turned his back to me and put his hands against the railing of the balcony, leaning into the breeze, into the wild bosom of the forest. From somewhere behind us, the roar of a motor advanced, then faded away. I thought of Bonnie, flinging her bottles, cursing Jill—and now, coming over to my house every night. Coming over to the house of a crook, and wriggling out of her grey uniform. I shook my head and wondered how I'd accomplished so complete a mess.

"But I could swallow it," I heard Sonny say.

"What?" I asked.

"My pride. I could swallow my pride. If that's all it came down to."

He bowed his head. Watching the back of him, slumped and defeated, I wondered if Sonny ever prayed, or considered suicide. I'd done plenty of the latter, almost none of the former, and had figured the ratio to be reversed in Sonny's case.

He turned now, and like that, it was his back leaning against the railing, and the barbecue juices from his hands smudging his dress shirt which was already streaked with charcoal and sweat. His expression was almost perplexed as the words tumbled out of his mouth:

"He phoned me the day you came back to Shepherdsville. Called me maybe an hour before you got here. He'd already heard about the pardon. And he laughed and said, 'Mister Director, my respect for you just went through the roof today. I don't often run into fellas who make good on a twenty-some-odd-year-old debt.'

"And when I told him I didn't know what the hell he was talking about, he said, 'Coleman, Mister Director. Hadrian Coleman. The fella that's kept your little secret all these years.'"

I gaped at his utterly neutral expression. "Bullshit," I said. "That's impossible. I never told a soul. You know that, Sonny."

"I know," he said calmly. "I know. And I never did either, God knows."

Then he held out his hands, which were trembling. "Red Wickersham," he said. "That was his name. Tempesta met him a few years ago. Says he's a junkie with AIDS now. But he can still remember, and he can still talk, and Tempesta can produce him at a moment's notice."

I scowled and said, "I have no idea who you're talking about."

Sonny expelled breath. He leaned towards me. "Think, Hadrian," he said. "The little redheaded punk who was on the chain gang picking blueberries that day? The one I was making fun of? Remember?"

With reluctance, I brought myself back. Before long, I saw him, the scrawny new boot with his terrified eyes; and Sonny on the mulecart beside me and the judge.

"Hadrian. He remembers. He remembers me laughing at him. He remembers I was there that day."

"Oh . . ." I lost all focus for a moment.

What revived me was the closeness of Sonny's anxious breath. "Wait," I said. "So Red Wickersham told Tempesta you were at the blueberry fields. It's some ex-con's word against yours. And besides, who gives a damn? So what if your name got left out of it? That doesn't implicate you in anything. I was the one who killed Castlebury."

"Well." His expression remained bothered, even sickly. "Anyway, I told Tempesta we'd have to talk about this in person. So he came over to my office."

I watched him carefully. "And?"

"And he knows everything. Everything!"

His voice became a frantic, haunted whisper: "He knows I was there at the scene of the murder and you protected me. He knows Thunderball brought you up to be his houseboy a year later. He knows that I pushed to have you pardoned after you escaped. And—"

"Well, so what, I still don't—"

"*Will you shut up and let me finish!*"

I shut up. Against the dark, his face seethed like a meteor.

"And he knew your cellmate Digby."

For a second, I didn't understand. "Well of course he did," I began. "I mean, Tempesta was on our cell block. He knew me. He knew Digby. He knew . . ."

Then it hit me, even as Sonny said it: "Digby told him, Hadrian. He told him how the whole thing went down. How Wexler jumped you from behind and you swung around and stabbed him with his shank, and Digby mopped up the blood after you ran off."

He said, in a voice suddenly vacant: "Which, of course, is completely contrary to what Digby said on his deathbed."

The question I'd been wanting to ask for days came bursting out of me: "Did you ask Digby to lie?"

Sonny waved me off. "Digby was happy to do what he did," he said tersely. "Let's just leave it at that."

Then he stepped towards me. He squatted down in front of me. Dropped a knee to the floor. Put his hands on my knees. And looked up into me. And though I could see his chin stubbling with the evening, see his lids bruised with fatigue and worry, I finally saw just the boy beneath the milky green eyes fixed upon the core of my soul.

"Hadrian," he said, slow, quiet, but very sure. "Tempesta has got us both. Don't you see that? It's not just me he's got. He's got you, too. He could throw us both in jail. He could finish us off."

The voice tightened a bit: "It's him or us, Hadrian. We've got to finish him off. Before he does the same to us."

We were that way for minutes—he on one knee, imploring my shadowed face. Then I whispered:

"No."

He whispered back: "Yes you can."

"I can't."

"You have to."

Suddenly I was burning, and through clenched teeth I said, "The hell I do. The hell I do! I did my time for one murder, and I got pardoned for the other. Tempesta can't touch me. My slate is clean."

My slate. The words sounded almost evil. I swallowed. He blinked hard, and when he opened them, his eyes were careening wildly in his sockets and he hissed, "So that's it. You'd throw me to the wolves for trying to help out your sorry ass. If I hadn't gone to bat for you, I wouldn't be in this fix."

I swallowed again. But then I said, "Don't hang that on me, Sonny. You took a bribe from a con. That's why you're in this mess."

"Hadrian, will you—"

I shoved him away from me. He fell on his back, and I jumped up, and he rolled back towards the balustrade, his arms uplifted as I stood over him, snarling, "You pardoned me for one reason and one reason only. And that's to save your ass by killing Tempesta."

"No!"

"Bullshit, Sonny!" I flung a hand at him, dispensing with him, and turned away. "Boy, you've got a lot of gall," I said. "And after those years I pissed away, *because of you*—"

"Whoa!" and he was laughing as he scrambled to his feet. Sonny flipped back his hair, defiantly stuck his hands in his back pockets as he thrust out his chest at me. "Who's hanging what on who? Don't you blame me that you went loony tunes out there in the blueberry fields and decided to make a damn jack-o-lantern out of Castlebury's face! I ain't taking credit for that one!"

"I kept your name out of it," I spat back. "I could've said you were there. And maybe it would've made trouble for your dad and gotten you thrown out of college. But it would've sure made *my* day in court a lot easier."

"Well, hell, Hadrian! Can't we just speak the truth here?" He flashed a rotten winner's grin. "Yeah. You saved my life. And thirty seconds later, you ruined *your* life. Can we just agree on those two things and quit pointing fingers?"

My brain felt suddenly unspooled. I reached for my chair to steady myself.

"Agree with me on this," I managed. "You got me the pardon so that I'd feel beholden to you and I'd have to agree to kill Tempesta."

"Listen to me!" he hollered, suddenly inches from my face again. "Will you listen to me? I got you the pardon because you're my only friend in the whole goddamned world!"

I sat in my chair.

"And lest you think, *friend*, that I am so consumed with selfishness that I would never for a moment think about you, consider this thought: If Tempesta told the world you'd killed Wexler after all, don't you think the Shepherd County D.A., to say nothing of the governor himself, would feel just a little bit duped? Don't you just know they'd have Bo Worley on you like stink on shit? They'd introduce new charges on you in twenty-four hours! And then, *friend*, you would be back in the pen—only this time, there wouldn't be no Thunderball or no Sonny to help your white ass out. Hah! You'd be a *real* con then."

I closed my eyes. He was right. Everything he said was right.

"For God's sake, Sonny," I still said. "I can't do this to myself."

But I'd said "to myself." Not "to Tempesta." I was already halfway there.

"He'll do it to you," he assured me, and he stooped to face me again. His gaze was as steady and flat as a butcher blade. "You don't mean shit to him, Hadrian. If taking me down means taking you down—"

"Then don't let him take you down," I said. "Give him what he wants."

"You can't ask me to do that!" he shouted. "He'll always want! He'll blackmail me out of existence! You can't ask me to be his goddamned slave for life!"

"But," I protested wearily, "you're asking me to risk my life—"

"And mine! Hadrian—we are talking about this together. This is both of us."

His hand was on my shoulder. "But you want me—"

"I can't ask anyone else. My God, who could I ask?" His fingers dug into my skin; his eyes bulged to bursting. "Who can I trust, if not you? I can't trust my deputy. I can't trust my wife. I can't trust anyone. Not anyone. Only you."

And then he quickly added: "Only us. It has to be only us."

But the word "us" was like a dead language now. I sat there, and though his hands still held me and his anxious breath surely whistled against my cheeks, I was very far from Sonny—like that day, some twenty-three years ago, when Thunderball came to visit me at the Creel Unit and urged me to take my lumps for a year, to be patient, and by all means to say nothing—to forget about Sonny. To be a good con. Meaning, be the raggedy, filthy ghost in the sugarcane fields, the mute child learning to be deaf in the rec yard and the chow hall, the mummy on the rack at night. Be alone, forget all others, speak not their names . . . and one day, one day . . .

Then I said quietly, because I had to say it: "I don't know how to kill."

Sonny said nothing in reply. Not so much as a noise. Nor did I say anything else. And that made it a done deal.

And now, Sunday, I watched my sister Mimi leaning over the edge of the balcony—her stomach full of Jill's food, her life full of crooks, but she could always see past that, poor child, even now as she squinted against the August light. "A swim," she was saying, her voice so crisp with the certainty that this was the remedy of the moment. "Don't you think? Wouldn't a swim be killer?"

I waited for Sonny to say something to her. But when I looked over at him, I saw, to my surprise, that he wasn't staring at my sister's backside. He was looking at me. It dawned on me that he had been looking at me all this time.

I turned away. To my sister I said, "Okay. Let's go find a pool."

She squealed, lunged for me and kissed me again. Sonny rose up from his seat. "Jill!" he called out, in a tone that sounded somehow lost. "Company's leaving! Let's get back into town! Hey, *Jill*!"

5

They had it all wrong about her—everything: every dim observation, every uncharitable speculation, every filthy rumor that said all there was to say about them and nothing, nothing whatsoever about her. The hayseeds and college boys who ambled up to her, drawn by the brilliance of her ponytailed blonde hair and the darker glow of those unfathomable barefooted legs melting out of her white cut-offs, and wanting to see if behind the edgy feline sunglasses twinkled an invitation, if behind the barely sealed lips lay a smile, or at least a few words, like "Sure," or "Maybe," or even just "Shut up and give me a light"—the boys who came her way, the way of the professor's daughter, didn't even know what they were seeing or what she didn't see in them. They withdrew steaming, denouncing her as a slutty prude, a bitchy misfit, or whichever other impotent, idiotic slanders came to mind; and they spread the stories first started by the other women in Shepherdsville, the corn-fed hordes whose inferiority to her amounted to an everyday cruelty, fevering them to spawn their brood of delirious lies.

They said she regularly visited the tar-paper shanties east of town, where the black boys took turns with her, or romped with her all at once, while she screamed out laughter and guzzled their oily bootleg hootch, so that she would return to her professor father's mansion late at night reeking of turpentine and sweat and her own spoiled flesh. They said she saved the black boys' pubic hairs, which she would keep under her pillow and later use as knitting material, and that every few months her father's chauffeur drove her into Houston to abort the

latest mulatto fetus. Such information came courtesy of a local gyne-
cologist named Pluckett, who had lost the girl as a patient owing, perhaps, to his notoriously excessive handiwork; came as well from her
father's former maid, who had been fired for shedding pubic hairs of
her own while entwined with the estate's gardener on the girl's very
own bed; and from Luellen Folger, the warden's niece, who had seen
the girl chatting with the Negro bagboy at the grocery store and
judged this to be an erotic overture since she, Luellen, had once been
so inclined with a different Negro bagboy, who after they were discovered ran for his life, but not fast enough, and whose remains now
rested on the west bank of the Minerva River, in the Negro cemetery
which the white boys regularly littered with beer cans after bedding
down their dates nearby.

They said she spent her family's money on imported French per-
fume which she would then pour down her bathroom sink, by the gal-
lon, so that you could taste the stuff in your drinking water the next
day—her way of spiting the less fortunate, so it was said. They said she
had been thrown out of every private school in Houston, and that
Hockaday in Dallas only took her after her father agreed to finance a
new school library—which she managed to stock with French pornography, paganistic dogma, and works by Ayn Rand, Henry Miller, and
Timothy Leary. They said that while in Dallas she had prostituted herself to a jazz musician with mob connections, to a rich oilman with a
shoe fetish, and to a police detective who had been Jack Ruby's best
friend. They said her report cards were a fraud, that her acceptance to
Harvard had been rigged, and that when poor Aynsley Reeves the
lawyer's son followed her there, she promptly transferred to Yale and,
depending on whom you believed, either sent Aynsley's love poems
back to him in shreds or published them under her own name. They
said that her hair was fake, her tan was fake, her teeth were capped, her
small breasts were nonetheless surgically enhanced, her hymen had
been surgically restored, she was a scandalous drinker, she screwed
Yankees, she hated animals, animals hated her, she liked to do it in air-
planes, in limousines, everywhere but in Shepherdsville, with the good
local boys, like a good local girl.

It was all untrue. But the lies were more like crude slapstick—not
telling the half of it, of how wrongly they had her. For they didn't see
how her father's house—which they all insisted was haunted by Shep-

herdsville's founder, Joshua Estelle—was in fact haunted by every Estelle *but* Joshua, by their collective pomp and misery in the wake of their progenitor's honest genius for entrepreneurship; and that it was in an effort to escape these ghosts that she made for the park on summer days. There she sought out the sunlight, only to find herself shadowed by fools. They surrounded her, figuring the strongest or handsomest or richest of them would win out, unable somehow to see that she had already in her young life seen quite enough of beauty and power and wealth. She wanted something else, and they couldn't see that, though it was there to be seen.

How? Just in the way that her long, unbejeweled fingers held her cigarette in a limp dangle, the grip not so sure after all. Just in the way that the one leg bent upward from her recline, like she'd jump to her feet in an instant, and in the meantime despair for the lack of any reason to jump. Just in the unelaborate arrangement of her ponytail, or in the simple white T-shirts she always wore, or in the toenails she painted only because color was in such short supply in this town of grey and white . . . or in the lips barely grazing each other as if she were trying, trying to speak, trying, trying to make herself heard by the someone who might observe, through her jade lenses, that her eyes were never fully closed, that she was willing to see, if you could see her.

Sonny saw her better than the rest. He must have, for as he would later tell it, it was an unlikely pick-up line he improvised the day he bounced up to the throng by the park in his bermudas, grinning greasily from cinema popcorn. "Hey," he said, addressing the other boys who thrust their myriad lighters towards her cigarette. "Any of y'all want to light my fart?"

The others turned on him, hazing him with cries of "Prison brat!" and "Jail rat!" and he must have seen right through the pack and made note of that one bronze leg bent just an inch further, because he didn't stop. "That's right, boys, I'm the son of the prison boss," he declared, his handsome teenaged face radiating insolence. "And one day you'll be working for the man, so why don't y'all just line up and start kissing my ass right here and now?"

Sonny stood his ground as they advanced on him. One of them gave him a push, as did another, and that's when the miracle happened.

She spoke.

"Leave him alone," she said.

They swiveled towards her, astonished, and waited for her next words.

"Leave us both alone," she said.

Sonny stayed with her that afternoon. He cracked prison jokes, told prison fables, played the fool like the town's most desperate con. Before long, both her knees were raised. Then she was sitting up. Then she was laughing, and finally on her feet, kicking him in the shins with her bare toes, pounding his flabby shoulders with her slender fists, shoving him, pleading, "Will you get out of here, you filthy malingerer? Tell your father if he lets you out of your cage again I'll have you tied up and shipped off to a circus!" But she could not stop laughing, nor could he, until some time after he left the park and was ambushed on the way home by the other boys, who gave Sonny just enough bruises on his face for her to want to kiss him the next time they met.

He'd seen something they hadn't, which was that she could not bear her life and yet could not slip its bonds. And perhaps she herself hadn't seen that all it might take to transport her from her unique doom in Shepherdsville were a few coarse jokes, told with brash off-color by the beaming offspring of a prison boss. But he knew it, of course, and that's how Sonny got Jill.

Yet even he, though he got her, got her wrong. For Sonny was never one to measure depths, much less to comprehend them. He didn't see how unmoved she was by her loveliness, how little comfort it brought her. He didn't see the longing beneath the laughter, the hesitation before the smile; and he utterly failed to see, beneath the pink vapor of her cheeks, that she burned—not so much from being scorned as from her own unshakeable sense of alienation. She had no place whatsoever in the town that her forefather had named, and the likelihood that with her would die the last of the Estelles could not help but imbue her with a keen sense of failure and premature loss. He didn't see why she so often fled Shepherdsville yet each time returned. It had nothing to do with Sonny. He knew that, at least. But there was more to know, more to learn from those lips that Sonny could coax into parting open with uncontrollable laughter—but which he could never prevent from rearranging themselves, after the last laugh, into that familiar manner, the two pliant brackets of the girl's mouth forever fixed to reveal, for those who could see it, a solitary, unspeakable ache.

I could see it. I saw it every night, one hundred twelve miles away from her, in my six-by-nine cell at the Albert Creel Unit in Sugarland. I could see it and speak to it—sometimes aloud, by mistake, which would prompt my cellmate, a car thief named Halbert, to kick the underneath of my top bunk and threaten yet again to sharpen his shank against my throat—adding sometimes, because he wasn't all that bad a con, "Talkin' to her ain't gonna put her here, little boy." But Halbert had it wrong, too. At the very least, she was closer to me than she'd ever been before. For I'd only laid eyes on her three times before the sentencing. And in that first year, as the youngest inmate in the Texas prison system, a lamb thrown to lions, I had found a way to stay alive. The way to survive would be to hang my eyelids low. Look this way and that with hooded vision. See, otherwise, only my feet. My hoe. My chow. The taped line I could not cross as I walked parallel to it, back to my cell, to await the evening slamming of the gates and the extinguishing of the lights. Then, and only then, could I fully open my eyes—and in the darkness of a fifteen-year-old killer's hell, see what none of the others could see.

The day would come several weeks after my sixteenth birthday, which I had celebrated with a visit from my mother. She brought Mimi, who peed all over herself with anguish when the CO at the front picket took away the birthday balloons she had brought me. My mother gave me the book I'd asked for. It was a history of the Estelle family, written by Jill's father Tobias and published by East Texas State.

"I hope you like it," she said, emotions bridled as she held the book up against the plexiglas visitation screen so that I could see it. "I read the first few pages. It looks . . . well . . . thorough."

"It looks boring," corrected Mimi, who wore our mother's sweater around her waist so that the pee stains on her dress wouldn't show. She twirled on the visitor's stool, and her dark chocolate curls wagged. Everything about her mocked the greenish gloom of our surroundings. I nearly blurted out for her to cool it, that they might get thrown out. But my eyes were hungry for life, and so I grinned and nodded as Mimi went on, "*I* wanted Mama to buy you a picture book. I found one in the bookstore that was sooo pretty. It was all about the piney woods, and it had these color pictures of cypresses and tupelos and snakes and spiders and wildcats and all those other things you and Pawpaw used to see when you'd go—"

"Mimi, please, I didn't think it'd be right for Hadrian, I," and when she looked up at me the tears were pouring out of her red eyes. "I'm sorry," she said, clenching her fists in her lap. "I'm sorry, I know you told me not to . . ."

Sighing, she propped up a smile. "You look like you're putting your weight back on," she said.

"Not like this one," I said, pointing at Mimi. "Hey, fatty. You getting enough to eat now that I'm not stealing your biscuits?"

She spun around once on her stool, then skidded to a stop and set her big dark eyes on me. "I'd give you all my biscuits if you'd come home now," she said.

It was my turn to look away. I heard my mother whisper something reproachful, and Mimi whined, "But I would!"

Before our time was up, my mother said, "That awful Shipman girl called me this morning. She says she's doing a story on you for the University of Texas newspaper."

"I know," I said. "Warden Pierson told me yesterday."

My mother's face hardened. "I told her I had nothing to say," she said. "You won't be talking to her, will you?"

"Warden Pierson says Director Hope wants me to," I said.

Her eyes flooded with tears again. "Why?" she demanded. "What good would it do to bring all this up?"

"Mom," I said, leaning towards the plexiglas, "Director Hope says Sissy's going to write it anyway, whether I talk to her or not. Warden Pierson's giving her thirty minutes, and Director Hope's told me what to say."

"Which is . . ."

I shrugged. "Just general stuff. That I'm sorry for what I did. That I'm studying. That they're treating me okay."

"But they're . . . they're not!" she said, and I could see the blood running up her neck. "They're making you work in the fields 'til you get sunstroke, and they're feeding you food a dog wouldn't eat, and they take your sister's balloons like they were weapons. . . . Hadrian, how can you say—they read all your mail and they—"

"Mom, now listen," I said. When she'd calmed herself, I lowered my voice. "Director Hope told us we've got to be patient. He said this would happen. He said someone would write something about me on the—on the anniversary. He said to just act like everything's as you'd expect, and they'll write some boring story, and everyone'll forget about me, Mom—and see, Mom, *that's* when he can bring me back. Not before. Not while everyone's still got their eyes on me."

She shook her head tearfully. "He won't ever return my calls," she said.

"Mom. Quit calling the director. Calling him's not going to help."

"Guess what happened to Sissy Shipman," sang out Mimi. "Foots Taylor dumped her."

"He did?" I exclaimed. "Wow."

My mother smiled when I did. "He met a girl at A&M," she said. "A girl from a very prominent San Antonio family. They're already talking about marriage. Of course," she murmured, "I don't get out much. But I hear she's very nice. Certainly nicer than Willie Shipman's daughter."

"It's good you told me," I said. "I would've asked Sissy how Foots is doing."

"Do I have to let her interview me?" my mother asked in a voice so doleful that Mimi stood and hugged her.

"No," I assured her. "You don't have to talk to any of them."

At last I asked the question that had been on my mind for months: "Is Sonny seeing anyone?"

Mimi said, "Yup. Jill Estelle. The purtiest girl in town."

I nodded, looked down.

"They say so many terrible things about her," my mother said.

The guards stepped forward. Time was up.

"They're wrong," I said as we all rose.

And I was right. On the first of December, five weeks after my interview with Sissy Shipman was reprinted in every newspaper in the state, assistant warden Kirby Morris visited my cell two hours after the lights had gone out for the evening. I leaned over from my bunk and watched as the gate to my cell slid open.

"Get your things, Coleman," he said.

They put me on a bus no different than the one I'd ridden from the Harris County courthouse to Sugarland over a year ago. But this time it was just me and the driver, whose eyes I could see flicker back to regard me in his rearview as he drove. Fully twenty minutes passed, as the white converted schoolbus rumbled through those accursed sugarcane fields and finally into the pasturelands abutting Highway 6, before the driver popped the question that was just about to drive him crazy:

"You know somebody upstairs, kid?"

And I didn't say anything back. But it was a rare smile that appeared on my bony face that cool early winter night as we pushed northwards, from the coastal plains and into the pines, which even through these iron-grated windows I could smell. No metal or glass could keep that smell from me.

"Take those leg irons off him, you jughead. Where you think he's gonna run to? Back to Sugarland? The boy's home now."

Prison Director Purvis J. "Thunderball" Hope flashed a sort of sneering smile in my direction and then returned to his glower as one of the COs stooped to unlock my shackles. "And uncuff him, for God's sake. This here's a sixteen-year-old boy. You worried about protecting me from a sixteen-year-old boy, Riley? You don't think I could hold my own against a goddamn *child*?"

"Nosir, or yessir, Mister Director," stammered the second guard as he fumbled with my handcuffs. "I mean, I reckon you could take him, sir. I just figgered that—"

"And that's where the trouble started! With you figgering! God amighty," he swore in disgust. With a wave of his backhand, he added, "You two jugheads figger that heap of metal out of my office and figger it around your necks and figger yourselves into the river. Y'hear me?"

"Yessir, Mister Director," the two men in grey chorused in high, wobbly voices, and stepped on each other's heels as they beat a path for the front door of the director's mansion.

Thunderball watched them go, his fists balled up in the front pockets of his shapeless khakis and his lips pursed in disfavor. "Shit on a stick," he finally said, his narrow eyes fixed on the empty doorway. "I got some of the best men in Texas working for me. And then I got some that're dumber than a Got damn paperweight."

He turned to me. That famous underbite now sawed at his upper lip as he appraised me, TDCR Inmate #356023, a mere scaffold of a teenager lost inside my prison whites and oversized black rubber shoes. I pretended to be looking at the floor. Naturally, I'd seen Thunderball in the past: twice on this very property, and once at Creel, just after my sentencing. The day he showed up at Creel for the purpose of having a few words with me was an otherwise typical one for him. During his three-hour visit, he fired one assistant warden, demoted another, suspended or fired three COs, took a fourth CO with him to lunch, slapped one inmate to the ground, ordered a second to be administered ten licks with the bat, removed a third from the Oven, replaced him with a fourth, and gave every inmate in cellblock 6 the week off from work for keeping their dayroom especially tidy. After he left that afternoon, word went around that Warden Pierson had suffered a nervous collapse and would not be in the following day. But Pierson, who knew how the grapevine worked, made sure to be in his office the next morning to take the call that inevitably came in from Thunderball, who barked, "What's this I hear about your Got damn nerves, Pierson?"

The other two times I'd seen Thunderball seemed a lifetime ago. I was free then, ridiculously free, and scampering around the mansion with Sonny, flinging rocks from his second-story bedroom window at the freshly processed ex-cons on the street below and then running for cover downstairs. The director wouldn't have remembered me back then, the way I ran right into him and bounced off of him and fell to the floor like a rag doll; but what I especially remembered was the way Sonny's teeth chattered, the way he giggled nervously as he stood before his father, a flabby lamb before this great unyielding silo of a man who looked at me only for a second—and with a look that suggested I wasn't even worth *that* much attention—before regarding his only child with equal measures of perplexity and revulsion.

The words came out slowly, deliberately. "If I took a horsewhip to some con for throwing rocks at my son," he said to Sonny, "would you say that was unfair?"

Sonny seemed to have trouble controlling his breath. "N-no sir," he managed.

The director's teeth pulled at his upper lip. "Those men out there," he finally said, nodding towards the street. "They just got processed out. I'd just finished telling them, 'You boys go out there and you walk a straight line.' And no sooner do they start walking than my own son tries to incite 'em to violence."

His voice suddenly exploded: "Now you tell me! You tell me what's fair! Should I go fetch those boys to horsewhip you? Or should I horsewhip you myself? Answer me!"

Sonny was still grinning, even as the tears flowed down his chattering face.

"Please don't hurt him, Mister Hope," I blurted out. "It was my fault. I—"

"I didn't tell you to speak!" he growled. "Now you get on home! Get gone!"

I scrambled to my feet and stepped backwards to the door. Sonny's whole body was rattling, I could see. His tears kept pouring. But why was that stupid smile still on his face?

I closed the front door behind me. Then I waited, my hand still on the gigantic brass doorknob, my ear pressed against the wood. Finally, I heard Sonny's father speak again, in a lower but no less disdainful voice:

"You get gone also. You ain't worth whipping."

It seemed a foregone conclusion that Sonny would be grounded the next day. But I walked up to the mansion anyway, and when I rang the doorbell, it was to my relief that Mama Jean Hope answered. She was a tall, big-boned lady with a wearily knowing stoicism about her, not to mention a cutting sense of humor. But she was also a renowned softy, especially when it came to her only son.

"Why, good afternoon, Hadrian," she said, sighing a bit as she wiped her hands on the apron she wore. "Don't tell me you've come to fetch Sonny."

"Yes ma'am."

"Well, and I thought you were smarter than that," she said. "His daddy gave him fifteen. Ten for good behavior. You didn't think he'd let him off with probation, did you?"

"No, ma'am. Mainly I just wanted to see if he was okay."

She managed a dry laugh. "Purvis wouldn't lay a hand on my baby," she said. "I'd show *him* cruel and unusual. How's that Pawpaw of yours doing? Getting meaner every year?"

"He's a little sick now," I said, though I did not suspect that my grandfather would be dead in three months.

"Awww. Well, you tell that rascal to get well. Tell your mama and the Doc I said hi, too. I'll have Sonny call you when he's out of solitary."

We said our goodbyes. Just after she closed the door, the west gate to Big Red directly across the street slid open. I stopped in my tracks as Thunderball Hope stepped out of the prison sallyport and onto the street.

"You," he barked at me, and I could only stand there as he strode forward in that all-encompassing, crablike way of his, khakis flapping, belly jiggling, his short thick arms swinging like wrecking balls. He did not slow his pace until he was maybe two feet from me, at which point he came to a dead halt.

He stood there for a moment, breathing heavily. Finally, he barked, "You're Doc Coleman's boy, that right?"

I nodded. "Yes sir, I am."

"Well." His teeth worked at his gums. I found myself wondering if it was possible to chew one's own mouth off. His eyes now did not appear unfriendly, but I did not count on this to be a lasting condition.

"Your daddy's one fine man," he said. "I'm sure he raised you to be loyal to your friends. Be brave. Stand up for the weak. All that good shit."

He grimaced a kind of smile, and I couldn't help but smile back. "I guess so," I said.

"Well, and far be it from me to tell another man how to raise his boy. So I ain't gonna tell you how to act. But I'd like to ask a little favor of you."

His tone was not exactly beseeching. Cautiously I replied, "Um . . . sure."

The prison boss leaned towards my face, so that I could smell the coffee on his breath and see the charcoal bags, like an accumulation of ancient bruises, beneath his narrow eyes. "Don't stand up for my boy," he said. "He needs to learn to stand up for himself."

Making a spitting noise, he mumbled, "You'd think he was a Got damn cripple the way everyone babies him. His mama. His teachers. Even the Got damn houseboys . . ."

Then he looked straight at me again. The next words constituted an order: "Sonny gets in trouble, you let him get his own self out of trouble. You hear me?"

"Yes sir," I said, blinking.

"That's for his own sake," he said.

And did he really say the next sentence, or did I only imagine later that he'd said it: "And for your own sake, too . . ."

Regardless, as I stood in front of him now, his youngest ward, I could clearly see, as he slid a set of almost comical-looking granny glasses onto his bulbous nose and squinted hard at me while chewing the blubber of his upper lip, that he was now remembering that very encounter as well. His hard gaze slightly faltered. I saw his great chest rise and fall, heard a resigned gust of breath sail out of his nostrils. All this time he had been standing beside his desk, fists in pockets, feet spread apart, a casual but defiant posture. Now he sank slowly, until an immense, crudely built cypress chair—clearly the craftsmanship of an inmate—groaned loudly as he settled into it. His hands moved up to his face, prayerfully. A warm if somewhat sad sensation washed over me. I had nothing to fear from this man.

His eyeballs slowly rolled upwards to study me again. "How in the hell did a scrawny thing like you break Castlebury's neck? He was twice your size, at least."

Before I could decide what to say, he waved me off. With the same meaty hand, he adjusted his spectacles, eyeballing me through them a final time before he took them off and tossed them onto the desktop. "You're one of those types that don't like compliments," he concluded as he folded his hands upon his lap. "Same way with me. I hate 'em. Never know what to say after I get 'em. I hate giving 'em, too."

Then he nodded towards the far corner of the study, where the nicest piece of furniture in the room sat. It was a walnut liquor cabinet with a red marble top.

"Fix me a gin and tonic," he said.

I had lost track of time, but I believed it was somewhere between eight and nine in the morning. Slowly I walked towards the cabinet. Some empty glasses, an ice bucket and the relevant beverages sat atop the marble.

"Ice first," he called out. "Then the gin."

After I'd finished tipping the alcohol bottle, I reached for the tonic water. "See how much gin you got in there?" I heard him say. "That's half what you need."

I made the correction, and then finished off the drink with tonic. "Just bring it here," he then said. "I like to do my own stirring."

I brought him the drink. Without stirring, he took a hard, heavy swallow, sucked on his wet lips, then nodded solemnly. "Sit down," he said as he wagged his drink in the direction of an empty chair.

As I sat, he picked up the telephone receiver from his desktop. Without identifying himself, without any greeting at all, he said into the receiver, "Tell Fitch to get on over here," and then hung it up.

"You eaten yet?" he asked me.

"Yes sir. They fed me right before they brought me over here."

He sneered as he asked, "Food's pretty awful here, ain't it?"

"Not as bad as the Creel Unit, sir."

He nodded, unbothered. "Creel's for the hard cases," he said. "Guess you noticed."

"I did, yes sir."

"Creel, Chadwick, Carter, and that shitass farm they just named after me. Those are the toughest." He nodded towards the window of the study. "Now Big Red, that's a different story. It ain't exactly Holiday Inn, but it ain't Creel, either."

I nodded. "It looks . . . it looks better, yes sir."

He took another gulp of his drink. "See," he said as he crossed his legs, "Big Red's where we take all the tour groups. All the politicians. All the charity types. All the Christers. Big Red's where we take all the do-gooders. To show 'em how good we do."

And then he let forth a long chuckle: "Hehehehehe." A low, dirty laugh that seemed itself to give him pleasure, and thus perpetuated itself: "Hehehehehe." I smiled by way of letting him know that I felt as he did about do-gooders, whoever they were.

His eyes were still gleaming when he said, "So Big Red's gonna be your new home. Warden Folger's a good man. Ain't the brightest one I've got, but he ain't the dumbest, either. And he's fair with the inmates. You don't give him any trouble and y'all oughtta get along fine."

"Yes sir."

"I wished I could've gotten you here earlier," he then said, a little more somberly. "Couldn't be helped, though. You gotta pick your spots. And see how we did? Played it just right. Willie Shipman's girl did her story, wire services picked it up, everyone read all they wanted to read. Now the story's over. Ain't no more writing to be done about Hadrian Coleman. They've done forgot about you now. Yup. Played it just right."

"Yes sir," I said, but even before I said it I noticed that his face had clouded over once more, and he'd uncrossed his legs and folded his arms over his chest, which was heaving long, dreary breaths again.

"I owe it to you," he said quietly, with some difficulty. "I owe a lot more to you than I can give."

Then he looked at me expectantly. But I simply had nothing to say.

He nodded to show that he understood. "I love that boy of mine," he said. "Don't ask me to tell you why, 'cause I damn sure don't know. He ain't got the sense God gave a monkey. Still, I do love him."

Clearing his throat, he added, "But I ain't gonna sit here and tell you his life was worth doing what you did to yours."

I looked down, tried to focus on something, but through the blur all I could see were my cloddish black shoes, two primitive objects against the off-white carpet.

"Anyway," said Thunderball Hope. "Beginning today, I aim to do all I can to make it up to you."

The front door swung open. In walked a black man in his mid-thirties, wearing a blue dress shirt with the sleeves rolled up to mid-forearm. He was short and somewhat portly, but his saunter was relaxed, almost cocky. Seeing me, his thin lips spread across his face. "This our local boy?" he asked.

"Just fetched him up out of Creel," said Thunderball. "Hadrian Coleman"—and the way he said my name compelled me to spring to my feet, even though Thunderball himself remained in his cypress highback—"this is Deputy Director Cal Fitch."

"Pleasure," said the young man as he extended his hand. "I knew your dad. Know your mom, too. She's in my Sunday school class at First Baptist. Nice lady. She talks about you a lot."

"Calvin goes to the white church, y'see," remarked the prison boss as he slurped at his drink. "His mama raised him to be just like us."

I looked sidelong at the deputy director. He was smirking. "No one's just like you, Thunderball," he said. "By the way, the feds came by yesterday late. They wanted to talk to you about that drowning over at the Hope Farm last month."

"Shit. Ain't nothing to talk about. Damn inmate fell into the stock tank and drowned."

"Well . . ." Fitch's glance shifted my way.

I studied the floor, waited. The next words I heard were among the most significant of my young life.

"You can talk in front of him," Thunderball said.

I looked back up to catch Fitch's casual nod as he continued, "Well, except that makes four drownings at the Hope Farm this year."

Thunderball drained his glass. Plopping down the tumbler, he shrugged elaborately. "Guess we've had high water," he said. Then: "Hehehehehe."

Smiling, Fitch waited patiently for the director to finish. Then he said, "It hasn't rained since February. The problem's not high water. It's our farm manager over there."

"Jumbo Whaley?"

The deputy director nodded. "The four inmates are his, Thunderball. And the FBI hasn't connected the dots yet, but they will. They're going to want him."

Thunderball spat dryly. "Well, they ain't gonna get him," he said. "No better farm manager than Whaley. He's getting a full day's work out of the meanest sons of bitches in the state. You tell the feds they can kiss my ass."

Fitch folded his arms across his chest. "They're going to look into it," he said.

"Well, don't give 'em nothing to look at. Tell Jumbo to go fishing the day they show up again."

"That's not an option," said Fitch flatly. "If they get him off-premises, then we've lost control over the situation. They could drive him down to the federal building in Beaumont and scare him into taking a polygraph. Let's do this, Thunderball. Let's go to their side of the table. I'll debrief Jumbo, and then I'll write up a statement and have him sign it. Have the hoe squad COs do the same thing to take the focus off of Jumbo. Meantime, you might want to consider my transferring every inmate who was present during the four incidents."

"Do it," said the director. "Scatter 'em."

"And if the feds want to see you?"

"Tell them my door's always open."

Turning halfway to me, Fitch said with his broad grin, "Director Hope tells all his employees, 'Anytime you want to see me, my office door is always open.' Thunderball, when was the last time you visited your office?"

"Middle of March," the director wheezed, and it seemed okay for me to join in the laughter.

When he'd composed himelf, Thunderball explained to me, "Calvin's the only one I let come in and out. Otherwise, if someone wants to see me—well, they're gonna have to wait 'til I want to see them. And when I want to see them, why, I either come to them, or I bring them right here." He gestured vaguely about the room.

Then he pointed a sharp, thick finger in my direction. "Your work is here," he said, and though he said it loudly enough, I caught a narrow gleam in his eye that I knew was only for me. "Sunup to sundown. Sometimes later. You'll have trusty privileges. Meaning, you walk across the street by yourself in the morning, and you walk back at night. You wander off, the A picket guard will put you down for a dirt nap."

He stared at me meaningfully. "Yes sir," I said.

"You won't eat over at Big Red," he continued. "You'll eat here. It ain't gonna be what I eat. But it ain't gonna be what *they* eat, either." At this, Fitch chuckled quietly.

"Vermiel!" the prison boss suddenly hollered.

From back in the bowels of the house: "Yessir?"

"Get on in here."

Presently, a middle-aged black inmate shuffled in. He was square-headed, muscular, several shades darker than Fitch, and he wore an apron that was smudged with blood. "This here's our new houseboy," said Thunderball to the black man. "Hadrian Coleman."

Casually, he added, "I imagine you've read about him."

The inmate's eyes bulged. "I imagine I have," he said. He stepped over to me, extending a hand that, when I clasped it, exploded in a cloud of flour. "Howdy, Coleman. Vermiel Crenshaw."

"Vermiel's the best chef in East Texas, and that includes the free world," said Fitch. "Every time he comes up for parole, Thunderball makes a few new entries in his disciplinary jacket."

"Is that true, boss?" the inmate demanded with mock horror, before laughing richly and exposing a row of impeccable white teeth.

"It's on account of those—what the hell did you call 'em—sweet-breads you fed me that one time," said the director. "Still can't get the taste out of my mouth. Like a damn cat throwed up on my tongue. Anyways. This is your new boy. Use him in the kitchen, in the yard, in the laundry room, in my study. Use him everywhere. I got him schooled on the gin and tonic. You do the rest."

"I'll break him in, sir," said Vermiel as he winked at me.

"You do that. And you teach him everything you know. He's got fifty. Gonna be with us for awhile, looks like." Thunderball looked down at his hands as he said it.

"Yessir," said Vermiel, averting his gaze as well.

"Alright then," said Thunderball, and waved at the inmate and the deputy director. "Both of y'all get gone. I got a final word with our young houseboy here."

"Be seeing you," waved Vermiel as he headed back towards the kitchen.

Fitch gave me a soft pat on the shoulder. "Look forward to chatting with you later," he said as he eased out the front door.

The director watched him go. "That fella," he said once the front door was closed. "You can learn a lot by listening to him."

"Yes sir," I said.

"I ain't just talking about prison bullshit," he said.

"Yes sir."

He shook his head, whistled out breath as he fidgeted with some papers on his desk. "That Fitch," he said. "I don't know what he'd be without me. I got a pretty good idea of what I'd be without him. Cooked, that's what I'd be."

The underbite went to work on his lips again. Then he said, without looking up, "Sonny's away, case you didn't know. He was flunking out of East Texas State, so we shipped him off to El Paso for a couple semesters. See if the change of scenery does him any good. But he'll be back here for the holidays in three weeks. Living here, like before."

I considered this.

The director sighed. "You know," he began, but then the words failed him, and he waggled his glass of ice for me to refill it, which I did.

I handed him the fresh drink. Nodding, Thunderball said, "I don't know if I would've done what you did." He took a sip, swallowed noisily. "But once you did it—once you got your story and stuck to it . . . Well, I hope you understand, there wasn't no point in Sonny contradicting it."

"I know," I said quietly.

"He didn't commit no crime that day. At least, that's what he says."

I shook my head. "It was just me," I said.

"Well. So I've told him, 'Forget you were there. Just forget.' But of course, that's easier said than done. He wanted to write you. He wanted to visit you at the Creel Unit. I wouldn't let him."

I nodded.

"What I mean to say is . . ."

Only because the pause seemed to go on forever did I look up. The old bulldog face was beet red.

"Got damn it . . . What I mean to say is, you're my boy's best friend. Shit," he chuckled mirthlessly, not for my benefit. He was look-ing somewhere towards the ceiling. "I wish I had the kind of best friend you were to him. Shee . . ."

Then he looked straight at me.

"Forgive him." Spoken in the manner of a command. But it was a plea.

"I already have." I said it, not having the slightest idea whether what I said was the truth.

But he, my new boss, the boss of bosses, was pleased by the reply. He stepped my way, put a beefy arm around me and walked me towards the front door, the tumbler a little stab of coolness on my right shoulder. He opened the door and we stepped out together onto the verdant lawn, like father and son, strolling languidly towards the sally-port of my new home, the Shepherdsville Unit, Big Red, while Thun-derball Hope said to me, in his most intimate voice yet:

"Been meaning to ask you. In two weeks, Sonny's girlfriend's coming over for the holidays. Mama's invited her over to trim the Christmas tree right before he gets home. I don't know nothing about her. Just that she's one of those Got damn Estelles."

So, I thought as I stood frozen before the sallyport: This is my reward. My punishment.

"You know anything else about her?" came the director's voice.

I fought off the dizziness. "Only what I've seen," I said.

My six-by-nine was standard issue, but in place of a cellmate, I was given a little wooden school desk donated by Shepherdsville High. Warden Scotty Folger, as gabby as Warden Pierson at the Creel Unit had been taciturn, was my first visitor. "Director Hope says you're his boy, so I'll just stay out of the way and let y'all have at it," he said while sucking away on an immense chaw of tobacco. "Anyone in here gives you trouble, though, come to me."

He slapped me on the shoulder, and in a lower voice added, "No sense getting ol' Thunderball involved every time a hard con wags his pecker at you. Don't you worry: ain't nobody gonna make a bitch outta you long as Warden Scotty's in charge."

Folger spat into a styrofoam cup, then wiped his lips against his shirtsleeve and grinned as he leaned off of his bad leg. "Damn, I sure as shit wished I'da been there when you broke that cocksucker's neck," he exclaimed. "I woulda sawed his head off and stuck it on the hood of my car and drove it around town for a few laps. That's the only proper way to treat a prevert."

As he left, the warden tousled my hair, which had finally grown out of my first year's burr cut.

Few of my waking hours would be spent in my cell at Big Red. At five every morning, a CO would roust me out of my bed. Fifteen minutes later, I was outside the red brick wall, strolling unescorted through the predawn silence of downtown Shepherdsville, towards the red brick mansion across the street. I entered through the back door. Vermiel was already in the kitchen and well into the preparation of Thunderball's six o'clock breakfast. I'd never so much as cracked an egg before, but by the second week I was mixing pancake batter, frying the hash browns and turning the omelets while my mentor flipped through the pages of *The Shepherdsville Light* and *The Houston Chronicle* and jotted down unfamiliar words so as to build his vocabulary for later encounters with his crossword puzzle books.

Vermiel had entered the system in the late 1940s as a fine cook, and was now a great one. Mama Jean Hope had stocked the kitchen with volumes of recipe books from all over the world for his edification. She had taught him how to read. Now, thirty years later, I had become her new project. "From two to five every day," Mama Jean told me that first day, "we're gonna sit you down over there"—she pointed to the sunny breakfast room adjacent to the kitchen—"and a tutor's going to be on you like white on rice. But not like I am. Every week I'm going to give you a book to read. And you're going to read it, and you're going to tell me what you've read. You're going to make use of this time, Hadrian. You know why you are?"

And she looked over my shoulder with her sleepy eyes before saying to me, quietly but intently, "Because you're not like Vermiel. You're going to get out someday. Don't you ever forget that."

It was reflexive kindness on Mama Jean's part. She did not know, nor would she know, exactly why her husband had taken such an interest in me. Along with everyone else, she simply assumed that Thunderball was giving me the cousin treatment out of pity for my mother and my youth, or to repay the many community debts owed my father, or to appease my old pal Sonny, or because I had relieved—if to excess—Shepherdsville of its most repugnant elected official.

I had it pretty sweet. But it didn't take long for me to understand why some of the old cons I'd met at the Creel Unit refused trusty status, refused to do light work in downtown Sugarland, refused their furloughs—refused any glimpse, taste or touch of the freedom they were finally, at the end of each day, denied, and why they instead kept to the rec yard, the dayroom and their cell, to those feeble cubic inches that were theirs.

Two weeks into my stay at Big Red, I was vacuuming the gin-stained carpet in Thunderball's study when a U-Haul truck pulled up to the front of the mansion. Edging towards the window, I turned off the machine and watched the inmate lawnboys scramble over to the truck and relieve it of its cargo: an enormous evergreen tree, which they brought inside while Mama Jean stood beside the doorway with her arms folded across her waist and monitored their efforts. "Gently, now," she admonished them in her usual fatalistic melody. "Don't make a great big toothpick out of it. What's your hurry there, Mister Winfield? You've got another twelve years, don't you?"

For the afternoon it stood there in the mansion's grand entryway, an unadorned green behemoth. When no one was around, I stood in front of it, and felt the bristles with my hands, and closed my eyes and summoned a wordless prayer.

I was in the kitchen with Vermiel, preparing a light six-thirty dinner for two, when the doorbell rang. I kept listening.

"Come on, Coleman," said the chef. "You expecting that salad to toss itself?"

I smiled, made a show of manipulating the wooden fork and spoon. Mama Jean and the visitor were talking in the entryway. Sounds of high, feminine jocularity—the one voice twangy and brittle, the other more graceful, but together a duet of plainly frazzled nerves. Thunderball had bowed out of the get-together at the last minute, citing emergency budget meetings in Austin, though I'd helped him load his deer rifles into the trunk of his car early that morning. "I ain't put together for this kind of thing," he growled while his inmate driver started the engine. "I hate her father, I hated her father's father, and most of all I

hate decorating Christmas trees. You tell Mama Jean anything different than me going to Austin and I'll slide your butt in the Oven."

Now I turned to Vermiel, who was testing the lamb with a fork.
"Have you met her before?" I asked.

"Who?" he said as he grimaced at the meat. "Oh. Sonny's girl, you
mean. A few times, yeah." He shook his head at the roast, removed the
fork and stuck the dish back into the oven.

"What do you think?" I asked.

He wiped his hands on his apron. "Few more minutes," he mumbled.

"Cut it out, Vermiel."

"Oh. What do I think about her?" He grinned as he bent down to
the lower oven to check on the potatoes. "I think she's rich. That's
what I think."

"Is she nice?"

"Huh. Rich is always nice. And always not nice, too. Don't you—"

"Shhhh." They were walking into the dining room.

"Oh, I don't really mind the cold up there," I heard her saying. "To
be honest, it's a joy after living through all those saunas that pass for
summers in East Texas."

"I don't know," I heard Mama Jean reply. "Every time I see a
snowflake on the TV, I get a chill. And the people . . ."

"They're quite astonishing, actually. They read, for one thing, and
not just the *TV Guide*. New Haven's hardly bigger than Shepherdsville.
And yet you compare its newspaper, or even the campus paper, with
our town's poor little daily tattler . . ."

"Well, I think Willie Shipman puts out a fine publication. It's about
the only one left that isn't a rat's nest of liberal propaganda, which I
know is very popular among young folks, at least until you start paying
taxes."

"Actually, my father's quite liberal. And he pays more taxes than
anyone in Shepherd County."

There was a pause before Mama Jean Hope replied, "Well. When
he pays taxes, he's got a little pile left over. Now, I hope you don't really
think Yankees are the only people who can read without moving their
lips. I suppose you didn't know it, but I've been the director of a
monthly reading group here for the last fifteen years."

"How charming!"

"Well. I don't know if it's that. It's mainly a gaggle of wardens' wives who need a rest from all the prison gossip. If you're interested, maybe we can squeeze you in a spot when you come home for summer break. Right now, we're reading that new novel everyone's talking about. *The World According to Garp*. Shoo! I'm halfway through, and I can't tell whether I like it or hate it. Have you read it yet?"

"Um . . . yes, in fact, I have."

"And?"

"To be honest, I thought it was incoherent and shallow."

"Oh. Well. I guess I haven't gotten to that part yet . . . Lord, I'm starving. Vermiel!"

"Yes'm!" he called back as he wheeled towards the oven. "Coleman's coming right out with the salad!"

Bowl in hands, I pushed through the louvered doors to the dining room. They were seated across from one another, just under the chandelier—spotlit, the interrogator and the interrogated, though neither was having an easy time of it. She wore a blue knit sweater and matching skirt. But what I first noticed was that her hair was done up in a bun, pinned back simply, and that her neck, which I'd never contemplated before, was swoopingly long, the color of pale roses. Her hands sat on either side of her placemat, the long red fingernails just barely rustling. Otherwise she seemed poised, almost brutally so—until she looked up at me, and saw a figure in baggy whites, and flashed an embarrassed smile before quickly looking away.

Mama Jean, for her part, seemed stricken with relief at my appearance. "Just set that there, honey," she said.

"Yes ma'am," I said, as I set the bowl directly in between them. "The lamb and potatoes are coming right out."

She looked up then. It had to have been my voice—the voice not of a hard con, but of a kid. When she lifted her eyes to me, the wind sailed right out of my chest. They were penetratingly dark, an indigo purple. I knew they'd be that way, and still I wasn't ready for them.

"Uh, Jill," came Mama Jean's awkward voice, "this is Hadrian."

Her eyes suddenly widened, and the chandelier light poured into them. "Hadrian Coleman?" she exclaimed. "Sonny's friend?"

Tongue-tied, I blushed at the ground. "When did you come back to Shepherdsville?" she said. "Does Sonny know? Oh, he'll be so excited! He's talked about you so much, he . . ." And then, evacuated of all words, her lips came back together into that fragile arc of melancholy—and I'd realized then that I'd had it wrong also: she wasn't so disconnected after all, she could feel us, she could feel *me:* that frown was *for me!*

God, that was something.

"I'll be back with the iced tea," I said, and retreated to the kitchen, where, with the blood rushing to my head, I mumbled to Vermiel, "Could you bring them the rest? I have to go to the bathroom." I kept walking through the back hallway of the kitchen, pulled open the heavy door to the walk-in cooler and closed it behind me. Inside I slammed my fists against the frosty wall until they burned.

Vermiel found me there. He stood in the doorway in his stained standard-issues, a half-eaten potato in his hand as he regarded me where I sat on the floor atop a sack of rice.

"What the hell's got into you, Coleman?" He asked the question gently.

"I'm sorry," I muttered without looking up.

"That ain't answering my question. What the hell's got into you?"

And then: "Damn, boy, you're bleeding. Was that you making all that racket? Let me see that hand."

My hand in his looked like an egg in a nest. "Come on," he said. "Let's get you a Band-Aid. Can't have you bleeding all over my apple pie."

When he turned and saw that I was still sitting there, Vermiel leaned against the doorway, one leg crossed against the other. I watched as he gobbled up his potato, then licked his fingers one by one.

"Let me tell you something about love, Coleman," he then said. He belched, spat out some potato gristle. "Love don't set you free. It may feel like it does. Then one day you look around and you see everything you been doing is something love told you to do, and that's when you know you ain't nothing but a goddamn slave. Now listen here."

He brandished a sly grin. "I got a stack of magazines in an old grain sack underneath the kitchen sink, where I keep the lard," he said. "You want to fall in love with one of them girls, you be my guest. But with anybody else . . . Shit, boy! Don't you got enough prison going on in your life already?"

"She's beautiful, though," I blurted out. "Isn't she."

"Course she's beautiful! Jackie Onassis ain't bad either. Why don't you go after her next? Shit, Coleman," he said as he grabbed a fistful of my shirt and hoisted me up. "You ain't nothing but a skanky con. That's all you are."

I had just begun to wash the dishes when Mama Jean strode into the kitchen. The moment she came to a standstill, she lifted her eyes heavenward and heaved a sigh. Seeing that we were watching, she smirked. "Wonderful dinner, Vermiel," she said. "The guest said the lamb was 'divine.'"

"Divine," considered Vermiel with a grin as he cleaned his knives. "I like that."

"She's gone to 'freshen up,'" added Mama Jean wearily. "Personally, I don't see how she could get any fresher. Me, I'm about wore out. I hadn't had so much fun since I had my teeth cleaned."

"Aw, come on, Mrs. Hope," Vermiel chuckled. "After all. She's purty and she's rich."

"I guess it's too much to be asking for a personality," she said, and turned to me. "Hadrian, you can have the rest of the pie to yourself if you'll help her trim the tree. Would you mind? I've just got nothing to say to the girl. And God knows it must be killing her, having to talk to a cretin like me."

"Yes ma'am," I said. "Be happy to."

She aimed an annoyed grimace at Vermiel. "What're you laughing at?" she demanded. "Oh, hell. I know what you're thinking. You and Purvis both. I have *never* said that no girl's good enough for my Sonny."

"That's true," said Vermiel with a semblance of a straight face. "You've never said it."

"Besides." Her smile became wry. "This one isn't a girl, anyway. I don't know what she is. Well, God help us all. Vermiel, throw me the key to Purvis's liquor cabinet. I'm taking a drink with me up to bed."

Jill was standing beside the tree, untangling the strings of lights. She was a tall girl, but beneath the evergreen she looked like a forlorn little orphan. Her expression changed when she saw me coming.

"Any minute now I'm sure I'll electrocute myself," she said. "This seems more of a manly endeavor anyway. Why don't you do this while I put the hooks on the ornaments?"

I sat crosslegged beside the tree. When she dragged the boxes of ornaments over to me, and then sat nearby, so that my clown shoes were inches from her almond loafers, I felt an awful sense of panic overtake me. But I returned to the lights and did the work slowly until my hands stopped shaking, at which point my confidence grew, and I told myself that I was quite an expert at light-untangling, quite a man. . . . Sidelong I could see that she sat to one side, her long legs sheathed in white hosiery and folded underneath her. As she threaded the hooks through the ornament loops, she frowned, as if the task were on the order of neurosurgery. For the first time all evening, I felt like laughing.

"You're quite famous, aren't you," she suddenly said.

When I reddened, she added, "You shouldn't be embarrassed. The day you were sentenced, I remember my father pounding his fist on the dining room table and saying, 'Send him to prison? They should make him mayor!' He'd had his run-ins with Judge Castlebury. Killing him, according to my father, was the greatest civic deed Shepherd County's seen in at least a century. He'll be so jealous when he hears I've met you."

A moment later, she added, "And of course, Sonny always speaks well of you."

A hard laugh shot out of me. "That's big of him," I said. To hell with it, I thought, and braving that delicate pout of hers, I showed the Estelle girl my ugliest sneer.

"Don't blame him, Hadrian."

My heart cringed as those notes of loyalty were sounded. "Sonny's father forbade him to contact you in any way. It was terribly frustrating to Sonny."

She arched a disapproving eyebrow. "His parents smother him. She smothers him with protectiveness. He smothers him with pure ridicule. I don't think I've ever seen anything like it. It's awful. I'm sure he's happier in El Paso."

"He's got good parents," I declared, to my surprise. "You don't know them well enough to say."

"Oh, is that so?" There was a playful gleam in her smile now. The thrust had been parried. This was better than tree-trimming. "I just spent an hour getting to know *her* rather intimately. Let's see. She thinks Yankees lack the East Texan's vise-like grip on proper English. She thinks that it's objectivity one reads in the *Shepherdsville*

Light-as-a-Feather, which is nothing more than a weekly paean to the Texas Department of Criminal Retribution. Not that I'd expect her to complain about *that*. She thinks John Irving's an author—why, he's nothing more than a hairy-chested comic strip artist—"

"—who's got a thing about bears," I added.

She cocked her head in astonishment, while I silently thanked Mama Jean for loaning me the novel the week before. "Exactly," she finally said. "Exactly. But above all, she thinks her son still needs to be breast-fed, still needs to be dressed in the morning and put down for a nap in the afternoon. Still is utterly incapable of making an adult decision for himself. Meanwhile, he—" and she gestured towards the study, where a single bulb burned over the liquor cabinet—"could not be more of a brute. Is it true that he's actually proud to be running the most unspeakable prisons in America? Is it true what I've heard about that, that medieval furnace they roast inmates alive in . . ."

"The Oven?" I grinned. "It's probably just a myth."

"Well, he's proud of his myths. He's proud of the blood on his hands. He's proud of everything except Sonny."

Her face was scarlet. I had not imagined that she could get so worked up.

After drawing a breath, she sealed her lips into a frown. Then she said, "I don't know. Maybe it all evens out. She spoils him; he torments him. It just doesn't sound like a normal life to me."

"Jill," I said.

My mouth tingled to say her name aloud.

"Jill. Tell me what a normal life is."

Her head slowly, slowly turned. Her golden eyelashes fluttered two, three times. I held myself steady. I did not flinch. I owed it to those waking dreams at the Creel Unit not to flinch.

"I've seen you before," she then said. "Haven't I. And I don't mean in the newspapers."

She slid around on her hip so that she was square with me. Her stockinged knee was grazing my scruffy white pants. But she was absolutely focused on what there was to see beneath my eyes.

"You were with Sonny that first day," she said, realizing. "You . . . you ran away from me . . ."

My whole body was trembling, but I could not turn away from her stare.

Her lips seemed to want to curl into a smile. "That was . . . that was such a, a *different* day for me," she said. "After all those foolish young men, hovering like vultures . . . And then someone comes up to me . . . And someone else runs away . . ."

Oh my God, I thought, as a tear rolled out of my eye.

Her eyes began to water. *Please don't ask*, was all I could think. *Please don't ask why I ran.*

She didn't. I knew she wouldn't.

"Oh dear," she whispered instead, as a tear of her own fell.

They both stampeded in at once, boy and dog, Sonny and Sparky, the college kid and the yellow Labrador, and together they brought me to the ground. All I could do was hope that it was the dog doing the licking.

"Look who the cat drug in, Sparky!" he hollered. "Let's make a punk out of him! You go first!"

He'd gained the pounds I'd lost. It took some doing before I could wriggle out from under him and get him under my knees, while the Labrador drooled and licked and barked. But get him under me I did, neatly dodging a last squirming knee toward the groin area, and suddenly there we were, the biscuit-head pinned by the con, and him giggling redfaced underneath me.

"You like it on top?" he managed.

"I just like you on the bottom," I said.

He panted for awhile as I eased up just a little. His face was still red, but I had a better glimpse of it now. He didn't look bad. In fact, he looked far better than I'd remembered. It was the brilliance I'd forgotten. His teeth flashed back at me.

"We even?"

"Not even close," I said, and started to tickle him, and he began to shriek out giggles.

Suddenly his eyes went wide. "No!" he protested. Before I knew it, a dull sound was all around me, and I felt myself hit the ground.

A moment later, I came to. Mama Jean was hunched over me, pressing a kitchen towel full of ice to the back of my head. "He's alright, he's coming out of it," she was saying, while up above me a CO stood with Sonny's bags at his feet and a prison bat in his hand—his face disordered, babbling, "Mister Director sir, I just saw white and the damn numbers on his back, I didn't stop to ask—"

"You didn't stop to do shit!" Thunderball roared somewhere off to my right. "You didn't stop to hear my boy laughing, you didn't stop to see that dog wagging its tail—you didn't stop! You just wailed in!" And suddenly the wild blur of him, thick arms coming down like tree limbs in a hurricane: "Now how'd you like it if I—came—wailing—in—and didn't—stop—"

"Jesus, Dad," came Sonny's voice off to my right, amid the thumping.

"Shaddup! I oughtta come after you next!" And then he turned back to the guard, who was prostrated against the front door, arms crossed in front of his face while he gurgled in soprano.

"Purvis! Purvis! Stop this!" exclaimed Mama Jean. "It was just an honest mistake! Purvis, it's—it's the holidays!"

"*I hate the Got damn holidays!*" he exploded, and the world went foggy again. But I was conscious enough to hear the door slam, the hollerings fade with the footstep, and then, finally, just the ringing in my ears, along with some other steady, breathy sound.

A wet substance dragged against my face. It was Sparky's tongue. It lulled me to unconsciousness.

Sonny and Jill visited me in the prison hospital that evening. I saw all the inmate orderlies turn to regard their approach. It didn't surprise me that they looked so good as a couple—the same height, the same hair color, hands held tightly together. What did surprise me was that I felt good seeing them this way.

He held out a bunch of yellow roses. "I stole 'em from Dillard Bunch's garden," he snickered. Then he leaned towards me and inquired confidentially, "So is it true what they say about frontal lobotomies? You feel more at peace with the world?"

"I feel just at peace enough to kick your ass," I said.

Jill smiled distractedly. It occurred to me that this was her first experience around a roomful of inmates.

"How long do you have to stay in here?" she asked.

I managed a smirk. "Depends on what you mean by 'here.'"

Her lips sagged and she looked at the floor.

"Honey, the doctor said he'd be out by tomorrow," Sonny admonished her as he squeezed her hand. "It's just a damn concussion and a few stitches. He didn't lose his spleen or anything."

Now she smiled. "You don't even know what a spleen is, do you?" she asked. "Tell me what a spleen is, Sonny."

"Okay," he said, straightening. "All right. A spleen is something that Hadrian does not lack."

She smacked him one on the shoulder. "Ow!" he cried. "Guards! They're attacking the director's son again! Break out the tear gas!"

Before leaving, Jill asked Sonny to step outside. He swatted me on the foot and her on the backside before bouncing off, howdying inmates and doctors and COs alike as he exited.

She leaned against my bed and put a cool hand on my forehead. "It's just the way they do things, isn't it," she said. Her voice was remote, but there was a tremor to it. "When in doubt, start splitting skulls."

"Not really, Jill," I said. "Not with me, at least. I've been lucky." I offered up a smile.

"Lucky," she half-whispered, and then she looked away. "Yes, I can see how lucky you are."

She turned her back to me. Her head bowed, and a hand reached up to it. An inmate orderly poked his astonished tattooed face in. I motioned for him to get the hell away. He continued to peer in for a moment before ambling off.

I laid my hand against her slender back. "God," she sighed as she wiped her eyes. She did it slowly, painstakingly, and in the process she composed herself.

When she swiveled back towards me, her eyes were only a little red. "I've found one thing about which Sonny's father and I agree," she said. "I hate the goddamned holidays, too."

"You should see it in the pen," I said. "It's a nightmare. They scream at night, they try to kill themselves. Last year at Creel we had seven suicide attempts on Christmas Day. Santa's helpers were running from cell to cell cutting 'em down. They saved all seven necks, from what I heard."

Her hand, warm and moist, reached just above my shoulder. "Don't you ever do that to that sweet neck of yours," she said.

That unyielding look of hers.

"I'm past that," I finally said.

In our silence, the air was cluttered with moans and snores and yapping curses. As a con, you develop a talent for deafness. Usually I was fairly adept at it. But now my ears throbbed with the miserable din.

After awhile, Jill pushed herself off the bed. "I have two more matters to take up with you," she announced. Her expression was of mock reproach. "Sonny's mother said you don't want your mother and sister invited to the Hopes' Christmas Eve party. Why is that?"

My stomach seized up. "It wouldn't be good for them," I said. "Besides. I don't want to be there myself."

"What? You can't leave me in the lurch like this! You're going to cast me out into those shark-infested waters—those bucktoothed wardens, and that pathetic nincompoop Aynsley who spent a year writing me the worst poetry imaginable . . . Hadrian. Please . . ."

She tugged at my gown, and I couldn't help but laugh. "You're not the one who'll have to wear white," I said.

"But—but I could! We all could!"

"Oh, give me a break."

She was resolute. "Leave it to me," she declared. "I'll get Sonny on it right away. It'll be the theme!"

"Jill—"

"It already is the theme. Isn't it? Before the commercial tidal wave of red and green? Mary and Joseph in white? The shepherds in white? And of course the swaddling—"

"*Jill.*" I said it through gritted teeth so that I wouldn't yell. "Please. Just shut up. You ain't gonna get Thunderball Hope to wear white, and you ain't gonna get his wardens to wear white, and for that matter, you ain't gonna get my mother to wear some number across her back to remind her of what it's like to be her son. So just, just . . ."

"You're right. You're right." Her hands were on either side of her head as she stared at the ground. "God, I'm an idiot. You're right. I'm sorry."

Then she was sitting on the bed again, tugging at the collar of my gown. "I want you to come," she said. "Stay in the kitchen if you have to. I'll come in and see you and Vermiel. Okay? Will you do that? Will you save a girl's life the night before Christmas?"

Her face was so serious. She was really quite funny.

"God, you're as bad of a pest as Sonny," I finally said. "Okay. But I'm staying in the kitchen."

Bouncing off the side of the bed, victorious, she continued: "Aaaaaand secondly, I need to solicit your opinion. I've bought Sonny a sweater for Christmas. I'm sure he'll say it's too preppy, since I was the one who picked it out. I think it's very stylish, but what do I know? I'm only a girl. Will you look at it before I wrap it?"

My heart lumbered to the bottom again. I shrugged. "I don't know anything about sweaters. Why don't you show it to his mom?"

I was ashamed the moment I said it. She drew back a little.

"I'd rather use the sweater as a noose than leave myself open to his mother's snide comments, thank you," she said.

It appalled me, how swiftly this could happen—one minute her beside me, and me swimming in her perfumed breath; then, an instant later, me watching as she shrank into herself. I tried to reach over, and bolts of pain went through the back of my bandaged head. Then, just as everything seemed to slip away, the words tumbled out of my mouth:

"Don't you do that to your sweet little neck."

And there we were, back to staring at each other again.

"Bring the sweater over the day after tomorrow morning," I said. "He gets up at ten. Anytime before then is fine."

She didn't say anything. Her gaze drifted.

Then, like an arrow, her face raced to my cheek, and her lips grazed it. "'Bye," she whispered, and whirled through the hospital curtain.

The prison director's Christmas party was a moment to anticipate, being not merely an opportunity to wear green and red (instead of the usual town colors), but also a chance to mingle with the mighty while being served by authentic convicts, in the setting of a mansion that seemed to find its calling on such an occasion. Various elected officials were known to drop in, along with powerful friends the director had procured in the course of dispensing favors to their incarcerated beloved. There was a reason assigned to each invitation, and that made for great rumor-mongering in Shepherdsville—though no one, not even the uninvited, ever asked aloud just who it was that was paying for this gaudy affair.

On the morning of the party, a downtown stroller who happened to be traversing historic Big Red might stand with his back to the brick wall, gaze across the street and wonder if the inmates had staged a

coup. For there they were, in the trees and on the rooftop and in and
out the door, armed with hammers and ropes and nylon cords . . .
They were, of course, being put to work: stringing lights, construct-
ing wooden snowmen, wooden shepherds, crowning the mansion with
wreaths and holly, and at the very tiptop of the roof, affixing an
enormous Star of David whose lights were so searing that Big Red's
A picket guard would be obliged to wear his shades throughout the
evening. Ten convicts—five males from across the street and five
females from the Farenthold Unit—were huddled together in the
mansion basement, practicing their carols under the frantic direction
of Shepherdsville High's choir teacher. Vermiel had his own squadron
of kitchen elves. Mama Jean was bolting from room to room with me
in tow. Thunderball, meanwhile, was immersed in budget meetings
at a deer lodge east of town.

Sonny had also made himself scarce. But just before seven, he and
Sparky barrelled through the kitchen door. One of the inmate recruits
jumped, and his platter of cheese jangled loudly against the floor.
Sparky promptly descended upon the scattering of cheese.

"Get that damn dog out of my kitchen," directed Vermiel. I
grabbed ahold of Sparky's collar and nudged him through the back
door. Sonny wore a T-shirt and a Shepherdsville High letter jacket. I
wondered how he'd acquired it, given his athletic deficiencies. Perhaps
he'd pried it away from one of the jocks in exchange for a prison bat,
since the weapons were in great demand among the East Texas State
fraternity boys. The jacket, with its myriad baseball, football and track
patches and the gaudy orange insignia SHS WARDENS, seemed out-
landish against his soft frame. I couldn't decide whether the comic
effect was intentional. Sonny certainly didn't look self-conscious, with
his cheeks bright red from the cold and his yellow hair sweeping
against his forehead as he laughed for no clear reason other than the
fact that everyone else in the kitchen looked so damned unamused.

"God dawg, Vermiel, I hope you got more food than that," he said
as he lustfully surveyed the platters of delectables situated along the
drainboards. "Ain't you seen the guest list yet? Biggest bunch of
mooches in Shepherd County."

"If I can keep you down to five platefuls then I 'spect we'll be
alright," Vermiel said as he whirled from oven to drainboard to sink to
oven, turkey and baking pans and potholders seeming to orbit around

the blur of him. "Coleman, check on my help out there and make sure they're doing what they're supposed to be doing. And take Mister Touchdown with you."

A couple of inmates burst out laughing at the reference to Sonny's jacket. "Hey-*hey*," Sonny yelled, suddenly scowling. The kitchen became very quiet.

He pointed a sharp finger at the two inmates. "Y'all might as well start basting yourselves right now, 'cause as soon as Warden Folger walks on over here I'm gonna have your asses in the Oven. You hear me?"

Even Vermiel was speechless. Sonny's normally placid face was clenched. His eyes bulged with blind fury. The two inmates stared nervously at the floor. One of them was holding a platter cluttered with champagne glasses. They tinkled like window chimes as the platter trembled.

I had little warning of what would then overcome me. "Don't fuck with the help," I snapped. "The only oven Warden Folger cares about tonight is the one in here. Now come on," and I grabbed Sonny by the back of his leather jacket and shoved him out the louvered door.

Once we were on the other side, Sonny hissed at me, "Who in the hell do you think you are, showing me up like that in front of those cons?"

"I didn't show you up," I shot back. "You ain't rank. You ain't jack shit. Why don't you go change your damn clothes before your mother has a seizure?"

"Wh—" His cheeks swelled with hot air. He was standing maybe a foot away from me. *Go ahead*, I thought. *Go ahead and give me an excuse.*

Instead, he took a step back. A curdled grin moved rancidly across his face. "Why don't you go change *your* clothes?" he asked, still grinning as he kept walking backwards and then up the staircase.

I opened my mouth to shout out some reply. But just then the doorbell rang, and on cue the inmate choir, positioned in a somber semicircle around the Christmas tree, fell into "God Rest Ye, Merry Gentlemen." Mama Jean rushed to the doorway. "Your suit's on the bed, Sonny, now hurry!" she called out. And, "Purvis, will you get in here?" The louvered doors swung open behind me, and past each side of me glided the inmate waiters with platters held aloft. The rooms were suddenly alive with guests, music, the pouring of drinks and dispensing of food, coats being taken and cheeks being kissed.

I stood there for a moment, a pale shade blinking back the profusion of holiday cheer. On my way to the kitchen, I caught a glimpse of Thunderball Hope lumbering towards the entryway from his study, already out of his mind on Tanqueray.

I did not go out after that. Instead, I posted myself beside the dishwasher, accepting the pans and casserole dishes Vermiel handed me. Occasionally I'd turn the water off and catch my breath, and in these moments I could hear familiar voices through the doorway: Thunderball and Mama Jean, the ever-bullshitting Warden Folger, the compelling, unhurried drawl of Foots Taylor, Cal Fitch's discreet chuckle, and a nervous but resonant voice that I eventually recognized to be that of my lawyer, Colbert Reeves.

Above all voices, including those of the choir, was Sonny's. With the bombast of a sideshow barker, he carried on and on until he'd explode with laughter, and they all laughed back by way of applause. He jawed, he quizzed, he flattered, he bantered, he guffawed. He never came up for air. And they loved it, surely; but from where I stood, hunched over the scalding water, and from where he had scaldingly put me, his voice sounded like the very melody of falsehood. God, how I hated him at that moment. Something came over me, but I was in no position to stop it, I'd already tried, it had its own mind and now it had me—the air spattered with purple, and then a roar caromed, and all the while the blood sloshing around in my skull, twin geysers of red boring twin scars, fists of jagged glass . . .

"See, we told you he was harmless. Notice, for example, his zen-like approach to dishwashing."

Startled, I looked up from the suds. Aynsley Reeves stood there, ill-postured in his father's greasy hand-me-down seersucker, bespectacled, the puny makings of a mustache bristling as he smirked. Beside him stood a short, mousy brunette in a slightly moth-eaten green sweater. "Sheila Polunsky, meet the state's one and only, uh, 356023," he declared as he squinted at the number on my shirt pocket. "Hadrian Coleman, meet my one and only fiancée."

"I, well," and I held up my soapy hands, and the young woman nervously mumbled that she understood. "Congratulations," I then said. "I didn't know."

Blushing, Aynsley's fiancée shrank against him, and as he threw a stiff arm around her, he said, "We just announced today. Actually, we're just starting with you." He beamed.

"Aynsley!" gasped Sheila. "Didn't you tell your parents yet? I thought you'd told me you'd told your father!"

"First we start with my father's client. Then we work our way up. Have patience," he said, and gave her what was meant to be a reassuring squeeze, though she responded with a suffocated burble. After flashing a you-can't-please-'em smile, he explained, "My girl's from Pittsburgh. We met at a college debate tournament. Sheila gave a very compelling argument for introducing a weighted-voting system into the United Nations. I'm not ashamed to say she trounced me. Call me a fool for romance, but there it is."

Aynsley's fiancée gaped, exposing a mulish overbite. "What's to stop you from just running out the back door?" she inquired.

I forced a smile, shrugged and returned to my scrubbing. Aynsley replied, "I'm sure he's afraid we'd gang-tackle him, dearest. Have we already had too much eggnog? Your—oh, for Christ's sake."

There was another presence in the doorway. I paid no mind until Sheila stage-whispered, "Is that her?" and Aynsley muttered, "Who else would it be?" Then I looked up. Jill wore a red silk dress with matching lipstick and fingernail polish. Against the color, her flesh seemed wintry. She offered a smile to Aynsley, who turned to his fiancée and said, "We'll get you that other drink now," then said to me over his shoulder, "*Feliz Navidad.*" Jill stepped to the side to accommodate the couple's headlong rush to the door.

She shook her head as the louvered door swung. "I don't know why he's pretending to be so injured," she said. "He and my father can still entertain each other with their marathon Shepherd County history discourses, and that's all he ever cared about anyway. Hi, Vermiel." She smiled at the chef who, perched upon the drainboard, looked up from his crossword puzzle and grinned back. "Your dinner the other night was—"

"Divine," he finished lavishly. "Mrs. Hope passed on the compliment. Thank you, Miss Estelle."

Jill blinked. "Is that what she said I said? I've never used the word 'divine' in my life." She grimaced. "That woman must really hate me."

Lifting her gaze to me, she scowled prettily. "The holiday spirit is upon us like the Black Death," she observed. "How are you?"

I gestured to the stack of dirty platters and pans. "'Scuse me, Miss

Estelle," said Vermiel as he frowned at his paperback book. "What's a nine-letter word for 'beacon'? It ends with an 'e.'"

"Try 'semaphore,'" she said, and spelled it for him. Then she leaned over the stainless steel basin separating us.

"Sonny told me he said something very nasty to you," Jill softly said. "He didn't say what. He really feels terrible about it."

I shrugged and looked away. "He knows where to find me."

At that moment, his voice could plainly be heard wafting merrily over the buzz: "I told him, 'Bubba, you cowboys in El Paso may be tough in a damn saddle. But y'all come on down to East Texas some time. We got river rats and hillbillies that'd make y'all look like y'all came out of ballet school!' Hawhawhawhaw!"

Jill winced, and I was almost embarrassed for her. I reached for another pan.

"You know how he is," she persisted. "When he gets nervous—"

"If you want to believe that," I cut in, "fine. You can believe whatever you want to believe."

And then I turned my back on her. "Hadrian," she began, but I turned on the water as high as it would go and dove my arms back into the suds. Sidelong I watched her quietly disappear.

The rest of the evening passed without further visitors, other than Mama Jean, who peeked in and, with a harried expression, declared, "Thank God it looks like they've stopped eating. Vermiel, you and Hadrian take the rest back to Big Red tonight. Or throw it out, I don't care. Just so it's not in this kitchen. I don't want to see another turkey 'til Thanksgiving."

Outside, the clamor continued, carols and cackles and all the usual happy talk, and eventually I noticed the absence of Sonny's voice. Replaying all that had been said, I felt utterly saturated with gloom and self-loathing. I knew he hadn't meant it. I knew he was sorry. And I knew, in any event, that Jill was blameless but for the fact that she loved him. As did I—I loved both of them. There was just enough love inside of me to stoke my suffering.

Vermiel sidled over and began to help with the last stack of cookware. He hummed "O Little Town of Bethlehem" as he scrubbed. The choir had ceased singing; the noise outside was ebbing, and the front door slammed with greater frequency. I noticed that Vermiel was working at double my pace. The clock above the oven read ten minutes before eleven. It seemed a great deal later.

Vermiel looked up. "You hear that?" he asked.

"Hear what?"

The chef wiped his hands on his apron and headed towards the back door. After opening it, he leaned outside. I heard him talking. I turned off the water to listen.

Just as I did, an arm from behind Vermiel swung around him, a shirtsleeved blur. "Think fast!" came the unmistakeable voice, followed by the unmistakeably bad throw, and the hurled object fell a good ten feet in front of me. But "Think fast again!" and the second toss was better, and as I caught the can of beer, I could hear Sonny's snickers trail off into the night.

Vermiel closed the door. He palmed his can against his hip. Smiling, he said, "Let's put these in the walk-in 'til everyone's gone."

And shortly after eleven, the front door slammed a final time. Following this, Mama Jean's fatigued drawl could be heard: "You get to work, Santa. We're opening the gifts at nine in the morning. I'm turning in. Oh, Vermiel? Hadrian? Y'all do what you can out here. It looks like pure hell."

Thunderball was reposed in an armchair, snoring gently with an empty tumbler cradled in his lap. He remained there throughout our cleaning, dusting and vacuuming; and he was still there when Vermiel and I guzzled down our Chistmas beers and the chef excused himself for the night. Only when Vermiel shut the front door behind him did the prison boss stir. He sputtered, smacked his lips and focused a single red eye on me.

"They gone yet?" he mumbled.

"Yes sir. About an hour and a half ago."

"I be damned." He made no effort to sit up, though presently the other eye opened. "Jesus," he then muttered, and handed me his empty glass.

"Get me another," he ordered.

"Yes sir," I said.

"Naw. Never mind." He eyed his watch, grunted. "Fuck a truck. I better get out the rest of the Got damn gifts, if they ain't been stolen yet."

He waggled a finger towards the tree. "Something for you under there," he said. "She told me it wasn't contraband. You better open it here, though."

I followed the direction of his finger. Of the multitude of gifts scattered under the tree, there stood out a rectangular box wrapped in mirrorlike green, with a red velvet bow. I walked over, set down the tumbler.

"Open it," said the director. His voice indicated drowsy interest. He sat up and scratched his ear.

I pulled off the bow, then peeled away the wrapping. With a tug of the finger, the tape around the box gave way.

"Well?"

"It's a . . . it's a sweater." Cobalt blue, but with a pale yellow circle just over the left side of the chest. Full moon burning through a universe of night.

"Lemme see it. Hold it up."

As I did, a small card fluttered to the ground. I bent down and snatched it up. Sidelong, I could see him watching.

Dear Hadrian, it read, *you didn't really think I made you try this on for Sonny, did you? Merry Christmas. Love, Jill.*

I exhaled slowly. Then I put my note in my back pocket.

"I guess you're not gonna tell me what it says," he said.

"It's . . . it's not an escape plan, sir," I said.

He nodded, yawned. "What're you gonna do with that?" he asked. He waved at the sweater. "Can't be covering up your number."

The words sank in, and the sweater slid out of my hand and onto the floor. I couldn't even look at it. Nor at him. Outside, the lawn and the street glimmered with the spangles of reflected Christmas lights and the cold, hard beams of Big Red.

"Jesus wept, Coleman," he then growled. "I may be the devil, but I ain't Scrooge. Take your damn shirt off, put on the damn sweater, and put your inmate shirt over it. Do it."

I did it. And a moment later, I stood in the front yard, bathed in lights—a shadow aglow, with the moon trapped against my heart—before finally crossing the street, and wishing the sallyport guard a merry Christmas as the gate opened and Big Red swallowed me up.

After Sonny flunked out of college at the University of Texas at El Paso and returned to Shepherdsville, my proximity to him was closer than it had ever been. Yet my perspective was hopelessly muddled. I served him his meals now, washed his clothes, bathed his dog; I took down his phone messages from Jill. The everyday playground of which he spoke was forbidden to me. And when he entered my world—put on the payroll as a Big Red correctional officer—the results were disastrous: he slept on the job, frequently abandoned his post and, on one occasion, was cajoled by a gang member into mailing a letter containing instructions to gun down a rival who'd just made parole. Warden Folger begged me to intercede with Thunderball, and I did, and the following day Sonny's father requested that the CO turn in his grey uniform.

In short, I witnessed my best friend's development sometimes in a daze, at other times in a fever, but never with unobstructed clarity. And so the onset of his ambitiousness caught me unawares. If anything, the events following Sonny's abortive stint as a prison guard lulled me into believing that he'd gone permanently fetal. After being canned by his own father, Sonny sulked for weeks. He spoke to none of us, including Jill. Thunderball was particularly at a loss. Everyone in the mansion had heard his fulminations the day Sonny had returned home from El Paso diploma-less: "You won't try! You're just a spoiled, lazy, child! A Got damn baby! It's all you're ever gonna be! Jesus! I'm gonna call up the inmate workshop right now and have 'em build a giant-sized crib for you to sleep in!"

Thunderball had laid down the law to Sonny that day: "You are going back to East Texas State in the fall. But in the meantime, you are off the tit. You want room and board, you're gonna pull the wagon like everyone else. Starting Monday, you're wearing grey!" But three months later, when I brought word to the father that his son had become the single most dangerous threat to security at the Shepherdsville Unit, it became clear that Thunderball could contribute only to the further humiliation of his progeny. And though introspection did not become the man, he spent much of that summer in a fog of surly brooding, a phenomenon that drew my fascination and pity . . . causing me to miss whatever it was that happened to Sonny as well, right under my nose, and thus, to draw all the wrong conclusions about his intentions, which were far more relentless, encompassing and vengeful than I could ever have imagined.

It began with him winning the war of wills with Thunderball—though at the time, the whole spectacle looked too pathetic to amount to anyone's idea of a victory. The prison boss at last joined the rest of us in propping up Sonny. Seeing little point in letting his son become a miscreant, the director bade his deputy, Cal Fitch, to summon the finest minds the penal system had to offer. Fitch produced, among others, a mathematician who had butchered his wife, an advertising copy writer who'd kept preteen boys in his wine cellar, an astronomer-burglar, a philosopher-fraud and a tragic young woman from the Farenthold Unit who knew American history but not her own, having succumbed to amnesia the moment she gently slid her newborn into Lake Whitney.

They tutored him at first. Then they drafted his homework. Finally, they wrote his term papers start to finish. Owing to their surreptitious heroics, Purvis Hope, Jr., received his B.A. in medieval history from East Texas State University, a mere two years behind schedule. "That's Bachelor Hope to you, bubba," Sonny took to boasting, and all I could think was: poor Sonny. He'd flopped in his father's business, which was the only game in town. He still couldn't change a flat tire or draw a straight line. He could sell, perhaps, but only if the product was Sonny Hope. He knew that his father was disgusted, that his mother was chronically depressed; and he had to know that Jill would, before long, find no further consolation in Sonny's blitheness, and withdraw from him as she had from all the others.

Improbably, I found myself actually believing that I would not trade my life for his. I was now eighteen—three years a con, a trusty with a G.E.D. and well into my second semester of college correspondence courses, no longer the system's youngest, and in my own way, one of its strongest. My native gift, I had come to discover, was a modest but useful one: I could be trusted with secrets. Whether I could ever trust myself was another issue, of course. Random nights found me swimming in the familiar blue-black abyss, and on my birthdays, I didn't even attempt to sleep. But by and large my preoccupations were braided with the longing, forlornness and unquenchable hungers of any eighteen-year-old male. I'd achieved something, which was the ability to live a young man's daydream—and so I did, and thus did not see what was coming.

Professor Tobias Estelle stood fidgeting on the porch of the mansion. He was three minutes early, and apparently annoyed at himself for this. So he remained where he was, and from the window of the director's study I watched, since I'd never before been afforded such a close look at the town's wealthiest man. Prior to my incarceration, I'd seen the professor walk his route to the university, and had frankly felt let down by the spectacle of him: tall but misshapen, with frail shoulders, high hips and a pot belly, outfitted in a shabby tweed blazer, uncreased khakis and Hush Puppies, his thin longish hair greased back but for two strands that slapped against his lenses as he walked. He had a half-drowned, rodent-like look about him, all the more so because of the shock of peppery whiskers that completely obscured his upper lip. Today, up close, I could see that the professor sported two embellishments, a red bowtie and a pocketwatch which he consulted every minute or so. But I could see something else, through benefit of experience with human nature. The professor, I deduced, was not wearing such clothes because he had no choice—but rather, because the opposite was true.

Tobias Estelle's great-great-grandfather, Joshua, a twenty-six-year-old sheep farmer from Kentucky, had founded the town in 1838. "A shrewd, unbending speculator," as my copy of *The Shepherdsville Estelles: A Quiet Greatness* (penned by one of the professor's graduate students) put it, "Joshua's lone regret was the sale of a hundred and twelve acres in eighteen-forty-six to a consortium of Dallas investors. The selling price was most to his advantage, and the land itself but a sliver of Joshua's vast county holdings. A year later, however, the consortium successfully bid to have the state's first penitentiary built on one of the plots in question—an undistinguished twenty-two-acre tract on the southern flank of town. The remaining ninety-acre tract was also sold to the state in eighteen-fifty-two, and today is the site of the Purvis J. Hope Prison Farm."

Joshua died in 1867, a victim of the plague that took half the town. But he left behind a fortune so staggering that not even his nitwit descendants could rip through it all, though they gave it their best effort. The next three generations saw scores of near-bankruptices as each Estelle took three steps forward, five steps back and still came out obscenely ahead. Jill's grandfather, Edwin, may have been the biggest boob of them all. Seeking in 1938 to commemorate the centennial of Shepherdsville in throwback fashion, Edwin imported three thousand sheep from the Orkney Islands and pronounced himself a shepherd. His talents, it turned out, ran more to genocide. By the second year,

Edwin's pastures were heaped with white corpses, victims of food contaminated by the runoff from Edwin's brandy distillery (which itself produced the county's most undrinkable hootch). The sheep venture neatly reduced the family fortune by half. To make matters worse, Edwin's two eldest sons would both be killed in Paris during the war. (Though not by warfare; they'd both been found face-down in the Seine, their bodies naked and bound tightly with fishing line.)

That left Tobias, who was sickly, unambitious and financially incompetent. He did seem to like school, however, and so he spent most of his young adulthood abroad, collecting degrees. Tobias married in London, was divorced in New York City and remarried Jill's future mother, an Austrian chocolate heiress named Andrea Schiller, in Florence. They relocated to Shepherdsville in 1957, three months before Jill's birth. Andrea lasted there until just after their daughter's third birthday. After that, the facts gave out, leaving the vacuum to be filled by the usual Shepherdsville improvisations. Was Tobias a closet homosexual? Had Andrea seen in the eyes of her daughter some brand of roiling genetic pathos? Incest, devil worship, cannibalism (after all, no one had actually *seen* Andrea leave town) . . . Whatever had befallen her and Estelles past, the town was left with Jill and her father, who taught a single graduate history class each semester at East Texas State, and otherwise secluded himself at the dilapidated mansion on Estelle Avenue, until today.

The professor looked up at the picket tower, squinting with discomfort at the guard overhead. The Estelles had been famous foes of the prison system's expanding presence in town. But the family had lost every round. Tobias himself had fought the creation of a Criminal Justice Department at East Texas State. He threatened to yank the family's trust, until his lawyers advised him of the legal consequences. Then he threatened to quit the School of History, and was in effect told, "Be our guest." The Estelles had founded the university, along with everything else in town, but that was yesteryear. Shepherdsville's future lay in prisons. That final defeat had been in 1970—and at the hands, I now realized, of the very prison boss upon whose porch the professor now stood.

The clock in the living room tolled seven. Professor Estelle referred to his pocketwatch, nodded at it, replaced it in his pocket. But he didn't ring the doorbell, as punctuality might not send the desired message. I wondered, though, just how long he might have to languish out there before it all seemed right and proper. And so I went to the front door and opened it, making as if to step out for some type of errand.

The professor all but jumped into the bushes as I opened the door. "Well, then," he stammered. A hand went up to his mustache, and he eyed me with concern.

"I'm a friend of your daughter's, Professor Estelle," I said, and put out my hand. "Hadrian Coleman."

His face split open in delight. "Good lord, yes, of course," he said as he threw his soggy hand into mine. "Jill speaks very highly of you. Well, and—well, truthfully, *I* speak very highly of you."

Tossing a scornful look at the picket guard behind him, he whispered, "The sick barbaric fascists. Enslaving the very best, empowering the very worst. You'd think it all a farce, but there are lives at stake, are there not? To say nothing of the life of the town. In any event."

His voice was surprisingly deep and acerbic. "I assume they're here," he said.

"The director and Mrs. Hope? Yes sir. They're inside."

"And Jill and Sonny will be here after the movie." He smiled unhappily. "That should give us plenty of time to become the very best of friends."

Again he looked back at the tower. "Listen," he then said. "I'd certainly like to know something. Jill says she loves Sonny because he makes her laugh. Well, I've met Sonny, and I don't find him the least bit funny. Quite the contrary. He's rather embarrassing, isn't he? Unless I'm missing something."

"Well," I began, and then stopped and smiled and folded my arms and stared out at the lawn. "I mean, yes sir, I think he's—I think he can be funny. Maybe a little . . ." I stopped myself. "He's changed some. Since he made warden, I mean."

"Warden," he scoffed. "As if that truly elevates him. As if that's a change for the better. And as if that's supposed to bring me some relief," he went on as he removed his spectacles and wiped them against his white shirt, "knowing it's not the class clown my daughter's engaged to, but instead, a warden."

The world inside me took a vicious sidespin.

"Engaged?"

"Yes. Engaged. You don't think I'd be standing in the shadow of this, this Tower of Babel, if I didn't have to, do you?"

"No . . . No, I guess not."

I didn't even realize that I had sat down on the porch step until the professor had joined me there.

His voice was apologetic. "I would've felt certain they'd have told you," he began. "The Hopes and I were told yesterday."

I tried to focus, tried to think about where we'd all been yesterday. I realized then that Sonny hadn't been around. He'd waited until evening, when I'd gone back across the street. And this morning, Sonny had scooted out early, not stopping for breakfast, instead yelling out, "Gotta interview for a new assistant, catch you later." And shortly before noon, Mama Jean had made an appearance in the kitchen. Her face looked drawn but resolute as she told Vermiel, "We're having a guest for dinner tonight. Professor Estelle. But nothing too fancy, okay?" And then she'd left as well.

"In any event," the professor said, "I told Jill that I was against it. And that's exactly what I intend to tell them. I'm not having my daughter marry some prison thug. I don't care if he's an amusing thug or not."

Under other circumstances, I might have fallen over laughing at that characterization of Sonny.

"Is that where you live?"

I saw that he was looking across the street. I nodded.

"How long have you, um . . ."

"Five years, seven months."

"Hmm. It's terrible, isn't it?"

I had a stock answer for that question. Today I didn't use it.

"It is," I said.

"And when do you get out?"

I turned to him. "Professor Estelle," I said, "I'm in love with your daughter."

"I gathered that," he said smoothly. "When do you get out?"

"I'm up for parole in August of '89."

A moan perished in his throat. "That's more than nine years from now," he observed. "What will that be—fifteen years? Fifteen years for killing a monster."

"If I make parole," I said.

"Hmm. Well." He groaned his way to his feet.

I was still sitting. His face leaned down towards mine.

"I'm sorry," he said awkwardly. "But I need for you to show me in."

"I'm against it. I just want to go on record right now."

"Toby, you can go on whatever you wanna go on and it ain't gonna mean squat. Shit, I'm against it, too. You think they're doing it for *our* sakes?"

"Well, I will do all I can to make my opinion count. I'm sorry, Director Hope, but I—"

"Call me Thunderball, Toby."

"Don't call me Toby, please, my name is Tobias. And as I was saying, with all due respect, your son does not yet strike me as a mature adult, he—"

"Mature? He's a warden, for the love of God!"

"Well, yes, I was happy to hear from Jill about his promotion over there at the farm, I'm sure he made quite an impression on just the right people, but I don't see exactly, now wait—"

"Purvis, sit down! Sit *down!*"

"Goddamn it, he's a warden! He supervises two thousand felons! Now, maybe you think it takes more maturity to supervise thirty little college brats, but I'm gonna tell you something, Estelle. I'm proud of my boy. He done worked his way up, from CO to assistant warden to where he is now. He done worked his way up, To*bi*as, and if you can say the same for yourself or your daughter, why you just—"

"I resent that! I have earned three Ph.D.'s and one master's!"

"Please! Both of you!"

From the other side of the louvered door, Vermiel and I sat motionlessly as Mama Jean Hope regained command. "Now will you two behave like grown men? We're not here to take a vote. Our votes don't count."

The catch in her throat was evident. "It's not our decision," she continued. "Maybe we all wish it was. But what we do have to decide is whether or not we're going to show them our support."

A long silence followed. Then the professor spoke. "I'm afraid it's not that simple," he said. "There are certain . . . well . . . ramifications."

"Like your money? Fuck your money, Toby. Sonny doesn't want your damn treasure chest."

"Purvis."

"Well, that, in fact, is for us to decide, Director Hope. But money isn't what I was referring to, anyway."

I could hear Thunderball's chair creak as he leaned forward.

"It's the name, Director Hope."

"The name? What name?"

"Our name. My name. And, if you will, it's another name that concerns me. The name Herrera."

"Her—you mean, that piddly-ass lawsuit? What the hell's that got to do with any of this?"

"Our name, that's what it's got to do with it. I do not want to see an Estelle chain herself to an institution that is about to be declared inhumane and unconstitutional."

The director roared out a laugh. "You got it all figgered out, don't you? Hadrian! Get in here and bring that wine with you!"

I nearly sprang out of my shoes. Vermiel put his hand over his mouth to hold back his laughter. His other hand shoved me through the doorway.

The director hunkered at the far end of the dining room table, as always, with his wife seated to his left. The professor sat across from Mama Jean, but a good three feet away from the table, and his indignation was undisguised. Thunderball's joyous outrage I had seen a thousand times before. It was Mama Jean's face that fascinated me most, because it changed the moment she saw me—from a hard, flushed mask of nausea and shot nerves to something that resembled . . . shame? Was that it? It was. She had known, and hadn't told me, and that was wrong. The whole thing was wrong. And somehow, her expression suggested, the whole saga came back on her.

"Hadrian," barked the director. "Pour the professor some wine."

"Hello, Hadrian," said the professor, and put a hand over his wine glass. "I'm fine, thank you."

"Just set it down there in front of him, he'll change his mind. Now listen, boy. Toby here—"

"That is not my name."

"Toby here," he repeated, with obscene relish, "thinks Sonny ain't fit to be married to Toby's daughter on account of Chu-Chu Herrera.

He thinks ol' Chu-Chu's lawsuit's gonna prove us all out to be cavemen."

The director gestured grandly. "Now you tell the professor," he said. "You've been with the system, what, almost seven years now? Hell, the system raised you! So you tell him. Are we cavemen?"

I smiled faintly. "No sir."

"Tell *him*, Coleman. Not me. Are we running some house of horrors?"

I turned hesitantly to the professor, who slapped his hand against the table and said, "You're putting him rather on the spot, Mister Director, and besides, I'd venture to say Hadrian's a special case. He's not out in the sun spreading fertilizer."

"Really, Purvis," agreed Mama Jean as she rubbed her forehead. "This isn't fair to Hadrian. He doesn't know anything about—"

"The hell he doesn't! He knows damn near everything! You Got damn right he's a special case, Toby, he—"

"Purvis, he's told you, now quit being a horse's—"

"—damn catbird seat, he's seen both sides, he's right in the damn middle! He's your expert, professor! Now tell him, boy."

I rubbed my hands against my white trousers. "It's not barbaric, sir," I said, though I felt my face reddening as I looked at him. "I mean, it's not a fun place. But they treat us okay, as long as we follow the rules."

An odd smile materialized on his face. "And if you don't?" he asked.

"Well, then, God help your ass," interjected the director. "This ain't the Boy Scouts, Estelle. These cons are the worst scum in Texas. You don't run them, they'll run you. They'll take over. Look at New Mexico. They burned that buddy to the ground! You think that's what the law-abiding taxpayers of Texas want to see? Crooks having a field day? Stringing up the guards? Burning the prisons? Pouring out into the streets? I know you academic types think the criminal justice system should be like summer camp. But we ain't dealing with co-eds, professor. They are every last one of them *vermin*. Except maybe for Hadrian here," he added quickly, but then continued, "And my job is to keep vermin in line. It ain't to nurture them. It ain't to apologize to them for what society or that nasty judge did to 'em. I ain't beholden to them, Professor Estelle. I'm beholden to the law-abiding citizens of the state of Texas. They've entrusted me to a job which I've had for fourteen years now, and which I intend to keep God willing for another fourteen, and another fourteen after that. But I'll be the first to say it: it ain't a pretty job. Tending to vermin never is. Am I getting through to you, professor?"

Jill's father wore a tight smile, all but invisible underneath his mustache. "My line of work must seem very trivial to you, Mister Director," he said.

Somewhat weakly, he added: "Or Thunderball. That's certainly a real-world appellation, isn't it. Unlike, say, Tobias."

An unease presided. For the moment, the director was noticeably disarmed. The guest wiped his mouth on his napkin. "Wonderful meal, by the way," he said to me. "My compliments to the chef."

He turned back to Thunderball and Mama Jean. "Funny how history doesn't seem real-world to some," said Tobias Estelle. His voice had regained its acerbic lilt. "The Constitution, being a living document, has its own history, naturally. One can either read the lines through which its blood courses—or, at one's peril, one can ignore them. Now, I'm a historian. I'm not a legal scholar. But that is my point, in a way. Expertise is not required to allow one to see the Constitution's guaranteed protection against cruel and unusual punishment. Nor does one need to be an expert, one need only be able to read, to observe how the courts have continually and vigorously buttressed that protection. Yes, I'm aware of the New Mexico situation—which, as you well know, was a function of overcrowding and misappropriated resources, not of limp-wristed paternalism. But more significantly, Mister Director, I am aware that forty-eight other states in the union do not have burning prisons. Nor, however, do they have unconstitutional prisons. At one time, of course, many of them did violate the Constitution. And it's a matter of historical fact, Mister Director, that the courts have taken them to task. One by one. Your prison, Mister Thunderball Hope, is the very last hold-out. The last of the outlaws. But it will be taken to task."

The director's face broadened into an ugly grin. "Well, that's a damn lovely speech, Tobias," he said as he clapped his hands. "But—"

"Excuse me," cut in Mama Jean. She looked my way. "You can take the dishes now, Hadrian."

"Leave 'em and take a seat," rasped Thunderball. "We may need that expertise of yours."

"Purvis, I don't think it's—"

"It don't matter what you think, Mama, he's my con, now sit down!"

His grin came too late to convince anyone he'd been joking. I sat.

Thunderball's fat hand gripped the wine bottle and tipped it towards his glass. He slid it my way. "Don't worry, Tobias, I've checked," he said. "Constitution don't say I've cruelly or unusually punished my houseboy by giving him a glass of wine."

The professor folded his arms but said nothing. I stared at the glass. Being offered it and drinking it were both prison code violations, of course. Mainly, though, I found myself suddenly indisposed to accept Thunderball's charity.

"Now tell the professor," he boomed. "Sure, you ain't working the hoe squad at present. But you have, haven't you?"

I nodded. "My first year, yes sir."

"And you know all the inmates at Big Red."

"A lot of them, yes sir."

"They talk to you, don't they? You're their go-between. They take their grievances to you, you take 'em to me. Ain't that right."

"Yes sir."

The director winked. "Tell the professor what the colored inmates call you."

"Coolman." I blushed, but I also smiled. The nickname indicated how far I'd come, and I wasn't ashamed of it.

"So Hadrian here's plugged in," the director announced. "He's heard it all. Tell us, boy. You heard anything about us chaining inmates to walls and bullwhipping 'em?"

"No sir," I said.

"Or cutting their fingers off? Or castrating 'em?"

"No sir."

"Do they sleep out in the fields, or do they sleep inside?"

"Inside, sir."

"And how many meals we feed 'em daily? One? Two?"

"Three, sir."

"There you go," declared Thunderball, his eyes bulging as he turned back to face Jill's father. "Oh, one more thing. Do you know Chu-Chu Herrera?"

"I've met him a few times, yes sir," I said.

"And?"

I shrugged. "He's doing fifty like me," I said. "But he's got six or seven priors. Armed robberies, I think. He's a little guy, tattoos all over him. I heard he's tried to kill himself a few times. He's jumped a couple of guards. He's a little on the nutty side, I guess you could say."

"Have you seen him recently?" cut in the professor.

His eyes were keen and unblinking. "No sir," I said, "not in six or seven months. He's in ad-seg. Administration segregation. Solitary confinement."

"He violated rules," said the director in a bored voice.

"Hah!" exclaimed Tobias Estelle, and stabbed the table with an index finger. "The rules of silence, you mean. You're keeping him from the inmates and the law books and the reporters, that's what you're doing."

"Baloney," said Thunderball with a dismissive wave. "I got his damn disciplinary jacket right there in my study. I'll get Hadrian to fetch it if you like."

"Oh, I have no doubt you've found some meager justification for isolating him," retorted the professor. He let out a spray of cold laughter. "But for what it's worth, Thunderball, I've read Herrera's complaint."

The director shrugged. "Good for you," he said. "It's a public document."

The professor then turned to me and asked, "Have you seen water leaking through the walls of the prisons?"

I looked at Thunderball, who waved his hand permissively. "Yes sir, on a couple of walls," I said.

"We're in a budget crunch, professor, in case you haven't noticed," remarked the director.

Jill's father ignored him. "And the rats," he said to me.

"A few," I said.

"The finest eating establishments in Shepherd County have rats, for God's sake," snapped Thunderball, no longer amused.

"Perhaps the ones you eat at. And the dayrooms have been turned into bunkers, haven't they?"

"Yes sir. We've gotten awfully crowded, sir." I looked Thunderball's way for approval, but his eyes were fixed on the professor.

"And," Tobias Estelle went on, "they've run out of uniforms and shoes, so some of the inmates are forced to serve their sentences half-naked, without—"

"I told you we're in a budget crunch, Got damn it! It ain't my damn fault the legislature's tighter than a Chinaman's daughter!"

"Yes, I can see," said the professor as he cast an expansive gaze about the mansion, "just how much you're suffering." Ignoring the director's curses, he said to me, "And they do run out of food, don't they? And they do shut down the air conditioning in the dead of summer, don't they? And the hospital is crawling with roaches and rodents, mosquitoes and maggots, isn't it?"

Again Thunderball erupted, but Tobias Estelle was on a roll, and his voice had just the right nasal resonance to pierce the former's objections. He went on: "And the bat we all know about, it's legendary of course, I see the fraternity boys on campus all pretending they're Thunderball Hope with their cruel little toys. But this Oven. That exists too, doesn't it? Some aluminum furnace that wilts their brains without leaving any telltale marks. You know about that too, don't you, Hadrian?"

My mouth opened on its own. "He don't know about that kind of make-believe bullshit, Estelle," interrupted Thunderball, "and you got one hell of a lot of nerve after we bring you into our house and extend our hospitality to you and all you can do is go on about how we're a bunch of damn Nazis! I don't care how much money you're sitting on! You got the manners of a billy goat!"

Before the professor could reply, Mama Jean came out of her stupor and said sharply to the guest: "Don't. Don't, either of you. Now stop this. For the last time, this has nothing to do with prisons or family names, it has—Oh, God. That's them, isn't it."

A car door had slammed. Two pairs of heels clicked up the walkway. A galootish snicker was followed by a squeal of protest and, "The guard saw that, now will you keep your nasty old hands *away*?" Then another muffled squeal, and a sudden quiet. They were kissing.

Remembering what tonight was all about, I stood up and began to gather the dishes so as to make haste back to the kitchen. The Hopes and their guest wore looks of pain and guilt.

Still, before the doorknob turned, the professor vowed, quietly and evenly: "I will fight this. I will do all I can to keep this from happening."

A heartbeat later, they were inside, Sonny dragging Jill in by the waist as he reported of the movie she'd dragged him to the campus theater to see, "I wouldn't've traded a stick of gum to see the damn thing. Shit, Jill told me it was all about Shepherdsville—"

"I did not," she corrected, rolling her eyes. "I only said—"

"And the whole damn thing was in Italian!" he complained. "Some jerk named Fellini, he's got this thing for freaks of nature and . . ."

When he saw I was there, Sonny's face went slack. "Oh. Hey, bubba."

I stood by the louvered door, loaded down with dirty dishes. Jill let go of her fiancé's hand. As her face turned, I caught the wet glimmer in her eyes. She lifted her hand up to her mouth. Sonny's smile was fearful. I'd seen him smile that way to his father. He was begging. So was she. I didn't say anything. I just pushed my way through to the kitchen, and dropped the plates into the suds. I stood there, gazing dumbly at the soap bubbles. The thrumming hurt inside of me took only a second to reveal its origins. Just as quickly, I knew what to do.

I stepped away from the dishes and back through the doorway. The five of them were as I'd left them. There was only one move, and it was mine to make. So said a voice I'd never heard before: *This is how you ascend to the land of the living. This is the only way. You shed your feelings, your self-interest, maybe everything left in your life. You do this so that something might be saved, in the end. And then maybe you could say you'd paid in full.*

And they may have cringed, both Sonny and Jill, as I came upon them. But it didn't really matter how any of us felt at the precise moment that I threw my unsure arms around them both and said— maybe too softly, but it took all I had just to get it out of me:

"Congratulations."

That was April. On the first of May, I convinced the director to recruit another trusty to help with the gardening. His name was Manford Wallace, and he didn't know a spade from a salad fork. Wallace was an East Texas boy like me, but from even deeper into the woods, the offspring of an enormous brood that couldn't read ten words between them. The other inmates called him Bobo, and though he was a very big man—at least 250 pounds—and was a confirmed pyromaniac, he was pitiably lamblike away from a matchbox, and so they took turns walloping him in the rec yard. The COs got in on the act. When one of them sneeringly displayed to me the papers he'd confiscated from Bobo Wallace's cell, I gawked in disbelief.

Returning the papers to the inmate one evening, I said, "Wallace, where in the hell did you learn to sketch like that?"

The big man, hunched over his bunk like a fagged-out gorilla, shrugged and offered a toothless smile. "Guess I always been bad to find the purtiness in a girl's face," he said.

As I nodded, a thought took hold. "You like your job at the mattress factory?" I asked.

Wallace giggled a little. "Shee," he said.

"What do you think about gardening?"

"Well . . ." and he reflected for some time before he shrugged.

A week later, it was a done deal. Bobo Wallace spent his mornings pawing halfheartedly in the flower beds. From there, he watched her come and go for two weeks as she strolled from the avenues up Walls Boulevard. Held in her own elegant oblivion, she had no clue that her movements were drawing more than the usual scrutiny—least of all that the slack-jawed brute at the edge of the mansion's walkway was looking into those mulling half-closed eyes, at the disquiet settled upon her lips, and taking what he observed back into the bowels of Big Red. When Wallace handed me the pencil sketching two weeks later, I had to sit down in his cell for a long time.

I'd never given Jill a birthday present before. In the meantime, their wedding was four months away, and I had tried to imagine something suitable as a gift. But my heart wouldn't open up. After having said what I'd said—"Congratulations"—and felt their bodies melt gratefully against mine, and having seen the professor and the Hopes rise awkwardly and hug them as well, I returned to my cell that night and thought, for the first time in years, about hanging myself. It wasn't her. It wasn't even Sonny. It was me, and what I had done to bring upon myself this most ancient form of punishment . . . But the drawing was all that was left to say, all that my heart could say to hers. Or this I thought all the way up until the morning of Jill's twenty-third birthday, when I awoke to find myself in a state of despair so dire that I knew I couldn't part with the sketch of her. It had to be mine.

I watched the world grow older, and so little of it changing. From the kitchen window every late morning, I observed the continuing procession of ex-cons as they took those first free strides from Inmate Processing to the bus depot, spattering the air with the same acrid boasts; and at all hours of the day I saw the new ones arrive as I had, in armored schoolbuses, hobbled with chains and trying to look as tough as the walking dead can look. I saw out into the free world that the new kids, starched and short-haired and inexplicably smug, had become the faces of my dad's college yearbook from the late forties. I saw the cars get bigger, the skirts get longer, a living rerun before my eyes. Shepherdsville was just as Pawpaw had predicted it would be: fancier and dumber than ever.

Or so the view appeared from my overgrown birdcage, on the days when the changes in me reared up themselves like the walls fending off all but a few taunting rays of light. I had hardened and narrowed into a shape and texture that suited the life that was now mine to lead. By now I understood why Vermiel spent so much of his free time immersed in the refuge of his cookbooks and his crossword puzzles. I understood as well what he had meant about love and prison. Whole weeks went by without me looking at the drawing. I didn't talk much to Jill or Sonny anymore, and I didn't much care if they saw that I had at last become what I had no choice but to become. I enjoyed the company of the director, but more for how my closeness to him improved my life as a con. I knew as well that, though Thunderball had become attached to me—and for reasons that by now had nothing to do with what had brought me here to him originally—he also knew I was a con, and now and again he treated me as nothing more than his houseboy. That was his prerogative, and it made things easier for all of us.

Cal Fitch was something else again. The deputy director enjoyed lingering in the mansion hallways with me. If there was an angle to his cordiality, I couldn't see it. He told me things no con had any business knowing. Standing in the living room one day, arms folded, his black neckless head disappearing halfway into his collar, he had a good laugh when I mentioned what all the rank at Big Red had been saying for some time—namely, that the new warden at the Hope Farm, one Sonny Hope, was making a mess of things.

"So Sonny's not cut out to be warden," he finally said. "Neither was I. Never lost any sleep over that."

Then he said, "We're moving him into Administrative next week.

He'll do good work over there. You watch. You see who's left standing when the roof falls. It won't be the rank over at Big Red, I'll tell you that."

Blinking, I said, "You don't mean the Herrera lawsuit. Thunderball says it'll get laughed out of court."

Fitch turned his compact body just an inch or two. He looked right into my eyes, and I saw a sudden absence of the usual bemusement—and instead, a welling of pity.

"Thunderball," he predicted simply, "will eat those words."

On a bristling October afternoon, I stood on the porch of the mansion and did what I could to draw inspiration from the copper sun and its hard, brilliant aloofness. Sonny stood beside me. He struggled for a moment with his bowtie, cursing its tightness, then flipped back his hair and pulled at his tuxedo jacket. I had figured he would look like a yellow-crested penguin in his wedding outfit. But in fact he looked quite handsome, even dignified. The cleft in his chin and the dimpled creases in his cheeks sharpened in his round face. Squinting into the sun, hands fisted in his pockets in the way of his father, he cut a contemplative, even baronial figure.

"It knocks you down to size," he said quietly, rocking back and forth on his heels. "Moments like this. Moments that are a hundred times bigger than you are. Not much you can do but pretend you're up to it."

He looked my way. "You know what I mean?" he asked.

I nodded. "You'll do fine," I said.

Out of the corner of my eye, I could see his gaze drift to the ground.

"You're the only one," he murmured.

His face went rosy as he returned my stare, the mint eyes watering. "You're my best man," he blurted out in a cracking voice. "Goddammit, Hadrian. I wish the hell you could be there."

Then he said, "But I understand."

Does he? I wondered. Could that be possible?

"You're almost halfway home," he said as he wiped his eyes with the back of his tuxedo sleeve. "Right?"

I shrugged. "That's for the parole board to decide."

"Well. They'll decide what they're told to decide."

Just as quickly, the cockiness ebbed. "When you get out," he mumbled. His voice raised an octave, and his eyes filled with copper light. "Bubba, when you get out, I am going to throw you the biggest goddamned soiree. Booze and hookers and—shit," he grinned, those teeth crystalline against the sunlight, "you'll get such a workout, I'll have to push you around in a wheelchair for weeks . . . And I'll do that, boy howdy, will that ever be a pleasure . . ."

I propped up a smile for his benefit. But he didn't dare look at me anyway.

"Foots'll be there at the wedding," he then said as he adjusted his cummerbund. "They say it's all over but the crying for Bluffer. Can you believe that? Ol' Foots as a legislator."

I looked at my watch. "It's about five," I said. "You'd better get on pretty soon."

"Do you think I'll make her happy?"

The sun darkened to red.

"No one can make someone else happy," I said.

"I think I can," he declared, and sidelong I could see his mouth lock into a tight-lipped grin. "Her dad's gonna be surprised. He thinks Sonny's just some chucklehead prison brat. He thinks Sonny just wants his pile."

Scuffing his shiny rented tuxedo shoes against the red brick porch step, he said in a lower voice, "By the time it's over, I'll have more than his whole fucking family ever dreamed of having."

I tried to laugh, but what came out sounded frosty: "Do you really think that's what Jill wants?"

He looked up, surprised, and I held him in my sights until he looked away, nodding balefully. "I know," he whispered. "I know."

He cleared his throat. "Listen. That thing I said to you before the Christmas party a few years back . . ."

"Forget it." But I'd said it too quickly—he knew I hadn't forgotten. In a more controlled voice, I added, "Things were different then."

"They were," he nodded. "Damn. Was I brat and a half or what . . ."

Suddenly he stood in front of me, and tugging softly at the front of my white shirt, he blurted out, "I know I don't deserve my luck, okay? Okay?"

He winced, but still held me up against him. "There ought to be a law against my luck, I know. Just—just don't hate me for it, Hadrian. Please. Your luck, it's gonna change, damn it. It will. It just—it will. Goddamn it, I'll see to it!"

"Oh," I laughed, "and just how—"

"She loves you too, you know," he suddenly said, and as if his own words had slapped him, he spun away from me, and in the same motion he advanced rapidly down the walkway and then down the street, towards First Episcopal, where the bells were already ringing.

The mansion was empty when I stepped back inside. Even Vermiel was at the church. The choice had been mine. I knew I had decided wisely. And I knew then, as I stood in the entryway, that wisdom was damnably hollow. I found myself ascending the staircase, up into the forbidden private quarters of the mansion.

I had not been in Sonny's bedroom since we were both boys. It still looked like a boy's slovenly sanctuary, with strewn clothes and candy bar wrappers and a couple of dog-eared *Playboys* splayed out underneath the bed. From this very room, only minutes ago, he had stepped out into the unforgiving terrain of adulthood . . . Or did he, I thought: would he ever really be ejected from this overgrown, unkempt womb, marital and vocational vows notwithstanding—just what kind of luck was his, anyway?

Never before had I wanted to be Sonny. But his bed, which was unmade, felt like a feathered cradle when I stretched out upon it. And for awhile, I slept what was surely his sleep rather than mine.

I woke up in the darkness, jerking forward. I couldn't read my watch. Heart pounding, I scrambled out of his room and down the stairs. A key was scraping against the lock. I made it to the kitchen by the time the door opened.

The house was suddenly flooded with the voices of Thunderball and Mama Jean and Cal Fitch and Scotty Folger and others similarly crocked. "Hadrian!" Sonny's mother called out. "Come on out! We brought you some wedding cake!"

"And some beer! Get on out here, boy!"

A moment later, I did, and nodded and smiled as they carried on about the striking blonde couple, the proud way he exclaimed "You bet I do!" and the way Thunderball blubbered throughout the proceedings; and how even the professor, when he gave his daughter away, winced a tightassed sort of smile; how Sonny lifted Jill off her feet as he kissed her, then muttered audibly, "My Gawd, we done did it, girl!" which brought the house down; how the evening was just right, coolish even, featuring a sky blistered with stars, and you had to hand it to old Toby, he threw a hell of a wingding at the country club, that was real champagne, and the weaselly bastard showed a touch of suaveness as he wheeled Jill around the dance floor—and speaking of Jill, manners did count for something and there wasn't a soul she didn't approach and thank for coming, right down to the COs and Sheriff Worley who stalked the premises with that shiny hunk of tin right on the lapel of his polyester blazer; how the couple scampered off amid a blizzard of rice, into a rented limo that would cruise them around for a bit while everyone caught their breath, took off their ties, started hitting the whiskey back home, waiting for one last appearance from the soon-to-be-honeymooners . . .

"They're coming here?" I asked them, but the words had no sooner left my mouth than the door flew open. In sprang the Labrador Sparky, now ten but showing new life as he cut a swath for his master, who stumbled in, redfaced and hooting, with the bride in his arms. I turned away, but too late. Like the popping of a great flashbulb, I saw the engulfing twirl of white silk, the lace veil thrown back, the dangle of pearls, and the cascade of golden hair; I saw the white heels aloft, the silk stockings like shoots of exotic white wheat, swaying in submission to her conveyor; and I saw, finally, the pale gloved arm, and the fierce magnificence of the ring gleaming on the finger. Too late, way too late, I looked down to the white of my trousers. Only for a second. Because I could hear them all cheer as the newlyweds mounted the staircase. I could hear, by the dim concussion of their hollering, that their backs were to me. And without hesitating further, I made for the door, stepped outside, and with long, wooden strides, crossed the threshold to Big Red, where the sallyport gate slid reliably open, the cold brick womb taking me in, as it always would.

But never again after that night. The following morning, I spoke to Warden Folger, who spoke to Cal Fitch, who spoke to Thunderball. That afternoon I boarded a white schoolbus, manacled, and rode crosstown to my new home, the Hope Prison Farm, where I would be just an ordinary con, sharing my six-by-nine with another loser named Digby, eating slop and keeping my head down. Only my new job would bespeak of my former clout. At my request, I was assigned to be a kennelman for C. C. Holliday, the tracking-dog sergeant. I fed the dogs, groomed them, raised their pups. And I laid tracks for them in the early morning, in the dew, lumbering through the fields in my protective padding, and finally hunkering in a spot for an hour or two, listening to the prison cattle low in the distance. I'd occasionally hear trucks from the mulecart roads, and on some mornings, I believed I could just make out the gurgling of the Minerva.

Otherwise, I did nothing but sit there, like a mute, discarded mattress in the pasture—waiting 'til I'd hear the baying of the hounds, closer and ever closer, until in a sonic rush they'd be upon me, frothing and roaring and tearing at my padding while I lay there limply in the grass, this close to death, and only in those brief moments, fully alive.

6

The land splaying out at the dead end of the paved road was as bald as a tumor. WELCOME TO TRUST, read the sign in plain black letters. A hundred yards down the temporary gravel thoroughfare, an array of parked cars baked under the August sun. I left my Impala there. Ahead lay a skeletal universe: cranes angled in all directions, scaffolded monstrosities-to-be, girders heaped here and there and dozers scudding through clouds of red clay. Another sign appeared through the dust: TRUST IS THE ANSWER! To what question, I wondered, before the grimly satisfying notion settled in, to the exclusion of all else: *Yes. There is plenty here to stir me up.*

The tour was already in progress. I fell in, accepting a hard-hat from the grinning young fellow in the navy blazer that bore on its lapel a button declaring, PRIVATIZE NOW! I pulled the brim of the hat over my forehead. There were hundreds of us. I looked at no one else, paid no heed to the tour guide as he led us across the foundations of the new empire and honked on with his shameless exclamations, "unprecedented" this and "state of the art" that, while I braced myself for the main event and in the meantime imagined all this as it had been before Ricky Tempesta, in his zeal to mock the mockery that was Shepherdsville, robbed it of every oozing stump, every pine needle, every breath of life. Well. The favor would be returned. I was here to see to that.

"Are there any questions?" came the tour guide's voice. "No? Well, then, let's get out of this heat, waddaya say!" The spectators were herded into the one semi-completed building on the complex, an as-yet-unpainted domed metal edifice with an inscription overhead: Trust Institute of Criminal Justice. Hundreds gasped in relief as a blast of air-conditioning enveloped us. "Any seat is fine," we were told as we entered the auditorium. When I took one in the second-to-last row, the young man who had handed me the hard-hat grinned helpfully and said, "You might want to sit closer up. Doctor Tempesta puts on quite a show."

Doctor? "I'm sure he does," I said. But I didn't move, and the young man shrugged and walked off.

Then the lights dimmed, and a lone figure appeared onstage to hearty applause. I remained where I was. Even from this distance, I could clearly see how Ricky Tempesta had changed. Like a middle-aged wolf whose lean, lonely days of meager backwoods predation were well behind him, he now enjoyed a routine of easy prey, and with that luxury came a sleeker coat, a lower belly and an unhaunted, even drowsy countenance. *Go ahead, come closer*, those eyes said. *I won't bite you out of hunger, or even anger, because I'm set up sweet now, I've got my pick of the lambs and the rabbits and the fatted calves, and the sun shines on my ass every blessed minute of the day now. No, I'll just bite you on account of I'm a goddamned wolf.*

But all else remained in place. His first gesture, an upthrusted index finger from a right arm turned so that the forearm faced the audience—what correctional officer at the Hope Farm had not been summoned in precisely that manner, not waiting for the finger to bend in a beckoning waggle, the point indeed being to spare the master any exertion lest the money be redirected towards another CO equally corrupt yet swifter to demonstrate it. "Point One," he declared—so much for greetings and thank yous—"is that we would not be here if Trust already existed." The auditorium fell silent. Tempesta spoke without benefit of notes, and as his voice rose over us with evangelical fervor, I wondered if I was the only one in the room who could hear the poison bubbling up from his zesty oratory. Who needed ears? Simply to glimpse those needle-like fingers gripping the lectern as if it had blood and breath to squeeze out; to see, below the tortoiseshell glasses, the nose broken so many times in so many back-alley brawls that it had taken on the contours of a thousand knuckles; to observe that hideous mangle of skin on the right side of his neck, twisted and seared by a long-dead foe's fire-hot industrial pliers . . . But wait, I then realized:

the trademark wound was no longer there. Or rather, it was obscured. Hidden beneath a minister's collar. Doctor Tempesta. A coldness raced through me. He was the devil. He had to be. At such depths, no other creature could survive. And only in the low trade of prison-building could a Ricky Tempesta flourish.

"Dim the lights, please." Now he stood framed by a backdrop of slides purporting to reveal the sundry scandalous glimpses of Sonny Hope's Trustless prison system. But the images seemed to close themselves around Tempesta in a grisly embrace. There he was, a con, just as I knew him. The coldness passed through me again. Was this intentional taunting, the way he cast himself against his natural environs and dared the gathering not to see or care? He'd done everything, short of wearing prison whites, to show them what Ricky Tempesta was all about. Hell yes, it was intentional, I decided, and with the dawning of this recognition I felt something stir in the cavity of my soul—something awaken, rise slowly to its feet and stretch the muscles that had slumbered all these years. Without a doubt, I could kill him.

". . . because you don't just gig one snake and lop its head off and pronounce Shepherdsville a Garden of Eden—no *no*! We would then be like the sower Christ speaks of, flinging his seeds that fall by the wayside or upon stony places. Wasted! No, it's good ground we seek, folks. And the proof that it can't be found in Shepherdsville is standing right here in front of you."

Tempesta fell silent for a beat. He struck a leering pose, and as his jagged face tilted into profile, I could see a small diamond stud winking from the lobe of his left ear. "For three years I bore witness. Three years, while incarcerated at the Hope Prison Farm for a crime I did not commit, while waiting for the Court of Criminal Appeals to declare me an innocent man as I knew they would—all that time, I heeded God's message to me. 'For that righteous man dwelling among them, in seeing and hearing, vexed his righteous soul from day to day with their unlawful deeds.' Like Lot from Sodom and Gomorrah, the Lord delivered me from the Texas Department of Criminal Retribution. But first, my friends—first, He gave me a mission. Next slide, please."

I thought Fitch and Sonny had prepared me for what came next. And yet I sat in childlike stupefaction as Tempesta, buoyed by his morbidly delighted audience, took the truth as I had personally witnessed it and plunged it headfirst into manure: "I held out crumbs, and they came crawling out of every rathole. *Whatever you want, boss.* Well!" and only at the back end of his glorious booming laugh did I detect the acrid gurgle of old. "It was a quite a test of my imagination. Lord, I had them bring me stereos and refrigerators and carpets and antique furniture—things I had no use for, particularly in a prison cell, but I'd ask for 'em anyway, just to see how much trouble the COs would go to for a few bucks under the table. Oh my! Folks, you should've seen them lugging that contraband into my cell! How they aimed to please! And then, poor Warden Grissom . . ."

A spasm of laughter overcame him. "It just tore him up to see his underlings doing better than he was." Tempesta cradled himself, tried on a look of anguish. "Folks, the Hope Prison Farm warden just spelled it out for me. *Money for girls.* That's what he said! I couldn't believe it! Man alive, where was Warden Grissom when I was a freshman in college? And it's all in my book, *Why We Need Trust,* which is for sale in the alcove—it's all there, how the warden had no earthly idea that the girls I was sending for were my cousins and my hometown friends, and that we'd just sit in the library and laugh the hours away . . . Since, after all, folks, it *was* a joke! But on you! On Texas!"

The slide projector was now extinguished, and aside from the obscure glow emitted by the lectern lamp, a brooding darkness hugged the room. Tempesta's voice rose sternly. "And nothing, nothing has changed. Where, you ask, is Mitch Grissom today? Why, he's got himself a cushy job at the TDCR! Because that's the way it's always been, my friends. The Texas prison system takes care of its own. That's why I'm not gonna stand here and criticize Director Hope as a person. He's a product of the system. He's rooted deep. He's gonna throw those wild seeds down upon the usual stony places. *But.* When Sonny Hope says, 'Hey, we can run prisons just like a business, too . . .'"

He pursed his lips as if to spit. "Why, that's like a damn scorpion saying, 'Well if you just wanted me to tickle you, why didn't you say so?'"

They banged their hands together as they laughed. "What a dick," came a voice right next to me.

I jumped. Sissy Shipman had taken the seat directly behind me. Stuffing her notepad into her purse, she said, "I don't even know why I bother carrying this with me. He's been using the same lines all year long. If I hear another pun on the word 'trust' I think I'll take a blowtorch to the place. So what brings you here, Coleman? Did your pal Sonny send you out here to spy on the opposition?"

I looked carefully at those grey button eyes to see if anything lurked beneath them besides the usual fatigued sarcasm. "I heard Tempesta was building a new town," I shrugged. "Guess I had to see it for myself."

"That's right," she remembered with a smirk. "You two were down on the farm together. Don't tell me you're hoping he'll offer you a job."

"Thinking about it," I smiled.

She sighed. "You are one weird dude, Coleman. Some people, you hand them a free ticket, and all they do is make a paper airplane out of it."

"Thanks for the write-up, by the way," I said. "It was nice."

"Yeah, we'll have to do it again sometime," she said as she snapped her purse shut and surveyed the crowded auditorium. "Look at them. If the Klan had ever figured out how to turn a profit, we'd all be wearing robes."

"You don't think Tempesta's made any good points?" I asked.

Sissy lowered her voice a notch. "He's made one good point," she corrected me. "All the problems in the TDCR are systemic. Reform at the bottom, reform at the top—attacking it on just one level won't do a thing. If you really want change, you've got to take the whole thing apart."

"So . . ."

"Oh, please. *Nobody wants change.* Least of all Tempesta. That piece of cloth around his neck doesn't look half as good as a noose would. *That's* the change I'd root for."

Her smile was both fetching and frigid. "Coleman," she then said, "if you hook up with Tempesta, then you're an even bigger idiot than I thought you were."

The expression on my face must have given something away. The spite left Sissy's face. She leaned towards me, saying into my ear, "Don't you know that he's—" But then her next words were lost to the applause as the lights went up and Ricky Tempesta thrust his forearm into the air and took in their approval with a cobra's smile. Dozens moved towards the stage, open hands and business cards extended. Four men in suits materialized and hastily formed a ring around Tempesta as he dismounted the stage and hitched up his jacket sleeve to consult his Rolex. I turned back to Sissy Shipman, but she had already left the building.

I waited by the exit door. From thirty yards away, over the din of his suitors, I could hear Tempesta's flurry of insincerities: "Absolutely! Oh, let's do it! Just give me a call and we'll set something up! I'd love that! Means the world to me! Terrific! Absolutely! God bless!" Each word like a cattle prod jabbed into the ribcage of the monster inside of me. I could do it now, I thought as my right hand fell into my pocket and squeezed the cold marble womb that held the switchblade. I could stick him like a pig, and then let his bruisers stomp me into the carpet. An instant later, the planet would be markedly better off. Him with the world at his feet, me at the feet of the world—and then, just like that, the both of us carcasses. Both of us a single stab away from eternity. My blood and his, gurgling in harmony. Why not now, after all? *Get it over with . . .*

Stepping towards the fray, my eyes fell on a man who wormed his way up to Tempesta and looped an arm around the latter's becollared neck. The man was outfitted in suspenders and a striped shirt. He put his lips to Tempesta's ear. As he began to whisper, his eyes darted about. The moment I realized that he was Wick Aspromonte, he recognized me as well.

Aspromonte jerked reflexively away from Tempesta. Contriving a smile, he called out, "Good to see you Hadrian call me and let's get a bite gotta run 'bye now!"

I saw Ricky Tempesta's expression freeze at the mention of my first name. His gaze ferreted through the entrepreneurs and lobbyists and other sycophants. The eyes narrowed as they found their target. It was a familiar gleam they cast. The look on his face said that I hadn't changed, either.

He pushed through his ring of bodyguards and held out a hand. "Brother Coleman," he said, half-chuckling. "I'd been wondering when I'd hear from you."

He had? I took his hand, remembering too late that Tempesta was one of those individuals who liked to squeeze until they heard something snap. Fighting off a wince, I said, "Well, you remember how hectic those first weeks are."

Still smiling, his jaw nonetheless tightened. "Sure," he said. "Sure.

Now that you mention it, someone told me how hectic you've been. Getting hectic with that big-legged girl over at the Hicks Unit. Beerbagger, or whatever her name is."

So this is how it would be, I thought. "Hah-hah-hah-hah-hah!" Tempesta then laughed. Slapping me on the chest with the back of his hand, he said, "Let's get a bite and catch up."

Sidelong he scanned the environs. "How about in Houston," he said. "We'll meet in my lawyer's office in an hour and a half. He's downtown. We'll walk to a place from there. Andy, give Coleman here one of your cards."

A balding man with a thin grey mustache handed me a business card. A. P. Whitfield was the name. They were both out the door before I remembered who had sold Sonny the riverhouse.

"I was glad to hear about you and that CO girl," Tempesta grinned, revealing a mouthful of well-marbled steak. "I couldn't remember if you'd gone punk."

In the comfort of the corner booth, with his goons seated a table away, he had shed all of his artifice to reveal the oilfield trash he'd always been. The linen napkin he had tucked into his cleric's collar was speckled with the food he sprayed about as he laughed. "Really," he giggled. "I honestly couldn't remember."

Looking down at my plate, I said, "I guess it would be hard, Ricky, remembering every single con who sucked your dick."

Leaning across the table, his face creased with awful glee, he continued, "Now, your good buddy Sonny, I believe he nailed that Beerbagger gal a few times himself."

I wasn't going to look up. "You'd have to ask him," I said.

"Oh, well," he snickered as he went back to his food, "I believe you know Sonny and I don't do much talking these days. How do you like it, by the way? Trust, Texas. It's got a ring to it, doesn't it?"

"I want to know more about the ring around your neck," I said.

"Oh, this?" He fingered the collar delicately. "Freshly ordained. I know I've been blessed. I'm just trying to give something back is all. Not that I'd expect someone like you to appreciate that concept."

"I remember that Bible you used to carry at the Hope Farm," I said. "That big King James version, with the hole you cut into it to stash your walking-around money."

"Just doing the Lord's work, Coleman." His laughter was toxic. "And it's only the beginning. It's gonna come. The legislature's gonna ratify it. I'm gonna turn Shepherdsville into a ghost town. And your boy Sonny's gonna be out on the street. You watch."

Sonny had fronted me the money for the suit I was wearing. Still, at this posh downtown Houston steakhouse, the waiters looked at me as if I had come in through the kitchen. They regarded Tempesta more appreciatively. He was their kind of clown, the kind that oozed cash. Gold cufflinks, wrist chain, tieclasp. Linen, Italian leather. Starch. Salon tan. A quart of thirty-weight in his hair. All those capped white teeth glittering when his grin split open the bottom half of his head like a gash. The cleric's collar only augmented his decadence.

"So he wants you to spy on me," he said. "That's why you were there, wasn't it?"

I summoned a disdainful chuckle. "Don't be a fool, Ricky," I said. "I'm sure he knows your speech by heart. There aren't any secrets."

I knew that would prompt a look.

"There's a world of secrets," I heard him say.

I shrugged, worked away at my steak.

"That was one sweet favor he did for you," said Tempesta. "Giving you your freedom."

Chewing, I said, "Nothing an appellate judge wouldn't do for you, Ricky."

He rubbed his stiletto chin. "You *were* smart, now that I think about it," he mused. "You played the angles pretty good."

"I was just another con, Ricky."

"Well." He considered this. "Maybe so. You never kissed my ass that I can remember. You never asked for nothing. Just hung out in the dog kennels." He cackled for awhile.

Then he leaned towards me. "But you saw it," he said. "Everybody had a hand out! Everybody! The people of the state of Texas, they shouldn't stand for it! See, that's why . . ." And Tempesta, poised on the edge of his seat, made to launch into the same speech I'd just heard or some variation, only to catch himself—though not to avoid repeating himself, which would never bother someone so self-adoring. It was the nature of his audience that stopped him short. I'd seen it, all right. Yes I had.

He jerked the napkin from his collar and tossed it onto his plate. "Why don't you tell me why you're here," he said.

I took a sip of water. "I could use work," I said.

"Hah!" The laugh invited stares from other tables. "Oh, come on, Coleman. Who do you think you're talking to? Quit lying and tell me what you want."

"I want a job." My voice was shaking. "I don't have any money. I've got a sister to take care of."

"That big-tittied girl who used to visit you at the farm? Her I'll take care of." His grin widened impossibly.

"I'm just asking for a chance," I said.

"A chance to do what, Coleman?" Tempesta folded his arms across his chest, hoisted up a thumbnail and picked at his teeth. His voice could not have been more condescending. "What would you do for me? What do you know *how* to do, anyway—other than run off? I could hire a beagle to do that."

His gravel-nosed, crescent-eyed face was close enough for me to gouge with the fork I was holding.

"Well? I'm waiting, Coleman. What would you do for me?"

I pushed myself out of the booth. "Eat shit," I mumbled, and tossed a fifty-dollar bill onto the table and wheeled to go.

"Hey! Don't you need this to feed your poor sister, Coleman?"

I shouldn't have turned. When I did, he crumpled my fifty and hurled it at me, and it hit me squarely on the nose. Tempesta's body-guards exploded with laughter. Otherwise the restaurant was stone silent. He had me. For now, he had me.

Tempesta's cufflink flashed like a shark's tooth as he pointed at me. "I don't know why the hell Digby bothered," he sneered. "Your life wasn't worth saving."

The words clanged against my ears. I restrained myself. *Not here. Not yet.*

Like the bum that I was, I bent to retrieve the wadded-up fifty, which was Sonny's anyway.

The phone was already ringing as I walked inside my parents' house.

"Give me the rundown, bubba," said Sonny.

"You didn't tell me he'd become a man of the cloth," I said.

"He's got a real glow about him, don't he? Piece of shit. What do you think of his little village?"

"There's not much to it."

"Oh, but the man's got a vision, let me tell you. Condos, a shopping mall, a movie theater—and the nation's first privately operated death row facility, just right down the jogging path. Jesus fucking Christ. Herrera guidelines? What Herrera guidelines? Might as well just dig a lion's pit and throw every con in it. I guess it *is* kind of funny."

His voice suggested otherwise. "Wick Aspromonte was cuddling up to him," I said.

"Oh, they all are. *All* of them. Like rats to Limburger. After all Sonny's done for—I mean, Wick Aspromonte wouldn't even be in business, he'd be scrubbing bedpans in Newark. Did I tell you? Aspromonte had a chain of adult bookstores up east, they were letting the underaged in. The state of New Jersey shut 'em down, got him on a morals charge. He had a record! And who got their prison boss Pip O'Malley to call in a favor to the governor—who got that little weasel a fucking pardon? And then set him up sweet with his first two minimum-security contracts right here in East Texas? And the dumb son of a bitch hires Tempesta as a developer, gets swindled by him, gets a few more contracts from Sonny . . ."

His voice became thin. "I mean, what *is* it? No matter what I do *for* them, no matter what he does *to* them . . . Goddamn, I never seen so many whores!"

Then: "Well. Sonny won't forget. Did he see you there?"

"We had lunch," I said.

"Wh—Damn. Did, did . . ."

"Relax, Sonny." I closed my eyes. "It'll happen soon."

"How soon?"

"The next day or two."

He sighed. "Lovely. I got another call. Talk to you." The line went dead.

I hung up the phone, turned, and noticed then that Mimi was curled up on the couch. She wore jeans and a black bra, and her mouth was slightly open.

"Hey," I called out. "You dead or alive?"

She groaned and shifted to face me, though her eyes remained closed. "Dead," she said. "Was that Sonny?"

"No."

Mimi lifted her head from the pillow, which had reddened and wrinkled her cheeks. Her curls swung wildly about her face. "What's wrong?" she asked.

"Nothing." I rubbed my eyes. "Both of us had better get jobs soon."

"Let's go get a drink first," Mimi purred.

I strolled over to the couch. "Make room," I said, and backhanded her rear a good one.

"Aaagh!" she shrieked. "They should've given you the chair, you're so mean."

Her legs curled up to accommodate me on the couch, which was warm from her body. Holding the pillow over her breasts, Mimi moved her mouth all around her apple face as she assessed her condition. Then she settled back and emitted a drowsy squeal. Such an adorable wreck, my sister. I felt stabs of regret from all sides. Already I'd missed too much of her, had stained what should have been a rosy little life for Mimi. And now, with a chance to put things right, I had matters all set to blacken her world again. It wasn't in her to blame me for the curse I'd put on every Coleman. But for what would come next, even Mimi would find it impossible to forgive me. Too late now, however. I was already there.

"Your kids," I said. "Jesus, what an uncle I am. I don't remember their names."

"Whitney, Tabitha and Circe," she recited.

Circe. God. "Where are they now?"

"Over at Britt and Tanya's."

"Those the titty dancers?"

"Oh, now, they're real sweet. And they love my little girls. So will you. I thought I'd bring 'em down here this weekend . . ."

She eyed me hopefully. "Wait a few more days," I said. "It's just . . . it's not them. I just need to straighten things out."

Mimi sat up and stretched her legs across my lap. Her voice was dreamy and sad. "Do you miss the Doc?" she asked.

The question seemed to come from another world entirely—one I couldn't possibly face. "I don't even really remember him," I said.

Her face paled for a moment. Then she laughed. "You liar," Mimi exclaimed, and chunked her pillow at me. With an emphatic bounce of her breasts, she sprang to her feet. "First round's on you."

From somewhere down the hall, she added: "Second round, too!"

We drove into town in her turquoise Geo. My sister switched the radio channels with one hand as she steered with the other. She seemed to know the lyrics of every song. I noticed that the needle on her gas gauge was just grazing E.

"Pull over and I'll fill it up," I said.

She traced my stare. "Oh, that? Don't worry. It's broken."

"Great."

"Tomorrow," she pledged. "I swear, I'll look for work tomorrow. Maybe we'll run into Sissy. She told me she'd see if the *Chronicle* had anything."

Mimi jabbed me in the stomach with a long-nailed finger. "I think Sissy likes you," she teased.

"Shit. Sissy Shipman doesn't know how to like," I said. "She'd eat her young."

"Bonnie says you're good in the sack." She giggled.

"I don't want to hear about it." The thought of Bonnie Bierbauer made me suddenly ill.

"Did you have any girlfriends?" Mimi then asked. "When you were—you know. When you were hiding out."

Only because she asked the question so innocently did I manage to restrain my anger. "No," I said under my breath.

"Really? Why not?"

"Because I couldn't fucking afford to get close to anyone, Mimi. Jesus."

"Damn, what a grouch," she remarked lightheartedly as she returned to the radio dial. She found a Top Forty station and cranked it up so as to expunge the mood I'd set. Then she flashed me the toothiest of grins. I patted her on her thigh. She took my hand and squeezed it. Sweet Mimi.

"Look," she said, gazing up at the sparkling office tower at the entrance to town. "That's where Sonny works, isn't it? Maybe he could get me a job. Don't you think I'd make a good guard?"

I tried to let the notion pass. But it wouldn't. "Just stay away from Sonny," I snapped. "Okay? If that's not too much to ask."

Mimi's mouth fell open in surprise. "I thought you liked Sonny," she said.

"I do like him." I pulled my hand away from hers and flipped off the radio. "I just think you ought to stay away from him."

"Well," she laughed nervously, "too late for that. I saw him last night."

"You *what*?"

"Hadrian, now don't get all worked up, we just had a few drinks and cruised around for awhile, it wasn't—"

"Stop the car," I ordered.

"Hadrian, we didn't screw, if that's what—"

"Pull over or I'll jump out!"

When I got out of the car, I leaned back through the passenger window to face my sister, who was crying. "Mimi," I said emphatically, "you are playing way, way out of your league."

They were angry tears. "Oh, is your league any better?" she yelled back at me. "Besides, I thought I was doing you a favor!"

She was sobbing, but I laughed anyway. "Doing me a favor? What the hell are you talking about?"

"Oh my God!" she wailed incredulously. "You really think I'm dumb, don't you? You think I don't remember that book you had Mama buy you for your birthday—the one about her family . . . The way you couldn't take your eyes off her this past Sunday . . . You just think all that stuff goes right past me, don't you?"

Her glare, wet though it was, was triumphant. "That's ancient history," I shouted back, "and goddammit Mimi, they're married, and you have no right—"

"Stop it!" she shrieked. Her entire body was shaking. "Just stop it!"

Mimi set her head against the steering wheel. Cars whizzed by us. I became aware of the tall shadow off to our west. I wondered if Sonny could see us down here, fighting over him.

Her voice was steady now. "God," she muttered. She turned her head slowly my way. "What did you do all those years, anyway? Don't you know the first thing about . . . about *yourself*?"

"Oh, fuck you," I snarled, and she shot me the finger and I stepped back as she punched the accelerator. I didn't watch her go, but I could hear the moan of her engine fade off into the south, towards the bars near campus.

I looked up at the office tower.

"Leave me alone," I whispered.

At The Guilty Dog I sat alone on a barstool, my back to the karaoke machine and to the tortured warblings of Scotty Folger. Tonight I would rejoin my charted path. But not just now. I let my mind pull away from its hinges and muddle ablur through a deepening, darkening universe. All meaning had become elusive. I didn't even know why

I was here in Shepherdsville. I put the question to my memory. Eyes shut tightly, I began to conjure up a rippling vision of mulecart roads—and then of Del Sparks's ranch, of the icehouse on Bernadette Creek . . . That was the way in. The same way I'd taken out. And why was that . . . And why had I run, wouldn't it all be different if I hadn't . . . Wexler and his shank: it was the only moment that seemed reliable to me, because it was random, which was the way things were, the way things happened every day down on the farm. Some mean old con in the throes of spiteful rage. And now: had I become him? Was there any more to me than a staggering lunge at someone else's heart? . . . I'd heard Digby's yelp of warning, and I turned just in time. After that, even Wexler, gulping through his blood on the cold floor of my cell, knew better than I how I'd turned his blade against him. "Just get a move on," Digby had said as he snatched the sheets from my bed and began mopping up the blood. "*Go.*" And I did, though nobody told me to keep going—Digby, I knew, had only meant, "Go to your work, go to the kennel, just go away from *here*," because no one had ever escaped the Hope Farm and absolutely no one made an attempt without months of planning. Yet even then, I knew why I had to keep running: fifteen years earlier, it was me left behind with the blood, and I'd been wading in it ever since—though it can be no other way for the killer, all this recoiling from the bloodshed being a fool's pursuit . . .

There. That was something I'd learned, I thought dismally. I wore their blood, Wexler's and Judge Castlebury's, just as I'd worn a number on my back. The awareness of this had snuck up on me, as a killer would. I'd awakened to it some time after Sonny and Jill announced their engagement. All of Shepherdsville, on both sides of the walls, knew me as a murderer. Never mind the life in question, and whether the world was better off without it. Never mind the criminals in my ranks who had committed acts far more ghoulish than any I could contemplate. My act, the taking of a human life, was an affront to God. It was a usurpation of divine ordering. And it would put me in the ranks of the most unholy, forevermore.

Though in the meantime, the distinction was not without its privileges. Even at the Creel Unit, when I must've looked like the juiciest young lollipop to the hard cons, they kept their distance. And they always would—all of them but Wexler, and see what happened? He fucked with a killer, God rest his scabrous soul. And now Tempesta was doing the same. Sonny had been so right. The way he'd mocked me . . . How swift, how sure my taking of Ricky Tempesta's life would be. Like black magic, this native gift. And how could such a trait possibly disappear? How could it possibly be traded in, with one's prison whites, at Inmate Processing, in exchange for fifty bucks and a bus ticket? Who would be crazy enough to think you could run from it?

But, I thought: *Mimi, what had she said* . . . My darling disaster of a sister, from whom I'd never learned a thing—why did her words pierce so surely: *Don't you know the first thing about yourself?* My mind and stomach throbbed in unison. Could she be right about all this? Could it be that when in my daydreams I stood before a river of red and beheld my reflection—was it not mine after all, but rather the reflection of someone or something else, standing in between?

"Damn it," I snapped quietly, and reached for my beer mug. I sipped slowly, felt the liquid slither down me. Damn it, I'd heard something. That's what was eating at me. I'd heard a clue. Maybe even the answer outright . . .

"So tell me, Coleman," came a voice.

I jerked up from the bar. Sheriff Bo Worley pushed at my shoulder to sit me back down. He took the stool next to mine and placed his Resistol on the bar. Then he rubbed the grease off of his beak-like nose with two calloused fingers, and wiped whatever he'd come up with on the back of his pants. With the same hand, he adjusted the toothpick in his mouth. Not for a second did his keen stare deviate.

"Tell me," he repeated. "Save us both the fuss. Who you gonna kill next?"

It was as if he'd been crouched inside my thoughts all this time.

"Just killing time, Sheriff," I finally said.

Worley turned a hair to his left and spat out some gristle from his toothpick. "You ain't even hiding it," he remarked. "Ain't been looking for work. Ain't been to church. Ain't changed your ways one lick. Just getting drunk in a prison bar like you was already wishing to be back inside."

Working up a smile, I said, "You look like you could use a drink yourself," and foolishly I reached for my wallet.

"Not with you I don't." He leaned towards me. I could see the network of corpuscles and gouged pores in the crevices of his leathery face.

"I want to know," he repeated intently, "who you are gonna kill."

My face burned. His intensified. Slowly he let loose a smile. If I could have spoken anything just then, the name "Ricky Tempesta" would surely have flopped out.

But another was heard from. "We beg your indulgence, upright sirs, but Proprietor Folger has enlisted our aid in promulgating a thematic revolution here at The Guilty Dog. It's Barbershop Quartet night, we've decided, and we wondered if you two songbirds could be prevailed upon."

Aynsley Reeves demonstrated just how insulting a grin could be. I felt then and there like kissing each one of his horse's teeth.

The sheriff glared at the TDCR general counsel. "You need to get on, Reeves," said Worley. "We were talking."

"Instead of singing!" reproached Aynsley, his grin only wider now. "And that's terribly insular, a positively esoterrifying state of—"

"Just can it, will you?" yelled Worley, loudly enough to stifle Scotty Folger's karaoke croonings. The sheriff slid off of his barstool and positioned himself perhaps two inches away from Aynsley Reeves, who raised his eyebrows and clenched his jaws in mock terror.

"Jesus Christ, look at you," said the sheriff. His upper lip curled. "You're as pathetic as your old man."

"Ouch!" yipped the general counsel, and somehow he dared to look straight up at Worley—and with an expression that would inflame a prison chaplain. "Double-ouch! Was that verbal haymaker intended to kill our whole family? All done very smoothly, we must say, Sheriff Worley, well within the strictures of the penal code, though our own First Amendment protections—wait, don't go away mad, Sheriff!"

With a rough swooping motion that managed to knock over my beer mug, Bo Worley swiped his Resistol off the bar and stomped his way out the door.

Aynsley Reeves blinked his eyes several times. "Is this stool occupied?" he asked.

"It's yours for life," I assured him, and thereby resigned myself to Aynsley's dronings. I sank into an altogether different stupor, blurry and for the most part agreeable. Meanwhile, the general counsel rattled on about inmate writ writers and the relative merits of in-cell segregation, the latest gang tattoos, a CO whose sex change had prompted new uniform guidelines, Sissy Shipman's latest Open

Records Act request and the various methods of subverting it . . .
It was all karaoke to me. At a certain point, I noticed Cal Fitch easing his way in. He saw us as well, but took his time performing the
usual back-slapping and dirty-joke-swapping. When he finally did
make it to the bar, the chief of Inmate Processing tossed me a genial
but perfunctory hello and then turned to Aynsley. For five minutes
they engaged in quiet consultation. When the general counsel said,
"We may well have a copy of that on our person" and reached down by
his feet for his satchel, Fitch turned towards the bar as if to fetch
another drink.

"Come by my office in a half-hour," was all he said.

Fitch leaned against the desktop, arms drawn against his squatty chest.
His head was cocked to one side.

"Do you have the slightest idea what you're doing?"

He knew about my lunch with Tempesta. I didn't have to ask. Nor
did I have to answer his question.

"Jesus, youngun," he said gently. It was a hurt smile he wore.
"You're fixing to waste a good pardon. Aren't you."

Then he held up his hands. "*I don't want to know,*" he said, and those
long, thin lips arranged themselves into an arc of elaborate disappointment. Overhead, the fluorescent lights of his cramped office room
hummed like an insipid mechanical brain. I sat down heavily in a large
chair. The moment I did, it creaked miserably. I whirled around,
looked at it for the first time.

"I'll be damned," I said. "Do you know how many millions of times
I dusted this old chair?"

Fitch nodded. "Thunderball let me have it the day he got canned,"
he said. "Told me, 'Well, hell, Calvin, it ain't gonna go with anything
you have.' And I told him, 'That's right, Thunderball. It's gonna stand
alone.' I don't need to tell you how he reacted to that."

I'd never sat in it before, I realized.

Fitch let his hands fall to the desktop. "Sissy Shipman called me
today," he said. "She's on to the land connection between Tempesta
and Sonny, though she doesn't know it yet. But she took the first big
step. She's linked him to that lawyer, A. P. Whitfield."

My stomach turned. "How did she do that?" I asked.

"She followed you from Trust to Whitfield's office in Houston."

I nodded and felt the liquor surge towards my throat.

He shrugged, squinched his eyes by way of calculation. "It could take a day, a week or a month. She might find other land deals first. Maybe with bigger fish than Sonny. Or she might go straight to the Trust land deed. Or to the riverhouse. She wanted my help. I gave her a number in Houston. That'll move her away from the county court-house records here. For how long, I don't know."

I said nothing.

"Two little words," he said, quietly but firmly. "Think again."

I shook my head. "It's not that simple."

"Hey. You want to know what's simple? Six digits on your backside. Doesn't get any simpler than that."

He held open the door for me, then closed it behind me.

That evening, while Mimi was still out, Bonnie Bierbauer came over. She followed me into the living room in her grey CO uniform, and before she could sit down, I told her we wouldn't be seeing each other anymore. She demanded reasons. I didn't give her any to speak of. She began to cry, and then she took a few swings at me and called me all the usual names. A half-hour later, I was alone again.

Then I went driving.

I veered south from downtown, skirting the courthouse and the buildings of red brick, and for the first time since my return, I idled down the avenues. On a weeknight such as this, the town's historic homes seemed bereft in every sense of the word, left to slouch darkly under the magnolias until the first dawn putterings of the domestic servants. Virtually all of the homes had been given a makeover since I'd last seen them twenty-three years ago: walls kicked out, garages expanded, pool rooms and wet bars and hot tubs added, exteriors brightened, the yards littered with deck chairs and grills and satellite dishes; and some houses had simply been leveled and replaced with structures plucked straight from a catalog out Midwest. I advanced down the streets at a respectable crawl. Gone the Whittingtons, the McMillans, the Ellises, the Sandersons, the Gants, and almost all Estelles. An avenue for each of the first six families. How sweet and boundless Shepherdsville must have seemed to them back then, before the walls came up and the jailers and the bureaucrats rushed in, dragging the cons behind them. I couldn't imagine such a place—nor imagine, as far as my life went, how it could have made a damn bit of difference. Or so Bo Worley would've been happy to remind me, I figured as I crept along in my Impala. Some are made, others are born. The sheriff had been unwavering in his belief that I fell in the second category. Certainly I'd done nothing this evening to convince him otherwise. And if he had it right about me being a crook from the cradle, then perhaps it was just as well that I'd never drawn a breath in an unsullied Shepherdsville.

Still, I thought, I would've liked to have seen it. Instead, there remained a solitary vestige to ponder. I took the cross street and then turned onto Estelle Avenue.

It had not been my plan to stop. But from the moment the property fell into my view, I could feel the years shed themselves away. The figure who slipped out of the car and onto that imposing street was fourteen again, skittish and bewitched, but treading ever closer. The sooty white manor, moss-bearded and jacketed with ivory, peered out at the insignificant figure below from the twin lids of the second-story balconies. It rested there, upon that three-acre swamp of ageless tupelos and magnolias, much like its occupant, every day adding to its atrophy. But it had a real life, unlike all the others down the way. It bared its history, and it could tell stories. I stood there at the curb, hands still at my side. The boy had known all he needed to know about the Estelle house—namely, that it was a magnificent but lonely house, placed there to be out of place, and all the more beautiful for its splendid isolation and mortality. Before I truly understood what there was to love about the Estelle girl, I loved the Estelle place. And in my passion for it, I had come to believe that she and I might have a chance, somehow or other.

I didn't blame the house. It hadn't failed me—more likely the other way around. I fell prisoner to the view of the second-story window on the far right. Twenty-three years ago, there would've been one light, beside her pillow; and though across the lawn and through the silk curtain the eyes could make out only the fibrous outline of a book and the narrow hand that turned its pages, the heart could see her face in full. It could see the face, speak to the face. It could almost make the face speak back. Something crumbled like a sand castle in my chest, and a sigh heaved itself out. In my cell, I'd always managed to forget how desperate I used to feel, standing here among the great shadows of Estelle Avenue. Only now did it occur to me that the days of promise were the most excruciating of all.

But I knew I would take those days again.

There was a light on downstairs, near where the den would be. I figured that Professor Estelle was up reading or muttering to himself. Someone had made mention to me of his poor health. Aynsley or Sonny, maybe, but not Jill. We'd scarcely spoken since my return. Maybe twenty words passed between us at Sunday brunch. She'd been moody that day, as had I. The Trust land had been hers until Sonny made the swap for the riverhouse. Did she know Tempesta had been involved? Or perhaps she knew Sonny had been cheating on her. More likely she'd just gotten tired of his bombast, or of stepping on a con or a CO every time she turned around, or of hearing the sallyport gates slam at dinnertime and obscenities sail over the wall to commence the morning . . .

"Hadrian? Is that you?"

My heart rocketed. From the driveway, Tobias Estelle padded towards the front lawn in his nightrobe and his loafers. Fixing his lenses upon his face, he exclaimed, "Why, it *is* you. I knew you were back, of course. How are you, son?"

He offered his hand, perfectly unbothered by my unexplained presence here on the edge of his property. As we shook, I noticed that in his other hand he held a large book, but its title had been worn away. I also noticed that his fingers trembled badly and his legs were as thin as my arms. "You look good," I said.

"Oh," he demurred, but the remark pleased him. "Do come inside. I was just about to have a bowl of lime sherbet. It's Blue Bell."

The invitation, so harmless and blasé, brought a tearless sob to my throat. Back I withdrew. For tonight was the night, the night of the end.

"Actually, I was just on my way to see someone," I said.

The professor nodded slowly, already detached from the invitation he'd tendered. "Jill's gone off again," he said. "I can't remember where."

"New York, I think Sonny told me."

"That sounds right."

He looked up at me, and I saw that his eyes welled with an aging father's sorrow. "You know," he said, "Jill has always loved to travel. New York, London, Rome, Buenos Aires. But this year, she's been gone almost every other week."

He searched my face. "Well," I stammered, "like you said, she's always loved—"

"It's no longer for the love of travel, Hadrian. It's for the hatred of something else."

We must have looked at each other that way for a solid minute. It struck me how close I felt to this man, and how confidentially he spoke with me, when we'd only conversed twice in our lives.

"I didn't want to be right, you know," he then said, finally looking away, off into the darkness of his great unkempt lawn. "A father wants happiness for his daughter. Being right . . ." He winced and shook his head. "It means nothing."

Bitterness seeped into his voice, though he managed a frustrated smile. "I've asked her why they won't have children," he said. "She always would tell me, 'Sonny's all the child I can handle.'"

He shook his head at the ground. "That was never funny," he said. "A forty-year-old man acting like a little boy. I never saw the humor in it."

"I remember," I said.

He frowned briefly. Then his eyes lit up. "Ah yes," he muttered. "On the porch at the director's mansion. The day we all became one big, happy family."

A dry laugh. "That rabid mongrel of a man. Talking up the integrity of his chubby-cheeked pup. Was he the only poor idiot in town who didn't think his son would be his downfall? He never for a second fooled me."

There was an embarrassed silence before he added, "I guess he fooled my daughter. Though not any longer. See, that's why she won't have children! It's not because he's immature! It's because she knows"—and now his teeth were gritted—"that her baby would have a father who would be more than willing to sacrifice his family to get what he wants!"

"Not just family," I heard myself say.

He looked at me, momentarily startled. "No," he then said. "I imagine not."

There was something about this conversation that was humiliating to us both. Eventually I cleared my throat and said, "Well, I'd better head on."

"You loved my daughter once," said Professor Estelle, his eyes gleaming.

I stared down the avenue. "I shouldn't have told you," I said.

"Did you think it offended me?"

"Goodnight, sir."

He gave me a pat on the shoulder with his heavy book. "You still love her," he smiled, a little strangely. "And I'm still not offended. This is Shepherdsville, after all."

He drew his robe around him and shuffled back to his sanctuary.

West of town, the roads were new and narrow and deer flashed across them and vanished over hills of freshly mown grass. The houses themselves were built out of a sparkling hill country limestone, but had the swooping appearance of ski lodges. Nothing out here was more than five years old. Still, the cool white stone wobbled eerily in my headlights like ghost missions from another time and place.

The address Sonny had given me to Ricky Tempesta's house led me to the western edge of the fledgling neighborhoods, where a private drive dead-ended a mile or two outside of the Shepherdsville city limits. From the road, only the driveway was visible, and so I left my car at the curb and walked. At the edge of the driveway I noticed that the property was fenced, but that the security gate was swung open. I stood there for a moment, staring at the combination pad and wrestling with the riddle. Probably Tempesta had guests but hadn't entrusted them with the passcode. I stepped through.

The house was just like the others except that there was more of it. Every room was lit. I crunched slowly along the gravel driveway. Two cars were parked at the edge of the front porch. The black Jaguar I guessed to be Tempesta's. The other, a two-door Mazda, was a mystery. I crouched behind a tree a few feet away from the driveway and viewed the ex-con's spread. The house was brand new, despicably large, half-obscured by transplanted bluejack oaks, sweetgums, white ash and even palms, lending the property the suggestion of a craggy old manse inseparable from nature's bosom. Ah, what money could buy . . . My knees in Tempesta's well-combed dirt, I thought about our lunch: the way he chomped slavishly at his food, the glint of his pimp cufflinks, that perverse sparkle in his eye when I groveled for a handout from a man I wanted to get close to for the express purpose of murdering him . . . He'd set me off, and I had spent the rest of the day simmering coolly, resigned to our new fates, his and mine.

So. Tonight. I took a deep breath, the better to plunge into an airless black. I looked down as my hands, moist with sweat at first, hardened with a chill that was not a chill of fear. The clamminess rose up my arms, down my chest. Just as suddenly, warm ripples overtook me, and then I was fine. Taut, composed. Some part of me stepped away to look at the rest. What it saw was a shadowy diamond, unblemished in its state of malice. When I looked up, obeying some unaccountable urge to locate the moon in the sky, my eyes went right to it—a metallic sliver tonight, poised like a sickle over its prey.

When I turned my attention back to Tempesta's house, I felt something desert me. It was my life, or everything that had tried in vain to touch and turn my life. *No need to say goodbye,* came some brittle voice within me. *No need to bother. That was their mistake, bothering about me.* Then, almost in panic: *Don't think of them, forget them, no names here, we are in a nameless territory, forget everything* . . . Another deep breath of the piney air. Now he and I were one: killer and killer, both hellbound, not a victim between us. We would both go down—only I would enjoy a few more minutes spent dumbly pondering his guts jiggling at my feet. A good deed? Someone might think so. I wasn't fit to judge. I was only fit to act. And as I reached back to my back pocket, I tried the sound of it in an acrid whisper:

"Murderer. Murderer."

I pulled out the switchblade. It had been with me for years now, but I couldn't remember where or how I came upon it, and now I didn't even want to look at it. Irrelevant, but for its moment. And maybe even not for that. The key was me. Me and the ugliness that I *knew*, better than I could know anything, would come storming out the moment I got close. Like out there in the blueberry fields. Where I was baptized in purple quicksand . . . My temples pounded, and I noticed that my tongue was as dry as shoe leather. Something trembled up my body. Doubt. *Get out, you have no place here* . . . I willed the name to the surface. *Tempesta.* The fluttering dissolved into a joyful madness. Oh, and it would be a pleasure, to take him as he would take me or anyone else in the wrong place at the wrong time. As I would. While I was out at the dog kennels, he was shuffling hookers in and out of the library. But he knew it just like I did: we were no more different than any two wild dogs in a pack, and if the urge hit either of us, we would lunge, and our jaws were no different, our twisting bodies indistinguishable. What fool would bother to sort us out . . .

I took the first step. Then the front door opened.

Tempesta stood in the doorway, staring at the back of Sissy Shipman as she uttered a clipped "Good night" and walked towards the Mazda. Instantly the night seemed to change colors, and I felt the switchblade handle go wet against my palm. Sissy's face was careworn, missing its usual cutting bemusement. The host, dressed in jeans and a white dress shirt and framed extravagantly between the darkness and the light, was smiling all too sweetly, and he unfolded his arms long enough to fling a casual wave as she put it in gear. He disappeared behind the front door just as she idled past me. I could see her holding up something to her face. Maybe it was a hand mirror, but I didn't think so. She was gone before I could tell for sure.

When I looked back at the house, I saw that Tempesta was staring through a front window. The curl of his right arm told me he was holding something as well. He stood that way for maybe half a minute, utterly frozen.

Then, as if spring-loaded, he whirled violently, and whatever he held in his hand he threw against a wall. I heard the object shatter, the voice bellow out a curse, and then the house was silent once more. A moment later, the front lights were extinguished one by one.

As I scrambled down the driveway, it came to me. A tape recorder. That's what Sissy Shipman was holding up to her face. She'd come away with something Tempesta didn't want to give up. And this would have some bearing on Sonny, and on me. And while I was mulling this over, I suddenly remembered my car. She would have seen it on her way out.

With nausea and horror I confronted it, the pathetic spectacle of my Impala, which she'd already tailed once—this time sticking out halfway into the road, yoo-hooing the whole goddamned planet. I fell against it and banged my fist hard on the hood. "Goddamn you!" I yelled, just once aloud, but it echoed mercilessly within me: *Goddamn*

*how worthless you are, is there nothing you can't ruin you worthless piece of
shit . . .*

And there, while prostrated against my raggedy Impala in the
throes of self-disgust, my ears were treated to the unlikeliest noise. It
was laughter. Mine. Laughter that had been coming for days now.
Laughter granted to me by no less an authority than the governor of
the state of Texas. But Shepherdsville and Sonny had choked it off,
until now. Now it poured out like wild honey. I could not feel myself. I
was weightless. I was nowhere.

My God, I was free.

Mimi was home when I returned. I peered into her bedroom. She was
curled up alone, with the blankets kicked away to ward off the heat of
the evening.

When I sat down on her mattress, the only part of her that moved
was her mouth. "Go away," she mumbled.

"I'm sorry," I whispered.

She smiled and said nothing else, but the smile was enough. I called
it a night.

Despite what had transpired yesterday, Cecilia Shipman's byline did
not appear in the *Chronicle* the next morning. There was no mention of
Tempesta, none of Sonny or even of his prisons. I examined every
page, top to bottom. I checked the page numbers to make sure I hadn't
received a defective edition. I flipped to the front, double-checked the
date, the year, the name of the paper. Finally, I pulled out the sports
section.

It was a Saturday. I sat at the kitchen table in my boxer shorts and
my T-shirt, drinking coffee and catching up on the baseball scores.
With a daffy sort of amazement I considered this normal state to which
one could return so readily, even from so great a distance. Now and
then I would eye the telephone. Any minute now it would ring, I knew.
I had no idea what to tell Sonny. The truth—that I'd been spotted
twice by Sissy in Tempesta's vicinity, unwittingly leading her towards
the land deals while at the same time drawing attention to myself as
someone with some kind of sinister interest in the ex-con—was so cat-

astrophic that I wasn't even sure he'd believe it. Instead of getting Sonny out of trouble, I'd dug him an even deeper hole.

And as for myself . . . It was possible that Tempesta, so as to deflect further injury, had informed Sissy that he'd heard straight from Digby that I was in fact Wexler's killer. Yet the truth, even if Tempesta was to be believed, was not so damning. I'd killed out of self-defense. I hadn't asked Sonny or Digby or anyone else to lie on my behalf. I'd done nothing wrong. And regardless, I'd been absolved by the governor. If Bo Worley wanted to dredge up some new charge against me—well, it wasn't as if he wasn't already trying. Maybe the sheriff would find something. The law had a way of finding things. But Worley wouldn't find Tempesta's blood—not on me, anyway.

"And why, you stupid shit, did you not figure all this out beforehand," I sighed as I tossed the sports page onto the table.

"Figure out what?" came Mimi's groggy voice from down the hall. She flushed the toilet, then stumbled into view, yawning, eyes swollen nearly shut. The cotton short-sleeved shirt she wore was the one I'd left on the bathroom floor last night.

Mimi plopped heavily into a chair and laid her head on the breakfast table. I got up and poured her a cup of coffee, set it down an inch away from her nose. "Where'd you end up last night?" I asked.

She reached out, gathered up the newspaper and made a pillow out of it. "Well," she mumbled, "I met some cute criminology major over at the Grizzly Grille. But his girlfriend showed up and she tried to bite me, and then when he wouldn't leave with her she tried to set the whole place on fire. They caught her lighting up a couple rolls of toilet paper. I think she was one of Kirby Morris's daughters. Some prison brat. So I went over to The Guilty Dog and sang karaoke 'til it closed. Scotty Folger said I just missed you."

My sister peered up at me with one open eye. "Bonnie was there. She said you dumped her."

I tried to smile. "Was she mad?" I asked. "Your coffee's getting cold."

Mimi hoisted herself up into a sitting position. "She felt a little better," she said, "after I told her what an asshole you were."

"I knew I could count on you."

My attention wandered to our surroundings: the veterinary science journals still stacked on the bookshelves, the idiotic hunting-motif upholstered armchair, the television our mother had put to overuse after he'd died. Even the coffee smelled like him.

"I do miss him," I said.

Mimi was sitting up now, watching me. "I do," I said. "I miss not seeing him over there in that chair."

But upon imagining it—our father here among us, appraising his flesh and blood—my voice quavered with my heart as I added, "But I'm glad he's missed seeing me. Lord, I'm glad. It would've been too much for him. It would've drove a stake through his heart. No, seriously," and my words hurried on, because Mimi had opened her mouth to protest, "think what it'd be like if he was alive right now. He'd've been up at six. And at ten, his thirty-eight-year-old son, a jobless ex-felon, straggles out of bed. And at eleven, his daughter, who's been through four marriages and—"

"Five, but I—"

"Five marriages, and her kids are in the care of a couple of bisexual strippers, and what I'm saying Mimi is that he would hate the sight of us! He would hate it! Don't you think?"

Her eyes were bulging. "You are so full of shit," she said, and laughed with disbelief. "Doc would've loved to be sitting right here with his grown children, drinking coffee. *At any hour.*"

I tried to picture it. "But don't you—"

"Big deal, Hadrian," she said, exasperated though still smiling. "So he might've been a little disappointed. Big deal. Doc was a tightass. He just was. I mean, *everything* disappointed him."

Her words had such clarity. I could see him now. "It's true," I admitted. "No one could meet his standards. He saw failure everywhere he looked. Even in himself. Especially in himself. The way he raised us . . ."

Again the sourness crept in. "And that's why I'm glad he wasn't around to see how I royally screwed up my life," I said quietly. "God. It would've absolutely killed him."

I went back to my coffee and reached over for the paper when Mimi suddenly swept it off the table. I looked up. Her milky face was flared with hot pink.

"Would've killed him?" she hollered. "What planet are you on? What do you *mean*, would've killed him? Hadrian, you knucklehead! He already beat you to it! He worried his damn heart to death! You didn't do that to him, and I didn't do that to him! Hadrian, you were right there when the coroner said it! 'A heart attack waiting to happen!' He said it plain as day!"

Her pudgy fingers flew forward and slapped me over the top of my head. "Look at you!" she said, not quite laughing and not quite crying. "You are digging people up from the grave so they can help you hate yourself even more! And you think you're the reason why I'm such a fuck-up, don't you! Don't you!"

When I didn't say anything, when it became clear that I couldn't even look at her, she cracked me over the head again. "Well, I like the way I am! It's the way I want to be! Not like Bonnie or Sissy or Jill or any other woman in town! I'd rather be me than all of them! I wouldn't change a thing—not even having a brother who pisses me off so much because he thinks he's the root of all evil and he's made my life a living hell and—*arrgghh*!" and she smacked me one more time.

"Will you cut that out?" I said, but now I was grinning feebly.

Mimi let out another feminine snarl, pushed her chair away from the table and grumpily folded her arms. "You know," she said, "all my life in Shepherdsville, I'd hear people laugh about how there wasn't one guilty soul in the prisons—that all of those convicts, to hear them talk, were just innocent as lambs, never did a damn thing wrong, and they had no business being punished for something they never did."

She threw up her hands in despair. "*What happened to you?*" she demanded. "I mean, shit, Hadrian! You killed some pervert who would've killed you! You *are* innocent! Why don't you just . . . just *say* so, just once . . ."

Mimi's face went to blubber, and she sobbed. I sat and marveled. Then she reached out again, but not to hit me. Her hand fell gently on top of my head.

"All that time, you were innocent," she murmured, sniffing. "And look. It made your hair go grey."

I spent the day as I imagined Doc Coleman would have: cutting and edging the lawn, sweeping the porch, spraying the film of deceased lovebugs off of the windows with the water hose. The cars that drove past slowed at the sight of me. When they stared, I waved, and usually they waved back.

Later in the afternoon I unlocked the old vet clinic, which our mother had since used for storage. Nearly a quarter-century later, I believed I could still smell the horses, cattle and blue ticks. I sat on the examining table, legs dangling, and I stared at the boxes. They were crammed, I knew, with every sock and toothbrush that Doc Coleman had ever owned.

Another day, I decided. I was doing well just to be here, suspended among the remnants of his world. So immortal, it all seemed back then. And now in boxes.

My poor dad, came the thought, and tears with it.

At about five-thirty, the telephone rang. The voice on the other end said, "Whatcha know, bubba?"

But before I could begin to answer, Sonny said, "Man, you know what? I been up in this sweatbox all day, haggling with the damn privateers, negotiating cost-per-bed, walking 'em through the Herrera guidelines, doing the site-selection dance, and boy howdy I am plumb sick of working from Can 'til Can't. What I could sure use is a king-sized drunk. Just that. And not one word about you know who or you know what. Now son, can you handle that?"

He picked me up an hour later. The Sonny behind the wheel was half-ripped on Scotch, giggling, untethered. He wore a white pullover and jeans that in an earlier year might have fit well, and squeezing his blonde head was a Houston Astros baseball cap—not turned backwards, thank God for small favors—and a pair of sleek Ray-Bans.

"Open your pores, mojo, I got an itch for coon-ass food," he announced as I hopped into the Range Rover. And straightaway he slapped a cherry light onto the roof of the car, and we went wailing off eastward, skidding and screeching through the baygalls, roaring over the bayou bridges, and passing the bottle back and forth all the way to the state line, where Sonny slowed only long enough to put away the cherry light and fling the bottle into Texas behind us before he let out a zydeco scream and gave it the gas . . .

We returned, somehow, by the light of dawn. I slept all the next day. Some time well after the dinner hour, I awakened to the awful certainty that I had been dreaming a nightmare. My brain and my eyes boiling, I lumbered into the dark kitchen and picked up the phone. Then I dialed the number to the riverhouse.

After the fourth ring, a tired and slightly agitated voice said, "Hello?"

"Jill? This is Hadrian."

There was a pause. I believed I could hear her sit up in her bed and turn on the light.

"It's awfully late," she said.

But then she added, "How are you?"

"I'm . . . well . . . Did you get back from New York today?"

"Around noon, yes." She cleared her throat. "Sonny's not here, I suspect he's at the mansion if—"

"I was calling you," I said.

I could not hear her breath.

"I—I saw your father the other day."

"Yes. I know. He told me when I called him this afternoon. He said it was a joy to see you in civilian clothes."

"Yes."

I put my hand over my sweating forehead. "Hey, Jill?"

"Yes?"

"I've missed your voice. That's why I called. Just to tell you that."

"I've missed your voice too, Hadrian."

After we exchanged goodbyes, I sat up for much of the night.

7

The dark and gaunt stilted rows of pines rushed past me, accenting this one narrow way out of the trap that had been set for me. I pushed the pedal to the floor, and the Impala's engine responded with a high mechanical groan of protest. The car would go no faster than eighty, which was still enough to risk an encounter with Bo Worley's deputies. But I didn't fear the sheriff. In fact, the very thought of Worley and his joyless muscle of a face put a joyless smile on mine. I couldn't hold it against him for his opinion of me—I'd shared it, after all—and in any case, his judgment at least bespoke a reckoning of right and wrong. Worley wasn't my enemy. He'd never been. Not twenty-three years ago, when he dragged me like a sack of chicken feed out of Judge Castlebury's flatbed and clamped his cuffs on me, and not today, when he ached to do the same. For the sheriff's designs had been clear all along.

His jurisdiction, Shepherd County, lay just ahead. A few miles behind me, in Minerva County, I'd just finished roaring through Trust, searching for Ricky Tempesta. What he said to me a few days ago had gone unheard, until today—when I heard it again, spoken by someone else and about someone else. And now I drove white-knuckled and white-eyed towards Shepherdsville, through this stark, towering phalanx of pines, bound for Tempesta's house, so that I could hear the words a third and final time.

The truth had come to me in the town of Palestine, where Thunderball Hope now resided. This morning I woke up to the factual realization that I had to go there. I took the ninety-mile drive in a state of calm, burdened only by nostalgia. Sonny's parents lived in an unassuming suburban neighborhood, where dogs flopped about in the lawns and geezers in jumpsuits looked up from their freshly spooled and oiled fishing reels to eyeball the stranger in his itinerant sedan. At the end of a street I found their ranch-style house covered with green asbestos siding, shaded by a single monstrous oak. Mama Jean Hope stood there waiting for me, hands on hips, her head tilted fondly. Nothing about her seemed to have changed, least of all the taxed, arid smile she wore.

"I thought this day would never come," Mama Jean said as I hugged her. "God love you."

We sat on the patio of the back yard, which was vast and tree-cluttered, with a small creek bordering the property's western edge. "If you ask me, it's nothing more than a damn spawning ground for mosquitoes," she said as we sat in the wooden lawn chairs. "But Purvis loves that little stream. He loves all of this, out here. Most afternoons and evenings, he just sits and listens to the birds and the squirrels. It does him a world of good. You know, he never got much nature before."

I was struck by that thought. My ears pricked up to the obscure, gentle sounds of Thunderball's new life.

"He's better now," she said, though she frowned as she said it. "Those first few years were very, very rough. They were hell. But we got through them."

With a meaningful smile, she then said, "I'd offer you a beer, but we don't keep any alcohol in our house. Purvis hasn't had a drink in almost three years now."

"That's wonderful," I said.

"He says he's had more than his share, and that's the God's honest." Shaking her head, she added, "And I keep hoping the day'll come when he forgives Sonny. At least he's stopped making a fuss when I take the drive down to Shepherdsville for Christmas Eve. But I don't bring up Sonny's name anymore."

I nodded, taking that to mean that I shouldn't, either.

Mama Jean's eyes studied my face. "How is he?" she asked. "It's been weeks since we've talked."

I started to say what she wanted to hear. But the words shriveled in my throat. I stared out into the yard, imagining Thunderball slouched here at dusk, his hand clutching a glass full of some innocuous beverage as he succumbed to the tameness of his refuge. Despite the welcome news that he'd sobered up, I knew the ex-director's days were cobwebbed with bitterness—and I also knew, despite what Mama Jean had told me, that my presence here would dredge everything to the surface.

It had been ten years since the prison director arranged a final time to meet me at the northeastern edge of the Hope Farm, a good fifty acres away from the kennels, well out of anyone's sight. The day had just dawned, and I remembered standing in the dewy pasture in my kennelman's attire of padded clothes and hooded mask, not far at all from the very spot where I would make my escape a year later. Even that damp morning, I eyed the fateful gaping in the spirals of razor wire above the fenceline and thought to myself, for the hundredth time: *A blind man could do it.*

But the bulk of my sentence was mostly behind me, and back then I'd even given thought to telling Warden Grissom, on my way back to Inmate Processing, that he really ought to do something about that rag-assed perimeter fence near the northeast corner. Though he wasn't an affable bubba like Scotty Folger at Big Red, and in fact always seemed morosely preoccupied, Grissom had been consistently decent to me, never begrudging me my stroke with the Hopes. Once, when two of Sarge Holliday's canines managed to rip through my padding and chew into my left shoulder blade, the warden visited me in the hospital and brought me a newspaper—which in those days was hard to come by, given the increasing coverage of the Herrera prison lawsuit, which was deemed unfit for inmate reading for fear of riotous consequences.

Thunderball's ebony Cadillac appeared on the western horizon that morning. Presently I could see that his inmate driver, the fabled old campus strangler Manny Wilcox, wasn't behind the wheel. It was just the director, and though he drove capably through the meadow, his face even from a distance bore the distinct pallor of the doomed. He got out of the vehicle with a groan. His eyes were bloodshot and hooded with fatigue. I could smell the gin.

After we shook hands, he folded his arms across the chest of his khaki shirt and regarded my ridiculous dogboy costume with bland interest. "You just came out here to lay your morning track," he then said. "You didn't tell Holliday nothing about me."

There was the slightest quaver in the big man's growl. "No sir," I said. "Sarge Holliday just thinks I'm doing my routine, like you said."

He nodded, unconsoled. Squinting off towards the complex of inmate cells and agricultural warehouses, he asked, "When will he run 'em?"

"Usually about now the kennelmen wake them up and put them on their chains," I said. "They see the chains, then they start barking, and you figure it'll be about forty-five minutes or so before they make it out here. They just started barking about five minutes before you drove up. So . . ."

"I won't be that long," Thunderball said, and spat into the ground.

But then he proceeded to pace languidly about, dabbing his booted toes in the roots, kicking up divots of wet clay. Watching him dawdle, I found myself wondering what Purvis Hope had been like as a boy, when his cares came and went with sleep and he arose to a seeming eternity of dew-laden playgrounds—what games he'd played in the grass, in the days before he set himself to a life amongst cons and red bricks. Until now, I had never considered Thunderball as a kind of prisoner. But out here in the yard, with a mere 372 days standing between me and my parole hearing, I knew I wouldn't trade my sentence for his.

He opened his mouth to say something. But all that came out was a sound like that of a small fire being doused with water.

With effort he looked up at me. In a low rumble, he said, "It came out last night who the plaintiff's surprise rebuttal witness is."

His eyes gleamed with what I first took for morbid amusement.

"It's Sonny," he said. Then he turned and walked to his car and drove slowly, quietly off.

If an air of mystery had accompanied Sonny and his motives for taking the stand against his employer and his father those three days in September of 1988, there was no guesswork as to how the old man felt about the episode. I didn't need to be there at the Shepherd County Courthouse to conjure up the look of stupefaction in his narrowed eyes, or to see that jutting underbite mangle his lower lip while he gripped his chair at the respondents' table and listened to the truth spill out from the mouth of a babe, his only child: *The Oven is approximately four feet in width, depth and height, lined with aluminum, with no ventilation and no toilet, with three 150-watt fluorescent tubes which are kept on 24 hours a day, and which are affixed to the ceiling and secured there by a small cage. Its location varies from unit to unit, but it's typically situated behind the boiler room—though at the Hope Farm, for example, the Oven is adjacent to the ag warehouse, where the tractors are stored . . .*

. . . I believe, sir, that they were constructed in the early 1950s, on order of the director at the time, Mister Caldwell . . . No sir, I wasn't even born then. My source is secondhand . . . Yes sir. My source was my father, who was then the warden of the Shepherdsville Unit, also known as Big Red . . . Yes sir, he did personally witness the construction of the Oven at that unit . . .

. . . It was understood that the Oven was to be used for the most extreme disciplinary cases. Typically, inmates who attacked the staff and that sort of thing . . . Well, in that the guidelines were not written down, I would concur that its use was arbitrary, yes sir. Subject to each warden's discretion . . .

. . . No sir, I did not make use of the Oven during my tenure as warden of the Hope Prison Farm . . . Quite frankly, sir, I believed that it was a barbaric form of punishment . . . I believed this, sir, because, both as a correctional officer at the Shepherdsville Unit and later as an assistant warden at the Hope Farm, I personally witnessed its effect on those who were subjected to it . . . Baked alive is how I would describe it, sir . . . Yes sir, there have been several cases of permanent brain damage. I couldn't put a number to it. Those kinds of statistics were never kept by the TDCR, for obvious reasons . . . Yes sir, there have been at least three deaths that I know of firsthand . . . I do not know for certain if Director Hope had detailed knowledge of these cases, no sir . . . Yes sir, I did report the cases to the director . . . He thanked me and told me not to repeat the information to anyone else . . . Not until now, no sir . . ."

Three months later, after a host of wardens had scrambled aboard the bandwagon and confirmed Sonny's testimony with horror stories of their own, the jury found in favor of Chu-Chu Herrera, the Texas prison system was declared unconstitutional and the governor demanded and received the resignation of Purvis J. "Thunderball" Hope after forty-eight years of service with the Texas Department of Criminal Retribution, twenty-two of those years as its director. That the youthful hero of the saga would then publicly request clemency for the father whose career he had blasted to pieces must have been especially galling to Thunderball—a needless humiliation, since those of us who knew the fallen director also knew he would take down every state official with him if denied either protection from prosecution or full retirement benefits. From my six-by-nine cell, the view was all too clear: the floppy-haired maverick wanted the world to know that it pained him to be a traitor—that it wasn't in his nature, no matter what the fallen father was saying.

But, I would remind myself, when it came to Sonny there were always at least two ways of viewing his actions. He'd done the right thing, no matter his motives. And it took bravery none of us could've guessed he had. He had received death threats, had earned the scorn of his peers, and had lost a father forever. So I felt for both of them, and for Mama Jean and Jill as well, and I spent the next few months hoping Sonny would pay me a visit at the Hope Farm, though I knew it wasn't safe . . . which was why it stung me when word spread that Sonny, newly appointed as deputy director, had received a Hope Farm inmate in his new office—not me, but instead Ricky Tempesta.

"Well, shit on a stick! You can't keep a good houseboy down!"

If not for the voice, I wouldn't have recognized Thunderball. He looked frail, almost emaciated, in his flannel shirt and stained khakis, and his once-mammoth skull was now pinched and translucent. He had lost all but a few strands of his hair. Liver spots dappled his cranium. The hand that shook mine felt like a thatch of twigs.

But his bassett eyes welled with fondness as I reached to hug him. I patted his still-sturdy back, and he let out an almost feminine sigh. Already I was glad I had come.

"I got me a mess of crappies if you don't mind a fish fry without beer," he rasped once we plopped down in our chairs and Mama Jean excused herself to the kitchen. Thunderball grinned somewhat shyly. "Since I got myself cleaned out, I been able to taste things for the first time. For all I knew, Vermiel could've been feeding me goat turds all those years."

There was a buoyancy to his voice that I hadn't expected. I let him steer the conversation, which every few minutes dipped into his former world, only to swerve back to less precarious terrain. But it wasn't long before he squirmed in his chair, giggled a little and said, "I got to know how you busted out."

The story somehow became his. "I knew you found that northeastern perimeter! Got damn, I knew it! And then you hit the slough, didn't you! Just like I would've done! . . . I be damned, that old telephone wire trick—shit boy, we had an old con back in '43 or '44 done that, the dogs they got so confused there was actual tears coming out of their eyes! I bet you gave them *fits*!"

Lunch consisted of corn meal battered crappie fillets, hush puppies and cole slaw, along with a pitcher of lemonade. While Thunderball tore into his food, Mama Jean asked me about Mimi, about our parents' house and about my job prospects. She was pleased to hear I'd kept up my education, and after I ran out of things to say about myself, she began to talk about their lives. She said that Palestine was nice enough—gossipy and shuttered like all small towns, but nothing on the scale of Shepherdsville, and in any event they'd been decently received and at least no one whispered about them in their presence.

I smiled and issued my is-that-so's as she rambled on. But the more she talked, the more pronounced became the silence on the other side of the table. Every minute or so, her gaze would dart surreptitiously that way, and when she did her voice would harden for just that second, the words dropping like lead shells, before she resumed her breezy monologue. Still, Mama Jean wasn't a babbler by nature, and when she, too, ran out of words, the light on the patio seemed to falter just a bit.

Presently, Thunderball cleared his throat. He wiped his mouth on his shirtsleeve. "Tell the damn truth, I don't miss it," he declared.

Out of the corner of my eye, I could see Mama Jean grimace and look away. "Not one lick," he continued. "Hell. When I read about all those Got damn prison gangs, and those COs muling dope in and out of the units, and every damn con toting a *Black's Law Dictionary*, suing the system on account of they felt a draft somewhere in the dayroom when they got up to change the channel on the big-screen cable TV . . . Tell Hadrian what I say, Mama."

She smiled uneasily. "He says, 'They'd have to put me in white to make me go back.'"

"You got that right. Hey, and speaking of white: how is old Calvin, by the way?"

Before I could reply, Thunderball added, "I owe that boy a call. Every few months he rings me up just to check in. Old Calvin. He's the only—he, he's sure a fine fella, he doesn't forget a friend, he's different from all the rest of those worthless sons of bitches," and like that, the edge he'd been battling back overtook him, and I watched Mama Jean's face become ashen as the ex-director dug a bony finger hard into the table.

"It must be just killing old Calvin." He leaned his wizened face into mine. "It must just eat his ass out. Watching the damn system get bigger and bigger like a ten-ton gorilla with nobody standing over it, no one taking charge, the whole damn mess just out of control, and the—"

"Purvis," Mama Jean pleaded quietly.

"And the, well," and as his voice subsided he fought to compose himself, and grabbing his fork he stabbed half a fillet and stuck the oversized piece into his mouth as if to obliterate one taste with another.

But halfway through his chewing, he blurted out through his mouthful of fish, "And this new private prison town! Now ain't that the drizzling shits! We're gonna have some private business lordin' over our cons! And it'll be an ex-con doing the lordin'! Don't that just beat all! *Trust*! And we was worried about Nazis and Communists! Before you know it," and as he guffawed, a morsel of fish dribbled onto his chin, "we'll just do away with the whole Got damn judicial system, and privatize the damn courts! Make those wheels of justice more effi- cient—wouldn't *that* be a hoot! Make sure every case turns a profit, and if it don't, you just put a bullet through that crook's skull! Or better yet, just kill 'em at birth, shoot all the poor blacks and Mexicans, save everyone the—"

"*Purvis.*"

"No wonder they threw my ass out! Nobody was gettin' rich when I was around! You think I'd've let this fucking circus take place on my watch? No way, José! No Got damn corporation was gonna buy those cons away from me! There ain't enough money in all the world! *Those cons were mine, and they were gonna stay mine!*"

He threw his crumpled napkin onto his plate. "Well, and that wasn't gonna do," he growled. "And so they said I was against the Con- stitution. Hah! *There ain't no Constitution!* Look what's happening! Shee. They're gonna look back one day and they're gonna say, 'Boy, that Thunderball Hope, he sure was a softie, wasn't he? Why'd he even bother with those bats and those Ovens? Why didn't he just meet 'em at the gates with a machine gun? Housing all those cons—did you ever hear of anything more *wasteful?*' "

Thunderball smiled feebly at us both. He seemed at least as intoxi-
cated as any time I'd seen him while he was drinking. When we offered
him nothing by way of reply or encouragement, he sank into a bleak
stupor and glowered red-faced at his plate. I chanced a look at his wife.
Her face seemed drowned in dismay.

"No one's in charge," he mumbled darkly. "I never seen such a
mess. God, it must be killing old Calvin. Damn, I feel for him. I really
do."

There was no more eating to be done. Mama Jean stood, collected
our plates and stiffly retreated inside. I turned back to Thunderball. All
the gruff charm had fled him. His red eyes were on me, and his bulldog
jaw asserted itself as he held up his glass of lemonade.

"I almost forgot." He offered a full-fledged sneer. "Here's to your
pardon."

He completed the toast with a loud slurping of his drink, followed
by a prolonged sigh, heedless of the fact that I had not even lifted my
glass. Thunderball picked at his teeth while gazing off towards his
beloved creek. Today it was bringing him no solace.

Then he said, "Out there at Judge Castlebury's place. What you
did. Saving his life and all that."

With a theatrical wheeling of his head, he spat onto his crisp suburban lawn.

"You shouldn't have bothered," he said. "His life wasn't worth saving."

White light exploded in my eyes. I slumped back in my chair. *Not
worth saving*. Those were Tempesta's words. He'd said them, revealing
the trap. Now I heard. Now I knew.

And so I sped murderously back towards Shepherdsville, leaning like a
crazed jockey into the steering wheel, tilting at last towards the truth.
Just before the city limits, I slowed for the time it took me to reach the
interstate, whereupon I gunned the engine and proceeded due south,
the blur of white uniforms and flashes of razor wire like playing cards
obscurely fluttering as I passed the surly icons of the town one after the
next. Up ahead I saw a twirling of red and blue lights. It was a Shepherd County deputy, but he already had business in the form of a black
kid who stood glumly beside his red sports car on the shoulder of the
interstate while the cop ran his license number. At the southern edge

of the city, I exited west and eased off the gas pedal, though now my heart was pounding like a pneumatic drill against my chest.

The security gates to Tempesta's house were closed. I shinnied up and over them, then walked to the front door and rang the bell. There was no answer. The black Jaguar was not in his driveway. I stood on the porch and saw that my watch read three-thirty, but the numbers told me nothing about how much time I had.

Back towards the interstate, I pulled into a gas station and used the public phone. I dialed the number to the Trust Institute of Criminal Justice. Then the Houston number of A. P. Whitfield, attorney. Then Sissy Shipman. Then Cal Fitch. No one was answering. I made change inside, returned to the phone and looked in the phone directory for the Shepherdsville regional office of Global Corrections, Inc. The receptionist who picked up said that Mister Aspromonte was in a meeting right now.

"Actually," I said, "I'm trying to reach the person he's meeting with. Could you just tell Dr. Tempesta to call his office when he's finished?"

"I surely could," said the secretary.

"Thank you," I said, and after hanging up, tore out the page in the directory with Wick Aspromonte's office address.

The Jaguar sat in the far corner of the First National Bank of Shepherdsville garage parking lot. The hood nearly scalded my hand when I touched it. Tempesta had been on the move. The windows were tinted, but the sun roof had been left open. I put a knee on the hood, preparing to scale to the sun roof and peer inside. Then the car alarm went off and commenced a volley of screeches, wails and honks. I ran to the far end of the garage and hid in the stairwell.

Within a few minutes, I heard the bell go off from the garage elevator. I looked through the window of the stairwell door in time to see the taut figure of Ricky Tempesta step out into the garage. He wore a secular navy blue shirt and sunglasses. Recognizing that the car alarm was his, he held out his key button, pushed it to silence the alarm, and then proceeded quickly to the Jaguar, warily surveying his whereabouts.

"It was me," I said as I stepped out.

He froze, pivoted, and then sank instantly into a form of martial arts crouch, his hands at chest level. A part of me wanted to laugh. To think, as I had, that I could have gotten the better of a creature like Tempesta.

"I need to talk to you, Ricky," I said.

My tone was beseeching; it brought him out of his crouch. "You were trying to break into my car," he said.

"No." I stopped within ten feet of him. "I just needed to ask you something."

He shook his head, turned his back to me and reached for his car door. "Fuck you, Coleman," he said quietly. "I've got no time for you."

I stepped closer. He whirled, pulled off his sunglasses. The viper eyes regarded me carefully. "Do you want to get hurt?" he inquired.

"I told you. I need to ask you something."

"Is this about a job again?" he groaned. "Jesus Christ. Okay, fine. Go down to Trust and fill out an application." His eyes suddenly flared red. "There's gonna be plenty of slots to fill. Plenty of jobs. You tell your friend Sonny that. He's going down before I do! Tell him that! I ain't folding my tent! I'm not going anywhere! You got that, Coleman? It don't matter what that bitch writes!"

A shiver coursed through me. I hadn't read today's newspaper.

"Now get out of my way," he said as he opened his car door. "I've got a town to build."

"You said something to me last time," I said. "About Digby saving my life."

Tempesta's eyes seemed to lose focus for a moment. Then he snorted lightheartedly. "That was after you insulted me," he said. "Christ almighty, Coleman. I didn't remember you being so fucking thin-skinned."

An incredulous laugh rattled out of his wiry throat. "Is *that* why you're here? To have me take it back? Fine. I take it back. Now will you get out of my way?"

"I just need to hear it again," I said.

"What—about how I don't know why Digby bothered saving your life?" He snickered a little. "Well, try not to take it too personally, Coleman. But *I* wouldn't've bothered. I would've stepped back and let Wexler make a fruit salad out of you."

My whole body tingled.

Tempesta stepped into his car, started his engine. Then he rolled down his window. His hard, mangled face looked almost kind.

"Nothing against you, Coleman," he said. "That's just the law of the jungle. Hell, you know that."

I found my voice again. "And so," I said, "you never told Sonny you'd talked to Digby about what happened."

He looked genuinely puzzled. "Why the hell would I talk to Hope about—but look," he then said, the menace returning to his voice, "you tell your buddy I'm gonna be talking to him real soon, you understand? He's gonna vouch for me if he wants to keep his job. You tell him that!"

"And Red Wickersham," I persisted. "You never talked to him about Red Wickersham."

"Red who? You're delirious, Coleman. Step back or I'll run over your feet."

Just as he was peeling away, Tempesta leaned his head out the window a final time. "*You tell him we're gonna talk!*"

The tires skidded down the exit ramp. "I'll tell him," I said quietly.

Before driving to the mansion, I picked up a copy of the *Chronicle* and settled myself on a bench in the courthouse square. Now I saw why Sissy Shipman hadn't run with the story after tailing me and interviewing Ricky Tempesta last Friday. She knew there was more to get, and a few days later, she'd gotten it. As I read her front-page assault on the Trust founder—"Tempesta Did Deals with Drug Lords, Prison Director, Records Show" read the headline—I found myself looking up now and again, half-expecting to see Shepherdsville engulfed in flames. But on the courthouse steps, three grey-suited lawyers chewed the fat and nudged each other whenever the square's panorama revealed a female between the age of ten and seventy. Squatted at the attorneys' feet, three inmates listened in while manicuring the flowerbed dirt. A family of tourists filed out of the prison museum, postcards of Big Red in hand. Around the square, flatbeds from the country wheezed along, tailgated by college boys in their obnoxious sports cars—the two worlds chafing as before, as always. And regardless of where I fit in, here I was, in full view of Shepherdsville, an unspectacular but unoffensive sight: just another vagrant on a bench, gathered up into the town's collective daydream.

I listened to my deep breaths. Overhead, the courthouse bells gonged five times. I sighed and leaned back. I still had awhile to myself.

"'Scuse me, sir."

I looked up to find one of the inmates standing alongside the bench, feigning labor as he eyed me sidelong and spoke to the ground. "You finished with that paper?" he added.

Just then, a correctional officer from the other side of the courthouse hollered out, "Winslow! Get on back to Big Red, boy! You miss the five-fifteen count, your ass is going back into ad-seg!"

"Yessir boss," the inmate called back. As he turned back towards the prison, he muttered anxiously, "The man's got his eyes on me, but sir could you tell me real quick, what's it say in there about that private prison town they got going, I heard—"

"Winslow!"

"Right away, yessir boss!"

When he looked back at me a final time, I held out the paper and pointed to the headline. "Basically," I told him, "Trust bit the dust."

The inmate's face widened into reckless jubilation. "God bless you, sir," he declared, and with spade in hand he made haste towards his red brick home.

"He ain't made it home yet," Vermiel told me at the doorstep of the mansion. The chef looked past me and waved at the picket guard across the street. Then he hissed excitedly, "Shee-boy, you read today's *Chronicle*? That Shipman girl, she's got some brass ones, don't she!"

Then, in an even lower voice shuddering with intrigue: "And god-*damn*. Director Hope swappin' land with that shitass Tempesta? What's gonna happen, Coleman?"

I shrugged. "Something is," I said. "Do you have any idea when he'll be back?"

"Naw. He was up before dawn, got out quick, ain't seen him since. He was some kind of agitated when he left. Didn't eat but half his breakfast."

He shook his head, and then a dry smile appeared on his face as he looked directly into my eyes. "It don't surprise me," he said. "We go all the way back, just like you and him do. I seen what I seen. You know what I'm talking about?"

I didn't have to reply.

"That boy got into this line of work for all the wrong reasons," Vermiel continued. His voice was suddenly contemptuous. "Don't ask me what the right reasons would be, 'cause I sure wouldn't know. But I know his was the wrong reasons."

I nodded. "I saw Thunderball today," I said.

"You lyin'." The grin was fond at first. Then he shook his head again. "Can't say I miss the old man. The way he treated us . . ."

Then, after considering things for a moment, Vermiel added, "But I guess he cared about us, in his own funny way, didn't he? He had an interest. We were his cons. His boy's different. He just don't care about us, one way or another. We're just"—and the old crossword puzzle aficionado's voice caressed the next word—"*commodities.*"

"Hadrian!"

The voice came from behind Vermiel. It was Jill.

She stood behind the chef, obscured from my view. "Did Sonny get ahold of you?" she asked.

My heart stopped. It figured that he'd been trying to reach me. Sissy's story had only mentioned that Sonny and Jill once owned the Trust acreage, and that they'd purchased the riverhouse from Tempesta's attorney. "A bizarre coincidence, at the very least," was how the article had characterized it. That an actual swap had taken place, under clearly illegal circumstances between a TDCR inmate and its deputy director, had not been spelled out—but it stood to be, as long as Tempesta was alive and scrambling for survival. "I've been out of town all day," I told Jill.

"Well, I hope you don't have dinner plans. The Foots Taylors, the Aynsley Reeveses, the Kirby Morrises and Cal Fitch will be over at seven, and if I can scare up a few nuns and actuaries to enliven things, I will . . . but in the meantime, please say you'll be here."

Then our eyes met. Her expression was pale and disoriented. *Jesus,* I thought. *Of course she's read the story, too.*

"Excuse us, Vermiel," Jill said. "Hadrian, why don't we go to the back yard."

We sat on the red brick patio. Jill's right hand absentmindedly twirled her wedding ring on its finger. She wore an olive linen blazer and matching slacks, the right leg crossed over the left and her beige sandal drooping from her right foot as she rocked it back and forth. Her hair was pinned up behind her. She smiled somewhat as I pulled my chair closer to hers. She continued to play with the diamond ring. Looking at it, she then said, "You read her story, I suppose."

I didn't reply. "Imagine my reaction," said Jill, her voice compelling even in her weariness, "upon learning that the land Sonny had so cleverly bartered to a lawyer in exchange for that lovely riverhouse . . . was cloud cover for a bribe."

She shrugged. "The paper didn't say it," she said simply. "I did. That's what it adds up to. A rather obvious equation in a town such as this. Don't tell me I'm wrong."

Then she was laughing. "Do you know what he did?" she exclaimed. "Tell me if this isn't just like Sonny. He took the paper with him to work early this morning before I could get a chance to read it. When I phoned him at the office to ask about it, he said he needed it to make photocopies. He said the subscription at his office had run out."

Jill's mirth was genuine and alarming. "Like a boy hiding a report card from his parents! 'The dog ate my *Chronicle*!' And when I went to the grocery store to buy a paper of my own, I half-expected to see Sonny sneaking out with the whole armload!"

Her laughter dwindled, only to begin again. After a time, she fell silent and went back to her ring.

"What will I do now, I wonder," she murmured.

"What did he say?" I asked.

She frowned. "Oh, I didn't even bother calling him after I'd read it," she said. "He'll lie, of course. He'll say he had no way of knowing that this A. P. Whitfield lawyer represented Tempesta."

Then she arched an eyebrow. "He called," she said.

"Tempesta?"

She nodded. "We've never spoken before. Of course, I've heard he's an ogre. But I must say that I felt sorry for him. Don't ask me why. He wasn't especially nice on the phone. When I said Sonny had already left for the day, he refused to believe it. He accused me of harboring him."

A vacant laugh. "Which is what I've done all these years," she remarked. "Isn't it. And it's what he'll continue to expect me to do."

Her hand covered the ring tightly. "You're not the only one," I reminded her.

Quickly she scanned my face. "You knew all of this, I suppose," she said.

"I'm sorry, Jill."

"Don't be. It wasn't your place to tell me."

Her voice was nonetheless brittle. "Nor was it Ricky Tempesta's place. Though I did ask him outright."

Her face hardened. "The second in a series of indignities," she said with barren amusement. "First, to have all the dots connected for me by that Shipman shrew. Then, to concede to a total stranger, who happens to be an inveterate criminal, that I was totally ignorant of my husband's own criminal endeavors."

Shrugging, rolling her eyes, she added, "I mean, I assume it's criminal. Doing business with a felon in one's care. It certainly sounds somewhere below the up-and-up. I'm sure Aynsley will enlighten us . . . to add to the indignities."

Jill sighed. "To realize," she continued, "that by signing my portion of the family land over to Sonny, I have repeated the folly of my ancestor. That I, being the last of the Estelles, have, in the manner of Joshua, the first Estelle in Shepherd County, been duped into marring this countryside with prisons . . ." She covered her eyes with her hand. "It confirms what I've always thought about my family. That we were never any kind of . . ."

She fell silent. Then, beneath the shading of her hand, she said: "That we were only pawns here. Never any more than that."

Her hand then fell to her lap, and she lifted her eyes to me. "And then," she said, sighing more heavily this time, "to confront Sonny. Which I'll have to. Sooner rather than later. To wade through all the lies, all the excuses, all the how-was-I-to-knows . . . And, at last, to face my father."

Jill's eyes welled up. She looked puny in her chair. "Everything I couldn't see, or wouldn't see, he saw. Everything . . . And he won't have to say it. Not a word . . . But just, to face him . . . "

As her voice gave out, I slid out of my chair. Reaching for Jill, I fell to my knees at her feet, and she slumped towards me and I held her around her small waist as she sobbed. "How could he be so, so *immune*?" she gasped against my shoulder. "He never fell for Sonny! He saw him so clearly! So clearly, and so harshly! And all that did was make me fall for Sonny even . . . even harder . . . Oh God, Hadrian, what will we *do*?"

She said nothing else, and instead she slid from her chair, crumpling into my arms. And there we both sat on the smooth red bricks of the patio. As she wept, she wrapped her arms tightly around my neck and pressed her cheek against mine. I felt the fluttering of her breath, of her eyelashes. And somewhere behind me, I believed I could feel the bleary gaze of Vermiel—and somewhere beyond, the stare of the Big Red picket guard, and perhaps even the blinking astonishment of the mint-green eyes trained down from the highest perch in town.

But mostly I attended to the awful sensation of Jill Estelle Hope's heartbreak. *Good God*, I thought, *is this all I've known—and will there be a single heart left unsplintered before Sonny and I are through with Shepherdsville . . .*

He was nearly two hours late to his own dinner party. The others, including myself, filed into the director's mansion between seven and seven-thirty, with Foots and his wife Susie bringing up the rear. I'd never met the state legislator's wife before. But she shook my hand and with an embracing South Texas twang declared, "Foots has told me so much about you and your dad, I feel like we grew up together."

Foots himself squeezed my shoulder with his supple hand. "You got honest work yet, stud?" he asked in a low voice. Without waiting for my reply, and in a near-whisper, he said, "Why don't you call me tomorrow at my office. Something came my way. A job opening that's mine to distribute, you might could say. It'd be right up your alley."

Then, "Call me," and he swung away, hurling a sonorous "Hi how you?" to one of the other guests. My field of vision was consumed by the fidgeting sight of deputy director Kirby Morris and his horsehair toupee. "Wantcha to meet my wife Jeanine," he stammered, and brought forth a large, frazzle-haired woman in a tent-like denim dress.

Jeanine Morris's fleshy hand squirmed against mine. "I remember when you were one of Kirby's down at the Creel Unit," she beamed. "You were just a tot then, I recollect. Lord, I hated Sugarland. Nothing in that town but mosquitoes and niggers. I sure was glad when Kirby got his promotion to Shepherdsville."

"Yes, a pest-controlled environment if there ever was one, and with all the darkies in leg irons, as it should be," proclaimed Aynsley Reeves, who had been eavesdropping. "Of course, we give Cal Fitch free run of things. He's sho nuff a credit to his race, wouldn't you say, Jeanine?"

The general counsel adjusted his spectacles as he grinned brightly.

"Eat shit, Aynsley," growled the deputy director's wife, but she was blushing as she glanced across the entryway towards the dining room. I saw that Fitch was standing there, his arm around Jill's shoulder as they conferred quietly. She had changed into a pale blue silk suit, had redone her face and braided her hair. Jill looked up at me just then, as did Fitch. When Foots and his wife approached them, they responded with animated hellos. But I saw Jill glance at her watch, and I knew that we would be starting without Sonny.

Our hostess seated us at eight. I sat between her and Foots, with Fitch across from me to Jill's left. Vermiel's two houseboy assistants shuffled out, one pouring the water while the other took our drink orders. A few minutes later, the salads were produced. Jill casually exhorted us to dig in, and we did. But as we ate, each of us took turns casting glances at the empty chair at the far end of the table, with its plates stacked atop each other and the ice melting in its water glass.

Finally, Foots spoke up. "Aw, I'm sure he just got bogged down with that damned emergency bed-conversion project," he said. Putting his fork down, Foots offered a chagrined cackle. "Here's a case study in how politics and corrections go at cross-purposes. You've got the governor, on the one hand, who's all keen on building these some-would-say-innovative minimum-security drug treatment facilities for first-time offenders. On the other hand, you've got all these local judges up for re-election, and they're scared that if they sentence some druggie to a mini instead of a max, their opponent will use that against 'em. Soft on criminals—the usual refrain. So who gets caught in the middle? The executive director of the Texas Department of Criminal Retribution, that's who. First, Sonny's got to build five thousand minimum-security beds per the governor's game plan. Then, when those beds don't get used and we're backlogged on the maxes, it falls to Sonny to reconfigure every one of those new facilities—break down the dorms, put up cell bars and fences. And do it in 180 days, and do it cheap, so the taxpayers won't notice."

To Jeanine Morris, Susie Taylor asked in her warm drawl, "Does *your* husband speak in tongues, too?"

The other snickered gruffly. "I wouldn't know what to do with Kirby if I ever heard him talking about the weather, or sports, or whatever regular men talk about," she said.

"And he'll get it done," Foots went on, "'cause Sonny Hope knows what's at stake. But," he concluded with a wink Jill's way, "I imagine it puts him late for dinner a time or two. Jill, the state of Texas appreciates your patience."

She smiled, arched an eyebrow, but said nothing. Discomfort was general again.

"Pardon our long-arm-of-the-lawyer reach as we usurp yon crystal ball," piped up Aysnley Reeves after awhile. The general counsel then reached back and delivered a blue-ribbon Reevesian filibuster, a punishing laundry list of what-could-Sonny-be-up-to: "Up to his dimples in Herrera guideline revocation specs, or wading through consultation invitations from the governments of Florida, Washington, Toronto and San Juan, or throwing out the first pitch to the Rangers–Yankees game, or intervening in a waste management dispute at the East Nimrod Unit—seems the hog sludge found its way into the local water supply, though our educated guess is that the taste was only improved . . ."

"It's Tempesta," Kirby Morris suddenly said.

Everyone turned his way except for me. I watched the color diminish from Jill's face.

While his wife wiped a dollop of salad dressing off of his chin with her napkin, the deputy director blinked with happy astonishment over the attention he had attracted. "Dollars to doughnuts, it's this Tempesta business," he continued, and sat up straighter in his chair. "Ol' Sissy, she done cooked that buddy's goose. Hell, the whole agency's been talking about it all day long, hadn't they, Cal?"

Morris finally read what there was to read in Jill's expression. "Oh," he said with a wave of his hand, "no one I know thinks Sonny—I mean," and looking around at the rest of us, his voice faltered into a pathetic tenor, "heck, a small community like this, everyone's money bumps into each other's. Or, well, and anyway, that story of Sissy's, I mean come on, that's a damn take-down!"

He looked around the table again, eyes wide with near-panic as he sought to find just one concurring party. "Hell, that's it for Trust, Texas!" he insisted. "That's good news! We oughtta be celebrating—and, and, I bet that's what Sonny's doing right now! *That's* why he's late! He's celebrating! Don'tcha think, Cal?"

A starving dog could not have appeared more beggarly. Attention was thrown on Fitch, who hadn't said a word thus far. He managed a kind smile. "Best not to speculate, Kirby," he said.

"But—"

"Do *not* . . . speculate."

The barely controlled anger in Fitch's voice was apparent to the rest of us. Kirby Morris shrugged, mumbled something and returned to his food. Fitch did not. He was still staring at the deputy director, and his rooster chest rose and fell with hard breaths. I knew it wasn't Kirby he was mad at.

"Delicious salad," declared Susie Taylor at some point.

"I'd sure like the recipe," affirmed Sheila Reeves.

The kitchen door swung open a crack. Vermiel poked his head out. "Miz Hope," he said proddingly, "the fish is pretty well ready."

"That's fine, Vermiel," she replied. Her voice was opaquely cheerful. "So are we. Just—"

We all heard the noise, the breezy surge of the Range Rover's engine as it approached. Headlights flashed from the driveway.

"Well, what do you know," said Foots Taylor, and the others murmured their relief. Jill, seemingly mesmerized by the glow of the lights, made as if to stand. A second later, she eased back into her chair and looked away from the window. Now there was his presence, rather than his absence, to reckon with.

The car door slammed, and the figure of Sonny flashed past the dining room window. The moment the front door opened, each of us cocked our ears, anticipating a familiar outburst—an announcement of our good fortune at his arrival, a touch of ice-breaking slapstick, a snickering obscenity, anything. But after the slamming of the door, a thick silence followed. We waited. Then came a sickly tinkling clatter.

"Shit," we heard him say. Then we heard him stoop to pick up his keys from the hardwood floor.

Presently Sonny stood at the foyer of the dining room, keys still in hand. His yellow hair sprawled across his forehead in strands dampened by sweat. He looked at us, eyeing our stares, judging them. Then a grin commenced to move across his face. But it seemed to stop midway, in the billows of his cheeks—which were a pinched red, though not much more so than the rest of his face.

"I'm probably wondering why you all called me here today," he said.

In a rough motion, he slung his navy blazer over the back of his chair. The blazer slid to the floor the moment he sat down. "Looks really delightful. Really does. Couldn't ask for better," he said, addressing his empty plates. Then, an exaggerated "*Ohhh*," and beaming at Vermiel, who stood at the kitchen entrance with a platterful of red snapper, he said, in someone else's tone of booming formality, "*Gar-çon*, I insist upon seconds. Now fetch me another inmate out of the Oven and, or—well. You're one step ahead. Right this way please, *garçon*."

There was a general shifting of chairs and readjustment of napkins. After hesitating a moment, Vermiel said, "Yessir," and walked the platter over towards Sheila Reeves, the female guest closest to the chef. She smiled and murmured a compliment as Vermiel leaned over to dole out a portion.

"No, goddammit," Sonny snarled. Vermiel froze as if he had been shot. "No. Hold it right there. They've already been gorging themselves. Gorging themselves," he reiterated straight-faced, "and at the taxpayers' expense, I might add. It's high time a nickel got thrown ol' Sonny's way. I been reading about my loot, and now I want it. Bring those damn vittles over here. Now!"

Next to me, Foots muttered, "What the . . ." Fitch dropped his fork, began to work his mouth, sorting out the words. Jill gasped loudly. Her eyes burned like lunar torches.

Just as she opened her mouth, he cut her off with a pesky laugh. "It was a joke," he insisted. "A *joke*! Good grief. When did all of y'all start taking me seriously? Did I miss a memo, Kirby? Vermiel, serve up Sheila for God's sake, and save me for last, I don't even know if I've got an appetite after today's hell—though that snapper could turn me around, it definitely could. Sorry I'm late, everybody. Can 'til Can't. You know how it goes."

The sounds of breathing resumed as Sonny swept his gaze around the table. His grin was both eager and contrite. When his eyes met those of his wife, who sat rigidly in her chair, he winced and said, "Aw, honey, what can I say? It was the goddamn FBI. They don't even let you make one phone call. That stupidass in-cell integration federal court order," he said, looking to Aynsley for support as he went on, "the feds want us putting blacks and whites or blacks and Hispanics or whites and Hispanics in the same cells—which in a perfect world would be just ducky with ol' Sonny. But ain't no dandelions sprouting out of your patootie or mine, and you put a Crip in a six-by-nine with an Aryan Brother and those gutters are gonna run awful high, bubba. Can't talk sense to the FIB, though. So I got shanghaied by them, and it wasn't the first time and it won't be the last but I'm *sorry*, honey, really I am. Sorry to everyone. Don't run off with that, Vermiel, my appetite never strays far."

Aynsley cleared his voice. "It might have been prudent to notify counsel," he stated huffily, "in light of counsel's arduous labors towards resolving said federal contretemps."

"Well, and there'll be more arduousness, counselor, you can be sure of that, but the fact of the matter was, I couldn't notify you on account of the FIB caught me unawares and *detained* me. Okay?"

The edge had crept back into his voice. "The FIB," cackled Kirby Morris's wife. "That's a good one. I hadn't heard that one before."

"F . . . I . . . B," mused Jill.

Sonny studied Jill's searing glare for a moment. Then: "Eat, everyone!" By way of demonstration, he plunged into his food—much as his father had done this afternoon, and the recollection threw me out of balance.

"Delicious," said Susie Taylor, and Foots hummed his agreement, and the others put in their compliments as well. For my part, I had come here today certain of things I would say to Sonny. Now I had no idea what they were. Instead, I huddled in my chair, waiting for someone else's words—since it seemed, in the span of just these few minutes, that everyone was on to him by now, that he had been defrauded the moment he stumbled in. I waited, half-hoping that no one would say anything, and we would all parade out the door with thanks for the wonderful evening and let our separate consciences do with each of us what they will; or that it would come down in the fleetest possible crash: a guilty plea from the offender, throwing himself at our mercy, which we would gladly bestow, that our own complicity be forgotten. But as the forks clanked, the ice jiggled in the glasses and the plates disappeared one by one into the kitchen, I braced myself for the worst way out of this night—or thought I was braced, until Kirby Morris, of all people, opened the floodgates.

"I figured you were out late," said the deputy to his boss, with a defiant side glance towards Fitch, " 'cause you were out celebrating over that Tempesta article."

It took a lot to make Sonny's cushioned face go taut. But after a first flinch, akin to a stab of nausea, something metallicized in him. He straightened himself in his chair, and fixed his deputy with a look of pitiless fascination.

"Is that what you figured, Kirby?" he spat out. "That I'd been out celebrating?—and hadn't even thought to take you along?"

He made a swearing noise. Then he turned away from his blanching second-in-command.

"Hey, Fitch," he called out.

Cal Fitch smiled coolly. "Hey, Sonny," he returned.

Sonny's smile was more like a smear. "Why the hell aren't you my deputy?" he demanded.

Fitch shrugged, offered the same smile as before. "Been there done that," he said.

"Not with me you haven't. And why is that, Fitch? We could've made such beautiful music together. Built us the finest prison system imaginable. The best the world has ever seen. Not," he added as he placed a flimsy hand over the wrist of Kirby's startled wife, "that I don't already have me a fine, *fine* man by my side."

He patted Jeanine Morris's wrist for emphasis. "This here's a fine, fine man. But still, Fitch. What've you got against me, anyway?"

Fitch smiled pleasantly back and said nothing.

"Lay off, Sonny," interjected Foots Taylor.

Sonny gasped. "Why, I ain't even laid *on* yet," he protested. Wagging a finger, he continued, "I just don't like Cal Fitch when he's so damn quiet, that's all. That's all I'm saying, Fitch," he finished, and now his glare at the chief of Inmate Processing amounted to a blatant challenge.

Fitch offered a chuckle. "Well, then, you don't like me," he said. "Because I'm just a quiet guy."

"He was a quiet man," intoned Aynsley Reeves, "or so said his neighbors, until the day he let his bullets speak—"

"Not to Sissy Shipman, he ain't quiet," said Sonny.

The table itself groaned. Fitch was perfectly expressionless.

"That's right," Sonny said, and slapped the table and laughed. "You were Sissy's little helper on that Tempesta story, weren't you?"

Fitch's smile was weary. "Don't flatter me," he said. "I didn't know anything she didn't already have."

"That is *not*," Sonny's voice rang out, "what she told Tempesta. And you know how I know that? Because I talked to Tempesta this afternoon."

He turned more or less in the direction of Kirby Morris. "We were out celebrating together, Tempesta and me," he sneered. "Celebrating the libel lawsuits we both plan to file against Sissy Fucking Shipman and the *Houston Fucking Chronicle*."

Sonny licked his lips. "And you know what he told me?" he asked no one in particular. "He told me he'd had two very interesting conversations today."

He thrust out an accusing finger. "With you," he said, indicating Jill.

Then, in my direction: "And with you."

He tilted his head in mock inquisitiveness. "What's going on over there on that side of the table?" he wanted to know. Leaning forward, he added, "Are you three forming some kind of conspiracy against ol' Sonny over there? A little palace revolt? Well, come on! Say something!"

Jill beat me to it. Her voice was trembling. "Why don't you just tell everyone what he and I talked about?" she asked.

"I thought you'd never ask," he said.

Leaning back again, he nonchalantly addressed us all. "See, Tempesta's trying to blackmail me. He's in the skillet, and the temperature's rising, and he says if I don't help pull him out—if I don't tell the world that Ricky Tempesta's shit don't stink, that even if I oppose the Trust Plan I regard Dr. Tempesta as a high-minded idealist who never, ever would involve himself in anything crooked—if I don't stick my neck out for him, then he's gonna drag me into the skillet with him. He's gonna float the story that he was the shadow partner in the riverhouse Jill and I bought, and that the land Jill and I sold really went to him, that it was an underhanded deal we'd dreamed up while he was at the Hope Farm—all of which is an absolute fantasy, he knows it and I know it . . ."

His voice suddenly cracked. He peered into Jill's eyes. "But you believed him," he said in a half-whisper. "You believed the most odious son of a bitch in the state of Texas, instead of believing your husband. Didn't you. Didn't you."

Jill went white. She cast her eyes to either side.

"Don't look at your goddamned cohorts," Sonny snapped. "Can't you look your husband in the eye?"

"Sonny, you've had about five too many," said Fitch.

"Well then, have five more and catch up! Vermiel! Hey, Vermiel! Bring—"

"Not for us," stated Foots Taylor abruptly. His wife rose with him. "Jill, thanks for—"

"But wait," said Sonny, flummoxed, as he held out his hands, "we've got dessert, we've got more wine, more—"

"No, believe me, we've had a bellyful," said Foots tersely, and Susie managed a straitjacketed sort of smile and waved as the state legislator took her by the other arm and led her to the entryway.

Sonny flapped a bored hand in their direction. "Fine, go, it's been a gas, don't let it hit you in the ass," he sang out as the door slammed. "Jesus," he then mumbled, and surveyed the rest of us. "What?" he demanded, his brows furrowed with incredulity. "I find out that three people I've known all my life are conniving behind my back, and *I'm* supposed to apologize?"

"Uh," cut in Aynsley, clearing his throat and smoothing his seersucker jacket. "As charter nonmembers of the three in question, we should say our goodnights. There's a re-run of *My Favorite Martian* we really need to catch."

But Sonny ignored him. For the first time all evening, his attention had turned exclusively to me. He seemed, in fact, to be considering the whole of me, and of he and I together; and with every blink of his eyelashes, his focus intensified.

"You never were much for words," he commented, and chewed on a finger as he meditated.

Aynsley and Sheila were standing over him. But they weren't moving. Nobody was.

"I mean, I can't quite figure out why you chased down Tempesta to spew your guts out to him this afternoon." He shrugged, mumbled to himself, "Guess the mood for conversation hits us all at funny times."

His eyes returned to me. "But you just never were a talker."

"Oh, I've got plenty to say," I told him.

"No, you really don't," he said. His teeth appeared from behind his lips. "You may think you do. When it comes down to it, though, you don't settle things with your mouth. Isn't that right."

His eyes had become slits. I could hear the blood gurgle in my ears.

"Go to bed, Sonny," came Fitch's voice, and then I heard Jill's chair move, and her say something to the others, and the other chairs drag against the floor. But by and large I could hear only the sloshing, from one side of my skull to the other, and all else lost to the rising tide . . .

until his voice rose up higher, though not so loudly—only in a sure, coldly searing arc, the arrow with its singular mission, its designated target:

"Show us how you talked to Judge Castlebury," he beckoned. "Show us how you do your talking."

And then I flew, as did screams and furniture. But I was quickly earthbound—I was barely a child whose flailing body Kirby Morris easily restrained, while just out of reach, that baby face chorused:

"You see? You see? You see what you are?"

8

Under the sheets and blankets of the bed where I had slept as a child, I could hear the rain splatter against the roof and feel the premature snap of autumn. A bleak bluish light had crept into the bedroom by seven in the morning, but things did not brighten in the coming hours. Now and then I peered out from the covers, and through the dimness I could make out the relics of my youth bulked on shelves and hanging tilted from the walls. Then I would tumble back into sleep, or semisleep, with the room's familiar images hovering beneath my eyelids: the *Golden Book Encyclopedia* volumes filled with sketchings of dinosaurs and glossies of the Grand Canyon, the New York skyline and the Dakota prairies; the first record player my parents had bought me, accompanied by the red and blue plastic discs of cheery nursery rhymes; the autographed photo of Sandy Koufax in mid-delivery; an old woodcut Pawpaw had crafted of three blue ticks gathered around a cypress, baying at the raccoon arched high in the treetops; tarnished Little League baseball trophies, a long-vacated ant farm, sea shells from Galveston, a commemorative JFK silver dollar, a photo of me perched nervously upon a brood mare at the Taylor ranch . . . I stirred, remembering then that I was expected to call Foots Taylor today about the job he'd found for me. Then I pulled the sheets back over my head and fought to retrieve my sleep.

The rain did not stop all morning. Nor did the phone in the kitchen stop ringing. The caller would persist for minutes at a time, then hang up and immediately redial. It might have been Mimi, who didn't make it home last night. It clawed at my guts to imagine her in some kind of fix. Yet I was in no state to rescue anyone. Not after these three weeks in Shepherdsville. *Congratulations*, I told myself. *You've sure made quick work of things. Poor pitiful bastard—if this is what you do with freedom . . .*

I felt drained of all resolve, weak as straw, from the moment when Kirby Morris grabbed me by the waist and held me twisting in midair while Sonny sprayed me with taunts. He deserved to die then and there, and I deserved to kill him. But the demon that had so readily disposed of a far lesser foe, Judge Castlebury, would not answer my call this time. And where that had left me, by evening's end, was on this scrawny child's bed. My only desire was to shrink from the wilderness my life had become. But the damned phone would not stop ringing. Eventually, I shuffled into the kitchen and unplugged the phone in mid-ring. The silence was exquisite.

I lingered in the shower until I'd exhausted the hot water supply and most of Mimi's shampoo. Outside, a thunderstorm was in progress. I turned on light switches throughout the house en route to my bedroom, where I searched for something clean to wear for my visit to Foots Taylor's office. Nothing qualified, except for the grey double-breasted suit I'd bought with Sonny's money a week before. I pulled it out of the closet, held it up just long enough to imagine what would become of me if I ever wore it again. Then I tossed the suit onto the floor of the closet and shut the door.

My father's closet throbbed with the odor of mothballs. Nothing had been removed. From one of the hangers, I pulled out a checkered maroon-and-white long-sleeved cotton shirt—Texas A&M colors. It had been his children's last Christmas gift to him. He'd worn it all holiday season long, both to town and around the house, telling everyone whether they'd asked or not that the Aggie shirt was a present from his kids. That wasn't his way, I now thought. Doc Coleman didn't flaunt and brag. But maybe, I considered as I undid the buttons, his ways had begun to change that season. Maybe he'd discovered some wisp of a line deviating from that ramrod path he'd believed to be his one and only . . . And maybe he'd approached that new course, set one foot upon it and dared to test its trueness. He would've pulled back, of course. No one could fault him for that. But how fine, if tragic, a notion, that Doc Coleman chanced to stray a bit, before returning to the path that took him away for good.

I tried on the shirt. The sleeves were too short, so I rolled them up. I then pulled out a pair of his khakis, a rawhide belt and his everyday workboots. Standing before the mirror, I felt instantly ridiculous. But I couldn't help smiling.

I clomped back towards the kitchen in the workboots. But in mid-stride, in the living room, I froze. I had seen something. The invasion of another presence. Looking to my immediate left, my heart stopped cold.

Sonny was standing outside, looking through the window at me. He wore a dark suit and held a black umbrella above him. Through the rain-splattered window, his image was mottled and indistinct. But there was no mistaking the big-chested, round-faced figure, or the minty glare that burned out of him.

He'd been there for some time, I knew. We were maybe six feet apart, peering out at each other from our separate worlds—he in the cold and the storm, hulking over the flowerbed; me paralyzed in the house and clothes of a dead man. The rainfall cloaked his attitude. He was, at this moment, thoroughly incalculable. For the first time ever, I was frightened of him. We stood there for many minutes, saying nothing to each other; and the accumulating silence said all there was to say about me and Sonny.

Still, I waited.

His first words didn't so much penetrate the staccato of rain as blunder through it, hard and factual, from far away.

"Jill left the house," he said.

I could see just well enough through the downpour to tell that he was waiting for some kind of reply.

"Good," I said.

The change in his expression was like clay hardening in a kiln. "You never stopped loving her," he said. "Even when your best friend married her. Even when I made it possible for you to come back here a free man and start a life of your own. That didn't mean shit to you. All you wanted was to take what's mine."

His head turned just a couple of degrees. "Why is that, Hadrian?" he asked. "Why have you tried to take from me? After all we've been through together . . ."

"You're insane," I said.

I saw him flinch. Then a pale smile inched across his face. "You'd like to think that," he said. "But we both know what the truth is."

"Do we? Then you tell me the truth, Sonny! Let's hear it!"

The shrillness of my voice startled me. But its effect on him was entirely different. His eyes were focused, calm; for a long time he just gazed at me that way, not saying a word, while my heart pounded.

Then, abruptly: "Sissy Shipman's coming to my office at five o'clock today to interview me about the riverhouse. A courtesy call. The story's already in the can. It'll be in tomorrow's *Chronicle*."

He set his jaw. In a low voice, he said, "That story's going to be the end of me."

A reply was expected. Again I let the silence speak.

"Tempesta dragged me down with him," he went on. "Like he said he would. He laid it all out for her. Fitch did, too. Somehow he got wind of all this."

He smiled, but I knew what the stare meant. "Not from me he didn't," I said. "But you go ahead and believe whatever you want."

He continued to stare. Did he believe? And why the hell did I care?

Sonny muttered, so that I could barely hear him: "I don't want to see Sissy Shipman this afternoon."

At first, I wasn't sure I heard him right.

Laughing, I said, "Then don't see her."

His gaze fell to the mud at his feet.

"I want her dead before then," he said.

Then he looked up and said to me, "I want you to kill her."

I blinked hard. "You're joking."

"Do you think this is a goddamn joke?" he yelled.

"Sonny—"

"I want you to kill her, and I want you to kill Tempesta, and I want you to kill Fitch! I want them dead, and I want them dead today! All of them! Today!"

"Get out of here," I said. "Get away from me."

Instead, he took a step closer, drawing himself an inch away from the window. His hot breath sprayed against the glass, so that in his nearness he began rapidly to disappear.

"You're going to do this," he bellowed. "If not for me and all I've done for you, then for Jill. Do you know what this story will do to her? Think about it, Coleman! You love her? Fine! Show it! Do as I say!"

Beneath the film of his breath, he was a retreating ghost.

"*Now!*" he commanded, and then I heard a car door slam.

. . .

Waves of rainwater rolled through the streets of Shepherdsville. I plowed through the churning, creeping, fishtailing traffic. The courthouse square was empty. Lightning trembled beneath the clouds. Shepherdsville went wildly aglow, then fell back into a hounded darkness.

I slowed at the approach to the director's mansion. Both cars were gone. I sped up and headed west towards the avenues. A single porch light beamed from the Estelle residence, but no car sat in the driveway. I got out of my Impala and held my windbreaker over my head as I ran to the front door.

A middle-aged black woman in a blue uniform answered the doorbell. "I'm Hadrian Coleman," I said. "I'm a friend of Jill's. Can you tell me where she is?"

The woman squinted at me. "Who'd you say you were?"

I repeated myself, then added, "I'm a family friend. Ask Professor Estelle."

"Well. He's at school. And I don't know where Miz Jill is. She was here this morning, but she ain't here now. She's gone."

"Gone?"

The housekeeper shrugged and smiled apologetically. "She went off to the Houston airport. That's all I know."

Cal Fitch peered up from his desk at me. He motioned for me to close the door, which I did. "You all right, youngun?" he asked.

"I'm sorry about last night," I said as I sat down in Thunderball Hope's old chair.

His smile was pained. "So am I," he said. "But it damn sure wasn't your fault."

He leaned over his desk towards me. Quietly, he said, "It won't be long for Sonny, you know. Best thing to do is stand back at a safe distance and cover your eyes. See no evil."

Fitch then added, in an even quieter voice: "You can trust me. I've been through this drill before."

The former deputy director stood, scooped up a stack of pink message slips and eased his way over to a corner of his cramped office, where a small wastebasket sat. "This," he said, holding up one of the papers and then crumpling it and dropping it into the garbage, "is a message from Sissy Shipman. She's got the goods on the land swap. No surprise there. It's running tomorrow.

"And this," he then said as he held up, crumpled and disposed of another message slip, "is from Art Jacobs of the *Dallas Morning News*. And this one's from the *Austin American-Statesman*. And this one's from the *San Antonio Express-News*. They're all reporters from the capital bureaus. Tempesta must have gone to Austin and sung a damn opera. And not just about riverhouses. Oh, and this one's from the governor."

He folded the last one, stuffed it in his shirt pocket and offered a helpless shrug. "The governor knows I've been around a long time," he said.

But now he seemed burdened by this, and with his arms cradling his chest, two fingers reached up and massaged his bowed head. "Just the stupidest, most ticky-tacky stuff," he said beneath the palm of his hand. "Giving and getting. Nothing too big. But it'll come at him from all sides. Tempesta was smart. He's been gathering string on Sonny for just such an occasion. Now each paper's got a separate thread to play with. The Dallas reporter wanted to know if I'd heard anything about the director swindling some of TDCR's beef and spreading it around to friends in high places."

As I remembered the night at the riverhouse, something must have registered on my face, because Fitch eyed me curiously. Then he went on: "The Austin guy said he'd heard Sonny had awarded illegal contracts to two construction firms in exchange for a couple of lucrative speaking engagements. The reporter in San Antonio's chasing down a sex-for-promotion angle. Sonny dipping his pen in the company inkwell. Nothing major. Just little pins in a voodoo doll. But Sissy's story—that ain't no pin, youngun. That's a nail in the coffin."

He lowered his hand from his face and shook his head. "I led you wrong a few weeks back," Fitch said as he leaned against his unadorned wall and pretended to examine his fingertips. "When I told you I didn't think Sonny was fundamentally dishonest . . ."

His voice trailed off. "Cal," I said, "I've got something I need to tell you."

He returned to his desk. There he sat, level-eyed and tight-lipped, while I related how Sonny had asked me to kill Ricky Tempesta, and later, Sissy Shipman and Fitch himself. I revealed the truth about my killing Wexler so that he could comprehend how Sonny had convinced me to silence Tempesta—namely, by claiming falsely that Tempesta had gotten it straight from Digby that I, not my cellmate, had done Wexler the damage . . . which, of course, would have exposed Sonny's public lie that he'd been privy to a deathbed confession from Digby, but which would also expose me, pardon notwithstanding, to reprisals from the legal authorities.

Then, when I realized that Fitch could not completely understand why Sonny felt so certain that he could stir the loyal killer in me, I paused, took a breath, and retold the story, beginning it as it had truly begun, on August 5, 1974, in the blueberry fields of Judge Horace Castlebury. I used Sonny's own description of what had happened that day—that in a thirty-second rush of violence, I had saved his life and ruined my own; but, I told Fitch, the two acts were by no means separate. Having looked all the way down into my grief-hollowed self and seen not so much as a spark of promise, I had exaggerated the importance of Sonny's glow to my own life . . . so much so that I had reacted to the judge's assault on him with a doubled rage, avenging us both through the evening's carnage. For that fatal dependence, I could only blame myself. And it seemed only right and just to crown my upside-down life with the thorns of this misdeed, and meanwhile, let Sonny go on being precious Sonny—which was all that mattered anyway, it seemed back then.

Or almost all. I then spoke of Jill, and how I'd loved her since the first day I had fled her presence—making possible Sonny's courtship of her. I told Fitch what I'd never dared even confess to myself. I said that I believed Jill loved me, but that she, too, had come to view her years in the town of her forefathers as a kind of death sentence, and only Sonny could make Shepherdsville bearable for her. How he felt about her I couldn't say, but in the end it was probably irrelevant, since insofar as Sonny could love someone other than himself, he doubtless loved me, too. And he'd deceived us both, over and over. He had stoked our self-doubt, kept us hobbled, the better for us to serve him.

At that, Fitch suddenly removed his bifocals and covered his face with his hands. A soft moan of pain fluttered out from beneath his palms.

"Wait," he said.

He lifted his hands. The expression they revealed startled me. "Do you have any place to stay outside of Shepherd County?" he asked.

Before I could manage any kind of reply, he said, "Look." Then his gaze fell to his desk, and he cursed inaudibly. His normally unflappable face was now creased with worry.

"I don't blame you for not telling me all of this before, Hadrian. But damn, I really, *really* wish you had."

He stood up and began to pace. "Tell me again what Sonny said to you that very first night you came back to Shepherdsville."

I thought for a moment. "You mean, when he said he'd needed me back in the worst way?"

"See, Sonny gives himself away," he declared. "I just didn't have all the information when you first mentioned it to me. I figured he just wanted you to take care of Tempesta—which, at the time, seemed plenty bad enough. I was pretty sure he was recruiting you for a killing. You remember, I warned you. Couldn't spell it out for you then. I've been around a long time. You don't go speculating aloud that your boss is a conspirator to a murder plot."

"I should've seen it all from the start," I said.

"But here's what you still haven't seen," he said, and stopped his pacing to face me square. "Sonny needed you back? Why? To kill Tempesta? Well, yes and no. Yes, Sonny's in deep shit. Yes, Sonny saw you as someone who might get him out of deep shit. Did you hear the key word, youngun? *Might*."

I looked up at him, puzzled. But inside of me, the truth was beginning to surge like lava.

"Or," Fitch said, and leaned into me with an upturned finger, "might not. Because, you, youngun, are a major part of the deep shit he's been wading in. You know the darkest secret of his life—that he was a witness to a murder that wasn't a murder at all, and he never stepped forward to shed the light."

My stomach executed a single hard somersault.

"He ran off and left you. And damn it, Hadrian, I don't care how guilty you felt then or how guilty you feel now. That incident, as you're now describing it to me, is not in any way, shape or form a capital murder. Call it justifiable homicide. Call it involuntary manslaughter. Disfigurement of a corpse. But *think about it*," and his words came at me so seductively: "Think about how the jury would've reacted if Sonny Hope had taken the stand and said, 'I was there. It was me he assaulted. He had a gun. And he could see.' Think about it!"

"It's . . . it's too late," I said, shaking my head.

"Not yet! Not yet!"

I listened for the rain but couldn't hear it.

Fitch took a step back away from me. "Put yourself in Sonny's shoes," he said. "Because of his cowardice, his best friend's in prison. Remember, we're already talking about a kid who's been bullied by his old man for being a powderpuff. Your being where you are, in white—and later, *in his own household*—man, that's daily confirmation to him that Thunderball had it right. And so he lashes out at his daddy. Brings him low with his Herrera testimony. And that takes care of one demon."

"One demon," I murmured.

Fitch nodded grimly. "See, if I'm Sonny," he said, "I see you, Hadrian Coleman, as living proof that I'm a fraud. Unless . . ."

He waited for me to supply the answer.

"Unless," I said, the words coming to me as the realization did, "I'm nothing but a killer."

"In which case, he did the right thing to run off that night at the blueberry fields. For all he knew, you might've gone after him next. So you see where I'm going. Sonny Hope has a lifetime's worth of investment in the belief that killing is what Hadrian Coleman is all about."

While I was absorbing this, he stepped towards me. What he did next I was not prepared for. Squatting, he held my head on either side with his firm, supple hands. His eyes, level with mine, were suddenly liquid.

"Youngun," he said, almost mournfully, "you understand, don't you, that for the sake of his own sorry conscience, Sonny has done everything in his power to convince you, and therefore himself, that killing is what Hadrian Coleman is all about. Do you understand that?"

Soft though his delivery was, the message came as a body blow.

"Do you?"

"Yes," I said.

"And youngun," he continued in that same hushed but persistent tone, "you understand, don't you, that you have been acutely susceptible to his persuasions?"

"Yes," and with the word came tears.

Down came his two thumbs, and swept the tears away.

"But youngun," he said, laughing sweetly, "you don't believe that horse manure now, do you?"

Cal Fitch stepped back and let me be.

In a minute or two, I felt something being laid upon my lap. I saw that it was a box of tissues.

"I keep it for the inmates' mamas who come to see me," he explained as I blew my nose.

By the time I'd finished dabbing, the chief of Inmate Processing was back at his desk. He looked at me expectantly. When I nodded, so did he.

"Now, I'm fixing to tie all of this into the present," he said. "But before we get to that, I need the last chunk of history. You'll see how it fits in."

Dunce-like, I could only bat my eyelashes.

"The escape, youngun," he urged me. "Tell me about the escape."

To get to the woods, I had to cross Highway 392. Gasping for breath, I sank to one knee. It was ten-fifteen. There would be a roadblock, of course. As a kennelman, I'd been on manhunts before. They all had the same ending, despite the best laid plans, of which I had none. Until five hours ago, there'd been no need. I was on my way out. I'd done fifteen of my fifty years, and three weeks ago, the parole board had informed me that that was enough, that in a month I'd be a free man. In the meantime, Wexler had been denied parole for the fifth time. He'd thrown a weight at me in the rec yard, and I'd thought little of it.

I couldn't even remember stabbing Wexler. I could only recall his dying gurgles as he pawed at the handle of his own eight-inch shank embedded in the lower recesses of his heart. And then Digby bustling past me, wrenching the sheets from my bed, stage-whispering, *"Go!"* I'd gone, leaving my dogboy padding impaled on the northeastern perimeter. That had been the easy part. Now I crawled on my belly to the cover of a fallen oak, and from there I studied the highway. Just after a pickup whizzed by, I scrambled across the road.

I ran and kept running. The land on this side of the highway was densely wooded. Then, progressively less so. Plumegrass and wild rye gave way to an untended carpet of bluegrass. Behind a row of sweetgums sat a small wooden cabin with no vehicle nearby. The doors were locked. I pushed my way through a back window. Inside, I found cold beans, a camouflage jumpsuit and a pair of hunting gloves.

Not far behind the cabin, a pine plantation rose up from the clay. Less than half a mile through the pines came a clearing. Railroad tracks. My heart leaped. The words buzzing as through some ancient megaphone, spoken by an old kennelman named Kittycat Nelson—so named for his backwoods diet, they used to say, but the moniker stuck because of his success in eluding TDCR tracking dogs on three occasions. They'd finally transferred him to the Hope Farm, where escape was thought to be impossible. And that's where I'd heard his gummy baygall twang: "Dem dogs, dey bad to lose dey feets on dem tracks when dem flints gits to chewin' up dey pads." I was a few hundred yards north of where I'd begun to run down the middle of the railroad ties, when I remembered who else had heard Kittycat Nelson tell his tale that morning: Sarge C. C. Holliday, the boss of the Hope Farm kennels, who, I had to assume, was on my ass at this very moment.

Maybe he'd forgotten about Kittycat's monologue. Doubtful. Impossible. But I kept running, the flintstone crunching under my flying feet. My watch said eleven-thirty. Wexler had been dead for six hours; I'd been over the fence, and thus officially an escapee, for five. For what had to be four hours, prison officials had known I was an escaped murderer at large. I'd already seen evidence of their vigilance on Highway 392. But the question pounded along with my feet: Where were the dogs? I had half-expected to see the eight canine members of Pack A when I emerged from the cabin. Earlier I'd waded through a slough to throw off the scent, but that would take for only so long: Sarge Holliday would have known to drag the dogs a mile or two ahead of where the scent failed. He was TDCR's pre-eminent dog sergeant. There was nothing I could do to fool him for very long.

So where the hell was he? As I charged up the tracks, I tried to picture C. C. Holliday leaning back in his saddle, spitting, and telling my fellow kennelmen Sandoval and Peete, "Chain 'em up, boys. We've lost him." The image would not come. Sarge Holliday had no quit in him. And here I was, known by the pursuer, my scent so familiar to his dogs that they could pick me out of an ocean of cons . . . Here was I, the most helpless fool. But so far, undetected.

Some two miles down the tracks, I leaned against one of the telephone poles running alongside the east side of the rails. I was burning up inside the jumpsuit, and my feet ached from the flintstones. Overhead, the sun shimmered a lethal white. I dragged a sleeve across my sweaty face and waited for my lungs to find air. The moment my panting ceased, I could hear them.

The baying came from off to the southwest. In the stillness of the pine plantation, I could actually count the eight throats in the wild chorus. They were at the cabin, I figured, and groaning I turned back to the north in preparation for what I knew would be only another mile or two before Sarge Holliday would gallop up on his quarter horse, rifle drawn, and harry me back in shackles to the farm—to a new job hoeing, a solid twenty years' worth of Can 'til Can't, and I would be beyond help, beyond even Sonny . . .

The name deadened my stride. There on the tracks, I turned my head, closed my eyes and listened. I knew their voices many years running. They were the voices of my manhood, a manhood spent fleeing those voices through the prison meadows—how could I not know them, the dogs I'd named Elvis, Lucifer, Calamity Jane, Willie Nelson, Casper, Queenie, Mojo, Panama Red . . . No. *No*, I realized, my heart blasting against my chest. I listened again, turning my ear to catch the unmistakeable yodel of Calamity Jane. Hers was the best nose on the farm. She carried the tune. But it wasn't this tune. Calamity Jane wasn't there. Meaning Pack A wasn't there. Meaning C. C. Holliday wasn't there. Meaning, meaning . . .

"Fuck me running. The Chadwick Unit dogs," I gasped.

It had to be. No other prison unit within a fifty-mile radius kept kennels. These were Chadwick dogs. Led by one Sergeant Grady Buckaloo—much-lauded by sheriffs and mayors throughout East Texas for all the times he'd let them quail hunt on prison land, but a bonehead in spite of his handful of successes. Not fit to shine Holliday's shoes. But if this was him and his, then Buckaloo probably wouldn't even deign to radio my old kennel boss, so confident was he of his own dubious gifts. Meaning: C. C. Holliday, who could have me any old day like a slab of bacon on his plate, would be completely cut out of the manhunt. But, but why—surely he wouldn't, surely not Warden Grissom, surely not . . .

"Oh God," I cried. "Oh God! Sonny, you beautiful bastard! You made good!"

I leaped, punching the air. Could it be? Could it really be that Sonny had come through?—that TDCR's new deputy director had called off the Hope Farm's dogs, radioed the Chadwick Unit and in so doing, gave me just enough opening . . .

I took to the rails at a full sprint, vibrant, even ecstatic. I knew what was next, and it would break Buckaloo's back—Kittycat Nelson's best trick, and Sarge Holliday knew it too, but Buckaloo would have to hear about it later, how I ran a third and final mile along the tracks before pulling the work gloves out of the back pockets of my jumpsuit, and brilliant with the knowledge that I wasn't alone, that I'd been given the chance, I shinnied up a telephone pole; how, with far less effort than it might have taken for a far less desperate man, I advanced hand over hand along the telephone wires, dangling thirty feet above the jagged flint as I propelled myself, taking my mind off of the searing pain in my shoulders and fingers by estimating the distance between each telephone pole at twenty-five yards and thereafter resting at every tenth pole, but never for long, because I could still hear Buckaloo's canines, though faintly . . . And then, while clinging to the one hundredth pole, I heard an altogether different noise. I waited, plastering myself against the pole as the train whistle came louder, until at last the engine was chugging past me. I squinted, but the conductor wasn't looking back. He hadn't seen me. And with the train still rambling just below me to the left, I made one last go of it—left hand, right hand, one pole, two, three, left, right, ten, left, right—until the tracks deviated westward, and the telephone lines led me back into a forest, or at least to its edge, where, when my arms cried out that they'd had enough, I hugged a pole and looked down and discovered that I'd done good. I listened one final time. All that came to my ears were the scrambling noises of squirrels and the incessant echoing exclamation of a woodpecker taking it to a tree.

I steadied myself, crouched. Then I dove into Mueller's Slough.

My watch died in the water. But I estimated it to be around four in the afternoon when the slough conveyed me to the swift stew of the Minerva River. From the moment I slid into it, I knew what I was in for—knew, with the first futile tug of my arms against the current, that everything before had been but a rehearsal, and that every minute from now until I reached a safe stretch of dry land would place me close to death. I stroked as economically as I could, seeking gentler seams in the current. As often as I could find them, I reached for snagged boulders and trees and crawled across them. I rested as little as possible. These were the crucial hours, the last few hours of sunlight on this first day of flight. If, I told myself, I could just make it five, six, seven miles upstream, beyond where they would think to drag the dogs . . . then, maybe, it would be safe to rest.

Around ten o'clock, I dragged my aching, waterlogged body across the branches of a felled cypress in the river shallows. I didn't know how far I'd gone. I didn't care. I could go no more. I collapsed with my back against the trunk and my feet splayed out over the branches. For a few hours I remained there. I didn't remember closing my eyes. But when I opened them and gazed flatly at the pinpricked night, I saw a star course a lazy trail across the heavens. It began to grow larger. Then I heard a sound, and I slid back into the water. The helicopter continued its descent until it was buzzing perhaps two hundred feet above me, scouring the river bottoms with its unholy lightbeam. I hunched beneath the brush and waited. The water vibrated all around me. I was shivering in it.

In a few minutes, the helicopter was gone. Far off to the south, I heard the baying of dogs. But the sounds never got any nearer, and instead faded as I did, like driftwood downstream . . .

Wait. I awoke in the deep of the night, in panic. Things felt too right to be anything but terribly wrong. It took a second or two for me to understand. My weight on the cypress branch had dislodged it from the river bottom. It and I were now coasting downriver. Wild with anguish, I kicked myself away from the limb. In so doing, I caught my right tennis shoe in its crook. I pulled away. The shoe stayed. Downstream it and the branch went. A final glint of white rubber, and the shoe was out of sight.

I turned back ahead and started to flail again. There was no hope. A baby wrestling a bear stood a better chance of survival. I'd slept for maybe half an hour, drifted away maybe four hours' worth of numbing labor. Gasping, blubbering in the water, I reached for a boulder, pulled myself halfway up. Slid back down. I could just hold my face up out of the water. And after that, there was only enough energy left to say the only two words left for me to contemplate:

"Why bother . . ."

It was then that I thought of Jill. I did not visualize her as I'd last seen her, in that blur of white silk and lace in Sonny's tuxedo-clad arms. Instead, through the leaden eyelids of the dying, I saw her beside the

Christmas tree in the director's mansion. I saw her beside my prison hospital bed, leaning to kiss me. I saw her in each of the uncluttered moments that had been ours and only ours, omitting everything before, after and in between—and in a crowning rearrangement of history, I saw in the lawn chair in the park the goddess in fitful meditation . . . turning, seeing me there behind the tree, and then extending a feathery hand.

Which I took. Which took me upstream, in those desolate hours, when I had no one and nothing else. In the Minerva, against the Minerva, my strength multiplied. I plowed through the river, no longer bothering to find the accommodating pockets in the current. I just threw myself against the river, and kept on throwing, long after the blackness of the sky was pierced by a blood-red fingernail of light—long after the dawn exploded and daylight spread across the river bottoms, and the sun rose and conducted its day's worth of August tyranny. I outlasted everything the river had to throw at me—so that I may not have looked like much of a conqueror, or much of anything else, when well into my second evening in the water I found the fork that was Bernadette Creek and heaved myself into it. But I had won.

And it didn't sink in for several hours that I'd been fueled by delusions and worse. Well after I'd dredged myself out of Bernadette Creek and broken into the icehouse to steal food, money and fresh clothes, and even as I stumbled like a sleepwalker for four hours and four miles before I came upon Del Sparks's ranch and saddled up one of his horses which I steered into the easternmost edge of the state in a race against the coming dawn, and even as I dismounted and shooed the horse off, I still quaked from the lover's righteous tremors. These would only subside after I'd wandered the woods and suddenly found myself standing on the west bank of yet another river. The Neches. The sound of running water sapped everything from me. Along the riverbank I weaved crazily as the morning light pierced the darkness once again. Somewhere, somehow, I looked up to find a trailer house mashed deep into the pines like a fungus. I lurched up to it, rapped on the door and could hardly believe my eyes when it opened to reveal a skinny bearded fellow with a bandana tied around his head.

"I just need to lie down," was all I could say.

The fellow laughed, because inside the trailer was a methamphetamine lab, and neither he nor the others had themselves slept in days, and would I like to partake? "No, no thanks," I whispered, and without an invitation, I curled up on the hallway floor, hearing nothing—not my hosts, not water, not dogs, not helicopters—until a voice that sounded like mine, though surer than ever before, rang out accusingly from the cavity of my soul:

He saved you. Sonny saved you. And all you could think about was Jill.

I lay there, a guilty man prostrated before the day.

"There," said Cal Fitch, snapping his fingers. "That's where he stuck the meathook in your back."

"I don't follow," I said.

"You will. Start with this. Why did you run, Hadrian? Digby saw what happened. He would've testified on your behalf. In fact, he did later. Told all the investigators exactly what happened, and stuck by that story, the true story. Until . . ."

It hit me. "Until Sonny made him lie," I murmured. "Wait. Wait. So you're saying Sonny gave the order to use the Chadwick dogs because . . . Damn it, Cal, you've lost me again."

"Youngun! Listen! Sure, he wanted you to escape. But why? For your good? Hadrian. *Was* it for your good?"

"Oh, Jesus." I looked up, gaping. "You mean, he did it for himself?"

"Very much so! Put his whole damn career on the line! But not just for you, youngun. Oh, I'm sure a part of him thought he was saving your life. I've no doubt he's told himself that. But he also did what he did to make an outlaw out of you. To preserve your criminality. And yes, to put you in his debt—but that's secondary, don't you see? His entire life is bound up in evidence of your criminal behavior. You want proof? Here it is. He convinced Digby to lie, and in so doing, got you a pardon—and again, he did this at significant professional risk. And I'll bet you even thanked him."

"Well . . . yes."

"For what? Hadrian, have you hung that pardon on your wall? Have you gotten the red carpet treatment because of it? Does the world treat you any different now? *That pardon trapped you.* Not just by making you beholden to Sonny, but by making you live a lie. Sonny's lie. So let me lay it down. Okay? Twice now, Sonny has made a killer out of you. And you never were. But twice he made you one. Through his lie."

I nodded. "But he won't again," I said. "That's all over."

Cal Fitch sat erect at his desk, studying me. Then his head moved to one side, the other, the left, the right, like a bell clapper.

"It's not," he said morosely as he continued to shake his head. "It's not the least bit over."

Now his head retreated almost entirely into his collar. I stared at the headless Fitch, who inside his shirt let out a moan that I first took for disappointment. "Sonny," came the muffled voice, "needs you to be a killer more than he needs you to kill."

His head resurfaced. "Now," he acknowledged with an unbothered wave of his hand as he leaned back in his chair, "I'm not saying even Sonny sees that. Good chance he doesn't, in fact. I've no doubt he'd be pretty tickled if you mowed down me, Sissy and Tempesta. But we're not his biggest threat. You are. He can feel that even if he isn't conscious of it. In refusing to bump off Tempesta, Sissy and me, what in effect have you told Sonny? That you are not, in fact, a killer. How is the boy who turned tail and ran from the blueberry fields supposed to take that?"

I pondered this. "It's sad," I said. "I've all but ruined him."

"All but! Think! Thunderball all but ruined him, too! And who got ruined in the end?"

"Oh, come off it, Cal," I said. "Are you telling me Sonny's going to try to fix my wagon?" I let out a laugh. "He wouldn't even know how."

"Wh—? Damn you! Look at you! Sitting right there in the dunce's chair! A big old dunce, just like his daddy! Damn you both!"

He slammed his fist on the desk. Before I could do anything except sit up straight, Fitch hollered out, while continuing to pound on the desk: "That boy finished off his father so fast and so smooth, the old man didn't even know he'd been cut 'til he looked down and saw the blood shooting out of his chest! But that ain't nothing compared to the mess he's made of *your* life, Coleman! Taking an innocent boy and making him into a goddamned murderer! Twice! He's had a number put on your back and taken away your whole damn youth and the woman you love and made you hide eight years like a rat in a woodshed . . . And you mean to tell me Sonny Hope doesn't know how to fix Hadrian Coleman's wagon? Mercy!"

I nodded, laughing stupidly. "You're right, Cal," I then said. "Of course you're right. But—"

"But what?" Fitch demanded, and he flung his arms in the air with exasperation.

"Well, you said yourself that they're all coming after Sonny. His whole world's caving in. Shit, he could end up in white. He doesn't have time to settle anything with me, Cal."

Fitch nodded. "But you're in the middle of all that," he reminded me. "Like I said. I had it wrong about Sonny. His entire life is propped up by lies. You know that better than anyone. He will keep on lying to the bitter end. He lied to his wife's face. Lied to me, lied to Foots. He'll lie to the press and to the governor. He'll go down in a blaze of lies. But, Hadrian . . ."

He had my attention.

"It's the big lie that's always preoccupied him. He's always found time for it. Even at great risk, remember?"

I nodded.

"It ain't Tempesta Sonny's after. It ain't Sissy. It ain't me. It's you. Ever since that day at Judge Castlebury's, it's always been you."

I rubbed my hands against the arms of the chair. I retrieved the vision of Thunderball yesterday—desiccated, malignant with hate. Yet Fitch was right. Compared to me, Thunderball had gotten off easy.

"You should get out of the county," Fitch said quietly. "Bo Worley'd be happy to bust you for something, we both know that. In practical terms, Sonny's already framed you for murder twice before. Just a precaution, then. Get out of Worley's jurisdiction. Cool your heels for a couple of weeks. Or as long as it takes."

My head was throbbing. "Shit, Cal," I muttered. "I don't know where the hell I'd go off to."

"I do." Finally, a grin of real pleasure. "I've got kinfolks three counties over, just outside of San Augustine. They've got a peaceful little spread, and a little pond you can fish on."

"Cal, I couldn't do that."

He chuckled softly for awhile. Then he said, as his grin widened, "It'd be returning an old favor. It's my cousin's place. Billy Rivers. You remember that name?"

"Rivers . . ." I squinted, shook my head. "I've got a vague memory, but I can't place it."

Fitch folded his hands, licked his lips. "Thirty years ago," he said, "Billy Rivers's mule got shot in the belly by the Klan."

My whole body tingled. "And my dad . . . God. You are one scary bastard. That was your cousin? But, but wait . . ."

As it dawned on me, Cal Fitch folded his arms across his chest.

"That was my first year down here from Detroit," he said. "I was getting my master's in criminology from East Texas State."

His expression deepened. "My very first night in Shepherdsville," he recalled, "I went into George Worley's bar and I asked for a whiskey sour. And George Worley looked at me, and he said: 'You've got to be kidding, boy. I don't serve niggers at my bar. Now you get on home.'

"And he turned his back on me. And I thought I had made the worst mistake of my life, coming down to Shepherdsville, Texas. I gave George Worley some lip and stormed out, and early the next morning, he and his pals put on their white hoods and rode over to where I was staying at my cousin's house, and blew a hole through his mule."

He worked his lips as he stared off somewhere past me. "I stood over that poor bloody mule with my cousin crying by my side," he said. "And I thought, 'There's no humanity here. I'm gone.' And just as I finished packing my bags, I heard that Doc Coleman had saved that mule's life."

His eyes were grave but rippling with tears. "I've been around here a long time, youngun," he said. "Thanks to your dad."

Then he reached for the phone. "Let's give Cousin Billy a holler," he said.

And so I passed the ensuing days well east of the Minerva river bottoms, in the moss-robed acreage of Billy Rivers, his wife, their three children and their ten grandchildren. The air, both inside and outside the main house, was always syrupy, always choked with mosquitoes and love bugs, but I didn't mind. From the moment I pulled up, I wasn't anything but Doc Coleman's son and Cousin Cal's friend. And as Billy said to me, his eyes both sharp and glistening wetly, "We're real proud to have you."

They assigned me a bedroom, in the cool northmost side of the main house, and they lent me a fishing rod as well. The pond was a good four acres, and Uncle Billy had stocked it with Florida and Cuban hybrid black bass. Everything under six pounds, he informed me, needed to be thrown back. I laughed incredulously, which made the grandkids laugh, too—but at me. By the end of my first full day there, I had felt obliged to raise the minimum to eight pounds, which still afforded me six keepers. I volunteered to do the gutting and scaling, but Billy's daughter Retha got in my face and laid it out for me: "You already done half your job. Now get in that shower and do the other half!"

Before supper, Billy would ask for silence, and the family and I would join hands around the two long cypress tables set together. "Our gracious Lord, who hath given us the bounty of the earth and water," he would begin, his rich voice so obviously kin to that of his younger cousin Cal Fitch. Eyes shut, I believed I was beginning to see things for the first time. Then he finished, the platters went round and round, and so did the conversation and the laughter. No one asked me where I'd been or where I was going to next. They did ask me about Cousin Cal, and Billy prodded me with queries about Doc Coleman. Beyond that, they stuck to topics of fishing and weather and recent births and deaths. After the meal had gotten the best of us, the men sat on the porch and smoked and passed around a bottle of Rebel Yell. Then I'd pretend to turn in, and when the others had gone to bed, I'd sneak back out to the pond, watch the moon's reflection sizzle upon it like a great fried egg, and swoon to the baleful melody of the bullfrogs.

In bed I'd stare up at the moths on the ceiling. In all my life, I'd never been made to feel so at home. But I was not at home. I was, in a sense, where I'd been only a month ago—undercover, hiding for my life. It was all because of Sonny. That, at least, was clear. But when I thought of him that night in the blueberry fields, running from the crime but thereafter from himself, a cold burn shot through my chest. I told myself that I couldn't live that way. I was through running.

On the fourth night of my stay at Billy Rivers's country home, I was reclined fully clothed against the headboard, eyes open in the dark, when it occurred to me what I owed it to myself to do next. I gathered my few belongings, scribbled a hasty note of apology and thanks, and tiptoed out the kitchen door.

Two hours later, I was back in Shepherdsville.

The third time after I rang the doorbell, a hallway light came on in the house. I heard the drowsy, uneven shuffling of feet. Then a waxen, bespectacled face appeared in the front door window.

"Hadrian," mumbled Professor Estelle as he scratched at his pajama bottoms. "It's rather late, don't you think?"

"Please tell me where to find her," I said.

The flight attendant, a middle-aged but still perky brunette, fastened my seat belt for me, replaced my tray table and showed me how to work the headphones. "Channel 17's real soothing," she suggested. Then she patted my shoulder and whispered in my ear, "It's like sex. The less you worry about being in control, the better time you have, right, cowboy?"

I smiled weakly as she bustled down the aisle towards the cockpit. Then I strapped on the headphones and shut my eyes. I had never been on an airplane before.

Alone among strangers at an altitude of thirty thousand feet, I thought of everyone I'd barely known—cons, drifters, Bonnie Bier-bauer, my juvenile probation officer, Dillard Bunch, Chu-Chu Her-rera—and how each of them, through the brush of chance, had diverted me this way or that. I wondered if by the end of it all, my life would stand as one great, incoherent blunder, defined, as much as any-thing else, by the actors who had stepped in only to throw me off-balance. That's what I had done to Sonny, I thought, and him to me. Neither of us meaning the other any harm. All along, he'd probably been telling himself that it was all for my good. And Fitch had left me off the hook, but the question was too glaring for me to ignore: Where would we both be now, Sonny and me, if I had demanded he come for-ward and tell the jury about what he'd seen out at the blueberry fields? Would Sonny be in half the trouble he was in now?

The answers were obvious, and they played hell with my stomach. In short order, I bought and knocked back two beers. Sleep did not come. But I still felt jostled out of a dream state when the plane touched ground. I stumbled out into a world of fluorescent corridors, uniformed men with leashed canines, and hundreds of voices speaking a language that wasn't mine. I offered up my bag and my birth certifi-cate for inspection. In an hour I boarded another plane, more cramped and with brisker service. No longer preoccupied by the novelty of fly-ing, I gnashed at my fingernails—not my habit, but rather Sonny's, and for the thirtieth time today I wondered if other friends behaved in so vicious a manner as he and I had conducted ourselves for all these years.

I emerged from the second airport with my father's cloth suitcase in hand, into a swarm of arms outstretched for my fellow travelers. I pushed through the hugging masses. Looking down, I noticed that my shirt was splotched with sweat. I had never thought it possible to find a part of the world as muggy as Deep East Texas. From the curb stepped a middle-aged man in a short-sleeved cotton shirt and sandals. He gestured grandly towards his cab.

"Is air-conditioned, *señor*," he assured me. I handed him the address I had been given, and he, in turn, held open the passenger door.

Fifteen minutes later, while peering out the window, I asked, "Are we close?"

"*Claro que sí*, it is only—"

"Then let me out here," I said. "I want to walk."

The driver shrugged, pulled over. He gestured to my destination, a few blocks ahead. I gave him fifty *pesos* and dropped my suitcase onto the sidewalk.

Before me stretched the shaded main square of Mérida, Mexico. Though it was just shy of six in the afternoon and commuters surged to beat the traffic lights, a lustrous, dulcet tranquillity held forth. A horse-drawn carriage clopped past me, conveying an old woman and a basketful of mangos. Another woman with a basket crossed my way on foot. Inside were plastic bags bulging with *achiote* chili paste. Even from ten feet away, they gave off a brawny aroma that filled my mouth with primitive longing. Clumps of pensioners sat on benches in the plaza. They were short and very dark, with oval-shaped eyes that lent even the most shabbily dressed of them an air of imperial bemusement. I lifted my gaze, taking in the plaza's lush Yucatecan vegetation, and further beyond, the looming colonial palaces and churches that framed the square like a dreamy eruption of the heart somehow set to canvas. I had seen nothing like this before—though with that thought came the sudden belief that I had. It hit me then. This, I imagined, was what Shepherdsville almost could have been, a spectacle of exotic enterprise, before Joshua Estelle's original bungle that made possible the town's perversion. This was why she was here.

"*Caballero. Sus zapatos están muy sucios. Venga aquí, caballero.*" I saw that the man on the bench who had called out to me had some semblance of a shoeshine kit beside his feet.

He beckoned me with a vigorous wave of his arm. "Uh, well, gee," I mumbled, thinking: *Have I ever had my shoes shined by someone else before?* God knows I'd shined Thunderball's a thousand times. I looked down at my watch but did not actually check the time. My stomach throbbed as it had on the airplane. I felt like stalling.

For a few minutes, I watched from my place on the bench as the man squatting before me dipped his brush into a glass jar and painstakingly layered my scuffed shoes with black polish. Then I closed my eyes. Mérida and I were far away.

"Veinte pesos, señor." I had been asleep. Looking down, I saw that my shoes were now so glossy as to accent the dreariness of everything else I was wearing. I searched my pockets, came up with a twenty-*peso* bill, and along with the currency I handed over several coins the denominations of which I didn't bother to discern. The man nodded solemnly, and I retrieved my suitcase and departed the square.

Above me on Sixtieth Street, young couples sat on the individual third-story balconies of a glamorously appointed restaurant and sipped at their drinks while regarding the bustle all around me. I walked beside the shop windows. Wooden masks, silk hammocks, the ubiquitous short-sleeved *guayabera* shirts—but now, as I approached my destination, the merchandise and the animation fell away from my field of vision. I took the final blocks in a haste that did not become my environs, but where I was had suddenly become inconsequential to me in the face of the sheer recklessness of my being here. The sweat rolled off my chest in waves as I lengthened my strides, and I thought of the mess I must look like with my clothes and my grey hair plastered against me. But it was way too late to care about appearances.

The building occupied the corner of Sixty-second and Fifty-seventh Streets. The mammoth wooden doors gave way only after a concerted push. I found myself on a black and white tiled patio, situated around a garden exploding with flowers, cactus plants and rubber trees. Marble tables were positioned asymmetrically throughout, some directly under the sun, others set off in the shade. At one of the latter, two men sat smoking cigars and playing cards. They peered out at me from the hand of cards fanned out before each of them.

"Bienvenidos, Señor Coleman," said one of them, and stood. He seemed lighter in pigment than the others I'd seen. His peppered hair was thin but curly. Though unsmiling, he instantly betrayed a predisposition towards wry humor.

"I'm Anibal Torres," he said as we shook hands. "This is my humble and somewhat decrepit *posada.* And this is Francisco," he added, indicating the stockier, darker-skinned man still seated at the table. "Would you like something to drink? Perhaps a *cerveza*, or sangria, or maybe a little glass of tequila?"

"I'm fine," I said as I looked around. The high melody of clandestine songbirds drifted through the garden. Tucked into the vegetation, a fountain gurgled water into a wide and mossy basin. "How many hundreds of years old is this place?"

"Five," said the proprietor as he inserted his cigar. "I can bore you with the history whenever you are ready. But first, I am sure you would like Francisco to show you to your room."

"Yes. But . . ."

"Ah." Anibal turned to his assistant, and they exchanged a barrage of Spanish. "Señora Jill will be back in perhaps an hour. She has gone to the coast to watch the flamingos. Please. Give your bag to Francisco."

The winding stone staircase looked as if it would crumble, but was too fine a sight to induce panic. Cracked and dusty paintings of glowering images hung at every turn. Francisco stalked ahead, my suitcase in hand, murmuring Mexican verse. At the top of the third floor were two sets of double doors. Francisco fumbled with his keychain, then stepped over to the doors furthest from the staircase. He wrestled with the lock for a moment, then swung the doors open.

The room was impossibly vast, with twenty-foot ornately molded ceilings, baroque chandeliers, a four-poster mahogany bed and rust-and-green snowflake mosaic tiles. A clawed tub squatted in the bathroom. Green velvet curtains cascaded from brass rods. Francisco drew them back to reveal iron grille balconies. He nodded towards a small round table covered by white linen, which in turn was bedecked with fruit, a pitcher of water and a bottle of champagne.

"Is okay?" he asked.

"It's very okay," I said, and collapsed on the bed as soon as he left.

The room was still filled with green light when I awoke to the sound of feet softly ascending the staircase. I jumped up, rustled about for my clothes. My feet were still bare when the knock came.

Jill wore a white sleeveless blouse. Her yellow hair was pinned up off her neck. Though her face was rosy from the heat, the color made her appear invigorated, unencumbered. She looked me up and down, mouth slightly open.

"You found the place," she began.

Then her lower lip trembled, and Jill fell against my chest.

"Oh God, Hadrian," she sobbed. In my arms, she seemed to dissolve into sand.

She pulled away, just enough so that she could look up at my face while she rubbed away her tears with the back of her hand. "I don't know what to think about you being here," she said. "Which is to say, I'm glad—but I don't know what to think about that. Or about anything else." Her voice trailed off.

I gave her shoulders a soft shake. "But it's so beautiful here!" I said.

I had to look just to the side of her as I added: "You're so beautiful here."

The air, already moist, now seemed unbearably freighted. Jill stepped back and held up a straw picnic basket that had been sitting at her feet. "I bought some decent wine today," she said. "Not the easiest find in this part of the world, let me tell you. Of course, you can't go wrong with the tequila, until you go utterly wrong with it. Same with the sangria. It'll be a welcome respite. How was your first flight, by the way? You don't look particularly haunted by the experience."

Her nervous ramble made me smile. "It was like riding a bicycle," I said.

"Dinner's at eight," she went on. "And it's not to be missed. Anibal does the cooking himself. He's from Andalucía originally, and the Mediterranean touches are a welcome change from the—well, you'll see. I haven't missed Vermiel's cuisine, needless to say."

Then she smiled shyly, took three steps forward, leaned up and kissed me on the cheek. "It's wonderful to see you," she said, by way of assuring me. But I still could not help feeling like a trespasser.

"So how did you find this place?" I asked her at dinner.

Jill dabbed at her mouth with her napkin. "My father used to take me to the Yucatán in the winter," she said after she swallowed a bite of *ceviche*. "He was always fascinated with the Mayan ruins. You'll see why when we have Francisco take us to Uxmal. But I don't have the eye for detail my father does. He could marvel at a single doorway all afternoon long—never mind the door itself."

She giggled. "It could get somewhat tedious for a teenaged girl," she added. "So he'd leave me behind in the city, where I'd spend the day trying to find adventure. I found Anibal's *posada* during one of my meanderings. He was younger then, as were we all, and really quite dashing. He gave me my first shot of tequila."

The private smile begged the question. "Oh, no," she then said, anticipating me. "I was in good hands. Anibal's a misogynist at heart. Being from a prison town, I knew not to take it personally."

Jill then pursed her lips as she gazed at the great stucco walls streaked with smoke from old lantern smoke, like apparitions of romances past; then directly overhead us, where the fans dangling from the wood-beamed vaulted ceiling whirred at blinding speed. "Every time I leave here," she said quietly, "it's torture for me."

"Have you been here with Sonny?" I asked it as casually as I could.

She smiled. The very sound of his name, it seemed, had conjured up a welcome hilarity. "God no," she declared. "Anibal would never look at me the same way again. Though I have been to Mexico with him. Cancún, of course."

Her voice suggested annoyance, but the smile remained. "What a memorable time that was," she said. "There was an international corrections summit. Wardens from all over the world. In our company there were Cal Fitch, Kirby Morris, Scotty Folger, and several Dutchmen Sonny had taken under his wing. Let's see. Kirby went snorkeling and was ravaged by a school of jellyfish. Scotty Folger had convinced himself that every woman in Cancún had her price and got into a horrible barroom brawl when a waitress refused his fistful of *pesos*. Cal Fitch, God bless him, accompanied me to the pyramids at Chichén Itzá. We came back that day to find Sonny hopelessly sunburnt from playing volleyball on the beach. Oh, he looked so miserable! So I was saddled with the Texans and the Dutchmen for that evening, and when we returned to the hotel Sonny wasn't there. We searched everywhere. Cal Fitch returned with him at about two in the morning. He found him in a tourist bar with a sombrero on top of his head, smoking Cuban cigars with the chief of the judicial police, who happened to be the uncle of Chu-Chu Herrera and Sonny Hope's biggest fan."

She rolled her eyes as I laughed. Anibal sidled up, replenished our wine glasses and set down two bowls. "Here is the *sopa de limón*," he announced wearily, and trudged back off.

"It smells great," I said.

"It is great," she said. But in that interval, the foundation of our dialogue had buckled. Haloed in disquiet, Jill sat frowning in her wooden chair, head bowed, bare shoulders momentarily shuddering.

"I don't know what I'm going to do, Hadrian," she said. Her hands rose up from her lap, then fell again. "Every day I think about calling him. If we could just get by without saying anything of substance . . ."

It took nearly a full minute for the meaning of her words to register. When they did, I could not help but snap, "Jill, wake up, would you? You sound like a goddamned addict."

"Do I?" She smiled faintly. "I guess I do." She lifted her spoon. "It's a classic of the Yucatán. Don't let yours go cold."

"Look," I said, leaning towards her. "You're not alone. He's duped everyone. And no one more than me, Jill. You may not think that's possible. But I . . . well," and I forced myself to meet her wary eyes. "I have a lot to tell you, Jill. A lot. Not here, though. Later. God, why am I even talking about this now—how could I dream of spoiling this, all this . . ."

My voice was trembling. Jill reached out with both of her hands. She wasn't wearing her wedding ring.

"That's right," she said resolutely. "Let's enjoy this." And we did, more or less, for the food was wonderful, and the dimly fevered lights had a way of accenting us and only us—her most of all, I was sure, for even in her hesitancy Jill was immaculate. Her sleeveless dress was grey silk; I felt like a goddamned gym coach in her presence. But not a con. Not anymore. Here we were, wherever we were, and I even saw the candlelit reflection of myself in a wineglass, and when I tilted the glass to apprehend her reflection, our faces had drowned in wine . . . What was I doing here? And what had taken me so long? But let it last, let it last, spare us both each and every minute before the truth must smear this perfect light . . .

Still, I did tell her, late that evening, on a porch that spilled out from her bedroom and overlooked a deserted park, while I poured the tequila and she drew the sweater around her shoulders. I took her from the blueberry fields to the flowerbed of my parents' house just a week ago. We talked for an hour after that. Then I went back to my bedroom.

.   .   .

I almost slept through lunch. Anibal looked up from his newspaper as I clambered down the stairs. "I think that you are needing a tequila," he told me.

"I doubt that," I mumbled as I fell into the chair beside him. "Where can a guy get some coffee around here?"

"At once," he said somberly. The proprietor eased himself out of the chair and shuffled off towards the kitchen.

He returned with a smoldering cup of coffee, along with a small platter of scrambled eggs, delicate corn tortillas, and *chile pibil*. "Francisco took her back to Celestun," he said as he returned to his chair and his newspaper. "I don't know what it is about her and the flamingos. Every time she comes here, she heads for the water. Never gets wet. She only watches the birds."

"I've never seen one before," I said. "Are they really pink?"

"Like a baby's bottom. A baby's bottom with wings." He chortled a little, then turned a page.

When I finished, Anibal took my plates, then returned with the pot of coffee and a cup for himself. We sat together in silence for some time.

Then he said, with no inflection in his voice, "You cannot find your kingdom."

His expression was scrutinizing but nonjudgmental. "You are like me," he said. "Named after one of the great leaders in all of history. The great general Hannibal and the mighty emperor Hadrian. And here we are, in this almighty wreck."

I smiled. "Any time you want to trade places," I said.

"No thank you. The *señora* has told me about your little city." He shook his head, wincing, and I had to laugh.

"But even if this is no castle," he continued, dismissing the fine old *posada* with a backhand, "I have a kingdom. A kingdom to rule and a kingdom to serve."

He patted his chest. Then he made a fist of the hand, held it there between us. "A place," he said in a low, firm voice. "Just a place. One that is yours. A *place*. That is your kingdom, *señor*."

His sleepy stare held me. "I'm getting there," I finally said.

"Yes. Yes."

Then his eyes turned mischievous. "Do you want to get there on a horse, *vaquero*?" he whispered.

Jill sat alone on a marshy beach, staring out into the Gulf of Mexico. A hundred yards away, Francisco leaned against his car, smoking a cigar. All but mummified in their separate worlds, neither heard our approach, until an island not far from the shore suddenly exploded with the flight of dozens of pink flamingos.

She turned, then stood. The oversized denim shirt she wore had to be Sonny's. When she saw who it was, she flung her arms into the air and let out a delighted shriek.

"*Aiii! Los hombres de Marlboro!*"

I dismounted my quarter horse, whose back was indomitable, with rippling hindquarter muscles and a brilliantly arrogant red mane. Anibal's steed was Pegasus-white and far more cantankerous, though the Spaniard wasn't about to be bettered. Both horses glistened with fresh sweat.

"You had better take mine," Anibal said as he handed me the reins. "You remember where we picked them up? There are always taxis waiting there."

Jill snatched the reins of my horse out of my hand. "Who needs a taxi?" she said. "Just set the table for four, Anibal, with the appropriate carrots and sugar cubes." She stroked the red mane.

"Do not be late, *señora*," intoned the proprietor, "or you will be wishing for sugar cubes. Francisco! *Vamonos!*"

Before Anibal had reached the car, Jill had already mounted. "*A la playa!*" she cried, and coaxed her horse into a canter. I caught up, and together we raced along the brine-colored sand.

Anibal could tell that this dinner was different. He stayed back, let us pour our own wine. We poured and poured. Around Jill's neck sparkled a string of pearls. *Why did she bring them here*, I wondered— *what was she expecting, could she have known I'd come* . . . Our hands found each other's and would not let go. We ate and drank and poured one-handed, and talked over and over about the greatness of the ride and how wonderfully sore we felt. When she turned her head to catch the full of my stare, and ran her thumb along my knuckles, I knew I could say it.

It came out thin but decisive, a spear of truth. "I've always loved you, Jill."

Her eyes shone. She didn't flinch.

"That very first day," she said, marveling at the recollection. "When we decorated the tree together at the mansion. We saw all the way down into each other then, didn't we?"

"God," I laughed softly, and lifted her hand to kiss it. "Long before that day."

And I unspooled it, that epic thread that had sustained me throughout the Creel Unit.

"Hadrian," she stopped me early on. Panic brimmed in her eyes. "This is scaring me."

I lowered my eyes. But then I felt a tug of her hand.

"No it's not," she then decided.

We did not trade words on the staircase, nor in the upstairs hallway. She opened the door to her bedroom, and I followed. A brief memory fluttered past, uninvited—that of the two of them on the threshold, a swirl of black and white—but it was banished at the closing of the door. Jill pulled herself up to me by my neck. Our lips met. I had never imagined how the kiss would feel—imagined, instead, the world it would lead me into. My nerves melted, from my tongue to my toes. Unaccountably, a voice inside me screamed out a prayer: *Please don't let me let her down, Lord, please don't let me lose her* . . . Her lips pressed full against me; a little moan suffocated in her throat. God, we were both burning up. She pulled her face away from me, to look back behind her and measure how far we had to go to get to where we had to be.

"Will you get the light?" she asked. "But leave the lamp on?"

Her back against the pillows, Jill watched me approach her. I had never seen such a look. Devoid of absolutely everything other than that thing it was absolutely full of. She did not have to wait for long—though a voice inside me begged, *Slow, slow, measure every moment* . . . But there would always be that other voice, the long-fretting one, in concert with the fevered other . . . I heard her shoes slide to the floor, meant not to be heard at all. Mine followed. The first one, somewhat discreetly. The second, like an encyclopedia dropped on a library floor. She let out a husky whisper of a laugh. Stupidly, I thought of putting my shoes back on and doing it again, to hear that laugh . . . With a deft pivot of the hip, she was on top of me. Her eyes set against mine. No more secrets left. Jill's lips trailed down to my neck. Her fingers worked the buttons of my shirt. Then she kissed my chest, kissed the hairs that had gone grey behind bars well a decade after I'd cast aside all fantasies and dreams that such a thing as this might happen to a grey ghost such as myself. But "God," she whispered—to whom? to me?—and then: "Look how handsome you are." And then she wrestled with the belt buckle, her face comically determined, but she didn't ask for help. "Come here," I begged when she rolled my pants down off of my feet. *Look at that sly smile*, I thought as she rose up and then arched her back as the zipper slid down with her.

But it was different after that. Once we were naked, the grinning ceased and the world was struck tongueless. For the longest time, we held each other tightly, heartbeats joining in the shrouded light of what we both knew was not our home, not our love nest, but instead our hideaway—and now, to go forward, we would have to face that. And when we did, without a word exchanged, we both moved just a fraction, it seemed, and both of us gasped.

Later, we rested. Later still, we got dressed, figuring to go for a walk, but something incited us as we stood in the hallway and we all but tore each other's clothes to ribbons beside the staircase. In between those moments, though, Jill lifted her head from my chest to see if I was awake. When she saw that I was, she inched herself forward and then rolled so that she lay flat against me, all the way up to her neck.

"I want you to love me," she said.

Those eyes could not be doubted. "I do," I said. "I always have."

"It's not our fault," she then said, perhaps to herself. "We both know that. But this couldn't be right. What we're doing. This couldn't be right at all."

A coldness spread across me. "Don't, Jill—"

"Unless," she interrupted, and flaring her back she crawled up my body until her lips were directly over mine. I watched them say it again: "Unless . . ."

Her tongue traced the upper arc of her mouth. "Unless I love you," she finished. "Then it has to be right."

It was a whisper that followed:

"I do."

The lips fell upon mine. "It has to be right."

A kiss.

"I do."

Another.

"It has to be right."

I could not take my eyes off of her, could not stop listening to her, could not keep from touching her. But the desperation was articulate in its own way. We would not be here forever.

During my fourth night in Mérida, while Jill's body pressed up against mine, the dam shoring up my subconscious collapsed all at once, and I jerked upright from a nightmare.

She felt for me, calling out sleepily: "Hadrian?"

I was sitting up, holding my hair in my fists.

She turned on a light. "What's wrong?" she asked.

"I didn't tell her," I said. "I should've, and I didn't."

Jill sat up. "Tell who what?"

"Sissy Shipman," I said. "I didn't warn her that Sonny wanted her dead."

I rubbed my eyes. "I'm sorry," I said. "I just dreamed that he killed her."

She was wincing. "Sissy Shipman. *There's* another country heard from. Do you always dream about other women after—Where are you going?"

"I'll be right back," I promised, but I couldn't look at her, and slunk naked out the door, feeling both sick and confused. In my bedroom I fumbled through my wallet until I found the number of Sissy's home office in Shepherdsville.

She picked up on the fourth ring. "Cecilia Shipman," came the flat voice.

"Sissy. It's Hadrian Coleman."

"Coleman! Where have you been all my life? I've been trying to get ahold of you for over a week. Mimi says you flew the—Hey, what's with the connection? Are you in Mexico or something?"

I almost laughed. "Sissy, listen," I said. "I've got some things I need to tell you. About Sonny, I mean."

A laugh. "If I had a nickel for every time I've heard that sentence in the last week . . . So tell me. Is this the indebted houseboy leaping to his pal's defense? Or is this the last rat off the sinking ship?"

"I'm . . . I'm not going to defend him."

"Really? Too bad. I could use a little variety in my copy. So what've you got?"

I heard the distinct high fluttering of notebook pages. From the other side of the bedroom wall came sounds less traceable, but they suggested that Jill wasn't in bed anymore. *She's mad at me,* I thought. *Jesus, it was just a goddamned dream . . .*

"Hey, Coleman. Are you still there?"

"Sissy?"

"Yeeeees?"

"Do you ever feel like you're in way over your head?"

There had been some faint background noise from Sissy's end of the line. Presumably the television. Abruptly, it disappeared.

"Coleman, part of my job description is to destroy people that need destroying. But still, to destroy them. How much over my head could I get than that?"

"I'm pretty scared," I said.

There was a pause. "I believe you," she then said.

"Sissy?"

"Hadrian?"

"He asked me to kill you."

Through the wire, I believed I could hear her mouth open, then close.

"Well," she began, but the sigh was unsteady. Then I swore I could hear her lips crinkle into her smile. "But he got you wrong, didn't he?"

"Yes."

"You're a good egg, Coleman. Don't let anyone tell you otherwise."

"Okay, Sissy."

"Though if you do change your mind, could you at least give me enough time to go to the hairdresser?"

"I'd take great care not to muss your do."

"You charmer you. Do you mind telling me where the hell you are?"

When I didn't say anything, she chuckled and said, "I know you're not in Trust. No one is. Reverend Ricky will go down in history as the man who built the first city ever to become a ghost town two months after it was incorporated."

I knew, now, where I would have to take this. "Tomorrow night," I said. "I'll fly in tomorrow, and I'll come by your home. You still have the same address that's on your card?"

"It never changes, I'll never leave, they'll bronze me at this same fucking address. What time?"

"I don't know. Pretty late, probably. I'll call you from Houston Intercontinental. Sissy?"

"Yes, dear?"

"He'd kill us if he knew we talked."

"Well then," she said, and after a lusty laugh barreled out, she continued, "I guess that puts us in the same cozy canoe, paddling together up Shit Creek."

"I'm serious."

"I know you are. You think I'm not? Call me. 'Bye."

Jill was sitting up in her bed, reading or pretending to read a Mexican newspaper. She didn't look up.

"So you found humor in it," she said.

"What?" I stopped short of the bed.

"The dream," she said, and folded the paper against the blankets covering her lap. I saw, then, that she had put on a T-shirt. "I heard you laughing in the next room. You seemed scared out of your mind when you left here."

I sat down on the other side of the bed. Jill didn't move. Every inch between us now bulged up like a succession of pylons. Her gaze was intent, and there was a tautness in her neck. "That's not fair," I said.

"Fair?" she said, spitting out the word. Both her eyes and mouth mirrored a cold astonishment that distorted her entire face. "You bolted out of my room in the middle of the night and phoned that, that vile—"

"She's not vile, Jill. Jesus, for all the rotten things people in town have said about you, I'd—"

"I'm not talking about what people in town think. I'm talking about what I think. She's an awful person."

Her voice was frosty. "Anyway, I'm glad you've recovered from your bad dream."

"Jill, come—"

"Do you think you're the only one who's been having nightmares?"

she demanded as she threw the newspaper to the floor. "Do you have any idea what the last few days of my life have been like?"

I fended off the implication—that I'd been scarcely a firefly buzzing my feeble light through her world of darkness—and tried, instead, to imagine what she'd been through. But then I jumped to my feet, suddenly red-faced, and loudly I said, "The last few days? Do you want to trade? Hey, you just found our your husband made a shady real estate deal! Has he asked you to kill anyone lately? Do you feel like he's out to kill you? Come on, Jill! Let's trade!"

I could barely see her rage for my own.

"The last few days," I sneered. "Let me tell you about the last *twenty-three years*. While you were tanning in the park, or shopping for sweaters, or—"

"Will you stop!" she shrieked.

I would not and could not. "Or vacationing all over the world, moping in your mansions or your *posadas*," I hollered, "I was stuck right up the very asshole of the world. You couldn't even imagine it! But all that time I thought about you, goddamn you!"

Choking, I said, "While you were laughing it up with Sonny! Well, I'll laugh with Sissy Shipman or whoever the hell else I want to!"

My God, I thought, almost entranced, when I was finished.

She spoke in a barely controlled monotone. "You need to leave," she said.

"And you only pretended to love me," I then said, just before I threw myself out the door—after which I stood for a moment on the other side, waiting for her denial, or anything else from her. Then I went into my room, and slipped into the sheets I'd barely touched throughout the week. My heart was in fragments. From the other side of the wall, I listened for a noise. Any noise.

Well, how about that, I told myself. *You've finally done something on your own.*

Jill had left and Anibal was nowhere in sight when I awoke the next morning. I asked Francisco if he would take me to the airport. "Take taxi," he told me, his lip curled.

The driver took me past the main square on the way out of town. I looked out at the world I'd barely grazed with my fingerprints and tried to remember how I could ever have been in it. I pictured her out along the coast, staring out into the boundlessness. It was funny, I figured without amusement. All these years I'd thought of myself as a killer, and I wasn't. And instead, my one true love had become my first true victim, the first vulnerable person who had intended me no harm but got all the malice I had to give anyway. It was the last thing I could have possibly imagined doing. What I'd dreamed about all those years had been within my grasp, and I'd smothered it in my fist.

An even less funny notion occurred to me—that possibly this was what a normal life was like.

At the airport, a sense of panic overcame me, the sudden realization that I had turned away from the best life I could have imagined for myself. A stoic calm settled in somewhere over the Gulf of Mexico. We were like two moons, Jill and I, cast in parallel paths around Sonny. That I had fallen off my axis only made her further from my reach. I wondered, with a stab of sadness, if we would ever see each other again—and wondered, regardless, what my time here had meant, if I'd sent even the minutest tremor to that fatal orbit of hers, around the man I was now coming home to betray.

That's what it had felt like, from the moment I had heard Sissy Shipman flip open her notepad—though I'd also felt other things at the time, and gone a little giddy as a result, and Jill had heard me laugh . . . Of course, Sonny himself was the ultimate betrayer, but that brought me no comfort. His was the reflexive kind, as natural to him as one of his horse-laughs; and as Fitch had made clear, all of us had been fools to expect anything less from him. But what I would inflict was something else again: calculated, with the full expectation that it would devastate. My head pounded, and I requested some aspirin from the flight attendant, along with a Jack Daniel's. The plane was virtually empty, and before sleep drew itself over me, I rested my head against the window and succumbed to a child's fantasy—that of me as a lonely arrow, whistling through the stratosphere in some unfathomable arc, leaving a rainbow in my wake, and hoping that the world would rejoice in the colors I'd shed, and forgive me my arrowblade, dipped as it was in poison.

Houston was a reflection of the sky, dark but for its starry freckles, when I landed. At the airport pay phone, I called Sissy Shipman's number.

"If you want anything other than Scotch to drink, pick it up along the way," she said. "I've also got leftover turkey and some rice-based disaster my dog wouldn't eat."

"Keep it out," I said. "I'll be there in an hour or so."

"We'll have a big time. 'Bye, Coleman," and she hung up.

I stepped outside. Houston felt like a moist rubber glove around my body. I walked through the airport parking lot and its sea of vacated cars. Despite the flight, despite everything else, there was life in my step. Things were starting to fall into place, to assemble into a sort of path. *Find your kingdom*, Anibal had said. I was closer, I believed. In fact, I could have sworn I'd experienced this sensation before—that I'd walked these very steps. Or no, I realized, and the shades of the evening changed just as I found my parked car: No, I hadn't walked, I'd been driving the other time, it was a road, though barely one, and there was more light back then though its ebbing had felt more kin to evening . . . But what reminded me of it was the mounting clarity, the understanding of what I'd lost and what I had left . . . which should have warned me back then of what was to come . . . The shot ringing out . . . *He can see.*

He knows.

Sonny stepped out from behind my car. His smile had a twitch to it.

"Welcome back to the boondocks, bubba," he said.

The dimples disappeared. "Jill called. She told me what you were up to."

I had to smile at the grim inevitability of it all. "Did she," I said casually.

"She did."

He gusted out one of his long-hard-day sighs. Then, from the front pocket of his suit pants, he withdrew a .38 revolver and wiggled it in my direction.

"What do you say let's go for one last spin," he said.

9

"Yeah, you sure learn about your friends when the shit starts to sizzle," Sonny said as he crouched forward from the back seat and trained the revolver on my neck. I took a look in the rearview. His eyes were darting in either direction, and I noticed that his cheeks were a malignant grey. But his voice, loud and tunefully bitter, still possessed the breathless zeal of a twelve-year-old kid who'd just witnessed the neighbors having sex.

"It's been a whirlwind week in Shepherdsville, bubba. Every day's been like a day at the rodeo." The whites of his eyes shimmered. "First, the story about the riverhouse comes out. The governor calls me and orders me to sell the property. I tell him I've tried, but I can't, it's under my wife's name and I seem to have lost track of the girl."

A spidery grin, but he let it go at that and continued, "Then, come to find out the D.A. has empaneled a special grand jury. Meanwhile, Fitch and Tempesta have been spurting from every goddamn hole to the press. 'Course, I asked a friend for some help with those two, but I guess that friend had more pressing matters to attend to. Anyway, so in three straight days I get gang-banged by the dailies. Your sweetheart Bonnie Bierbauer, she comes out saying I promoted her to CO-II after she sucked my rod. My good buddy Foots, he announces he's purely shocked to learn that the beef I gave him last month was TDCR property that should've gone to inmates, and he's reimbursed the state and called for an investigation. Boy! I mean, can't friends be just *special*!

"Then, when the *Austin American-Statesman* writes that I awarded prison construction contracts in exchange for so-called lucrative speaking fees—I mean, ten grand is lucrative? Give me a fucking break. Wick Fucking Aspromonte gets ten grand for blowing his nose on opening night at the National Corrections Association's annual grip-and-grin, and he's not fit to carry my codpiece, I mean knowledge-wise we're comparing Newark, New Jersey, to the planet Jupiter, okay? Anyway, you'll love this. Soon as that comes out, my counsel, Aynsley Reeves, turns in his resignation, 'cause that's the kind of friend *he* is. Then yesterday, the grand jury indicts me for bribery, contract-fixing, theft of government property and for breaking a bunch of laws they hadn't even written yet as far as I can tell.

"And boy. Was it something. The handcuffs, the fingerprinting, the mug shots. I mean, all in all, I thought it made for a pretty full day. But I guess the governor disagreed, 'cause he fired ol' Sonny while the sun was still high in the sky. And then he ordered the grand jury to go back and find some more things they can hang around ol' Sonny's neck."

He coughed out a laugh of mock disbelief. "I told them, I says, 'Hey, how about hanging that lowest crime rate in ten years around my neck while you're at it?'"

Then he shook his head, retreating into his gloom. "I won't miss it," he vowed. "Not one goddamned minute of it. The phone ringing all day and night. Those fucking sallyport gates rattling my teeth every time they slam, and the inmates hollering"—and here his voice went Sambo shrill—"'I take yo ass to the hole you punk mothuhfuckuh, I make a bitch outta you right here right now!' while they're playing their five-on-five buttfuckball in the rec yard . . . Shit, and all those slimy lobbyists and vendors, all those wardens who hated my guts which is one badge I'll wear proudly, I tell you what. Hoo-hee. I'll bet they're all drunk as monkeys right now. Ding dong the witch is dead. Fine. Let 'em celebrate. Let 'em resurrect Trust and put it all on Tempesta. They'll get just what they deserve. I'm happy for 'em. I truly am."

I drove the Impala northward up the interstate towards Shepherdsville—taut, nervous, but curiously unafraid. Unlike my days in prison and on the run, when every shadow pulsed with menace, my enemy was here with me, and I knew him well. As to what would happen next, I didn't think even Sonny could say. So I maintained the speed limit, saying nothing, keeping my own movements to a minimum; but inside I felt clear-headed and almost, almost in control.

"So like I was saying, it was one of those weeks," he went on, though more sharply now, "when you learn a helluva lot about your friends. Especially your best friends."

Laughing, he sang, "Oh, I called and called. Silly me. I should've known that instead of rushing to your oldest friend's side, you'd be in the Yucatán fucking my wife."

At that, his voice became agitated: "Fucking my wife, and plotting to fly in after you were done with her so you could tell the world every rotten thing you could think to tell about ol' Sonny. Now that's friendship through and through. Wouldn't you say? Hey, wouldn't you? Answer me!"

He jabbed the revolver into my neck, pitching me forwards. Just outside, cars and pickups and eighteen-wheelers skated blissfully past us.

"If that's the way you want to look at it," I said quietly.

I couldn't chance a look back. But I felt him spit his hot breath against my neck.

"Tell me . . . *any* other way to look at it."

I decided to hold my tongue. He fell back against his seat, smirking at my silence. "Jill left me," he finally said, his voice at a low simmer. "But see, she's still loyal to me. She still loves her boy. She wasn't gonna let you destroy Sonny like that. I told her," he went on, laughing at first it seemed, until I realized that he was choking back tears, "I said, 'Boy, honey, they're really heaping it on ol' Sonny this time. When are you gonna come home and give me one of those patented back rubs?' Did she give you one of those, by any chance?"

He peered over the seat, studying my face. "Fuck you," he snapped as he again reclined. "I don't want to know." He loosened his tie. "Though you'd like to know how *she* answered my question, wouldn't you? Well. That'll just be part of the mystery."

I couldn't suppress my smile. "What mystery, Sonny?" I asked.

"Oh," he said, weighing the matter and then concluding, "I guess it'll have to stay under wraps. Would you like to know where we're going? That much I'll give away. We're going to the Minerva River."

He was watching. I tried not to react at all. After awhile, I said, "It's a big river, Sonny. Do you have any spot in mind?"

"None, really. I thought I'd let you choose. Though nowhere near my riverhouse, if you don't mind." His voice hardened. "We're liable to get coldcocked out there. Been vandals throwing things at it—night and day, ever since Sissy Shipman saw fit to publicize its location. All these bottles shattering against the gate. Hell of a racket. Not that it matters. I hadn't slept much anyway. Still, it's damned uncivilized, don't you think? It'd be different if they were throwing money."

He began to chuckle. "Imagine that," he said. "The peasants throwing money at the king," and as we drove the notion held fast to him, provoking bursts of laughter that seemed to grow progressively huskier, until he seemed almost unable to draw air as he mumbled, "Peasants throwing money at the king" over and over, before the words diminished and the laughter flagged, and all that remained was the cold fact of the gun in his hand and the miles that tumbled past us as we made for the river.

I had never heard so much silence from Sonny. I doubted if Jill or anyone else had, either. To see him there through the rearview, splayed out against the back seat like a bundle of laundry—mute, almost cadaverous even with the flickering of a thousand crazed thoughts and homicidal urges, so defeated at being the only Sonny Hope he knew how to be . . . I worried for myself. *Survive this, you must think only of yourself here*, came the order. Still, the familiar pangs surfaced as I searched in vain for the dimples and the acre of teeth, and as I waited fruitlessly for him to flip back, with that youthfully arrogant jerk of his neck, the hair that now hung like pale yellow cobwebs over his haunted eyes. His lips tightened, curling as if to fashion a smile; then, his resolve collapsing, he breathed hard through his nose and shook his head. Again he did this, and again, the smile stillborn and quietly decomposing. He seemed to be replaying the entire catalog of his travails and missteps, momentarily seeing a light that proved to be there only so as to cheat him from it. More than once over the past few weeks, I had seen him in a confounded state, but back then he seemed sweetly at a loss. The Sonny now resting numbly behind me was at last painfully aware that he was way past all the kid stuff, that there were adult consequences to bear. The Sonny I saw in the back seat was aging before my eyes. I looked away then, for fear of catching my own haggard reflection. But I couldn't duck the truth, which was that Sonny had never been completely alone in his guilt. There'd been me, Mama Jean, Jill, even Fitch—his accomplices, his sponsors, perhaps something more pernicious. Reaching out from our own grey worlds, we had embraced the boy, shown him the profit in playing court jester. I wondered if Sonny was aware of our culpability. He knew this: we had loved him, and now he had lost us all.

Finally, in a remote voice, he asked: "Have you picked out a spot yet?"

I looked back. He held the gun against his own cheek. "I thought I'd go over to where the river takes that sharp S-curve."

"Too close to town," Sonny stated. "I've got a better idea."

He cackled. "Really, I was hoping it'd be your idea. Drive me over to where you made your break. Where Mueller's Slough empties out," he prodded. "I think FM 1674 just about gets us there."

I stared out into the darkness of the interstate. "Okay."

When he didn't say anything else, I decided to ask it: "Is there a reason why we're going to the river?"

"Yeah," he sneered. "For inspiration."

"Inspiration?"

"And because I may need a nice quiet little spot where I can pin your fucking ears back with this .38 if things turn out that way. Just—just don't talk anymore."

I shut up and I drove—though I marveled bleakly at the demise that I was witnessing.

Having never driven to where we were going, I was forced to improvise upon exiting the interstate. The roads were unlit and poorly marked, and I worried that the false starts, backtracks and sudden turns would irritate Sonny. But he stared emptily and silently ahead, content to let me muddle through. I looked down at my watch. Ten-fifteen. Sissy would be checking her watch, too. Fatigue now fell on me. In this country we navigated, I had amassed a lifetime's worth of history, but tonight I felt none of it. Nothing registered but the duress I'd been placed under. Maybe he did have a plan, I thought, and perhaps one very much to my detriment. Maybe, though improbably, he would squirm out of this one, too. But it would only be an exercise, I figured, a hollow last laugh. He was gone. It only remained to be seen if he would take me with him.

At last I found a clay road that ran more or less parallel to Mueller's Slough. It dead-ended at a scraggly bluff—below which, I knew, churned the river. "We there?" Sonny asked gruffly when I cut the engine. He stepped out without waiting for my answer. With the barrel of the revolver, he signaled for me to do the same. The clay broke under my feet, and when I stumbled, I saw Sonny's gun flash as he wheeled towards me. I looked up, saw that his eyes were suddenly huge with panic.

"It's okay," I assured him as I held up a calming hand. "I'm . . ."

"Just a little fagged out from all that Mérida merriment? How truly sorry I feel for you. Just lead the goddamned way."

The distance was deceptive, considering that the clay was mushy from recent rains, to say nothing of the brambles and cypress knees that rose up to challenge every forward step. I heard Sonny, the consummate indoorsman, cursing behind me as we advanced. Soon enough, though, the open-throated chant of the Minerva filled the air.

"We pretty much have to take this slope at a run," I said, pointing to the way the land slid sharply down to the riverbank.

Sonny nodded, reluctantly deferring. "Go," he said, and we galloped downhill together; and I wondered, amid the flailing of our arms and the skittering of clay clods, if Sonny was too lost in his own doom to see how very closely we now resembled what we'd once been, ages ago—if he, too, saw the boys at play, and mourned their uncharted disappearance. In that twenty-yard descent, I listened closely beneath our propulsion and the river's incantations. Had he laughed, or cried, then gun or no gun, so would've I.

Instead, we stood on the shore and gathered our breath. A paltry sliver of moon angled overhead, burning a pale gash into the water. It might have been a fetching sight to someone else. The river thrashed like a lizard's tail. I wondered what would happen next—wondered, with a dull, bedraggled kind of dread, if the Minerva was the last thing in this world I would ever see.

"Upstream you swam," he observed, nodding once towards the water.

When I nodded back, he added, in a faraway voice: "Remarkable. I'll bet no one else had done it before."

A smile came to me. "No one else had to," I said.

"Oh," he said, waving off my reply with his revolver, "that ain't the point. Or maybe it's the same thing. The fact is, you had a nearly impossible task ahead of you. No one ever told you what it was. You saw it yourself. Saw it would take everything out of you. And you did it anyway. Remarkable," he repeated, his voice steadily rising, and I could hear something else, too. "The stuff of legend. And already no one remembers, or gives a rat's ass if they do remember. And even before that, they were remembering it for the wrong reasons."

He shook his head with pursed lips. Looking then at me, he said, "But then, they just flat *forget*, don't they?"

His head was tilted beseechingly. In a sudden jerking motion, he wagged the gun in the air. "They forget! They forget all the good! Who built all those beds for all the crooks to make the streets of Texas safe again? Sonny did. Who made our prison system lawful in the eyes of the U.S. Constitution? Sonny did. And who alone had the guts . . ."

Pacing, nearly hyperventilating, his face torched with moonlight: "The guts! To rid our state of a prison boss who was nothing more than a blackhearted fucking pirate! Who? Sonny, that's who! Guilty as charged, your Honor! Yeah, I'm guilty, all right!"

He took a step my way. Jerking his neck to flip back his hair, he grinned, but his eyes were whirling. "They should've given us medals, you and me! Think about it! You rid Shepherd County of Judge Castlebury, and I chased out ol' Thunderball! Who else had the hair? A couple of green townies, that's what it took! We saved Shepherdsville, bubba! You and me! They should've—goddammit, boy, I wanted everything to be ours," he suddenly blurted out as his face blubbered up with the tears.

I could only gape. "I really did," he said, wincing to fight off the weeping. "We deserved it all. Don't you think? And bubba—I wanted to share everything. And I would have, it was always what I wanted to do . . ."

He sighed and dragged his shirt sleeve across his eyes. "Remember that day in the park?" he asked, smiling almost timidly. "That day when you saw Jill, and went and got me out of the movies, and we looked at her together?"

Astonished, I forced a smile. But I was feeling something else. "Sure," I said.

"Well . . . you ran," he said, laughing apologetically. "You just up and ran. And I couldn't believe it! 'Cause I didn't want you to go! Man, I wanted you there! You and me and her—I always saw it that way, it just seemed perfect . . ."

It was the confusion clouding his face that finally got to me.

"Seemed perfect until what, Sonny?" I demanded. "Until I saved your life, and you ran off and left me? Yeah. We agree. Things got considerably less perfect after that."

He opened his mouth in protest, but I wasn't going to give him the chance. "Don't give me that you-ruined-your-own-life crap, Sonny," I said. "I bailed you out, and you had not one, but two chances to return the favor to me, but you ran and you didn't give a statement—you didn't do shit for me, Sonny. You left me to rot. And then you were all over Jill like a cheap suit. Where the hell were you going to make room for me? Did you reserve me a spot in the corner of the bed where I'd lie like the family dog? Fuck you, Sonny. There isn't a thing you've given me that a human being could possibly want."

He was still holding the gun, and he and I both knew it. But it now seemed irrelevant, even cumbersome to Sonny as it hung to his side while he cried out indignantly, "Jesus Christ, Coleman, are you high? My dad told you himself! He wouldn't let me testify! And I'm sorry," he blustered as he paced, not sounding sorry for me at all, "that for that period of my life I was under my dad's thumb. But," he snapped, pacing faster, "after that, after that goddamn you, I was your fucking guardian angel! Never gave you anything? My ass! I got you the job in the mansion, which kept you from being somebody's butt boy all those years! And then, then, I let you escape! I called off C. C. Holliday! You gonna tell me that wasn't a gift? And then," he carried on, not waiting for my reaction, almost joyously self-consumed, "I got Digby to lie about you killing Wexler! Now, who was that for? For me? To advance my career, maybe? By getting in bed with a con so I could get you that pardon? Like hell!"

Hands on hips, he affected pure indignancy. "Hah!" he exclaimed. "I've helped you all my life! *I've saved your life all my life!*"

Now I couldn't care less about the consequences. If my life had any value at all, I owed it this moment.

"Bullshit," I said. "Everything you acted like you were doing for me, you were doing for yourself. All of it," I emphasized as the glee froze on his face. "For your own gain."

He appeared blindsided. Then he reared back, addressing the moon itself. "Gain?" he hollered incredulously. "What gain? What are you talking about? Look at me! What has Sonny gained, for God's sake?"

"Everything you've since pissed away," I said coldly. "But first you gained it, all right. You gained it for yourself, and only for yourself. All this poor-ol'-Sonny horseshit," I spat out into his shocked expression. "Heaping it on ol' Sonny, not appreciating ol' Sonny—who are you kidding? What do you see that the rest of us don't see when you step outside of yourself and gaze upon poor ol' Sonny? Do you see the spineless, selfish weasel that the rest of the world sees?"

"Oh, bubba," he said, a grin rippling across his cheeks as he lifted his revolver. "Oh, you are really asking—"

"Yeah, I was gonna ask you, Sonny. Just what is that gun for?"

"It's for pinning your fucking ears back, you ungrateful . . . now just—"

"Then do it!" I yelled. "Do you need me to fucking show you how?" And then I lunged for him, saw him blanch and grit his teeth as I reached out only to curl back at the gunfire and the cold, decisive message of the bullet, which put me to the clay.

"Oh my God, oh my God . . ."

The voice was Sonny's, though it seemed to come from a distance. A high ringing had flooded my ears. I felt for my left arm. It was there. I opened an eye and saw the blood dribbling out of the wound just below my shoulder. The bullet had grazed me, nothing more. With a wince I rolled over onto my knees.

"Oh my God, bubba, are you okay?" I watched his legs pace. "Goddamn it, I never meant, you shouldn't've—oh God, you're bleeding like Jesus on the cross. Here, hang on."

I managed to look up and see Sonny set his gun down by his feet and proceed to unbutton his dress shirt. His voice was almost paternal: "Here, boy, we gotta stop that bleeding, I think otherwise you're okay, damn I wish you hadn't've—here, hang on, don't let anyone say ol' Sonny didn't give you the shirt off his back . . . Even if he did put a little lead in you first . . . Okay, here comes Nursie . . ."

I could see, sidelong, his approach—T-shirted, grinning fretfully, his dress shirt on one hand, and in the other . . . nothing. I averted my gaze. He bent over me, proffering his shirt, muttering, "Straight off my back, bubbaloo, straight off . . ."

In one motion, I threw my good right arm into his ankles, flipping him in midair. He landed heavily, with a loud vomiting of breath. Before he had even moved a muscle, I had leaped to my feet and seized the gun. The moment my fingers wrapped around it, currents of sweat cascaded down my face.

Sonny rose up groggily. For a single second there, he could have been in bed with a hangover, muttering at the alarm clock. Then he saw me with his revolver. Whether what he saw was actually me or what I had in my possession, I couldn't judge. The whole world seemed to be panting, shedding sweat—though it was only me, I knew by Sonny's aghast expression: it was me, nothing else, to be feared.

"Don't! Please! Don't!" he exclaimed, the shrieks sputtering out for lack of breath. He held up his left hand, which still clutched his dress shirt. "Please don't, Hadrian! God, please don't kill me!"

Inside me churned an emotion I could not identify. I took two steps and stood just over him, the .38 in both of my fists, aimed for his face. Sonny went whiter still. "Please! I wasn't going to shoot you, I didn't mean to, Hadrian, *please*! I gave you your freedom!"

His voice cracked, and something cracked in me. I erupted with a growl. Sonny rolled to his side, covered his head.

"You call what you gave me *freedom*?" I said. "Free to be your hired gun? To kill off all your enemies? Or go back to the pen? Is that your idea of freedom?"

Without thinking, I kicked him hard in the legs, and he let out a muffled scream. "You gave me no choice, you fucking lowlife," I said. "Because of you, I've had to live my whole life the way you wanted it! Like a crook!"

"No!"

"Yes!" and I kicked him harder this time, in the stomach. The air gusted out of him, and his face leaked tears of pain and terror. I leaned over his squirming figure.

"You did all you could to make a killer out of me," I said into his ear. "And now what, Sonny? Now what?"

I stuck the barrel into his ear. He didn't move.

"Say something," I urged him.

"I can't," he gasped. "I can't breathe."

"Jesus Christ. You big baby." I lifted the revolver and watched him roll onto his back. His chest heaved for several seconds until his wind finally returned. Something was crawling down my arm. It was the blood, still trickling out of my shoulder. I leaned over and snatched Sonny's shirt away from his loose grip. Then I backed away from him. Holding the gun in my throbbing left hand, I stepped on the shirt, pulled back and tore off a long shred. I wrapped it as tightly as I could. I noticed that my makeshift bandage had included his monogrammed shirt pocket. The initials rose up in relief out of the spreading blood. My heartbeat began to slow again.

"Then kill me," Sonny said.

Startled, I looked to find him at rest on his elbows, his hair straggled wetly across a face that no longer registered much of anything. "Go ahead," he said. "Why not. There's nothing else for me. I can't go to prison. They'd eat Sonny alive there. No way. Sonny couldn't wear white. Wouldn't be no angel watching over Sonny."

He let out an almost luxuriant sigh. "You were right," Sonny said. He flipped back his hair and stared morosely at me. "Everything you said. They're coming home to roost, all right. The whole damn sky, it's black with 'em."

Then his eyes watered, though faintly, and a tone of quiet pleading colored his voice. "But can you make it so it doesn't hurt?" he asked.

He shifted his weight to his side, so that he could hold out his hands in a last plaintive gesture. "I don't want it to hurt, bubba. Okay? Okay?"

His gaze fell to the gun. "Okay, bubba?"

"No. No, it's not okay," I said.

I stepped his way again. He shrank back only a hair. "It was never okay," I said, surprised to hear my voice shake as I gave the revolver a spin and dumped the bullets into my palm.

"Go find yourself another killer," I said, and flung the bullets against his chest.

When I turned away from him, I believed I could feel the world spin along with me. It was finally over. The chain had been broken, and now my movements were my own. But something was still turning inside, some crude longing. Barely a moment after I'd wondered what it could be, the answer appeared. I wished I could see my father. My lids fell over my eyes. I tried to imagine what tomorrow morning would be like. But then my thoughts were invaded by the voice of Sonny, whose presence here I'd nearly forgotten.

"What?" I said, turning back to find him on his feet.

He was hugging his bare arms above his T-shirted belly. "Help me," he said quietly.

The words, humble and ephemeral, nonetheless came at me like a tidal breaker. In an instant I knew why. For I had heard those words, when . . . When did I hear them . . . Surely a lifetime ago . . .

No. In astonishment I thought: Two months ago. Only that. And I'd heard them in just this way, as the breathy cry from one threadbare life to another, a whisper out of the wild: "Help me," the voice had said, and in its asking, I could feel my own errant life return to me. For I had foraged and burrowed like an animal, spread fertilizer, hauled junk, zigzagged through the South and then the Midwest like a serpent on its belly, scrambled aboard trains and garbage trucks, and finally scraped enough together to buy the half-mutilated Impala the front left tire of which I was mindlessly drenching with my own urine on the shoulder of a farm-to-market road some time later at night in the forests off to the west of Poplar Bluff, Missouri, when the words came wobbling out from amongst the trees and thereby made me human again:

"Help me."

I zipped up my fly and ran to the source. It was a young woman, naked and bleeding out of both sides of her mouth, curled up against a tree stump. Her long dark hair was a tangle of leaves and burrs and dried blood. Both of her eyes were nearly sealed shut from swelling. I took off my windbreaker, feeling momentarily self-conscious because the jacket was dirty, and in that motion the wafting sweat from my undershirt mingled with the metallic reek of spilled blood.

"What happened?" I asked as I covered her. "Tell me."

Her bruised lips curled so as to be able to speak out of the side of her mouth. "My husband," she mumbled vacantly.

"Your husband? He did this to you?"

"No . . . They shot him. I think he's dead."

I jumped to my feet. Through the thicket of evergreens I could hear no sound. But I believed I could see something huddled against the foot of a tree, twenty yards or so down the way. "Don't move, I'll be right back," I said just before I dashed away.

He was also young, but seemed unmarred except for the bloody condition of his nose. He wore a grey suit and patent leather loafers, one of which had fallen off somewhere. "Hey," I said, bending down to his sleeping face. "Hey, are you okay? Your wife's pretty banged—oh, Christ."

The gunshot wound was between his shoulder blades. I felt for his heartbeat, then his pulse. Stooping over him, I stared for a moment.

Then I threw my hands over my face and sighed. There was everything to calculate—but then again, no choice, really.

"Okay," I whispered to myself. I lifted the young man, not much more than a boy, carefully folding him across my shoulder. I laid him down in the back seat, on his side. Then I went back for his wife. She could stand, and as she leaned trembling against a tree, I tied a spare shirt from my trunk around her waist, and then I helped her zip up the windbreaker.

I took the drive back to Poplar Bluff slowly for the sake of the young man in the back seat. The woman seemed in a kind of trance. "They took the car," she said. "They ran us off the road, and then they got in with us. They made us drive out here."

With excruciating effort, she leaned around to see her husband. I watched her hand tremble as it brushed against his wounded body. She looked up at me. "Tommy wouldn't give them the keys," she mumbled. "It was a present from my parents. But then they showed us their guns. And then, when they . . ."

She rattled out a sigh. "When they were doing what they did to me, he tried to take a swing at one of them. And that's when they shot him. Oh, God. I hurt all over."

"The hospital's just another ten miles," I said. "You'll both be okay."

Her poor swollen eyes watered. "Do you think?" she asked out of the side of her mouth.

"I do," I said.

I drove on, aware that she had not stopped looking at me. "Do you live around here?" she finally asked.

I shrugged. "Not really."

"Well then. You must've come from heaven, because you saved our lives."

I patted her thigh and bit down hard on my lip.

"We were on our way to Chicago to see some friends," she said. Somehow she managed to convey an ironic smile. "Tommy here, he likes to take the scenic route. Not no more."

She began to sob. "I'd bet a dollar that accent of yours came from Texas," I said.

She nodded, giggled despite herself. "I'm a Houston girl through and through," she said. "You ever been to Houston?"

I smiled. "I was born and raised just a few miles up the road."

Uncannily, she perked up. "You're a Texan? Well, no wonder you're so nice." She leaned over the seat again. "God, I wish Tommy could hear this. What's all us Texans doing up here in the boonies, anyway?"

"You got me," I said.

"Well, and I ain't crossing the state line again, I'll tell you that." Her smile now had a bit of sass to it. "I'm Tina, by the way."

I hesitated. But somehow I already knew it was all over. "I'm Hadrian," I said.

"You know what the best part of all this is, Hadrian?" Her smile was crippled again. "We just got married. This is our honeymoon."

I grimaced. But the girl was laughing, or trying to. I stared out through the windshield. Finally, I said, "Well. Why don't you just write this one off, and try for a better honeymoon next year?"

Her swollen eyes grew bright. "That's what we'll do! Oh, what a good idea!"

Tina's hand then fell to my lap. "But only if you'll be there," she said. "In Houston. This time next year. Our first anniversary! Okay, Hadrian? If I give you our address, will you show up?"

I had to laugh at the impossibility of it all. "I'll sure try," I said.

A medical crew rolled a gurney and a wheelchair out beside the car. The shock was wearing off Tina now, and she was crying softly. I put an arm on her shoulder and eased her into the wheelchair. Bending down, I whispered, "I need to ask a big favor from you."

She looked up, her blackened face glistening with tears. "Don't leave," she begged.

"Shhh. I have to, Tina. Please. I can't stay here."

She knew something then. Frowning, Tina said, "Okay, Hadrian."

For a moment she looked at me differently—looked at me as I'd been looked at for years. "Is that your real name?" she asked.

"It is," I said. "But please forget you ever heard it."

Her eyes, all but caved in, were still just so stubbornly human. "I won't tell anyone," she said. "But I won't forget, either. You were a miracle to us."

I had to look away. "You've got it backwards," I said.

"Next year!" she called out as they wheeled her off. "Tina and Tommy Hepler! Don't forget!"

. . .

And yet, in a way, I had. Though through the dark forest where I found their bodies I had also found the way out, I had taken the path timidly, as if it were the way back into the abyss. And so it had become. But now came the words again, spoken by the best friend I'd come to know as my worst enemy—and now, as someone I barely recognized.

"Help you do what?" I asked.

Sonny shrugged. "Help me escape," he said.

I blinked. "How?" I asked.

"Hell, I don't know. I was hoping you'd suggest something. I mean, my choices are a damn sight limited, wouldn't you say? Give up, kill myself or run off. Damn. You got anything cold or strong in that glove compartment of yours?"

I heard a laugh rush out of me. Sonny was grinning. "I mean, shee-it. Got no choice. Gotta hoof it. You tell me, bubba. What was it like out there? Was it adventurous at all? Did you see the world?"

"I saw a lot of libraries," I said.

"Don't tell me that. I hate libraries. Did anyone take you in? Did any nice, long-legged librarian fix you fresh-ground coffee in the morning and show you how to play hide-the-bookmark at night?"

"Sonny," I managed through my laughter. "It was terrible. Really. Every minute of it."

His face clouded over. "Was it better than prison?"

"Barely."

"Better than death, though."

"I wouldn't know, but I have my suspicions."

"Give me your keys."

"What?"

"Your keys. Here, we'll swap." He threw me a heavy cluster of metal, which I caught. "They made me turn in the keys to the direc-tor's mansion—like I was gonna sneak in and throw a kegger," he snickered. "But those'll get you into the Range Rover, the riverhouse, the mansion's liquor cabinet, and through the back doors of three houses kept by three very accommodating young fillies. Come on, give me your damn keys!"

He wagged his fingers impatiently. "I don't know if this is a good idea," I said.

"For who?" He strolled over to me, and I admit it gave me the chills to see him so animated again as he flopped his arms about, saying, "Look, I know what I need to do, and now I just need to do it, okay? I ain't no Hadrian Coleman—I ain't gonna tame the wild Minerva, okay? I need wheels. And I'll lose a good two hours if we go back to Houston Intercontinental, where the Range Rover's parked. Besides, for all I know they've got a tail on me now. I mean, I got to *go*!"

He shook me by the shirt collar while I grinned dumbly. "Bubba, if you had half a brain you'd be dangerous! That Range Rover kicks ass! And look, if you don't want it, sell it—or leave it at the damn airport and claim your own car as stolen! Here," he said, and as he unfolded his wallet I saw that it looked like a Cajun po-boy, overstuffed as it was with cash. "Here's a hundred," he said. "When you get back into Fairfield, call a cab and have 'em take you to the airport. Or home, or to a damn titty bar, I don't care. Will you just do it?"

I tried to concentrate. "What about my suitcase?" I asked.

"Take the damn suitcase! Only give me a shirt so I'll look only half-desperate. Okay? You with me, bubba?"

"Lord knows why," I said, surrendering the key to my Impala from my keychain and handing it to him.

He wrapped his fingers greedily around it. "Don't ask for the gun," I said. "Because you're not getting it."

He guffawed. "You think I want the damn thing? I've had it for years, never fired it before tonight. How's your arm, by the way?"

"Better than your aim," I said as I adjusted the homemade bandage.

Sonny hitched up his pants as he gazed out across the river. "You know," he said, pointing vaguely, "we were gonna build a twelve-hundred-bed medium-security unit out here next July. Just a few miles south on the other side of the river. State of the art. The best intrusion-detection fences, fully computerized crashgates, automated food dispensers. Man. It would've been beautiful."

He permitted himself a hard chuckle. "They won't do it now," He said. "They can't. Tempesta? What a joke. Only Sonny could've put it all together."

He shook his head and said, "And now it'll be back to the Dark Ages without Sonny."

We started to go. But then he looked back again. I could only see darkness and the trembling white smile on the surface of the river.

"Did Jill ever tell you about that flaky grandfather of hers?" he asked with a chortle. "The one who flew in all those sheep from Scotland?"

"No," I said, smiling. "But I read about him. Edwin Joshua Estelle.

He took it upon himself to commemorate the centennial of Shepherdsville back in '38, I think, by importing three thousand sheep from the Orkney Islands."

"And they all got the shits and died," he snickered.

"Not for awhile," I corrected him. "They did fine for a couple of years." I looked at him. "What made you think of all that?"

"Oh," he said, looking down, scuffing the clay with his shoe. I saw that he was uncomfortable. Then I saw that the discomfort was barely masked pain. "Oh," he said again, but grinning this time, "turns out that property just across the river was owned by the Estelles back then. And right here is where that fool Edwin had his damn sheep. Right over across the Minerva. 'Course, then he lost out and got so embarrassed he sold all the acreage. Sold it to the TDCR. The only Estelle to trade directly with the prison system. Unless you count Jill."

Scratching his head distractedly, he said, "Anyway. She and I had it out when we made the plans to put that new medium-security unit out there. She said, 'Can't you find any other place to build it?' And I says, 'Convince your daddy to sell us a few of his acres and you got a deal.' She says, 'No way he'd do that. No way he'd sell to the TDCR.' And she said this acreage here was special to her. And when I said, 'Well, obviously it wasn't so damn special to Edwin if he sold it,' she said, 'It was very special to him. It meant everything to him. But Edwin had seen he wasn't any shepherd. He didn't know how to use the rod and the staff. And all the sheep had died because of him. But why does there have to be a prison here, of all things?'

"And I just said, 'Well, honey, 'cause there's a new shepherd in town.'"

He coughed out a single laugh. A sigh followed. Sonny juggled my car key absentmindedly as he gazed out. "But it must've been something, don't you think? All those little white sheep . . . Aw, hell, let's just go," he then muttered, and I followed him up the hill.

At the end of the clay road shouldering Farm Road 1674, Sonny put it in park. He wore my father's Aggie-maroon checkered shirt, which was long in the sleeves and tight in the midsection, but I didn't tell him. I pulled out my suitcase from the back seat and tossed it out into the dirt. Turning back, I saw that Sonny held out his hand.

"Are you going to be all right?" I asked as we shook hands.

His jaw was clenched in a show of bravery, and his eyes gleamed. "You've been there," he said. "You tell me."

I nodded. "You'll be all right."

He nodded back. A grimace appeared on his face. "If you hear from Jill," he began.

Then, "Well," and he waved it off.

Licking his lips, fidgeting in the driver's seat, he then blurted out, "I didn't deserve any of this, you know? I really didn't."

I looked away. Then, with a chill of memory, I turned back his way. His grin was pure devilment, pure Sonny.

"But maybe I had it coming," he said.

"Goodbye, you worthless piece of shit," I said in a choked voice as I stepped out of my Impala and closed the door.

I watched him back up the car. Then, from his open window, he hollered, "Think fast!" Something hit me in the chest, and then the car skittered off.

I bent to pick it up. It was one of the bullets I'd thrown at him.

I took the old route back, along the slough and then the crossing over to the railroad tracks. I walked alone and at my own pace, feeling light of foot but weighted down from within, and in no rush to go anywhere. There was no more need to rush—at least, I figured, not until I had to, and then I'd be part of the Big Rush, the one I'd seen from the windows of the prison mansion or from the dingy hobo refuges to which Sonny would now be consigned. I thought of him every minute as I walked the fateful tracks with my father's suitcase swinging from my hand. I could not visualize him surviving what I had endured, but he was tougher than any of us knew. Whatever else he was to me, or I to him, I still couldn't fathom. He hadn't said the word goodbye. Or thanks. Or sorry.

How strange, I thought. Not sad. Just how strange, how very strange, our friendship was. And how strange to be returning, as in a sleepwalk, down this path of flight—how strange to remember, of all things, this brisk and spontaneously realized trail where even the shadows now seemed to blush in apologetic welcome as I crossed through to the woods, the abandoned farmhouse, and then down Highway 392, which with yesteryear's roadblocks had me thinking I was just enjoying a brief and vivid hallucination when the red and blue lights flashed out of the darkness and the car braked just to my side.

As I walked towards him, Sheriff Worley stepped out of his patrol car. I couldn't see his face, only the hand that came up to stroke its chin. "I hear those keys jangling in your pocket," he said. "You gonna tell me you got drunk and lost your car somewheres?"

Without thinking, I jammed my hand into my front pocket and felt Sonny's keys.

I froze. Then, as the sheriff inserted a toothpick into his mouth, I looked away. But I believed I could feel his eyes fall upon the bulge in my other pocket where the revolver was—and then survey me further, noting the bloody cloth bandage on my arm, where the initials *SH* leered out of the mess.

What had Sonny said out there, I wondered sickly. Ah, yes: "I wanted to share everything . . ."

I tried to smile as I placed my arms behind my back. "Put 'em on me, Sheriff," I said. "I'm all yours."

10

They threw out the capital murder after the search for Sonny's body was brought to a halt on the seventh day, when a former CO named Mickey Phillips came forward with a rather enlightening tale. It seemed that on the morning that Sonny disappeared, the freshly indicted ex-director met with Phillips, whose dismissal from the TDCR a year prior for muling marijuana had been kept quiet, as those things usually were. Phillips was now an auto mechanic on the east side of town, and when he saw the director drive up to his repair shop that morning, he had the vague expectation, borne out of seven years' experience in the Texas prison system, that something was about to happen.

The two exchanged pleasantries, after which Mickey Phillips said he felt terrible about all the disasters that had befallen Sonny. Because he knew it was the thing to do, Phillips then asked his former employer if there was any way he could help. Sonny said that there was. He told Phillips he would need a ride to Houston Intercontinental Airport that evening at seven-thirty. More to the point, he asked Phillips to drive with him in Sonny's Range Rover—and then, after dropping Sonny off, to take the Range Rover back to the auto repair shop, lock it up for the night, and the following morning sell it to the chop shop operated by Banditos in the deep backwoods between Votaw and Rye. Phillips could keep the money if he promised to keep his mouth shut. And this Phillips did, until the news broke the following afternoon and the ex-CO figured out what he'd been asked to do, and what could happen to him—to say nothing of the fate of that hapless ex-con now languishing over at the county jail—if Phillips didn't pay a visit to the D.A.'s office.

But they still had me for unlawful possession of a firearm by a former felon. And because Sonny had naturally failed to show up for his own arraignment, the murder indictment was soon replaced by another felonious charge, that of aiding and abetting the escape of an indicted alleged felon. I pleaded not guilty to both counts, and my case was set for trial in January. The prosecutors moved that I be held without bail, as I was a proven escape threat. The judge, a bassett-faced coot named Clack, shrugged affably at me and said, "Can't argue with the history, can I, Mister Coleman? Motion accepted, and the accused will be remanded to the custody of the Shepherd County Sheriff's Department until the conclusion of this trial."

Bo Worley had died and gone to heaven. With uncustomary fanfare, he personally escorted me—decked out in leg irons, belly cuffs and an orange jumpsuit that was at least two sizes too big—to my new way-station, a six-by-nine peopled by three other inmates, two of whom happened to be chicken hawks in dire need of a punk, and the last being a five-time DWI whose chronic diarrhea kept the whole county jail awash in my cellmates' retchings. At least once a day, Worley himself would pop by to make sure I was miserable, and would strut off whistling. Whatever I had done to piss off the sheriff so greatly, my cellmates mused, must truly have been staggering. They held me in awe, while the jailers and deputies—thrilled that their boss was in such uncharacteristically high spirits—lit my cigarettes for me and smuggled in boxes of fried chicken from the courthouse cafeteria.

I had said nothing to Worley the night he took me to jail. I said nothing to his investigators, nothing to the D.A., nothing to the Texas Rangers. The day the D.A. announced the new charge of aiding a fugitive (punishable, in light of my priors, by life without parole), he had me delivered to his dusty fire hazard of an office overlooking the bus depot. B. J. Strong was the D.A.'s name, and after he saw I wasn't interested in talking about the weather, he ran his fingers through where his hair might have been were he not bald as an egg, and said, in a deeply concerned voice, "These charges against you are serious, Coleman. Just being an ex-felon carrying a firearm, that'll get you two to ten. And let's face it, you're just flat busted on that one. No ifs ands or buts. And we'll get you on this aiding-and-abetting charge, too. Judge Clack has already indicated he'll let in your history of escapes. Hell's bells, Hadrian. We've got you by the short and curlies! Now, you don't really want to die in a state penitentiary, do you?"

Strong's face was wracked with phony hurt. "Where's my attorney?" I asked.

"Oh, well, I'm just sure he's on his way," said the D.A., and a used-car salesman's grin spread across his hairless head. "But I thought we'd visit first."

I turned away from him. "Fine," said Strong, his voice now frosty. "You don't have to say anything. Just listen, then. It's not you I want, Hadrian. I want Sonny Hope. I want him where you are right now. And I believe not only that you can tell me where he is, but that you can tell me what he's done. See," he continued as he stepped around his desk and loomed over me like an albino vulture in a combustible polyester suit, "my hunch is that you've got the goods on your old pal. I think you personally can lead us to every place there's a Sonny Hope boondoggle. I'm right, aren't I?"

His expression could not have been more unctuous. "You do that for us—you cooperate . . ." He shrugged elaborately. "Two to three, max."

The door flew open, and at the enunciation of the first syllable, B. J. Strong's skull looked as if a cherry bomb had gone off inside of it. "Two to three, heck, where's the dotted line? By the way, was that years or decades? Either way, as Mister Coleman's counsel, may we just say, B. J., that your clemency is somewhat greater than ours, being as how by the end of the day, we will move not only for dismissal on the grounds of violating client's civil rights by interrogating without benefit of counsel—but furthermore, that you be made to scrub the Texas Bar Association's office urinals for oh, say, three to five, max?"

"Oh, calm down, Aynsley, Worley just brought him up here early by mistake," protested the D.A. as the recently departed TDCR general counsel took a seat beside me.

I had myself only learned of Aynsley's involvement in the case the day before. I was playing gin rummy with my three cellmates when, from the far end of the corridor, the familiar insolent voice rang out: "Quickly, father! Quickly! Lead us to the chamber of the wrongfully accused!" Everyone in the cell put down their cards, and at that moment I knew I had a chance.

There stood old Colbert Reeves, my former attorney of record—and behind him, similarly outfitted in seersucker, khaki and spectacles, but also wearing a smile that would scandalize a maggot, was Aynsley.

"I'm recommending you give my son a try on this one, if you're okay with that," said Colbert in his quavering but sonorous baritone. When I replied that I was very okay with that, Aynsley clasped his hands together and exclaimed, "My first case as a criminal defense attorney! Shall we pray?"

Once Colbert had departed and we were alone in the visitation room, I told Aynsley, as I had Fitch and then Jill, the complete saga. After I was done, Aynsley played with his mustache for a moment. Then, in that gratingly bright voice of his, he added, "Did you ever go to Sunday school as a lad?"

"For awhile. Why?"

"Tell me if they ever taught you this song," he said. With rapt solemnity he crooned: "Hide it under a bushel—*No!* I'm gonna let it shine . . . Hide it under—"

"For God's sake, Aynsley," I pleaded. "Can you explain just what—"

"I want you to sing that song every night with your three little cell-mates before you curl up in your jammies," he said as he fetched up his briefcase and signaled to the jailer.

His eyes were clear and knowing. "I want you to sing it until you see the wisdom of it as our defense strategy. Hide nothing. Open every door. Bring everything out. Let it shine."

I said nothing until the steel door began to swing open. "Except about Jill," I said.

"Just sing the song," he admonished me, and I could hear the insipid melody echo down the corridors: "Hide it under a bushel—*No!* I'm gonna let it shine . . ."

Now B. J. Strong said to my attorney, "Anyway, Aynsley, here's what I can offer. Your client debriefs on Sonny Hope, we'll drop the weapons charge and lower the other count to obstruction of a criminal investigation and settle for two years."

"Nyet," sang out Aynsley. "Nothing short of immunity. Otherwise we go to trial."

"Oh, get serious, counselor, you know I can't let your client walk," he snapped. "He's an embarrassment to the governor! A month after he's pardoned, he's sauntering around with a gun in his pocket! He's all over this Hope fiasco, now you know it as well as—"

"You must be under enormous pressure to fry our client," cut in Aynsley. "Well, bless your heart, you poor dear. But consider the potential embarrassment to our governor, Mister Strong, when our client walks away without having given you so much as Sonny Hope's favorite color. Six little words you should heed, sir: You-will-not-win-this-case."

The D.A. winced at Aynsley. But then he growled, somewhat haltingly: "Well. I'm goddamned sure I'm not going to let your client skate until I have *some* idea of what we're getting in return."

Aynsley nodded gravely and turned my way. "A moment with my client, then," he said.

"No."

The word came flying out of me. "No," I repeated. "I'm innocent. I want my day in court."

That day did not come for three months. By then, Thanksgiving, Christmas and New Year's Day had passed me by, and the metal beds in the county jail felt like Arctic slabs. My cellmates had all been released or shipped off to the state system, though Sheriff Worley saw to it that I always had extraordinary individuals in my company. No one gave me any trouble. Word spread that I had killed judges and cons alike with my bare hands. The young inmates would ask me if prison was as tough as everyone said. "Depends on how tough you are," was my mysterious reply. Worley could not understand why I hadn't yet been knocked upside. His mood worsened, but by now the jailers and deputies all thought it was a hoot, and stopped by my cell periodically to hear the stories about Ricky Tempesta, Chu-Chu Herrera and wardens put out to pasture.

It was not the worst of times. Still, the sheer ease with which I had readapted to life in captivity unnerved me, and every night when the darkness fell upon me like the cold-knuckled backhand of the Almighty, I lay awake pondering the distinct possibility that stupidity was the most heinous crime of all. On that count, I was, indeed, flat busted. His ruse—and that's exactly what it was; did it really matter if he'd conceived it subconsciously?—was masterful by any measure. But it had worked to perfection precisely because he had played on my misinformed belief that I knew him better than he knew me.

As it developed, Sonny knew me better than I knew myself. He knew I wouldn't kill him. He knew I'd give him the keys to my car. He knew I wouldn't be so suspicious as to take a cab to the airport that night and discover his Range Rover wasn't there. He probably even knew I was inept enough—with his gun (unregistered, as it turned out) in my pocket and his initials emblazoned on my flesh wound—to get myself arrested that very night. Without a doubt he knew, from past experience, that I'd be too appalled at myself to tell the authorities the truth, as if Worley would believe it anyway. By the time they figured out they weren't looking at a murder, but instead a flight from justice, Sonny and his fat wallet would be well out of Texas, possibly out of the country, while I would be wearing bright orange and lying on a metal rack like an oven-ready lamb. "Help me escape" had been his brazen request, and I had agreed to do so. Now here I was, with one of Bo Worley's numbers on my back. Well, it was Sonny who had my number. As if any further proof of this were needed, I even spent a few minutes every night wondering if he had meant me any harm.

Aside from my attorney consultations, I was allowed one visitor per week. These I reserved for my sister, though there had been a surprising number of visitation requests, ranging from Scotty Folger and my old dog sergeant C. C. Holliday to, of all people, Ricky Tempesta. Mimi had moved out of the house and into the apartment of a CO-II named Kip something or other. She was pregnant, she told me with a blushing grin, but she assured me that Kip would be a good father. I wasn't in any position to lecture—especially when she said that if it was a boy, his name would be Hadrian.

Seven weeks into my incarceration, the jailer notified me that Mimi was sending another visitor in her stead. "Whoever it is ain't gonna have your sister's dumper, I'll wager," mourned the jailer. Later that day, he informed me that Professor Tobias Estelle would be by the next morning.

Hunched against his cane as he tried to ignore the motley congregation seated on either side of the plexiglas, the mothball-redolent old professor could not have seemed more out of place. "Aynsley assures me you'll emerge vindicated," he said as he balefully appraised my garb.

Then, through clenched dentures, he muttered, "But it's too late for justice, isn't it? You should never have been in here. Never. And *he* . . ."

He shook his head and said quietly, "There's no justice on this earth for a man like him."

"Have you heard from Jill?" I asked.

His head was still bowed. "She sent me a telegram two weeks ago," he said. "It said that she was okay, and that she loved me. Nothing more."

He shrugged wearily. "I don't know where she is. Some investigators have been by. They've asked me dozens of questions. They seem to think that she and he . . ."

His face crinkled as if from indigestion. "Apparently she closed out her bank account. It's our bank, of course, so it was easy for her to do over the phone. It was a very large sum of money. Not the amount one would take on a short holiday to the Yucatán."

Professor Estelle looked up at me. "What he's done to our family is to end it," he said simply. "He has ruined Jill. But Hadrian, I hate what my daughter did to you. Aynsley told me she telephoned him from Mérida. You wouldn't be here if . . . So terrible," he moaned.

"Sonny's her husband," I said. "She didn't want to see me ruin the man she loves. It's as plain as that."

"Hmm."

"Your daughter's lost without him, sir."

I hadn't disguised the bitterness in my voice. But it seemed to have no effect on Tobias Estelle. He wore the pallor of a death row inmate.

"Then she is lost indeed," he said crisply.

He whispered, "Good luck," and hobbled out of the visitation room.

One other individual had been granted a special visit, which took place on the eve of the trial. I should have been tipped off that this was not an attorney-client meeting by the leer on the jailer's face as he led me to the conference room. There sat Sissy Shipman, notepad laid out on the table in front of her. The familiar smirk was tempered somewhat. Gradually it ceased to be a smirk at all.

"Hello, Coleman," she said. "You look like a highway construction sign in that get-up, you poor devil."

"Don't knock it 'til you've tried it," I said as I took the chair across from her. "It'd look good with your hair color."

She bobbed her hair playfully. "You think?"

Then she narrowed her grey eyes. "You stood me up, you prick."

I smiled. "I got held up," I said.

"Like I haven't heard that before." She looked over my shoulder, craning her neck. Then, in a lower voice, she said, "Officially, this is an interview. But I'm off the story. Gave it to one of the other galley slaves at the *Chronicle*."

"Really? Why's that?"

"Well," she smiled, "for one, I'm a material witness. Oh, don't look so alarmed. I'm on your side, dummy."

She blushed just a little—an amazing sight, to see that porcelain face with just a little fire to it. "Well," I said, "I look forward to your testimony, I guess."

"There's another reason." But she thought for a moment before leaning forward, grabbing my wrist with a surprisingly hot hand and whispering:

"The other reason is . . . that *I'm on your side . . .* dummy."

Then she stood, snapped her notepad shut, and with her lips set in a tight little arc of facetious mirth, she said, "End of interview," and swiveled towards the door. As the echo of her clicking heels receded, I wondered how I'd be able to sleep before my day in court.

"And finally," declared District Attorney B. J. Strong as he leaned over the jury box and addressed the twelve Shepherd County citizens sitting stone-faced therein, "we will show you how Sonny Hope's lifelong favoritism towards this man, his childhood friend, Hadrian Coleman, led to the big payback—the payback in which Hadrian Coleman, the prison escape artist who owed his freedom to Hope, aided and abetted the latter's escape from justice. It was an act that robbed the citizens of the state of Texas of their right to know the truth behind the scandals rocking the Texas prison system. And how ugly an irony it is, ladies and gentlemen, that this very act of robbery was committed by the very man who, mere months ago, was *pardoned* by the state for suspected wrongdoing. Pardoned, as you will hear the governor himself testify, at the behest of Sonny Hope.

"I wish we could right that wrong. But the wrong we can right, ladies and gentlemen, is to hold this man to account for his most recent crime—that of making possible Sonny Hope's escape, causing the truth to elude our grasp. I have faith that we will eventually bring Sonny Hope to account. But no thanks to his friend and fellow con-spirator, the defendant Hadrian Coleman. Thank you."

Judge Clack nodded placidly as the D.A. took his seat. "Mister Reeves?"

"Yes, your Honor." As Aynsley rose, I shifted in my chair, and with my practiced sidelong gaze I took in the packed house: reporters, prison officials, gadfly lawyers, Mimi and Scotty Folger seated together, Judge Castlebury's former clerk Dillard Bunch scowling directly behind the prosecutor's table, Sheriff Worley nearby, Foots Taylor's wife Susie seated next to Cal Fitch's secretary, Cousin Billy Rivers, Sheila Reeves, and other faces I'd seen in passing or at a distance . . . I had been here once before, as a child. Sissy Shipman, not much more than a kid herself, had been on the front row with the media. Now she sat at home, awaiting the defense's turn, when she would testify on my behalf . . . *and damn it, Coleman*, I scolded myself, *she had it right, you dummy. She's been on your side all along.*

"Good morning, ladies and gents," smiled Aynsley as he ambled towards the jurors. "As we established during jury selection, many of you know me in a prior life, as the general counsel for the Texas Department of Criminal Retribution. I am proud to hold myself up as a former high-ranking prison official who has *not* been accused of any crime. Yet. Uh, anything I need to know about, B. J.?"

He looked down, modestly fingering his mustache until the laughter subsided. "All of you have some affiliation, first-, second-, or third-hand, with the prison system," he continued. "That's the reality of this county. Shepherdsville's a prison town. As lawyers on both sides of the aisle will tell you, that cuts both ways. Still," he said, and leaned against the clerk's desk with his arms folded against his chest, "it's my belief that my client, Hadrian Coleman, is exceedingly fortunate to be seated before you today. And, at the risk of appearing immodest, may I say that he's exceedingly fortunate to have me as his attorney. Because when he told me the truth, the bewildering and head-spinning truth, I, the former general counsel of the Texas Department of Criminal Retribution, was thoroughly equipped to believe him. And when you hear Hadrian Coleman's story—and this trial will be, in effect, the story of his life—you, the residents of this prison community, will absolutely believe him as well. You will say to yourselves, as I did: 'This could only happen here, in Shepherdsville. And I know because I live here. And I see what I see. And though what I see seems at times unbelievable, I am living it. So I believe.'"

He jiggled his spectacles against his face. "So my client is fortunate. To find another jury that would possess the pure intuitive facility for this case at hand, I believe I would have had to travel many thousands of miles overseas, with shovel in hand. I would have had to dig up the inhabitants of Babylon, that other great prison city, ruled by Nebuchadnezzar, with his sequestered palace of hanging gardens and his unquenchable appetite for power. The Babylonians feared their king. But he brought the city great prosperity, which its citizens accepted, asking no questions—because, let's face it, Babylon wouldn't have been Babylon if anyone asked questions."

Aynsley smiled for a moment. Then he went on, "The Babylonians would have understood Shepherdsville, in other words, and they would have understood Sonny Hope. But they also had their own Hadrian Coleman. Jehoiachin was his name. A decent man held prisoner for no just cause, other than being at the wrong place at the wrong time in history. Nebuchadnezzar spared Jehoiachin the usual torments of that day and age. The king thought of his prisoner as his friend. He fed him well, and he gave him privileges the other subjects could only dream of having. Perhaps Nebuchadnezzar did this out of genuine affection. But from this distance, and in the context of the Scriptures, we come to see also that, though Nebuchadnezzar derived a sense of holy smugness from his gentle treatment of Jehoiachin, there was also a taunting, manipulative edge to their relationship. For make no mistake. Until he died, Jehoiachin was a prisoner, subject to the whims of Nebuchadnezzar. To cite Jehoiachin as a willing and active accomplice in the degradation of Babylon . . . well. It would be to call chains jewels, and cells boudoirs. It would be to call a slave a prince."

Aynsley looked back at me. I felt the jurors' collective glare as well.

"Hadrian wasn't the only slave to Sonny Hope," allowed my lawyer as he wrung his hands together. "You may know a few yourself. And if not, take a good long look at me, if you're able. I worked for Sonny for eight years. We grew up together. He was quite a character, Sonny was. He had this way of cajoling, of making you want to help him—to give the poor guy a boost, to hoist him up upon your shoulders . . . Until, before you knew it, there he was: up there, and not about to come down. And there you were, his beast of burden."

He looked at his shoes. "I'm not on trial here, thank God. Unlike

Hadrian Coleman, unlike Jehoiachin, I was never at the wrong place at the wrong time when the gallant emperor of the shining city found himself in need. I was touched by him, though, and so were many of you. And at the time, even when we felt that touch, and how it drove us down a peg or two lower . . . we looked up at that shining face of Sonny Hope's. And never once did it cross our mind, any more than it did the minds of the Babylonians, that we were staring up into the soft face of evil.

"The Babylonians are far flung and stone dead, and thus disqualified from this jury pool. But Hadrian Coleman is fortunate to have you here today, as his bona fide peers. Because every one of you has been born and raised to know the difference between the jailkeeper and the jailed. And every one of you knows how bars are bent, rules are twisted, lies are cultivated, and human dignity is sold down the river in Shepherdsville. Though yes—there exist a few universal elements to this case. One of them is vintage Americana."

Aynsley strutted towards the audience. He held his outstretched hand mere inches from the outraged face of Bo Worley. "The gnawing vendettas of small-minded local law enforcement, for example," he said. "I may well be wasting your time with the lengths to which I intend to prove Hadrian Coleman's innocence—since it will take you scarcely a few minutes' worth of testimony, I humbly predict, before you see that the D.A. has absolutely no evidence in his favor, that the sole basis of his case is Sheriff Bo Worley's long-standing desire to do in my client to avenge some pathetic family grudge. Any number of folks from any number of towns this size have been plagued with their own Bo Worleys. They'd see this charade for what it is, and after due deliberation they would tender a verdict of Not Guilty, and remind themselves to roll a few heads come the next local election.

"But I beg your indulgence. Because, as my client put it to me and to Mister Strong one day, this is Hadrian Coleman's day in court. He has waited his entire life for this day. He has waited for you, a jury of his peers, the citizens of Shepherd County, the throwbacks to another shining city—he's waited for you to hear the facts of his life. How as a boy he saved his friend Sonny Hope's life, and unjustly went to prison for it. How as an inmate he fell under Sonny Hope's dominion. How, at the very end of his unjust incarceration, he was attacked by a jealous inmate, and killed him in self-defense, and escaped in panic—a mistake any of us might have made, but one which Sonny Hope compounded by *allowing* Hadrian to escape, and then, by sealing him into a false rendition of what had happened. And why? So that the prisoner would remain chained to his keeper. We don't dispute Mister Strong's claim that Sonny Hope brokered Hadrian Coleman's pardon—we thoroughly agree, in fact. But Mister Strong has misread the contract. It was not, 'I've done you favors, now how about doing me one?' Instead, it was this: 'You have always done my bidding, and now you will continue to.'

"You will hear the TDCR's paragon of integrity, Calvin Fitch, testify that Hadrian Coleman came to him and confided that Sonny Hope demanded he kill three of the prison director's enemies—one of these being Fitch himself. Further testimony, both from Mister Fitch and another one of Hope's targets, Dr. Ricky Tempesta, will indicate that Hope warned Hadrian that he might well return to prison if he did not do as he was told. You will hear testimony, both from Mister Fitch and the third of Hope's targets, Miss Sissy Shipman of the *Houston Chronicle*, that the defendant refused to spill blood on Hope's behalf. Indeed, as Miss Shipman will testify, Hadrian called her to warn her that her life was in danger, that Sonny Hope wanted her dead, and that Hope would want Hadrian dead as well, if he knew what Hadrian intended to tell Miss Shipman that very evening. Sonny Hope kidnapped Hadrian en route to Miss Shipman's house. At gunpoint, Hadrian was forced to drive to a remote area. During a scuffle, my client overpowered Hope, and—though he was shot in the process—managed to wind up with the gun.

"At that point, my client had one of three choices. He could have shot and killed Sonny Hope, and thus be facing today the charge of murder. Or he could have somehow hogtied his quarry and dragged him off to the tender loving care of Sheriff Worley. All of our lives would be simpler if Hadrian Coleman had chosen either of the first two paths. He would be our villain or our hero, and we could all go home. But the path he chose was the third one. He let his lifelong captor go. He let Sonny Hope take the car, accepted Sonny Hope's car keys in return, said goodbye, and that was that.

"The state will offer no proof, because it does not exist, that Hadrian Coleman planned Sonny Hope's escape, that he harbored him, that he lent him advice, or that he covered for him. He just let him go. The bleeding-hearts among us might say he did what he did out of compassion for a desperate boyhood friend. The cynics among us will say he did it out of lifelong habit. Choose your poison after you hear the testimony of Sonny Hope's father, former prison director Purvis J. 'Thunderball' Hope, who will describe explicitly how Hadrian Coleman not only saved the life of Mister Hope's son by killing a perverted assailant, but how Hadrian steadfastly protected his friend from any exposure, any culpability—which silence would propel young Sonny Hope to the top of the heap . . ."

Aynsley Reeves himself fell silent then. He took off his glasses. Stuffing them in his pants pocket, he then lifted his squinting, blinking, pinkish countenance to the jury.

"God, it sounds so familiar, doesn't it?" he declared. "How many people, both inside and out, covered for Sonny Hope, turned the other way, kept their mouths shut, and finally, let him go?"

He raised a hand, smiled his wiseassed smile. "I'll step forward," he said. "I did all that. I never committed a crime on Sonny Hope's behalf, and neither did Hadrian Coleman. But we sure let him go!—didn't we?"

And then again, a quiet echo: "Didn't we?"

And blind Aynsley Reeves stood there for a moment, as if he had nowhere else to go.

As Aynsley had promised, the trial could have lasted a day but lasted four instead. Judge Clack seemed mildly surprised when Aynsley did not move for an instructed verdict of Not Guilty after the prosecution rested. Thereafter, the judge seemed preoccupied with scowling at the D.A. as they came forward, one by one, the pillars of the community of Shepherd County, to testify in my favor: Fitch, Sissy, Foots Taylor, Tobias Estelle . . . Then criminal investigators, Ricky Tempesta, Vermiel Crenshaw, the former CO Mickey Phillips . . .

I sat there as bewitched as I would have been had I been witnessing my own birth. My turn on the stand would come. But that long day for me would prove anticlimactic, bookended as it was by the emotionally charged appearances of two very different individuals.

Thunderball Hope had prepared for this moment. In a sense, it was his day as much as it was mine. His first stride into the courtroom produced a general murmur of awe. He had added a few welcome pounds since I'd last seen him, and had bought a well-tailored charcoal suit. But it was the air about him, pungent with defiance, the storied unapologetic underbite set in such a way as to assure the audience that in his mind it remained, a full decade after his exile from Shepherdsville, *My way or the highway Got dammit!* Yet by revealing, he would also be confessing, and Thunderball accomplished this with a show of dignity that both humbled and ennobled all those present.

"Do you wish you had encouraged your son to tell the truth about what had happened with Judge Castlebury?" Aynsley Reeves inquired.

Thunderball searched the courtroom, making sure everyone had his attention before saying: "You're damn right I do. I mean, I ain't no angel, Mister Reeves. But in my seventy-six years of not being no angel, keeping this here truth from coming out was the single most despicable act of my life."

"And you've had to live with that," Aynsley prodded him.

"Huh," he grunted. Thunderball looked down for a moment. But again he stared out at all those present. "A whole mess of people have had to live with that. But not like this fine fella here. Not like he's had to." And he gestured at me.

"But you tried, at the time, to make amends?"

"I did. I had him transferred back to Shepherdsville and made him my houseboy."

"Meaning, a relatively cushy job, better food, that kind of thing?"

"It was a plum job for most prisoners, yes."

"And for this prisoner?"

"It was the cruelest thing I could've possibly done to him. I didn't know it then, but I do now."

"How was it cruel?"

"Well, his friend Sonny, who'd gotten off scot-free, he lived there at the mansion. And Hadrian, whose own youth got took from him . . ."

Suddenly his words dissolved into a gurgle—a terrible, irresistible sound. "And . . . well. He had to sit there and watch his pal enjoy the fruits of growing up. Had to serve Sonny his meals. Had to pick up after him. And had to stand right there in his prison whites and watch Sonny woo the local girl Hadrian had always been nuts for."

"Jill Estelle?"

"That's right."

"Whom Sonny Hope married?"

"That's right."

"Tell us, Mister Hope. Did you come to know the defendant well?"

"I come to know him like he was my own boy."

"Then based on your close relationship, why do you think he freely protected your true son, from the moment of his arrest all the way up to his flight from justice?"

At that point, Thunderball looked my way. His eyes welled up. "'Cause he was one of those unusual types, Hadrian Coleman was," he began slowly, "who was really an awful good soul right down to his core. But he didn't think nothing of himself. His daddy, you see, was worshipped around these parts, and when the boy couldn't measure up, he figured he must be about worthless. He truly thought that. And in the meantime, he thought the world of my boy Sonny. Thought he was the greatest thing since sliced bread. And it just became his habit to throw his own self away, and let Sonny go on. And that's the way they carried on, those two, all the way up to now. Let Sonny go on, and let Hadrian take the fall."

"Do you still love your son, Mister Hope?"

He thrust out his magnificent jaw. "Yes, I do," he said.

"Can you tell us how it makes you feel, then, to be telling the court what you've just said about your own flesh and blood?"

"Humph. It ain't a joyous occasion, Mister Reeves."

"In fact, it's a grim situation for which you bear some responsibility, isn't it?"

"Just about near total responsibility, the way I look at it, yessir."

"But do you feel better now, sir?"

"Not yet," said Thunderball Hope.

After my testimony—which was halting and unspectacular, but at least did my cause no great damage—Aynsley Reeves called the final witness to the stand. Tina Hepler of Houston came forward. Her face bore a few scars from the episode six months prior, but otherwise she was spunky and unassailable.

"And how do you know the defendant, Mrs. Hepler?"

The answer, like the first tender gust of spring after winter, more than made up for a season's cruelty:

"As the man who saved my life and my husband's life."

It took less time for the jury to deliberate than it did for Judge Clack to chew out the D.A. for so profligate a waste of the taxpayers' money. And after rapping the gavel, he started in on Bo Worley, but I fell out of earshot. Aynsley got to me first, followed by my sister. Soon I couldn't see for the bodies pressed against mine, the spilling of tears and the tousling of my grey hair—and then, out in the hallway, the television cameras blasting out of a tunnel of white.

Foots Taylor's voice was in my ear, telling me, "I've still got that job for you, Hadrian, and it's perfect for you. Texas Youth Commission, working for kids who've landed in trouble and don't have male role models. It's long hours, and you'd probably have to relocate to one of the big cities, but I'm telling you, Hadrian, I've sealed the deal and—"

A small hand yanked the state legislator backwards by his suit collar. "Make yourself useful, Foots," said his former high school sweetheart, Sissy Shipman. Her words were clipped and urgent as she looked over his shoulder to the camera crews. "Throw the press a few chunks of meat while I slip our local hero out the back way."

As she wrapped an arm around mine, Foots looked us over in momentary bewilderment. Then, with that leavening smile of his, he leaned towards me and advised, "The moment she loosens her grip, you run for your freaking life."

He winked at Sissy, who made a face and gave him the finger, but already his back was to us as he waded into the tangle of lights and microphones: "Folks, I have a few words to say about what this trial portends for the Texas prison system . . ."

Before I knew it, we'd turned a corner. She took me down a staircase, through the snack bar and out a side door. The sunlight in the courthouse square nearly knocked me down. Sissy was moving briskly, almost running, dragging my arm, saying, "Well mother fuck, they're coming, there's my car, run, it's unlocked!"

We threw ourselves into her Mazda and laid rubber all the way along the square, laughing breathlessly and waving to the reporters at the top of the courthouse stairs. A moment later, we had joined the everyday traffic of Shepherdsville. Now we were ordinary, anonymous; and though I smiled and Sissy smirked as we drove, words came to neither of us, and I began to feel what others must feel every day as they lift a leg to take another free step, only to find themselves pleading, *God save me from this burden* . . .

"Five-thirty," said Sissy finally as she checked her watch. Eyeing me tentatively, she said, "Feel like a drink? The first seven are on me."

I laughed quietly. Then, *Be a man*, I ordered myself. I lay a hand on her leg.

She looked down at it, frowned. With an exasperated sigh, she slowed the car at a traffic light, switched gears, and finally took my hand in hers.

"Is this stupid or what?" she said to our hands. "I feel like I'm in high school."

"Let's go to The Guilty Dog," I urged her. "What do you think? Let's just jump into the fray."

"Are you . . ." But then her eyes sparkled. She let out a husky laugh. "At least you didn't say let's go neck in the ruins of Trust," she said. "What the hell. Into the fray."

She sped back towards the courthouse, returning her hand to mine after every shifting of the gear. "I heard Foots talking to you about that Texas Youth Commission job," she said. "You'd be a fool not to take it."

"It sounds pretty sweet," I admitted.

Then she began to squeeze my hand. "Oh," she murmured, almost a cry of pain. Then: "Well goddamn it, Coleman, can I just come out and say I don't want you to go moving off? I mean, son of a bitch!"

She arranged her lips into a smoldering pout. "Then go with me," I said.

Sissy blinked. "Well, listen to you, Speedy Gonzales," she cracked. But I felt her hand squeeze tighter.

She sighed morosely. "God, I could use a change of scenery, no question about that. I mean, look at this hellhole," she snapped with disgust, and pulled her hand away to indicate, with a defeated gesture, the square we had just abandoned, now deserted except for the usual gaggle of stogie-puffing attorneys, the usual two prostrated men in white, and a passing courthouse secretary the swishing of whose skirt captured the usual stares. It didn't look like a hellhole to me. Living beneath it for so long made passing through its streets and sidewalks, from sun to shade and back again, paradise enough.

That would wear off, I knew. For Sissy, there wasn't anything left to see but Shepherdsville's claustrophobia, its vanity and its fundamental dubiousness. Still, twelve of its good people had seen the town and the truth for what they were, and let me walk among them again, and I had Shepherdsville to thank for that.

But now it was Sissy Shipman I had to thank, because she'd always been there, hiding behind her notepad. And it dawned on me, as I watched her piercing eyes shoot daggers through the midsection of our hometown while she all but squeezed the blood out of my hand, that it wasn't just thanks I had to give her.

I lifted her hand, kissed it. She blushed a little.

But still vexed, she stammered, "Sometimes—oh, I don't know. Sometimes I think I don't even know the way out of this dump."

It was there for me.

"Is that all you needed to know?" I asked her, and a new kind of wildness overcame me. "The way out?"

Then I leaned over and kissed her blushing neck. "Let me drive," I said.

Robert Draper spent years as an editor and writer at *Texas Monthly* before moving to his current position as staff writer for *GQ* magazine. A lifelong Texan, he lives in Austin with his wife, Meg Littleton.

A NOTE ON THE TYPE

This book was set in Janson, a typeface long thought to have been made by the Dutchman Anton Janson, who was a practicing typefounder in Leipzig during the years 1668–1687. However, it has been conclusively demonstrated that these types are actually the work of Nicholas Kis (1650–1702), a Hungarian, who most probably learned his trade from the master Dutch typefounder Dirk Voskens. The type is an excellent example of the influential and sturdy Dutch types that prevailed in England up to the time William Caslon (1692–1766) developed his own incomparable designs from them.

Composed by Stratford Publishing Services,
Brattleboro, Vermont
Printed and bound by R.R. Donnelley & Sons/
Haddon Craftsmen,
Bloomsburg, Pennsylvania
Designed by Virginia Tan